THE RAIN WASHED people, stalls, and barrows from the market square, leaving only that one figure like a particularly stubborn stain. Drips fell from the tip of a pointed nose. And behind the clinging strands of damp hair, two large black eyes glistened like coal and gave the marketplace a look that spoke of coal's grit, griminess, and hidden fire.

This shivering, clench-jawed scrap of damp doggedness had a name, and that name was Mosca Mye. It was a name that would have been recognized in her home village, where a number of people would have had questions to ask about the burning of a mill, the release of a notorious felon, and the theft of a large and savage goose. A well-informed few would have known how it fitted into the tale of conspiracy, murder, river battles, and revolution . . . .

FLY TRAP

FRANCES HARDINGE

HARPER

An Imprint of HarperCollinsPublishers

Fly Trap

Copyright © 2011 by Frances Hardinge

All rights reserved. Printed in the United States of America.
No part of this book may be used or reproduced in any manner whatsoever without written
permission except in the case of brief quotations embodied in critical articles and reviews.
For information address HarperCollins Children's Books, a division of HarperCollins
Publishers, 10 East 53rd Street, New York, NY 10022.
www.harpercollinschildrens.com

Library of Congress Cataloging-in-Publication Data
Hardinge, Frances.
   Fly trap / Frances Hardinge. — 1st U.S. ed.
      p.   cm.
   Sequel to: Fly by night.
   Summary: Adventurous orphan Mosca Mye, her savage goose, Saracen, and their
sometimes-loyal companion, Eponymous Clent, become embroiled in the intrigues of Toll,
a town that changes entirely as day turns to night.
   ISBN 978-0-06-088046-0
   [1. Fantasy.]   I. Title.
PZ7.H21834Fmt   2011   2010027755
[Fic]—dc22   CIP
                                                                            AC

Typography by Amy Ryan
12 13 14 15 16   CG/BR   10 9 8 7 6 5 4 3 2 1
❖
First paperback edition, 2012
First U.S. Edition, 2011
Originally published in the U.K. in 2011 under the title *Twilight Robbery* by Macmillan
Children's Books, a division of Macmillan Publishers Ltd, Great Britain

To Martin,
for being my partner-in-crime, fellow adventurer and one
true love, and for being wiser than anybody has a right to be

CONTENTS

1

GOODMAN SPRINGZEL,
BRINGER OF SURPRISES

READ THE PAPER for you, sir?"

One small voice strove against the thunder of rain, the shuffle and huff of the passing mules, the damp flap of canvas as the last sodden stallholders gave up their fight against the dismal weather. Market day was coming apart like a biscuit in coffee, fragments of it running for cover with trays and baskets held over their heads.

"Oi! Gentlemen! Read the paper for you?"

The two farmers who had been hailed hurried on, without looking up to see where the voice came from. And so they did not notice a small figure that had found, if not shelter, at least a place where the rain simply pelted her instead of pummeling her. The upper stories of the courthouse, debtors' prison, and magistrate's house all jutted themselves forward like three frowning foreheads, and beneath this the figure hunched against the wall, bowing so as to shield a crumpled, sodden copy of a much-traveled *Pincaster Gazette* from the worst of the rain. Small wonder that the poor *Gazette* drooped so forlornly. Even in the cities reading was rare talent, and here in the little sheep-farming town of Grabely none of the inhabitants could read the tiniest tittle.

The rain washed people, stalls, and barrows from the market square, leaving only that one figure like a particularly stubborn stain. Drips fell from the tip of a pointed nose. Beneath a drooping bonnet with a frayed brim, hair spiked and straggled like a tempest-tossed blackbird's nest. An olive green dress two sizes too big was hitched at the waist and daubed knee-high in thick yellow mud. And behind the clinging strands of damp hair, two large black eyes glistened like coal and gave the marketplace a look that spoke of coal's grit, griminess, and hidden fire.

This shivering, clench-jawed scrap of damp dogged-ness had a name, and that name was Mosca Mye. Mosca meant fly, a housefly name well suited to one born on an evening sacred to Palpitattle, He Who Keeps Flies Out of Jams and Butter Churns. It was a name that would have been recognized in her home village, where a number of people would have had questions to ask about the burning of a mill, the release of a notorious felon, and the theft of a large and savage goose. In Mandelion, a city port to the west, a well-informed few would have known her name, and how it fitted into the tale of conspiracy, murder, river battles, and revolution that had turned the city upside down and shaped it anew.

Three months had now passed since the gates of Mandelion had closed behind Mosca. Those three months had brought in winter, eaten the soles of her shoes to a paper thinness, pinched her cheeks, emptied her purse, and most importantly of all, used up her last ounce of patience with her traveling companion.

"Mosca?" A faint, querulous voice sounded behind her, rather like that of a dying great-aunt. "If you do not wish me to perish from want, you might try to use a little charm. The flower girls manage to coo or sing their wares—they do not shriek like an attacking hawk."

The voice came from a narrow, barred window set in the wall of the debtors' prison. Peering in, Mosca could just make out a ponderous figure lying in its shirt sleeves upon a bed of straw. The man in question had allowed a tragic and injured expression to settle upon his plump face, as if it was he and not Mosca who was braving the elements. His coat, wig, and pocket-watch chain had all been sold, leaving his much-patched waistcoat on display. Eponymous Clent, poet extraordinaire, word wizard laureate, and eternal bane of all those mean-minded enough to expect him to pay his bills. Once upon a time Mosca had thought it a good idea to continue traveling with him instead of settling in Mandelion. They shared a love of words, a taste for adventure, and a dubious relationship with the truth, but such common ground can take two people only so far—and it was starting to seem as if it would take them to Grabely and no farther.

"What's your charm done for us, Mr. Clent?" snapped Mosca through her teeth. "Why don't you charm your way out of that cell? Why don't you charm us some dinner?"

"She mocks me," murmured Clent with a maddening air of stoic forgiveness. "It is her nature. Those of tottering intellect and meager spirit always turn against their best friends and protectors as soon as they face real hardship. She cannot help it, Fates." He sighed. "Madam, you might reflect upon the fact that you at least have your liberty."

"Yeah, it's lovely out here." Mosca glared up at the lowering sky of her liberty. "If I was any freer, I'd have influenza already."

"Or," Clent continued with a hint of bitterness, "you might reflect on the reason I find myself thus incommoded. After all, you would insist on bringing *him* into this accursed town."

Mosca made a crab-apple face, but here, sadly, Clent had a point. If it had not been for her, Saracen would not have been with them. For a good deal of her childhood, Saracen had been the orphaned Mosca's only friend and ally, and so she had taken him with her when she fled her damp and miserable home village. Since then she had resisted all Clent's attempts to sell him, lose him, or lure him into a pie shell. Mosca usually kept Saracen on a muzzle and leash, but on their first night in Grabely a laughing ostler had made the mistake of assuming that if something waddles it is funny, and that if it is funny then it is harmless, and that if it is harmless there is nothing to be lost by removing its muzzle. . . .

Clent had been thrown into the debtors' prison due to his inability to pay for the resultant damage to the inn. The ostler, who was somewhat damaged himself, was carried off demanding that Saracen be put in the stocks (into which his wings would hardly have fitted) and that he be publicly flogged (which nobody seemed willing to attempt). And by the time the townspeople had collected their courage and an array of long sharp objects, Saracen had escaped into the countryside.

Since that time Saracen had been making a name for himself. That name was not Saracen. Indeed, the name was more along the lines of "that hell-fowl," "did-you-see-what-it-did-to-my-leg," "kill-it-kill-it-there-it-goes," or "what's-that-chirfugging-goose-done-now?" Every time Mosca begged, stole, or earned almost enough to pay off Clent's debt, another bruised and bleeding farmer would limp into town to report a shattered roof or a stunned mule, Clent would be blamed for Saracen's doings, and they would find themselves right back where they started.

"Naturally I would earn our way if I could," continued Clent in the same dolorous tone, "but since the

Stationers stopped buying my poetry . . . what am I to do?"

Although nobody usually admitted it, everybody knew that between them the powerful guilds that represented the main professions and crafts of the land held the country together. The formidable Company of Stationers controlled the printing of all books in the Realm, and burned any book they considered dangerous. Most people were glad to leave them to this, for it was believed that reading the wrong book could drive you mad. The Stationers appeared the lesser of two evils, albeit one with a tendency to correct your grammar while burning your neighbors. Clent had once worked as a spy for the Stationers, and it was on their orders that he had traveled to Mandelion with Mosca at his heels. The Stationers had not, however, ordered him to help overthrow the city's government, and had been unamused by Mosca and Clent's involvement in Mandelion's revolution. Over the last three months they had shown their lack of amusement by refusing to buy any of Clent's work, not so much as a limerick.

"Why do you not cut off my hand if you will not let it write?" Clent had railed at them. "Why not cut off my head if you will not let it dream?"

"Don't think it wasn't considered, Mr. Clent," had been the curt response.

Remembering all this did nothing to improve Mosca's mood. At the moment the most marketable commodity

Mosca owned was her eyes—and the fact that she and Clent were the only people in Grabely who knew how to read. Newspapers sometimes washed up in Grabely, declarations and wanted posters were pinned to the door of the courthouse by the decree of the nearest cities, but they might have been covered in bird footprints for all the sense the inhabitants could make of them. And so every day for the last two weeks Mosca had been standing in the square offering to read newspapers, letters, wanted posters, and pamphlets to anyone who would pay her a penny. Mosca had always felt a passionate hunger for the books everyone else feared, but right now most of her waking thoughts were taken up with a far more ordinary sort of hunger.

Most people were interested in the copy of the *Gazette*, of course, wanting to hear more about the strange rebel town of Mandelion that had overthrown its duke and, with a reformed highwayman as its leader, still held out against the disapproval of its neighbors. Unfortunately after the first week there was nobody in town who had not heard every word in the newspaper, so Mosca had started making up more stories, and she was afraid that people were beginning to notice.

"Try calling out again, this time in a sweeter manner—"

"There's nobody here!" exploded Mosca. "There's nobody on the blinkin' streets! Nobody wants to know how the world's going! I'm sellin' the news to the bleedin' pigeons! There's nobody—oh, hang on. . . ."

A serving man had just come out of the courthouse, staring in confusion at a poster in his hand before pinning it against the door, upside down. When official declarations and bills were sent to Grabely, the local magistrate always ordered them to be posted outside his courthouse in the approved fashion, despite the fact that even he had no idea what they said.

"Mister! Mister! Do you want me to read that for you? Mister! Only a penny!"

The man looked at her, then swept his wet hair out of his eyes.

"All right." He tossed a penny. "Just the gist. Make it snappy."

Mosca tilted herself so her head was almost inverted and gripped her bonnet as she did so.

"It's a . . ." Unlike every other ounce of Mosca, her mouth was suddenly dry. "It's . . . it's an announcement of a . . . new . . . tax . . . on . . . table legs."

"Table legs!" The man swore and turned up his collar. "'Twas only a matter of time, I suppose," he muttered as he clipped off down the street.

Mosca turned back to the poster and gaped at it, white faced. What it actually said was this:

Eponymous Clent—Wanted for thirty-nine cases of fraud, counterfeiting, selling, and circulating lewd and unlicensed literature, claiming to be the impecunious

son of a duke, impersonating a magistrate, imperson-
ating a horse doctor, breach of promise, forty-seven
moonlit flits without payment of debts, robbing shrines,
fleeing from justice before trial, stealing pies from win-
dows and small furniture from inns, fabricating the
Great Palthrop Horse Plague for purposes of profit,
operating a hurdy-gurdy without a license. The public
is advised against lending him money, buying anything
from him, letting him rooms, or believing a word he
says. Contrary to his professions, he will not pay you the
day after tomorrow.

Eponymous Clent was known in the debtors' prison by his real name. That had been unavoidable.

Nobody ever did lie about their name, not least for fear of angering their patron Beloved. The Beloved were the little gods everybody trusted to take care of running the world, keeping clouds afloat, hens laying, and dust out of babies' eyes. There were far too many Beloved for each to have a whole day of the year sacred to them, and so instead every little god had to make do with a frac-tion of a day or night. If you were born in an hour sacred to a particular Beloved, it became your patron god, and you were given one of the names linked to that god. Everybody agreed that your name was who you *were*, your destined, god-given nature. Lying about it was as unthinkable as slapping a god in the face or trying to glue a new soul into your body.

Clent had been named Eponymous because he had been born under Phangavotte, He Who Smoothes the Tongue of the Storyteller and Frames the Legendary Deed. While he was shameless enough to impersonate anything from a high constable to a hedgehog, even Clent would not lie about his name. And so, sooner or later, somebody else who could read would turn up in Grabely and look at the poster, maybe read it aloud. . . .

"Oh, muck buckle," muttered Mosca. "We're sunk."

And then, not for the first time, it occurred to her that only Clent need sink, and that she did not have to be aboard when it happened.

The thunder of the rain hid the clatter of clogs on cobble as she ran along this wall and that, making her way toward the easterly road. It did not take long. The town was tiny, and soon her clogs were squishing into mud. The houses fell back, and she was gasping and sneezing and gazing out along a barren dirt track ribboning across the gray heath.

Ranged along the road like a rough-cut welcoming committee were Grabely's statues of some of the Beloved. These particular Beloved were hacked and hewn from wood, which the water glossed to a slick, dark red. Grayglory with his sword, Halfapath brandishing a sextant, Tombeliss beating on his drum.

The morning had been sacred to Goodlady Emberleather, She Who Prevents the Meat from Becoming Chewy and Unwholesome. The hours between noon and dusk on this day of the year, however, were devoted to Goodman Springzel, He Who Tips Ice Water Down the Collar and Hides the Pearl in the Oyster, the Beloved in charge of surprises both good and ill. Somebody had placed a crude wreath of leaves around his statue's neck to show that this was his sacred time.

Like everybody else, Mosca had been brought up worshipping the Beloved. Every habit of her mind told her that she *needed* to perform little gestures of respect to these miniature gods, in order to ward off disasters great and small. *But,* wondered her fierce, rebellious, practical mind, *what happens if I don't?*

Mosca's mother had died in childbirth, and thus the only parent she had ever known had been her father, the studious and uncompromising Quillam Mye. He had died when she was eight, leaving her an orphan. Some remembered him as a great thinker and a hero in the fight against the murderous Birdcatchers, who had ruled the Realm for a few bloody years. However, the wild and radical views on equality that filled his later books had seen him exiled, spending his last years in the miserable backwater village of Chough, where his daughter was born and raised. Mosca's childhood had always been tainted by the villagers' suspicion of her father. Had they known the full truth of his views, the people of Chough would probably have burned him when he first set foot in the village . . . for Quillam Mye had secretly been an atheist.

Ever since discovering the truth of her father's atheism, Mosca had discreetly stopped nodding to the Beloved's statues, reciting prayers to calm them, and leaving offerings in their tiny shrines. In spite of this it did not seem that rain made her any wetter, or that her milk curdled any faster, or that she was any more prone to attack by wolves.

And thus she felt no particular qualms about sitting down upon the wide, flat head of Goodman Springzel to consider her situation. She took out a wooden pipe and chewed angrily at the stem, but left it empty and unlit. It was a habit she had developed long ago, whenever she needed to clear her thoughts.

I'm done with Mr. Clent—done for good this time. All I need to do is find Saracen; then I'll leave that ungrateful old bag of lies to stew in his own juice.

But where could she run? To the west, back toward Mandelion? It was not that easy. She had friends there . . . but after the revolution a number of powerful and dangerous people had made it clear that Clent, Saracen, and she should leave Mandelion and never come back. Besides, even if she did strike out for the city, she might never reach it. The land around it was starting to sound like a war zone in the making.

A month ago all the big cities within spitting distance of Mandelion had passed hasty new laws decreeing that nobody was allowed to trade with the rebel city. The idea was to starve them out, but what it really meant was that suddenly all the little towns like Grabely that needed their trade with Mandelion to make ends meet found themselves with meager market stalls and dwindling granaries. And so some people had decided that life might be better in Mandelion itself and had tried to flee to join the rebels. Now many of the local towns and cities had beadles and other lawmakers patrolling the moors in search of such refugees, ready to drag them back to a worse cell than Clent's.

Could she last the winter in one of the nearby towns or villages to the north or south? Unlikely. Soon there would be no more apples to tug off the trees, any hint of good humor and charity would be pinched away by the cold, and nobody would pay to have a newspaper read to them. Knowing would become less important than eating.

Where did houseflies go in the winter?

"They don't," muttered Mosca with her eyes full of water. "They jus' die. Well, squash that for a start."

She would go east. Somehow she would find a way across the uncrossable River Langfeather that roared through its gorge from the mountains to the sea. She would trudge her way to Chanderind, or Waymakem—everybody said the living was easier there. But how to get past the Langfeather? The only bridge that spanned it for a hundred miles was governed by the town of Toll, and nobody could pass over without paying a fee quite beyond her means.

. . . but perhaps she would try her hand at getting money from a stranger one more time.

Looking back toward the edge of town, Mosca could see a figure sheltering in a broken barn, half hidden by the water that streamed in crystal pipes from the sodden thatch. He was tall, he held his shoulders slightly hunched as if his coat was too tight, and he was beckoning to her.

Mosca hesitated only an instant, then tucked away her pipe, sprinted over, and ducked into the little barn, hastily pushing the wet draggles of her hair out of her eyes to look at her new acquaintance.

His face was knife thin, long nosed. There was a strange stillness about him, which made Mosca think of a heron motionless beside a pool, waiting to became a javelin of feather and bone as soon as a trout was lulled to torpor in the water below.

"You know your letters?" The question was deep and gravelly.

"Yeah, you want me to read a newspaper? I got . . ." Mosca boldly brandished her fistful of sodden paper pulp.

"No, not that. Come with me—you need to talk to some friends of mine."

Mosca followed him into the adjoining barn, her eye making an inventory of the stranger's mildew-colored coat, good boots, and weather-spotted felt hat, her mind caught up in feverish calculation. She would charge this man and his friends too much, of course, but how much was *too* too much? How much would cause them to walk away in disgust instead of haggling?

There were four men in the next barn, sitting bowed on bales of hay, one of them mopping at his collar with a soaked kerchief, another trying to wring out his hat. They all looked up as Mosca and her guide entered the room.

"So that's the girl, is it, Mr. Skellow?" asked a young man with a mean mouth.

"That's her," answered the man who had brought her in. "What's your name, girl?"

"Mosca." Yes, now they would look at her and see a housefly, a snatcher of scraps, a walker on ceilings. There was no help for it. One could not lie about one's name.

"She doesn't look much like a scholar to me," objected the mean-mouthed man. "It's a ruse. She's no more a reader than we are."

"I can prove it!" exclaimed Mosca, stung. "Give me some letters and I'll show you! Or get me to write some for you!"

"All right," answered Skellow. "You there. Gripe. *You* know a letter or two, don't you?"

A bearded man in a brimless hat looked furtive.

"Only my given name," he murmured into his collar.

"Well, scratch it out on the floor. Let's see if she can see the sounds in it."

Mosca watched as the bearded man knelt and drew

lines in the dirt and straw scraps with his forefinger.

"Your name's Ben," she said when he was done. "But your B's back to front."

The men exchanged long looks.

"She'll do," said Skellow.

"I charge more when it's raining," Mosca added through chattering teeth. "'Cause it's a special service then, you see. Risk of drowning in floods, and ruining of clothes, and . . . and . . . pleurisy." She was pleased to see the impression created by the unfamiliar word.

Yeah, and I also charge more for people with good boots who hide in a barn on the edge of town instead of heading to the inn, even though they're wetter than herrings. You got something to hide and something important you need read, Mr. Skellow, so you can pay me for it.

"How much more?" asked Skellow.

Mosca opened her mouth and hesitated, breathing quickly as she assessed her chances. She held Skellow's gaze, then found herself naming the sum needed to pay Clent's debts, plus a little more in case he tried to haggle.

There was a cold pause, and one of the men gave a bitter cough of a laugh, but nobody moved to throw her out.

"You must," Skellow said icily, "be very, very afraid of pleurisy."

"Runs in my family," declared Mosca promptly.

Skellow stared at her for a long time.

"All right," he said.

Mosca could feel her eyes becoming larger and

brighter, and the effort required to avoid a delighted grin made her face ache. She had it, she'd bluffed it, she could feel her problems loosening with a click like manacles and clattering to the ground at her feet. . . .

Skellow reached for the purse at his belt and hesitated. "It's just you I'm paying, am I right? We won't dish out the coin and then find out you've got, oh, a master, or starving parents, or pleurisy-ridden brothers and sisters who need as much again, will we?"

Mosca's mind flitted to Clent, and the thought of him as her "master" rankled.

"No," she snapped with venom. "There's nobody. Just me. Nobody else I need to worry about."

"Perfect," said Skellow. He made the T at the end sound like a stone chipping a windowpane, and he smiled as he did so. The corners of his mouth climbed high up his cheeks, dragging furrows in all directions and showing rows of narrow teeth. It was the face of one who does not smile often because he cannot smile well.

And that smile was the last thing Mosca saw before a muffling, stifling weight of cloth was thrown over her head, drowning her in darkness.

2

GOODLADY PLENPLUSH,
BINDER OF BARGAINS

Idiot! Idiot idiot idiot! You flea wit, Mosca, you puddinghead, you muffin skull. Let your guard down, didn't you, you gormless grinning gull? Even when he agreed to a price he should have choked on. Even when he stood right there and near as skin asked you if there was anyone who'd miss you. . . .

There was a sack over Mosca's head, and a tight grip around her middle that pinned her arms to her sides. The roar of the rain drowned her screeched curses, and as the sackcloth around her grew sodden, she knew that she had been carried out of the barn once more, twisting, kicking, and hating with all her heart and soul.

Someone gripped her wrists and tied them behind her. Then she was hefted onto what felt and smelled a lot like the back of a rather damp horse. One of her clogs fell off with a splotch, and she doubted that anyone would stoop for it. A few juddering, unwilling horse breaths, the sound of hooves, and she was lurched into jolting motion.

She was rollicked along in this undignified way for what seemed like hours, hearing nothing but the rain and the clop of other hooves on either side. All the while she listened for the sound of new voices or a passing wagon, some cue for her to yell for help. But no, it seemed that all the world but Mosca and her captives had the wisdom to hide from the rain.

Just when her ribs were bruised with bouncing and her limbs soaked to the bone, she was tugged off the back of the horse and set on her feet. The sack was dragged off her head.

The town was gone, and all around was nothing but craggy moor. She was standing beside Skellow and two of his men in the shelter offered by a crab-apple tree, the grass still dotted with the amber pulp of rotting fruit. The clouds had come down to earth and oozed softly between the heaped granite, the throaty purple of foxgloves.

"Come on." Skellow took hold of her arm and gestured toward a shadow in the face of the nearest crag. Staring at it through her wet lashes, Mosca realized that behind the dismal trickle of water from above was the entrance to a cave. "And try to look grateful. Not many girls like you will ever get a chance to attend a Pawnbrokers' Auction."

Mosca might have found it easier to feel privileged if

she had not been sopping, half shod, and all too aware of a knife prodding her in the back as Skellow followed her into the cave. His comrades made no attempt to accompany them.

Mosca had heard of the Guild of Pawnbrokers, though until now she had had little expectation of attending one of their auctions. Once the Pawnbrokers had simply been a means by which desperate people could gain money quickly, leaving their valuables in the care of the pawnbroker in exchange for a small sum, in the hope of returning later and buying their possessions back. During the last thirty years, however, the Realm had seen countless times of trouble, and the Pawnbrokers had found themselves in possession of varied and valuable things whose owners were a little too dead to reclaim them.

Their subsequent auctions of these curious items had become legendary. Over time the auctions had become stranger, more secretive, and more exclusive. It was said that if you could only earn an invitation to such an auction, you would find all sorts of unusual and unimaginable things on sale—the skulls of kings, the services of assassins, crystal balls with wicked spirits trapped in them, deadly secrets, beasts with tusks and wings. . . .

Just within the cave, an iron hook had been hammered into the wall, and from it hung a dark lantern. In its narrow bar of light stood a walnut desk, at which a man in a smart waistcoat and cravat sat with his quill poised expectantly over a great leather-bound book. He looked like an ordinary clerk but for one thing—he had no head. Then Mosca drew closer and realized that he did have a head, but that it was shrouded in a black hood with eyeholes. Above him hung a frame on which were suspended three metal globes, the sign of the Pawnbrokers.

"Heydayhare," murmured Skellow in his gravelly tones, and the man nodded. Mosca guessed that this must be a password. "Name of Skellow."

"Expected." The hooded man checked something in his book. "What's that?" The quill pointed at Mosca. Mosca opened her mouth to speak, then felt the point of the knife press against her spine and closed it again.

"It's my scribe," said Skellow.

"Very well. You are responsible for its behavior during the auction." Two gray cloth masks were pushed across the desk. "Once past this point you must not remove these masks, nor must you speak a word to anyone but each other, and even then not loud enough for others to hear. If you break these rules, you will lose *all* rights."

There was something in the man's cold, incisive tone that suggested that breathing might be one of these "rights."

Despite herself, a little flame of curiosity started to burn in Mosca's chest as she walked down a narrow, rough-hewn passageway, the mask feeling rough but dry against her cold cheeks. *Well, these might be the last things*

I see, so I might as well get an eyeful.

At the end of the passage the rock opened out in all directions, and Mosca found herself standing on the edge of a huge cavern, some of it craggy and natural, some bearing the marks of picks and chisels. Dozens of lanterns dotted the darkness, each resting on a table at which a gray-hooded figure was seated. From the cave roof hung a far larger Pawnbrokers' sign. The globes were circular cages in which many candles had been set, so that the contraption helped illuminate the chamber like a peculiar chandelier and silently dribbled pale wax onto the cave floor.

Against the back wall stood a timber-frame platform, to which was still affixed a pulley that had once been used to lower buckets into a square shaft in the floor below. On this platform stood a pulpitlike structure, behind which stood a black-hooded figure in black overalls. Other similarly clad figures scurried through the cave, taking slips of paper from those seated at the tables and carrying them to the waiting hand of the auctioneer at the front. He in turn read each slip and called out a series of numbers in a nasal monotone.

Bidding on pieces of paper. No wonder Skellow needed a scribe.

Skellow was shown to one of the empty desks, and he yanked at Mosca's arm so that she was forced to kneel beside him.

The current auction seemed to be entering a state of

subdued frenzy, and Mosca listened spellbound to the auctioneer.

". . . thirty-five guineas . . . forty guineas . . . gentlemen, remember the sacred nature of these relics, surely a few guineas more . . ."

On the pulpit before the auctioneer was a candle in its last throes, scarcely more than a cratered stump. Mosca realized that this must be an auction "by candle." When the candle died, the auction would be over. As its flame flickered blue, several bid carriers broke into a run, and it was all the auctioneer could do to seize the flourished papers in order.

". . . we have fifty . . . we have . . . done! The candle is dead, gentlemen. The knucklebones said to have belonged to Saint Wherrywhistle herself go to Guest Forty-nine—"

"No!" An echoing cry filled the cavern as one of the gray-hooded figures in the main body of the cavern leaped to his feet. "This is an atrocity! Why will you not wait until we have more money? The knucklebones should never have been stolen from our cathedral in the first—what?—wait!"

A dozen black-masked figures had homed in on the shouter without the slightest fuss and laid hands upon him. In a second he was swept off his feet and borne forward toward the auctioneer's platform. Legs cycling furiously, the hapless rule breaker was hurled without ceremony into the waiting shaft, which threw back only his descending, despairing wail.

"Guest Twenty-four's rights revoked," the auctioneer declared sharply, tapping at his gavel with his hammer.

Skellow's cloth-covered face leaned close to Mosca's cloth-covered ear.

"Hush up," he whispered almost inaudibly. The injunction was unnecessary. Mosca had never felt more like hushing up in the whole of her life.

"Now," the auctioneer continued unflappably, "we are pleased to place on auction the services of one Romantic Facilitator." The mess of the last candle was scraped away with a knife, and a new stub lit in its place.

Skellow nudged Mosca vigorously with his elbow and pushed the quill and ink on the desk toward her hand.

What the blinkin' eck's a Romantic Facilitator? This chisel-faced maggot can't have kidnapped me because he needs someone to help him get a lady friend, can he? Mind you, how else would he get one?

However, she obediently wrote down the sum that Skellow whispered in her ear, and handed it to one of the swift-footed messengers in black masks as he hurried by. She thought about writing "Help, I've got a knife in my back," but decided against it. She had the feeling that nobody except Skellow would care.

"Five guineas." Mosca's eyes crept to Skellow's hood again as his bid was read out. Surely even Skellow couldn't be *that* desperate for a lady friend? And could he really have that sort of money?

For the first two minutes the bids came slowly,

intermittently. Skellow turned out to be someone who cracked his knuckles when he was nervous, and Mosca winced each time he did so, in case the sound was enough to see them shafted. Then the lip of the candle collapsed, hot wax spilling creamily onto the tabletop, and the room was galvanized. There was a frenzy of scribbling, then the pat-a-pat of feet as the bid carriers ran to and fro. Clearly Skellow was not the only person interested in the Romantic Facilitator.

Six guineas. Eight. Twelve. Frantically Mosca wrote down each sum Skellow growled in her ear. The candle's flame was growing squat and uncertain.

"Fifteen guineas!" hissed Skellow. "Write it fast! Faster!" The knifepoint jabbed at her spine. Hand shaking, Mosca scribbled the bid, waved the paper over her head, and watched, heart in mouth, as a runner tweaked it from her fingers and sprinted to join the gaggle clustered about the auctioneer.

The auctioneer had just time to snatch one last paper as the candle flame flared, buckled, and died, leaving a faint quill of smoke trailing from its wick.

"Done! Last bid before the death of the candle. . . ." The auctioneer unfolded the paper in his hands. "Fifteen guineas . . . sold to Guest Seventy-one." A runner trotted over and placed a small wooden token on the desk before Skellow.

The pressure from the knifepoint diminished, and Mosca let out a long breath of relief. The next moment, however, Skellow had taken her by the collar again and tugged her into whisper range.

"Write down exactly what I tell you," he hissed through the double layer of cloth. "You write a word awry and I'll spike you."

Mosca nodded and listened, her quill poised.

Dear Sir,

You are recommended me on account the auctioneers say you have a name good enough for daylight. We are wanting you about a matter of a gentleman in the town of Toll who would marry the daughter of the mayor but for the difficulties put in his way by her family who are not being amiable on account of some damage recently done to his good name. And it have been put to him that sometimes the course of true love does not run smooth but needs help, and sometimes a few coins changing hands and a bit of sword work like. And if you please I would meet with you at the old bastle house on Moordrick's Fell tonight to discuss how we can come by the lady and have her all safely wedded before she or her family can make any trouble about it. It is best that we discuss it there for it shall be devilish tricky to meet inside Toll. If I do not see you at the bastle house however, I shall look for you just after Toll's dusk bugle in Brotherslain Walk the day after tomorrow. And with this letter you will find moneys for paying of the toll and living comfortable in the city.

Rabilan Skellow

This was the letter that was dictated to Mosca. However, it must be confessed that it was not *quite* the letter she wrote. *That* letter, while similar in many respects, was a bit longer and a lot more creative.

Barely five minutes later, a response was brought by one of their black-hooded hosts.

> *Dear Mr. Scragface Pimplenose,*
>
> *Many thanks for your eloquent epistle. I am sure you cannot possibly be as grotesquely ugly as you claim, and I look forward to making your acquaintance. I always say that a man who can laugh at himself is a man worth knowing.*
>
> *Your star-crossed lovers sound quite charming, and I would be delighted to help.*
>
> *One little superstition of mine I hope you will indulge. I never meet with perfect strangers in desolate bastle houses or alarmingly named alleyways at twilight. This trifling quirk I developed shortly after acquiring a large number of enemies. I would therefore propose that, instead of meeting at either of the places you suggest, we meet at nine of the clock by the stocks in Lower Pambrick on Goodlady Joljock's morn. I shall be wearing a Fainsnow lily pinned to my pocket.*
>
> *Your faithful servant.*

Mosca let her black eyes dart from line to line; then she glanced up at the ominous outline that was Skellow, his pale amber eyes glowing softly through the holes in his mask.

"I'm not reading this to you," she hissed, "until I got some certainty that I'm gettin' out of all this alive."

"*What?* You . . ." Skellow winced at the sound of his own voice and looked about, but his squawk of indignation seemed to have gone unnoticed.

The auctioneer appeared to be starting the next auction. "Now we have on sale the services of a lady who has made her name in one of the quick-fingered professions. . . ." Black-masked messengers had materialized next to Skellow's desk with the air of one waiting to tidy it. Skellow rose, yanking Mosca to her feet.

"Outside," he spat.

Mosca tensed as they left the cave, looking for a chance to pull her arm loose and sprint to the cold and rain-sodden freedom of the moors. Skellow seemed to have read her mind, however, and kept a cruel grip on her until they were surrounded by his friends once more. A sharp shove sent Mosca back against the rocky face, and she found herself ringed by a set of very damp men who appeared to be losing their sense of humor.

"Read it!" Skellow thrust the letter toward her. "Or . . ." He was no longer making any attempt to hide the knife in his other hand.

"Or what? You'll kill me?" Mosca made fists in an attempt to stop her arms from shaking. "If you want me to read this letter, I'll need to be alive."

"Yes," said Skellow through his teeth, "but you won't need your thumbs."

There was a small pause during which Mosca realized exactly how fond she was of her thumbs and considered the many things she would be unable to do without them. These included untying knots and slipping keys out of enemies' pockets. Biting her lip so hard that it hurt, she snatched the letter back out of his hand.

"All right," she said sullenly, then lowered her eyes to the page again and started to speak.

Occasionally her black gaze would creep up for a furtive glance at the lean, dripping faces of her captors. Did they suspect that the words on the page in front of her were not *quite* the words she was speaking? No, she thought not.

After she had finished reading, Skellow stood in silence for a while, chewing the inside of his cheek.

"So . . . our Romantic Facilitator cannot come to the bastle house tonight, but is happy to meet with me in Brotherslain Walk like I suggested?"

"Happy as a mouse in a marmalade jar." Mosca gritted her teeth and fought to keep her gaze bold and unblinking. If Skellow sensed the lie in her words, he showed no sign of it.

"All right, then." Skellow gave a tick of tongue against teeth. "Come on, my boys. We're leaving."

Once again, the involuntary scribe found herself bound and bundled, bouncing along on the back of the same wet horse. She tried to twist her hands out of their bonds, but the cold and damp made everything harder and the chafing ropes burned like a brand of ice.

There is no way of measuring time that is filled with nothing but darkness, and knocks, and cold, and the rain's unending drum roll. *This might be the last thing I ever know* was the thought that went around and around Mosca's head, stretching each heartbeat to an eternity as if her frightened spirit was trying to draw the marrow out of every painful moment and live as hard as it could while it still could. She could not even hope for the ordeal to end, for how could it end well? What was she now? A tool that had served its purpose. Worse still, a tool that could talk.

She felt a tickle against her fingers and reflexively clutched at the bracelet tangled in the cords binding her wrists. The three carved totems that dangled from it were images of the Little Goodkin, the skeletal children said to protect any child endangered and lost in the darkness. Another child would have been chanting "Fenfenny, Friends Defend Me" and finding comfort in the rhyme. But Mosca had emptied her darkness of comforting, imagined faces, and such words were hollow to her. She clutched at the bracelet because it had been a gift from a coffeehouse mistress named Miss Kitely in a precarious moment and it still warmed her with a memory of friendship, but even this was small consolation.

At last the horse slowed and she was dragged off its

back. The sack was yanked from her face, and she found that the world had become a darker place than before. Mosca was set on her feet, and her clogless foot instantly sank into cold, wet mud.

Through the clinging mask of her wet hair, she could just about see that the horses had been tethered outside a bleak-looking farmhouse set alone on the moorland. It was built from large rough-hewn stones and its arrow-slit windows were chips of darkness. There were two doors, one set at ground level, one ten feet above the earth with a wooden ladder leading up to it.

Mosca knew that this must be the bastle house mentioned in Skellow's letter. A bastle house was a farmhouse designed to be its own little bastion. It was always dangerous to live near a border, what with the risk of invading armies or raiding parties sneaking across to steal cattle or whatever else they could get their hands on. The problem with the Realm, of course, was that it was *full* of borders. Decades before, it had splintered into smaller allegiances, each proclaiming the rights of a different absent claimant to the throne. Nowadays there was less fear of invasion, but along the borders buildings like this remained, some now derelict, like knobs of scar tissue to show where the Realm had been sliced asunder. To judge by its lightless windows, this bastle house had been abandoned.

For the first time, her captors' voices settled into a contented and relieved murmur.

"I'm frozen. Let's get in and light the fire."

"Some food wouldn't kill me either."

"What do we do with the girl?"

Silence. Mosca's black eyes flitted from face to face as the men exchanged glances.

"Keep her in the vaults for now," answered Skellow.

The sturdy ground floor door was heaved open, and with a *snick* and *hisshh* of flint, a lantern was lit. Mosca found herself looking at a dungeonlike space broken up into long, vaulted tunnels with iron rings hammered here and there into the walls. Only the crusted gray disks of long-dry cowpats showed that this space had been set aside to defend livestock, not to hold prisoners.

Mosca was taken by the shoulder and guided into the nearest "vault," hearing the antique cowpats give under her feet with a papery rustle. The loose ends of the cord tying her wrists were knotted around one of the iron rings set in the wall, with just enough slack that she could sit on the ground if she chose. Mosca, who had slumped against the rugged wall with every sign of meek exhaustion, furtively watched from under wet and spiky lashes as Skellow tugged at the cord.

Only when Skellow left the vault, taking the lantern with him, did Mosca's posture become less limp, less meek. Instead she bristled with attention, taking in every tiny sound from outside. The *shunk* of a bar being lowered across the door. The heavy grinding of an elderly key turning. Voices. The creak of footsteps on wooden rungs as Skellow and his friends climbed the ladder to the upper floor. The shuddering slam of another door.

Mosca blinked hard, willing her eyes to make something of the darkness. It was not absolute, for even on this level there were arrow slit windows, showing frayed ribbons of dull night sky.

Footsteps above; the scrape of a shifted chair. A wordless drone of voices. And then, at the far end of the vaulted tunnel, part of the ceiling opened with a clack, spilling candlelight onto the rutted floor. As Mosca watched, a soft plume of gray ash puffed its way downward, accompanied by a pattering of charcoal chips. Someone on the floor above had opened a hatch to sweep the debris from the fireplace into it.

Unbidden, there came into Mosca's mind a long-forgotten image of her aunt peeling potatoes, the long spiral curling down and down from the tuber and then dropping into the waiting bucket of throwings and leavings. The thought that she had been casually cast down like a piece of rubbish filled Mosca with a wild surge of unpotatolike rage.

Now that the hatch was open, the voices above were much clearer.

"Do you think maybe one of us should go down with some bread for that girl?" It sounded like the man named Ben.

"What's the point?" Skellow's voice.

The distant amber aperture vanished with a slam,

leaving Mosca in darkness once more.

What's the point? Those three words had told Mosca everything she needed to know. There was no point in feeding her because they did not need to keep her alive—did not *mean* to keep her alive. In Skellow's head she was dead already, and wasting bread on her would be like pushing food into the mouth of a stuffed deer head mounted on a wall.

Mosca could guess what had passed through Skellow's mind. How much had she seen and heard of his business? Too much for Skellow's liking and too little for her own. Perhaps he had never intended to let her walk away. He had, after all, asked her carefully chosen questions before concluding that she would never be missed and that no hue and cry would come after him if one night the moors swallowed her like a grape seed.

Worst of all, Mosca reflected, he was probably right.

3

GOODLADY WHENYOULEAST, MISTRESS OF REUNIONS AND REMEMBERED FACES

MOSCA HAD HEARD old stories of captives who were kept in oubliettes, cellars designed for prisoners whom one intended to forget. These had no doors, and the prisoner was thrown down through a hatch in the high ceiling. There was no stairway or ladder leading back to the hatch, because it would never be needed.

Even though she had seen her prison, Mosca's imagination started to crowd the darkness with the relics of such a dungeon. Perhaps she was not the first prisoner to be murdered there. Perhaps she had silent company, lying unseen in the shadows of the arches. Skulls yellow as pie crust under limp bonnets, stick shins jutting into slack boots, tattered tunics over dulcimer rib cages . . .

Nah. I'd be able to smell 'em.

In the room above her, voices droned for a time, fire

crackled, wood scraped on pewter, and someone even scratched out a few ditties on a fiddle. Later there was the hiss of a doused fire, the shuffle of feet on flagstones, and then quiet.

Quiet, and more quiet. The rain slackened and stilled. Silence, but for the chill quavering of owls, and guttering drips hitting earth outside.

Mosca let out a slow breath. Stealthily, her long, quick fingers and recently threatened thumbs twisted to pick at the cords around her wrists. A painful process, for there seemed to be countless knots to bite into her every time she strained against the bonds. Only after five minutes of silently mouthed swearwords did she realize that a particularly vicious knot caught between her wrists was in fact the small wooden head of one of the little skeletons attached to her bracelet.

Perhaps the Little Goodkin *could* be of some service to Mosca, after all.

With painful care she managed to squirm the little wooden figure out from between her wrists. Now there was a tiny amount of slack in the bonds, just enough for two lean and eager hands to writhe free.

In the silence Mosca shook her hands like dishcloths until the blood prickled back into them. She had heard the key turn in the lock of the door, and the arrow slits were clearly too narrow for her to squeeze through, so she crept to the end of the vault, where ash heaped with graying chicken bones, and stared up at the ceiling. The light from the arrow slits was just strong enough for her to make out the dark square of the trapdoor, inches from the end wall.

Mosca kicked off her remaining clog. She had been thrown down and forgotten, but she was not in an oubliette. This was a stronghold of sorts, but it was meant to keep people out and cattle in. And cattle, unlike Mosca, could not climb.

The rough-hewn face of the wall was Mosca's friend, even though the jagged edges were not kind to her cold fingers and bit into her knees and elbows at every opportunity. There were footholds and handholds aplenty, but they had to be groped for in the dark, and Mosca could feel her wet feet slithering against their perches. She tried not to look down nor up, even to satisfy the nagging need to know how high she was. *High enough to hurt if I fall,* whispered the tingle in her bones. And then, after a while, *High enough to break my ankle.* And finally, *High enough to smash me like an egg.*

At last the wood of the hatch met her fingers. She locked her face in a wince and pushed at the trapdoor, praying that nobody had bolted it. It lifted.

The trapdoor opened a crack, letting in the light of a dulling fire and an orchestra of snores. A bubbling snore like a bee dying in treacle. A rasping, lizard-hiss snore. A rhythmic, grindstone rumble.

Hardly daring to breathe, Mosca eased the trapdoor back so that it was resting on the stone flagstones and looked about her. A cooling, soot-bellied kettle hung over the glum red embers that lurked in the fireplace, furred with ash. A pack of Pincaster playing cards laid out on the floor for a game of Duchy's Favor. A row of dominoes set up on their ends along the floor. Two figures stretched beneath their own cloaks beside their muddy boots, an ear poking out here, a company of toes there.

Mosca pulled herself halfway out of the hatch onto her belly and wriggled her way forward until she could bring her legs up onto level floor. She rose to her hands and knees, and froze.

Against the door rested a time-ravaged basket chair, strands of its broken wicker splayed like spokes. In the chair lay Skellow, his mouth so wide open he seemed to be silently singing. From somewhere behind his cravat came the lizard-hiss snore.

Although nowadays Mosca did her best to avoid praying to the Beloved, at least until they provided her with decent evidence of their existence, she still reserved the right to mutter silent imprecations against them when her path was scattered with more thorns than she considered reasonable.

There was no escape through the door. Mosca picked her way carefully around the room, skirts hitched so that she would not knock over the line of yellow bone dominoes or set the wooden bowls rolling.

There—a small shuttered window set high in one

wall. Narrow, but wide enough to allow a Mosca through.

She climbed gingerly onto a stool, worked the shutter bolt free, and opened the shutters. Then she heaved the upper part of her body onto the windowsill and started wriggling through the gap, the night air rushing in past her so icily that it made her ears ache. There was sky ahead with stars drowned in it, black trees waving as if trying to mime a warning. . . .

Behind her there was a faint *clack-clack-clack-clack* like a skeleton impatiently drumming its fingers. In her mind's eye, Mosca could almost see the first domino teetering in the breeze, then falling to trigger the others. The lizard-hiss snore stopped abruptly, and then there was a hoarse cry, enough to tell Mosca that Skellow had woken, looked up, and seen that the nearest window was full of wet petticoat and frantically kicking legs.

There are times for caution and carefully planned descents. And there are times for hurling oneself out of a window willy-nilly and trusting to luck.

As it happened, luck decided to break Mosca's fall with a blackberry hedge. A few seconds were spent in bewildered flailing before she worked out why the sky was covered in dead leaves and why the ground had stars in it. Dozens of tiny thorns set in her clothes as she struggled to right herself. Only the sound of a door cracking back on its hinges gave her the panicky strength to yank herself free, leaving her bonnet to the brambles' embrace.

Which way to run? Anywhere. Anywhere not here.

"Get a lantern! Get a lantern!" Voices from the bastle house.

But it takes time to find a lantern in the dark, long enough for two quick legs to sprint away into the heaving labyrinth of gorse. It takes time too for sleep-fumbled hands to strike flint and nursemaid the trembling flame to the wick, long enough for small, cunning hands to snap off a fern fan the right size to shield a black-haired head from sight. And by the time three men stood at the door of the bastle house surveying the night, there was no sign of the fugitive, and no sound but for the restless wind and the disappointed fluting of owls skimming unseen over the mouseless moor.

There is nothing more miserable than being cold, wet, exhausted, and hungry without any likelihood of becoming *less* cold, wet, exhausted, or hungry. If the future does not hold that comforting promise of shelter, and dry clothes, and a bowl of hot soup, then the damp and cold are free to sink into one's very marrow, because there is no hope to keep it out.

Eventually, however, the dim starlight showed Mosca the twin grooves left by uncounted cartwheels, and she realized she had found a rough road. Following it, she at last discovered a clutch of slate-roofed, rugged-faced cottages huddling in the heather like eggs. Bonnetless and bedraggled, she limped into the village. It was silent, every window shuttered.

Mosca ran her numb fingers through her hair and tried to tame it into something less like a rookery, then knocked on the nearest door. There was no response, but on a second knock she heard a shuffling step and took a pace back, in time to look unthreatening as the door opened a crack to show a neat slice of nightcap, suspicious elderly face, linen bed gown, and fire iron.

"Please, sir—I been robbed." It was important to say this first. If she had had her money taken from her, she had some chance of being considered respectable. If she admitted that she'd never had any money in the first place, it was much more likely that she would be cast out and distrusted. Respectable people were funny like that. And after all, Skellow had promised Mosca money and not given it to her. What was that but robbery?

"Spare us, sores!" The old man took in her drenched dress and stockinged feet and did not seem inclined to hit her with the fire iron. "What happened to you?"

"I was taking some money and a message for my mistress. . . ." Mosca paused to note the effect of her words. Yes, the words "my mistress" had worked their magic, and she was transformed in the stranger's eyes from youthful beggar to diligent serving girl. And a mistress was even more respectable than a master. "And these men, they dragged me off and robbed me, and locked me up, and I think they was goin' to kill me 'cause I saw their faces, but I got away. . . ."

"Local men, were they?" The old man gave a speculative glance down the street.

"I don't know . . . don't think so, sir. I think they was here visiting. They . . . They come for the Pawnbrokers' Auction—"

The moment the words were out of Mosca's mouth, she knew that she had made a mistake.

"We don't know anything about the Pawnbrokers!" the old man declared, his bristled chin wobbling. Behind his face a door had slammed shut, and a moment later the door in front of Mosca did exactly the same thing.

"Hope yer roof falls in," Mosca told his door knocker conversationally.

A slammed door meant that this village *did* know about the Pawnbrokers' Auction, and they were eager to know no more than they had to. It occurred to Mosca that a guild that would happily throw its clients down mineshafts if they broke rules of anonymity would probably not be much kinder to anyone who snooped on the comings and goings around its auctions. Best to bolt the doors and fasten the shutters and wait for the auctioneers and their mysterious buyers and sellers to go away.

She limped on between the silent houses, trying to judge the friendliness of each. She was just about to raise another knocker when she spotted a glimmer of light ahead. Unlike its fellows, the last building's chimney churned smoke, and on a wall bracket swung a lantern, illuminating a gleaming sign that swung above the door, and upon which three painted dogs bore down on a painted stag. Beneath it the lettering read: «} z5Ɱ ƒ¢z¥5 } v' «C

A tavern! The village had a tavern, and one evidently willing to welcome visitors; however strange and dangerous they might be, even on this night. Winter was winter, after all, and money was money.

The door swung open to her knock. The smells of trout and muffins and blackberry sauce pushed into Mosca's insides like a spoon and scraped her empty stomach. A tall blond man in an apron stood in the doorway, the firelight behind him turning each golden hair on his muscular red arm into a tiny thread of flame. His eyes slid off Mosca and out onto the dark road behind her, as if hoping she was an errand girl for a coach, or at the very least a horseman.

"Yes?" he asked the empty road.

"I been robbed. . . ." Mosca saw the door start to close and had the presence of mind to push her clogless foot into the gap, a painful decision but one that kept the door open. "And . . . and I think my mistress said she was coming here. I was supposed to meet her, but I got grabbed and dragged off over the moor. . . ."

The door opened warily.

"Your mistress's name?"

Exhaustion suddenly fogged Mosca's mind. She snatched for a fistful of names, only to have them crumple in her hand like dead leaves, leaving her with nothing. She was just about to blurt out Clent's name in desperation when a woman's voice interrupted.

"Kale! What's wrong with you? Don't ask the lady's name!" The door was pulled wider, and Mosca found herself looking into the brown eyes of a woman not much taller than herself. Her neatness and pert precision of movement made Mosca think of a wren, a freckled little wren in a muslin gown. "We don't ask for names on this night—you should know better. Now bring the girl in, and we'll see if we can't find her mistress."

Mutely Mosca followed her diminutive champion to the fireside, where her legs decided that their work was done for the evening and crumpled under her. She was draped in a blanket that smelled of horse and had a burn hole in it, but which was gloriously, blissfully dry. Soon a wooden bowl of hot stew was in her hands, and in over-eagerness she burned her tongue so that she could taste nothing but metal.

On the other side of the room she could hear a murmured conversation between her two new acquaintances, who she guessed were probably the tavern keeper and his wife.

". . . let her in until we knew whether she was telling the truth."

"Oh, Kale! It's past midnight. You know what that means? These three hours are sacred to Whenyouleast, Mistress of Reunions and Remembered Faces. During those hours, if you reunite two people who have been separated by chance, then it means you'll have good luck the whole of the next year. So let's see if we can match her up with her lost mistress. I'm sure her mistress will pay for the stew."

Mosca had no idea how she would conjure a mistress out of thin air, but she was sure that inspiration would come more easily on a full stomach.

"Well, we've only one lady staying here, and she left hours ago and hasn't come back—"

As if to refute the landlord's words, there came a brisk knock at the door. Mosca stiffened as she heard the door open and the landlady's tones become sprightly and welcoming.

"Good to see you back, ma'am. Quite a perilous cold night for you to be out in. Oh, do come and warm yourself by the fire!"

"That would be most welcome, my currant bun." A warm summer breeze of a voice. "Ooh, as you say, a most perishing night, but well, business is business, isn't it?"

"Ye-e-es. . . ." The landlady was clearly unwilling to know too much about the business in question and swiftly changed the subject.

Mosca stiffened, her jaw frozen midchew. The new voice was not unfamiliar.

Two women came into the room. The first was the little wren landlady. The second was sturdy and sun browned, with a good-natured aura that seemed to pour into the room with her like warm custard. Under her cap, a thick plait of gray-touched auburn hair was twisted like a bread swirl. A dark green traveling cloak swathed her stocky figure.

". . . this girl is looking for her mistress." The flow of the landlady's speech continued, oblivious of the way her two companions had locked stares and frozen, like cats in a contested alley. "And since you're the only lady staying with us, we thought she must be yours. . . . Do you know her?"

"Oh, yes, I know her," answered Mistress Jennifer Bessel.

Mosca and Mistress Bessel had indeed met before. Their acquaintance had been very brief, and had involved rather more screaming, breakage, and hasty flight than is generally considered promising for a healthy friendship.

"Oh, now, that's wonderful!" The landlady clasped her hands. "Well, settle yourself down, ma'am, I'll take your cloak . . . and your gloves are all over mud, if you want me to take them away and clean them—"

"No!" Mistress Bessel's answer was sharp enough for the landlady to falter and look anxious.

In a flash, Mosca remembered why Mistress Bessel wore gloves. When they had last met, the gloves in question had been ladylike affairs in black lace, through which Mosca had just about been able to make out a dark mark shaped like a T on the back of each hand. It was enough to tell her that, once upon a time, Mistress Bessel had been branded as a thief. Mistress Bessel now wore good kid gloves. Evidently she was becoming more careful, and less willing to let people see the marks.

It was an opening, a tiny promise of a foothold, and Mosca reached for it.

"Hello, ma'am," Mosca said with a docile little bob of the head, her eyes wide, insolent black pennies. She let her gaze drop for a barely perceptible instant to Mistress Bessel's gloved hands. *If you cry me out for a criminal, two can play at that game.*

"Poor little currant bun," said Mistress Bessel, fixing Mosca with eyes the blue of a midwinter morning. "Look at the dear, draggled thing—don't you just want to wring her out like a dishcloth?" She turned to the landlady. "Now don't you worry about us, my lovely. My girl and I will take ourselves up to our room and be out of your way, won't we?"

Still retaining eager custody of the stew bowl and hugging her blanket around herself, Mosca followed Mistress Bessel's stocky form up a stairway almost too narrow for her. They entered a boxlike, windowless, dark-paneled room with a drably draped bed and a busy little hearth.

Once the door was closed and Mosca had crouched by the fire, Mistress Bessel fixed her with her gimlet gaze and then very slowly put her fists on her hips. Maybe it was a trick of the light thrown upward by the fire, but Mistress Bessel's face seemed thinner than Mosca remembered it, and more haggard. Perhaps the death of summer had not been kind to her either.

Mosca did not see the accusing glare as a reason to stop eating, but instead decided to scoop food faster, until her spoon became a blur. If there was a danger that she would have to flee into the night once more, she was determined to do so with as much stew inside her as possible.

"*You.*" All the warmth had drained out of Mistress Bessel's tone, leaving it as wintry as her eyes. "You *would* turn up now, like a witch's imp come to claim a soul. What hellcat coughed *you* up on my doorstep, tonight of all nights?" Her gaze dropped to the dribble of soup running down Mosca's chin. "I better not be paying for your dinner!" she snapped.

"You can't be short on money if you're going to the Pawnbrokers' Auction," answered Mosca through a mouthful of parsnip. It was a wild shot, but why else would the woman be out so late? Mistress Bessel flinched, and Mosca guessed that she had hit her mark.

Mistress Bessel gave a quick glance over her shoulder. "All right," she said in a low mutter, "where is he? If you're here, your partner in crime can't be far away. I've still got a bone to pick with him."

"Mr. Clent's in the debtors' prison in Grabely, and set about with creditors. If you want to pick his bones clean, you'll have to join the queue."

"I do not mean Eponymous!" Mistress Bessel glared at her, and this time Mosca noted a decidedly apprehensive look in her eye. "I mean that . . . *thing* of yours."

Saracen tended to leave a strong impression. Months before, while on their travels, Clent and Mosca had stayed for a brief interval at Mistress Bessel's shop. While Mosca was away on a shopping trip, Clent had tried to make a present of Saracen to Mistress Bessel. Mosca had had her own ideas about this, as had Saracen, and Saracen had ended up making a cripplingly strong impression upon Mistress Bessel, Mistress Bessel's apprentice, a counter, two tables, a window, and most of the contents of her shop.

"Saracen's not here." *Wish he was.*

Mistress Bessel relaxed somewhat, and then Mosca's previous words seemed to penetrate.

"Did you say that Eponymous was in Grabely? So . . . you're still gallivanting around after him, are you?" Mistress Bessel's face furrowed for a moment with an expression halfway between bitterness and wistfulness. Then the softer expression vanished, leaving only creases of suspicion in her brow. "So that's it." Her voice was a knife. "He sent you to find me. He still thinks he can honey-talk money out of me, after all this time. How did he know where I was?"

"He didn't! *I* didn't!" Mosca held up one wrist, where the red marks from her bonds were still visible. "I was in Grabely an' some beaky maggot grabbed me to be his scribe at the auction 'cause he couldn't read, and he'd have killed me afterward if I hadn't run off, and I *didn't*

know you were here and I don't know where here *is* and I don't even know how to get back to Grabely. . . ."

Mosca trailed off only when the air in her lungs was exhausted, but to her relief she saw the suspicious look in the stocky woman's face fade and relax a little.

Mistress Bessel settled herself in a hearthside chair, which received her with a creak. For a few moments she stared pensively at Mosca, her eyes widening and narrowing as if to allow in thoughts of different sizes.

"Well, why not?" she said at last with a sigh. She pulled her shawl up around her neck and suddenly gave Mosca a broad, freckled, summery smile. "Don't let me keep you awake with my chattering, blossom. You look like a bundle of wet kindling."

Mosca did not answer, partly through surprise at the change of tone and partly because her last hasty mouthful had caused her to sneeze barley into her nose.

"Pop your head down and get some sleep," said Mistress Bessel in her most motherly tone, "and tomorrow I'll take you back to Grabely and we can go visit Eponymous together."

Mosca had preferred it when she could hear the edge in her companion's voice. Now she felt like someone who knows that there is a scorpion somewhere in the room but can't see where it is. She did not much like the idea of settling down where Mistress Bessel could watch her sleep either, but what other option was there? Nothing but the moors and the owls and the cold and Skellow with his thumb-cutting knife.

Mosca pulled off her wet stockings and kerchief to hang in front of the fire, and nestled down in her blankets by the fireplace. She pretended to sleep, all the while keeping a sly watch on the woman in the chair. Mistress Bessel, however, seemed to forget her instantly, instead gazing with rapt intensity at the dancing flames, as if her own thoughts were performing for her within the theater of the hearth.

The plump fingers of one hand stroked the gloved palm of the other, as if soothing a wounded or frightened animal. There was a brightness in her eyes, as though she too had been wounded or frightened. The expression on her face made Mosca uneasy, in the same way that it is troubling to see a bell cord swaying in a wind you cannot feel, or to watch a caged bird twittering in fear of an intruder you cannot see. Mosca did not understand what the expression meant but was sure that she had glimpsed the same look hovering on the stocky woman's face when she had first been shown into the parlor, before she saw Mosca. Clearly Mosca was not the only one with worries, and whatever it was that haunted Mistress Bessel, it had nothing to do with Mosca Mye.

4

GOODMAN POSTROPHE,
GUARDIAN AGAINST
THE WANDERING DEAD

THE EVENTS OF the preceding night had taken their toll on Mosca, and she did not wake until midmorning, when the sound of voices and scraping pewter from the kitchens below finally penetrated the fog of exhaustion.

The hangings of Mistress Bessel's bed were pulled back and the rugs that covered the mattress pushed aside. Clearly Mosca's new "mistress" had already risen. Mosca's shed clothes had dried now before the fire, but their muddy-water drenching had left some of the fabric stiff and rough as canvas. There was still something luxurious, nonetheless, about pulling dry stockings on over her cold feet.

Lost: one bonnet, two clogs. Kept, in spite of the odds: two thumbs, one knife. Mosca poured a little water from a ewer into a bowl and quickly washed the blackberry scratches on her arms, the bluish bruises and cuts left by her nocturnal climb, and the red marks on her thin, pale wrists. She was alive. Somehow, impossibly, she had survived the night. Better yet, she now recalled with a malicious satisfaction, she had probably sent the murderous Skellow on a wild goose chase to meet his Romantic Facilitator in the wrong place at the wrong time.

And she was going back to Grabely. Mosca had talked to Mistress Bessel of returning there almost without thinking, just as she had automatically asked Skellow for a fee that would cover Clent's debts.

"I'm going back there to find Saracen," Mosca told a splinter in her fingertip. "That's all."

When she arrived downstairs, she found Mistress Bessel seated in the parlor, looking so warm and rosy that Mosca almost wondered whether she had imagined the haunted look she had glimpsed the preceding night. The plump woman appeared to be in earnest conversation with a black-clad man. When Mosca entered, he paused midsentence just long enough for his small gray eyes to glare at her from under his wild black brows with shortsighted intensity. This alarmed her until she guessed that he was hypnotized by his own fierce, flamelike thoughts and barely saw the things around him.

Mistress Bessel had her lips pursed to show that she was following his words with acute interest, but Mosca could not help noticing that her blue eyes looked a little glazed. She was wielding her porridge spoon in a way that struck Mosca as clumsy, though she could not pin down why.

"My own hypothesis"—the stranger clasped his long, bony hands in his lap—"is that the miasmatic theory can explain the sightings of ghosts. They are often seen in places where many people have died, yes? I believe that a special sort of noxious vapor is left by a corpse at the moment of death, tainting an area and poisoning the air. Everyone who lives in that area breathes the miasma each day without knowing it, allowing the tiny fragments to enter their systems and *attack the brain*. The brain bulges and buckles inside the skull like an oyster in a shell too tight for it, and out of it come visions, hallucinations, waking dreams—in short, the so-called ghosts."

"Why, that is quite marvelous, Dr. Glottis!" exclaimed Mistress Bessel. "Queer how it all makes sense when you explain it. So the brains of grave diggers and hangmen must be full to the squeak with miasmas and ghosts, then?"

"Ah yes!" The doctor looked dreamy for a moment. "How I would love to look inside the skull of a hangman! But one simply cannot get the bodies—according to the law, only executed criminals can be taken for study, and only a set number of those, and the Guild of Barber-Surgeons claims most of them." He sighed. "But at least here on the borders, a region that has always been rich in war and death, at least here I can wander and look at the inhabitants and satisfy myself whether"—he glanced toward the distant landlord and lowered his voice—"whether their *skulls are bulging.*"

Mad as a midday moon, thought Mosca.

Mistress Bessel finally seemed to notice Mosca. "Ah, there's my girl. Mye, Dr. Glottis is traveling to Grabely this morning on . . . business, and has agreed to give us a ride there. Run upstairs and pack our things, will you?" Clearly Mistress Bessel had decided to make the most of her unexpected "servant girl." "And Mye . . ."

Mosca halted on the stair, her tongue pushed into her cheek.

"Pack carefully." Mistress Bessel smiled, but there was a gleam of meaning in her eye. "I wouldn't want to find something missing this evening, would I?"

Slightly to Mosca's surprise, Dr. Glottis proved to be the proud possessor of a rather large cart, already heavily laden. Seeing the outline of bulky boxes under a mantle of sacking, Mosca's first thought was that Dr. Glottis must have been kicked out of his hometown for prodding people's heads in search of lumps and was now wandering adrift with the greater part of his furniture.

"What's under the cloth?" she asked Mistress Bessel as they were waiting for the landlord's son to lead the doctor's horses out of the stable.

"That," murmured Mistress Bessel while smiling at the distant doctor and giving him a little wave, "is not something a nice girl asks the day after a Pawnbrokers' Auction. I didn't hear *his* door close till an hour after we were abed. He's too much of a gentleman to ask why either of *us* are here—so keep your smile sweet and your tongue knotted, blossom."

Predictably, Mistress Bessel was given the comfortable seat between Dr. Glottis and his driver, and Mosca found herself bouncing along on the pile of swathed boxes. Her curiosity was too much for her, and she tweaked back a corner of the sacking. To her bemusement, she discovered that she was perched upon a stack of loosely tethered grandfather clocks, some of them showing advanced signs of age and many with chipped faces or missing hands. Could the doctor really have gone to the Pawnbrokers' Auction in the dead of night to buy a cartload of broken clocks?

Mad as a belfry full of bats.

The kindhearted landlady at the inn had insisted that Mosca take a pair of rough clogs and a battered old bonnet "so you won't catch a chill or make people wonder at you." With hindsight, Mosca was glad that her stew had been paid for by Mistress Bessel, and that the wrenlike little woman had not been cheated of the money for it. Mosca clutched the bonnet to her head as the cart jolted and jarred its way across the moor, the road before it little more than a conspiracy of stones.

The moor was less ominous in daylight, but Mosca still caught herself flinching each time a parchment-colored leaf spiraled down from a tree, or when a change in the wind splayed the dry grass that sprouted from the walls of stacked stones. Some trees were so knobbed and crooked that they seemed to be made up of elbows and knees. Skellow trees with thorns for eyes, watching her pass.

After hours of this, it was with relief that at last she saw in the distance the slate roofs of Grabely and the kinked spire of the town's little church. However, as the cart entered the town, Mosca became aware that the atmosphere there had changed. There was a subdued hum that did not come from the dozens of spinning wheels that the townswomen worked in the morning sun. Something had happened, something to cause a murmur of somber but excited gossip.

". . . took him to the Assizes at Notwithstanding . . . ," Mosca overheard, and her blood turned to ice. She pricked up her ears.

". . . the worst kind of thief as it turns out, infamous for this kind of thing, won't be seeing the light until his gibbeting day . . ."

Horror hit Mosca like a flash flood, drenching her in cold and taking away her breath. They were talking about Clent, it *had* to be Clent; she had run off and left him trapped like a rat with a poster right outside his cell listing his crimes, and somebody had come along who could read it, and after all the years of fast talking and whisker-close escapes the noose had finally closed around him, because *she* had betrayed and deserted him, and now he had been taken away to be tried and gibbeted and eaten by crows, and . . .

". . . they say his conscience sent him screaming to the law . . ."

Mosca's headlong panic missed its step, faltered and slowed. She could imagine Clent doing a great many things, but hurling himself into the hands of justice in a fit of conscience was not one of them.

"Mistress?" The doctor had ordered his driver to slow, and he now leaned to speak to the nearest of the spinning women. "Pray tell me—did you just say that a criminal had been taken to the Notwithstanding Assizes?"

"Yes, and I hope he hangs in chains! A good-for-naught grave robber. He had a dozen decent dead folks newly dug up from the villages round about, all wearing sacking instead of shrouds, piled in the old chapel out by the stream. But in the middle of last night he ran into the village screaming that a ghost was after him and collapsed on the courthouse steps. So they sent men back to the chapel and found the bodies. He'd have gotten off with a few nights in the cells, but one of the dead women was still wearing a silver ring, so that makes it theft, and a different kettle of worms."

"Imagine if he hadn't been caught!" added another spinning woman for good measure. "I'd never have felt safe on my deathbed again."

Mosca felt her own face go slack with relief. It was

not Clent. Whoever they were talking about, it was not Clent. She glanced quickly at her companions to be sure that her reaction had not been noticed, and found that Dr. Glottis was staring at the townswoman with a look of stunned horror not very different from the one Mosca had probably been wearing a moment before.

A dozen decent dead folks . . . Mosca's eyes dropped to the uncomfortable seating arrangement beneath her and silently counted a dozen clocks. It occurred to her rather forcibly that she herself would fit quite neatly inside the clock she was currently sprawled across. She shuddered and drew up her knees, trying to touch their wood as little as possible.

She now had a shrewd idea what the zealous doctor had actually paid for at the auction. Everyone else might be aghast by the thought of a grave robber roaming the countryside, but if she was right, the doctor was horrified that the man had been caught before he could deliver the dozen bodies he had promised so that they could be hidden in the clocks. Dr. Glottis seemed to have quite forgotten that he had passengers, and gave them not even a glance as they dismounted.

"Just take my things to the tavern, will you, blossom?" Mistress Bessel gave Mosca a purposeful little pat on the arm. "And I'll call in on dear Eponymous and give him my respects."

As her mistress sailed off in search of the debtors' prison, Mosca sighed and set about dragging Mistress

Bessel's travel trunk across the market square to the tavern. By the time she reemerged from the inn, Mistress Bessel had vanished, and the doctor was in feverish discussion with a red-nosed young man in a pie-shaped hat.

"But . . . is there no chance of looking around the chapel? Just a brief glance?" The doctor seemed quite frantic.

"It's haunted." The pie-hatted man spoke with the slow, deferential tone of one telling his social better something for the seventh time. "A wild and restless ghaist, the vexed spirit of one of those poor souls dug up by that ghoul they took to the Assizes. Nobody can go in without it attacking them and trying to drag them to hell with it. Nothing to be done but give Goodman Postrophe as many mellowberries as we can and leave it to him." Goodman Postrophe was the Beloved responsible for squirting mellowberry juice into the eyes of any dead that tried to return to their erstwhile homes, so that they were blinded and could not find their way.

The doctor hesitated; then his eyes took on a pitiable glimmer of hope.

"You say . . . a ghost? And you—you have seen this ghost?"

"Oh, I saw it and more, sir!" The pie-hatted man straightened proudly. "It would have had me if I hadn't fought it off. It was just after the, um, the quiet folks in the sacks had been taken off to be buried again, and

I was alone in the chapel, when I heard this dreadful flutterin' like grave clothes in a wind, and then I looked round and it flew at me, this horrible white shape trailing its grave shift. And I could tell it was trying to speak to me, but all that came out was this horrible garglin'. Then again, what would you expect, sir? Anyone buried decent has that band o' cloth tied under its chin to keep its cap on. How could the poor creature open its mouth to make itself understood?"

"Did you see its face?" The doctor was craning his head to one side, perhaps in an attempt to see whether the pie-hatted man's head was bulging strangely.

"There was no time for that, sir. One minute it was swooping at me, then it grabbed hold of me and tried to drag me to hell with the might of a hurricane."

"You actually felt it?" The doctor seemed fascinated.

"Well, yes, sir. You don't think my nose is this color naturally, do you?" The feature in question did indeed seem to be unusually raw looking.

"It . . . tried to drag you to hell . . . by your nose?"

"Yes, but I struggled with all my might and mettle, all the time flaring my nostrils as hard as I could to shake it off, and at last the wight let go with this ghostly, despairing . . . honking noise."

Mosca froze and stared hypnotized at the proud ghost fighter's nose. There was a series of dents and marks near the bridge of the nose that looked rather familiar, a little but not quite like teeth marks. She had never heard of a ghost honking or biting its victims on the nose, but she could think of one creature who would do so at the drop of a feather. She needed to act quickly, before anybody else came to the same conclusion.

"Now, if you'll excuse me, sir, I'd better go and pray so that my nose don't turn black and fall off." The younger man deferentially touched his knuckle to his forehead and trotted away, dragging his ghostly adventure behind him like a rich but invisible cape.

The doctor stared after his retreating form.

"Confound the fool," he muttered under his breath. "Why hide all his eggs in one basket? I suppose they did find *all* of them. It must say *somewhere.*"

And to Mosca's consternation, he turned and started reading the posters on the side of the courthouse. Until this moment it had not occurred to her that with the arrival of Mistress Bessel and the doctor, Mosca was now no longer the only person who could read the poster advertising Eponymous's crimes.

Mosca felt once again as if she was tiptoeing between dominoes, but this time the dominoes were house high and could press her like a flower if she let them fall on her. And topple they would, in the slightest breeze. Catastrophe was inevitable, as soon as someone linked Clent to the poster outside his cell, or investigated the ghost properly . . . or as soon as it occurred to Skellow to look for his intended murder victim in the town where he had first kidnapped her.

It seemed to Mosca that Grabely was swiftly becoming an excellent place to contemplate from a great distance.

"Eponymous . . . ," murmured the doctor to himself as he frowned at the poster. "Now where have I heard that name before?"

It was absolutely essential that Mosca say something, anything, to distract the doctor from his current train of thought, so that he would not remember Mistress Bessel speaking of visiting her "dear Eponymous." And then, quite suddenly, Mosca knew exactly what to say.

It was about half an hour later that Mosca entered the debtors' prison and was shown into Clent's cell. Slightly to her surprise, she noticed that he had apparently come by paper, quill, and ink, and was scribbling away with every sign of bad temper.

She settled down cross-legged on the ground beside him.

"That woman is dead to all sense of loyalty," he muttered. "A rosy apple with seeds of the purest poison. You would think that tender recollections might have caused her to pity my plight, but no. She was stonehearted enough to tell me that if I would not write her some respectable-sounding references in a variety of different hands, she would bring a suit against me for the damage that your infernal goose did to her shop, and double my debts. Of course I asked if she could spare the pennies for ink or whether she wished me to write them in my own heart's blood. . . ."

He glanced up from his paper, and then, as he took in Mosca's disheveled and battle-scarred appearance, the expression of outrage melted from his face, to be replaced by something less readable. His gaze moved over the scratches on Mosca's arms, the marks on her wrists.

Mosca stared at the floor, shrugged, and sniffed. "Got grabbed," she said gruffly.

"Beadles?" Clent asked, very quietly.

"No, just . . . just somebody with ugly business, who needed a reader. A reader who wouldn't be missed after." She could not quite keep the bitterness from her tone.

There was a silence, during which Clent watched his quill spread a blot on the paper without seeming to see it.

"You can hardly imagine that your disappearance would go unnoticed—"

"Saracen'd notice," snapped Mosca, "but what's he going to do, put out a reward? And if I hadn't ever come back, you'd notice, but you'd just think I'd run off."

Clent stared at her for a long moment. Then he let out a long sigh.

"It is true." His tone was weary and more than a little rueful. "When you did not come back last night . . ." He closed his eyes and shook his head. "I *did* think you had run away, Mosca."

And, Mosca's conscience reminded her, she had been

planning to do exactly that.

"This . . . individual with the ugly business." Something seemed to have occurred to Clent. "Is he likely to keep looking for you? Is there a chance that he will return to this town to find you?"

Mosca bit her lip and nodded.

"Then you cannot possibly stay in Grabely," Clent said simply, and his eyes shone with faint astonishment at hearing his mouth speak so plainly. He recovered almost immediately and busied his hands and eyes with the folding of his newly written papers. "Why I should have imagined that I would need a secretary *now*, while my papers are in the hands of the petty constable and I have no accounts to speak of—"

"That's what I came here to tell you," interrupted Mosca. "I *am* leaving."

Clent's hands ceased to move. He did not look up, his head remaining bowed over his letters.

"So are you," Mosca added. "Get up, Mr. Clent."

"What?"

"I got the money. You're free."

"But . . ." Clent's face was a picture of incredulity. "How in the world did you find the funds?"

"Well"—Mosca's countenance took on a demureness that did not seem to reassure him—"I had to sell something. I mean, the only thing I had left."

Clent's expression went through a number of different changes. Suspicion, wonder, astonishment, and, at last, hope chased one another across his face like successive sunrises lighting an opulent and rolling landscape.

"You have finally sold the goose?" he asked in hushed tones.

"No! Course not!" Mosca was shrill with indignation. "I couldn't do that!"

"Ah. No. Of course not." Clent sighed wearily.

"No. I sold you."

"*What?*" Clent instantly recovered enough of his composure and health to leap to his feet. "Did a cushion maker stuff your head with feathers? To what purpose are you delivering me from prison if you hand me straight into slavery?"

"It's not slavery," Mosca hastened to reassure him. "It's science. There's a doctor who likes to saw people's heads open to see if their brains are squirming about like oysters. And he was hoping to buy lots of dead bodies from a body snatcher, but the snatcher got himself nabbed. So this doctor had lots of money and nothing to saw. But he cheered up when I told him about my uncle in the debtors' prison who was perilous close to death because of a funny bulge behind his ear as big as a snuffbox. And apparently this doctor only gets to cut holes in *living* people's skulls when they're of unsound mind and their relations give permission. So when I told him that you were seeing ghosts in your soup and unable to speak anything but rhyme, he was pleased as punch."

"Poetry as a disease," whispered Clent. "Then let me

have no cure, let me die of it—before your barber surgeon can sharpen his tools. Is he waiting outside?"

"No, everything's all right, Mr. Clent. He's settling himself down to the biggest haunch of mutton you ever saw. He'll be at his lunch for an hour at least. Gave me a promis'ry note to say he owes the bearer the money—says he'll pay it off when he's seen you. Only I jus' gave the magistrate the note to pay the debts."

Clent collapsed back onto his rough mattress with a thud.

"An hour left," he murmured weakly. "The prime of my life treacherously sold by a little minx who probably didn't even haggle. And what, pray, are your plans for me between now and the end of the mutton haunch? Have you auctioned my last hour to a press gang or a road-building crew?"

"Actually, Mr. Clent," Mosca suggested quietly, "I was thinking we could spend the time running away a lot."

One last stop was required, however, before Mosca and Clent could shake the dust of Grabely from their feet.

The chapel stood a quarter of a mile from the town. Like many of the Grabely houses, the chapel had tall, ragged slate walls, the lower jutting slates tufted with plumes of fleece left by passing sheep. Its windows were fist-sized holes stuffed with bottle-top-sized rounds of colored glass, held in place by wire, all except for the biggest and highest window, a crude-edged, glassless opening in the rough shape of a heart.

"Bet he got in through there," whispered Mosca to Clent.

The chapel now had a sentry, the red-nosed ghost fighter she had encountered before.

"Nobody can go in." He straightened and gripped his crook as if it was a halberd. "Vicious ghosts."

"Ah, but my friend"—Clent took him companionably by the arm—"you overlook the power of innocence to overcome the unholy, the favor of the Beloved that falls upon every unthinking child so that no sprite or shadbaggle may . . ."

Mosca took advantage of the distraction to duck past the sentry, ignoring his cries of protest as she ran into the chapel. As she had hoped, his valor in the face of ghostly attack did not extend as far as risking a second encounter.

There was an odd smell in the chapel. *Damp,* Mosca told herself. *Damp and rat accidents.* She tried not to think of Dr. Glottis's miasma or of lumpish shapes laid out on the stone slabs in blotched sacks. They were all gone now, anyway. Carried out to be buried.

No ghost could be seen among the low wooden benches that served for pews, just splintered wood and shards of porcelain. No ghost behind the statue of Goodlady Halepricket, She Who Keeps the Heads of Sheep from Getting Caught in Bushes, though it seemed that the Goodlady had recently lost a leg. No ghost behind the door, just a collection of shears, hooks, and crooks, now flung into disarray.

"Hey!" Mosca risked a loud whisper. "It's all right! It's me!"

A fluttering, like the rippling of grave clothes in a breeze, and then a long, stealthy, dragging sound. A white shape emerged from a hatch that Mosca assumed led down to a crypt. The plaster walls threw back an echo of the gargling, glugging noise it made in its throat as it approached, its outline shapeless and rumpled.

Mosca knelt down and pulled off the white cambric altarpiece that covered the figure. This instantly revealed a long, white, python-thick neck, a bulging bully brow, and a beak the color of pumpkin peel. With a sense of relief that warmed her more than a dozen suppers, Mosca reached out and took the "ghost" into her arms.

When she gingerly emerged from the chapel, the sentry's reaction was less friendly.

"What . . . it . . ." He waved a disbelieving finger at Saracen. "It . . . it was that cadgebaggoting goose all along! Do you know how much damage—"

"Calm yourself." Clent's tone suddenly had a deep and rich resonance, as if he was declaring prophecy. "In mere moments we will be gone, taking Grabely's ghost away with us forever and leaving you to choose your path. Sir, you stand on the threshold of two alternative futures. In one I see you the toast of every tavern as the slayer of a ten-foot-tall, tiger-toothed titan of terror. In the other you will be forever remembered as the man bested by a young girl's pet."

They left the slayer of the titan of terror rubbing at the tender place on his nose, and clearly well on the way to deciding that discretion was the better part of candor.

Five minutes later the air of liberty had blown Clent into fine fettle in spite of the cold, and he greeted a cooper's cart with such magnanimous good humor that its driver seemed half convinced that Clent was doing him a favor in agreeing to accept a lift.

They were heading east, east toward the plump towns of Chanderind and Waymakem, toward the uncrossable Langfeather . . . toward Toll, Mosca realized. Toll, where some young woman dwelled, oblivious to the fact that a man named Skellow had plans for her future, plans he would kill to protect.

5

GOODMAN JAYBLISTER, MASTER OF ENTRANCES AND SALUTATIONS

As THE CART rumbled on, conversation gradually dwindled as the minds of the two human passengers contemplated the same question. Mosca and Clent were remembering, not for the first time, that while "away" is good as a travel plan, sooner or later there must be a "to."

Clent blew out through his nose and reached for a small black book that Mosca had seen before. Over his shoulder she could see him flicking to a blank page and writing, *Grabely—debtors' prison, brain sold, fowl play in chapel.*

Mosca had of course filched it from his pocket while he slept on earlier occasions, and as far as she could tell it contained notes on towns and villages that he had already visited and therefore could not safely visit again. It was full of scribbled place names and occasionally entries like *Lady Garnergaville's soiree!!* or *Duke for three days* or *Tried the troubadour caper in the fish market—dogs!*

Clent riffled through the pages with a frown and cleared his throat.

"Where are we headed?" he called to the cart driver.

"Well, I was planning to stop and water the horses at Hanging Sparrow, ten miles on," came the answer.

"Hanging Sparrow..." Clent leafed feverishly through his book. "Oh, merciful suns!" He leaned slightly toward Mosca and allowed some low words to creep from the corner of his mouth. "We cannot possibly go to Hanging Sparrow—an abominable place where forgetfulness is an offense punishable with the gibbet."

"What?"

"Well . . . it is if one wanders into it forgetting that one once fabricated the Great Horse Plague for purposes of profit within its walls." He leafed through the book again, muttering place names under his breath. "Twelve Apples . . . no. Starlington . . . no. Upper Dangwit . . . no. Child, I start to fear that we have sucked the very juice from this accursed county."

It did not surprise Mosca that Clent had not for an instant suggested returning to Mandelion. When sneaking her peek at his black book, Mosca had of course hunted down the entry for the rebel city, to find out which of their many escapades and disasters there Clent had thought worth mention. Instead, beneath the city's name he had written only a single word. A name, in capital letters.

GOSHAWK.

Mosca and Clent had fled Mandelion on the orders of a set of quietly insistent men in clean but well-worn overalls—representatives, in fact, of three of the most powerful guilds in the Realm. The Company of Stationers, the Company of Watermen . . . and the Locksmiths.

Locksmiths. They were more than peddlers of locks and strongboxes. They were shadow masters, ghosts, and they thrived on fear.

To outward appearances they were the epitome of respectability. What could be more upstanding than to sell the locks that kept honest men's goods safe? And the Locksmiths did more than this. They ran an organization of thief takers more skillful than any constable, and who, for a price, would hunt down criminals or retrieve stolen goods. They even offered to take over the policing of cities completely and rid them of crime altogether.

What was less well known was that the Locksmiths also ran the criminal underworld in most of the great cities of the Realm. What lock could hold them out? Yes, they would hunt down thieves—but only those who refused to join them and pay tithes to them. It was a bold soul who defied them, for they had hundreds of agents secretly working for them, each bearing the brand of a key on the palm of their right hand.

And from time to time a city ruler would lose heart

in his battle against streets full of cutthroats, moors bristling with highwaymen, and would hand over control to the Locksmiths. The smiling Locksmiths would bring in their own guards to keep order, and double the height and breadth of the city walls, and seal the gates up tight . . . and nobody ever heard anything more about the doings inside that city. The citizens within were doubtless safe . . . from everything but the Locksmiths themselves.

Mandelion itself had come within a stone's skip of becoming one of these cities, due to the maneuvering of one of the Locksmiths' most dangerous agents, an elusive, cold-eyed individual named Aramai Goshawk. Mosca and Clent had played a part in helping the city escape that fate, and they were uncertain how far Goshawk and the other Locksmiths blamed them for that.

There were a hundred reasons to avoid returning to Mandelion, but for Clent the other ninety-nine paled beside Aramai Goshawk. No, they would not be going back to the rebel city.

Mosca watched Clent for a few seconds and gnawed her knuckles while Saracen adjusted his unwieldy bulk on her lap.

"Mr. Clent," she said at last, "there's only one place we can go, isn't there? Toll."

Clent did not answer, but nor did he look particularly surprised. Instead he closed his book, sighed, and nodded.

"I fear so. If we remain between the rivers, then sooner or later we will starve or be caught, unless we can make ourselves invisible to the beadles or learn to eat stones. We cannot travel to Mandelion, and so . . . Toll. It is the only way across the Langfeather. I suppose you know that travelers must pay to enter the town on one side of the river and again to leave it on the far side?" He lowered his tone. "I do not suppose that capacious pocket of yours conceals enough money to pay two tolls apiece?"

Mosca chewed her cheek and kicked her heels for a few seconds. Then she delved into her skirt pocket and slowly pulled out four cambric handkerchiefs. She shrugged.

"Mistress Bessel had a handkerchief for each day of the week, so . . ."

"So that admirable viper in female form will now be able to blow her nose only on Mondays, Wednesdays, and Fridays. Not bad, but I doubt these little leavings will muster enough funds to enter Toll, let alone leave it again."

"No," Mosca muttered, "that's what I thought. Which is why I took her stockings too."

Clent's eyes widened as Mosca dropped two much-darned stockings between them. One bulged strangely about the foot and hit the wood with a promisingly coin-like *clink*.

"Might be enough, Mr. Clent. To get into Toll, anyway.

Didn't have time to count, 'cause she was coming back up the stairs."

"Yes. I see. How enterprising." Clent cleared his throat. "So . . . in the wake of various thefts, frauds, and goose-related blasphemies, is there anyone in Grabely who will *not* want to see us hanged?"

"Nobody springs to mind, Mr. Clent."

There was a short pause.

"Toll!" declared Clent, briskly, and with sudden zeal. "What a gleaming sound that town has! What a peal of polished bronze resonates in the mere word!"

He pondered, and then gave Mosca a sharp look.

"Child—you are forgetting something, though, are you not? Toll . . . that is where your kidnappers were heading. The brigands who appear determined to kill you?" The whole sour tale of the kidnapping had been related to Clent during the hasty flight from Grabely.

"I haven't forgot any of that." Mosca jutted her chin and stared at the distant trees.

I haven't forgot how I was tricked and tied up and carried off and poked with a knife and used as a scribe and thrown in a cellar and marked for death like a chicken for a pot of stew. I haven't forgot how all this was done 'cause I didn't matter. Well, I'll matter, all right. I'll matter so hard, I'll make them think the sky's fallen on their heads.

Clent regarded her shrewdly.

"Revenge is a luxury reserved for the powerful, rich, or unusually vicious." He broke into her thoughts.

"We cannot afford it. Mosca, be grateful that you have escaped this adventure with your skin."

But I don't want to be grateful. I'm tired of being kicked about like a pebble and told that I have to be happy that it's no worse. I've had enough. It's time the pebble kicked back.

"Mr. Clent." Mosca turned wide, black, guileless eyes on her companion. "We got a duty, don't we? To that poor girl with all the money—the one who Skellow and his boys are going to kidnap. Don't we?"

"Ah." Clent fiddled with his cravat ends. "Ah."

Mosca knew that his mind was skipping nimbly to the thought of reward. It occurred to her that she and Clent were a good deal like clock hands, one large and one small, often pointing and striving in opposite directions, but always linked and bound to come into line sooner or later. The mention of money had brought Clent into line, and quickly enough the long hand would overtake the short and run off into wilder plans, things that Mosca had not even considered.

"Yes . . . yes." Clent's tone was circumspect. "You are quite right, it is our duty. We *must* go to Toll, we *must* warn the damsel of her danger, point an accusing finger at her would-be abductors, modestly claim our just reward, and use it to pay our way out of Toll on the far side. And then! Ah, the fair counties beyond! The warmer winds, the trees bowing under late-swelling fruit, the streams gleaming with trout, and above all the welcoming smiles of—"

"People who don't know us properly," finished Mosca. "Exactly."

Mosca and Clent parted company with the cart outside a village called Drinksoll and continued their journey on foot.

Before long the route started to climb, and after an hour or so the first straggling pines and cedars came down to meet the road, their branches wild and feathery, their trunks ankle deep in bracken and soft dunes of dry, reddish pine needles. Gradually, although the air was still, Mosca became aware that she could hear a breeze-like breath in the distance, so relentless that it might have been a tickle of trapped air in her ear.

They did not have the road to themselves for long. Soon they were overtaking carts dragged by stocky little ash- and milk-mottled mountain ponies, their blinkers tagged with ribbons and bells to stop evil spirits calling to them from the roadsides. Alongside them tramped figures on foot, many muffled against the cold in cloaks and shawls of yellowing Grabely wool, their backs laden with packs and pots, baskets, and spinning wheels. Few talked, and there was a nervous, exhausted urgency in the manner of every traveler, their hopes trodden as thin as their shoe leather. Clearly Mosca's party was not the only one determined to escape the land between the rivers before winter set in properly.

The road climbed until Mosca's calves burned, and

the soft roar in the back of her ears grew louder and louder. As they neared the very top, it became several roars in one. A long, churning bellow, a thunderous echo, a thin and delicate hiss. Finally the road cleared the trees, and they emerged onto the stark, stony, sun-gilded crest of a knife-edge ridge.

Mosca blinked, blinded by the sun, her breath still recovering. Down on one side of the ridge, back the way they had come, was the county that had shunned and half starved her for the last few months. Its gray stone villages were little more than gravelly blots, its beet and pumpkin fields furrowed patches of brown corduroy, its drystone walls rippling over the lumpish land like seams in cloth.

On the top of the ridge itself, a shanty village perched like a shabby hat. Here, it was clear, the river of desperation had been dammed. Families skulked huddled under the same cloak, all eyes bleak with waiting. On the far side of the "village" she could see what appeared to be a large gatehouse of ocher-stained brick, beyond which the ground seemed to drop away. The roar that had been seething at the corner of her hearing was much louder now. Mosca guessed that this gatehouse guarded Toll's precious bridge at the end farthest from the town itself. Looking up, Mosca could see arrow slits and punctures in the stonework for pouring boiling oil on attackers.

Listening to the murmurs around them, Mosca soon

worked out the reason for the atmosphere of despondency. The admission toll had been raised, and many had trekked here for miles only to find that they did not have enough money to enter. Some families seemed to have been camping here for several days, each morning sending down a few of their number to hunt out odd jobs and try to scratch together the last few coins they needed. There were, of course, a number of people there who had come specifically to "help" them. Men and women with an eye to the main chance, hopping through the rubble of stones and tired figures like magpies, offering a meager price for anything the wanderers had left to sell—their boots, their heirlooms, their hair. Mosca's heart lurched as she wondered whether the little riches in Mistress Bessel's sock would be enough.

Mosca caught at the sleeve of one of the buyers as he passed. He cast a quick and watery eye over her stolen handkerchiefs, then a shrewd and watery eye over Mosca herself. The price he named was a pittance, and Mosca felt herself flush. Clearly he had guessed they were stolen.

"All right, my little linnet, I'll add a bit more if you'll throw in the goose." His smile was probably meant to be winning.

"No!" Mosca's cry was echoed by Clent, who took her by the shoulder and guided her away from the haggler. "Trust me, sir," Clent added over his shoulder, "I am doing you the greatest of services."

"Mr. Clent," whispered Mosca, "what shall we do if the money is short? Mr. Clent?"

Clent had glanced over his shoulder and frozen, one hand creeping to his cravat as though he feared to find a noose there. Mosca risked a look behind her and felt her heart plummet like a stunned starling.

Struggling to the top of the track and into the shanty village was a familiar figure, wisps of auburn hair escaping from its mob cap, its freckled face strawberry red with anger and effort. It was Mistress Jennifer Bessel. She did not appear to have spotted them yet, but she was barely twenty yards away and it could only be a matter of time.

Both Mosca and Clent instinctively ducked to avoid her view, and Mosca offered no resistance when Clent grabbed her wrist and dragged her away into the crowd and toward the gatehouse.

Once in the thick of the crowd, Mosca dared to raise herself on tiptoes, curious to see if she could peer past the gatehouse and catch a glimpse of the river and bridge, or perhaps even Toll on the far shore. However, here the crowds were denser and more urgent, and one short girl had no hope of seeing past the crush of adult bodies.

Worse still, there was little chance of two new arrivals pushing their way to the front. Suddenly Mosca's blood froze. From somewhere behind her came the shrill and all-too-familiar tones of Mistress Bessel. It sounded as if she was asking after girl with a goose.

"Coming through! Coming through! Message for the guards!" Clent called out hastily, and his words carved a narrow pass through the throng. When Mosca, Clent, and Saracen reached the front, they found what looked like half a dozen guards holding the crowds back from the portcullis and the great door behind it.

Arms aching with Saracen's weight, Mosca watched with her heart in her mouth as the coins were counted out of Clent's purse one by one into the hand of the leader of the guard. There was a pause. The coins were stirred with a forefinger. A nod.

As they were allowed past the line of guards, the mood of the crowd changed, and the glances cast upon them became outraged, even hostile, as if they had broken a rule somehow by having enough money.

A cranking grind, and the portcullis was winched a yard or so clear of the ground, and Mosca and Clent were encouraged to duck under it while the guards held the rest of the crowd at bay. They were through the gate, and the portcullis began lowering behind them, inch by jolting inch.

"Stop!"

Mosca flinched at the bellowed word and spun around. Pushing her way through the crowd behind them was Mistress Bessel, her ice blue eyes fixed upon Mosca's face.

"That's her!" Mistress Bessel jabbed a finger in her

direction. "That's them—the thieves—the skirling bandrishes! Raise the portcullis again! There is a magistrate in Grabely who—"

"Sorry, madam." The guard touched his forelock. "These people have just paid entry—they are in Toll now. The Grabely magistrate has no sway here."

"What?" Mistress Bessel stared in disbelief as the portcullis finished its descent with a resounding clang; then she glared through it at Mosca and Clent with such intensity that Mosca feared the metal grille might melt.

"Friend of yours?" one of the guards asked Clent in an undertone.

"Er . . . not precisely." Clent took a few surprisingly nimble steps clear of the portcullis. "Ha . . . this lady is, ah, a very sad case . . . fell into a melancholia and lost her wits after her shop burned down and incinerated her husband. . . ."

"And now when she's in her fits she thinks Mr. Clent here is her husband, so she follows him everywhere . . . ," Mosca shrilled helpfully.

In the face of this assertion, Mistress Bessel went the most radiant shade of fuchsia pink and proved incapable of anything more than throttled frog noises in the depths of her throat.

". . . and she will make up any lies to be near me," huffed Clent.

". . . even landed him in prison before now, so she could bring him flowers and poetry each day," added Mosca.

"You . . . scampergrabs!" Mistress Bessel appeared to have lost the ability to breathe. "You . . . scale-tongued . . . maggoty . . ."

"You see how it is." Clent kept his demeanor solemn and compassionate despite executing a high-speed backward caper. "Mad as a mushroom minuet. Alas. A tragic figure."

The guard peered out at Mistress Bessel. There was little in her stocky figure to suggest melancholy or wilting devotion, but at present there was plenty to indicate insane rage, and the guard also took a step or two away from the grille around which Mistress Bessel's plump fingers were now gripped.

"All right, I'll make sure the boys outside the gate know about her. And don't worry—unless she's got the money to pay admission, she won't be troubling you."

"I'll find you out, my honeybumbles!" Mosca could hear Mistress Bessel shouting as the gatehouse door swung open before them. "I'll reach you, my dumplings!"

"Follow me," muttered the guard. "I'll take you across the bridge so the Committee of the Hours can talk to you."

As she followed Clent and the guard farther into the gatehouse, Mosca could not quite resist pausing in the doorway to wave adieu to Mistress Bessel with one of her own handkerchiefs.

They found themselves in a short, unlit corridor with a large number of pikes and halberds that appeared to be propped in racks against the walls. Emerging at the far end through an open arch, they found themselves staring down the length of the bridge.

The bridge itself was an impressive effort in timber some twenty feet long, its planked walkway flanked by hundreds of Beloved carved from black wood, their faces ravaged by weather cracks. But it was not the bridge itself that took Mosca's breath away. Without warning, the ground had run out.

Where the bridge began, the earth dropped away into sheer, giddying cliff face. On the other side of the abyss rose another cliff, interrupted here and there with the chalky streaks of waterfalls and a few small trees that had decided to make the best of things and grow sideways out of the sheer face. Between them lay a plummeting gorge, at the base of which a seething white river hurtled, twisted, fizzed, and roared through a maze of warped, slick black rock. Somehow over centuries it had carved, scooped, and polished the rock bed into weird shapes and valleys and tunnels. The gorge itself was gauzed over with the mist and spray that drifted up from the churn of water. Here and there the chill winter sun painted the vapor with faint swathes of rainbow. Occasionally a white gull or coal gray jackdaw sliced through the mist below.

Mosca had heard a hundred times that the Langfeather was unswimmable, unnavigable, and all but unbridgeable. Now she started to understand why.

It was also said that the city of Toll had not been captured, razed, or successfully besieged throughout the whole of the Civil War. Raising her eyes to gaze upon the town on the opposite bank, Mosca could readily believe this too.

At the far end of the bridge stood a full-blown tower, flags flying from its zenith. The town beyond it was ringed with a great wall, its fortifications peppered with arrow slits and chutes, great dark weep stains marking the brick beneath them where generations of inhabitants had used them to throw out their waste. The town had been built on the tilt and had the unnerving appearance of having slid off the ridge down to its current location, stopping just on the lip of the precipice that would have sent it tumbling into the Langfeather. Beyond the wall, Mosca could just make out clusters of dark-tiled roofs, jostling like rook wings. On the northern side of the town, the wall suddenly became gray and ragged, and Mosca could see that it had been built into the remains of some ancient castle.

There had been other attempts to build bridges across the Langfeather, not only in these uplands across the roaring gorge, but also in the lowlands where the river was broad and muscular. None had survived, some burned during the Civil War or the Purges, some quickly losing their supports to the force of the water, others betrayed by the crumbling of the treacherous ground. Only the Toll bridge remained, through some freak of luck and craftsmanship, defended by Toll's walls.

"It's all right." The guard who had followed them through the keep smiled, misreading Mosca's awestricken expression. "Don't be scared to walk across. You can trust to the Luck."

Mosca's clogged foot hesitated above the first plank of the bridge. A moment before, she had had no reason to doubt the bridge. But "trusting to luck" didn't sound particularly safe.

"To . . . luck?"

"Not just luck. *The* Luck. The Luck of Toll. As long as the Luck stays within our town, we're all safe as sunrise."

"Ah . . . I believe I have heard of such things!" Clent sounded genuinely intrigued. "Certainly I know that some mansions and castles have a Luck, an object that it is said must remain inside its walls to guarantee prosperity. Often a glass chalice, or an ancestral skull, or a collection of breeding peacocks. So, what form does your Luck take?"

"Oh, no, sir." The guard touched the side of his nose. "We don't talk of the Luck in case we rub the luck off it." Mosca wondered if he even knew the answer to the question. In his place she would certainly have wanted to know.

"Now, if it weren't for the Luck," continued the guard, "that cliff over there would be crumbling away like good cheese, and the city would be tumbling off its ledge like a pie off a windowsill. And as for this old bridge, why, weather and time would have broken it apart like a bread crust. It'd be falling in flinders into the Langfeather, and us along with it. But thanks to the Luck, they're all sturdy as steel—"

"Wonderful," murmured Clent, whose knees had started to shake. "Admirable. Er . . . is there any chance that you could stop reassuring us now?"

The guard was happy to do so, evidently feeling that his work was done, and with new trepidation Mosca and Clent ventured out onto the bridge. The planks showed no particular inclination to give way underfoot, though some gave a slightly tuneful xylophone *thunk* when you stepped on them, and Mosca could not help noticing discolorations here and there that made her think nervously of rot. The air was cold and mint crisp, scoured clean by the white river below.

Mosca was rather relieved when they reached the tower at the far side without the bridge having crumbled away. As she passed through the arch, again she found herself blinking in sudden sunlessness. Then she was ushered through a side door into a dim, high-vaulted, stone-walled room draped with long, fading banners. At a desk in front of them sat a squat little man with a straw-yellow wig and a face so knobbed and purplish that he immediately put Mosca in mind of a raspberry.

"Names!" barked the Raspberry.

"Ah, greetings, if you will permit me to take upon myself the introductions for our party. I am Eponymous

Clent, whose poems and ballads may even have reached this noble town, and this is my secretary, Miss Mosca Mye—"

"Eponymous—that's Phangavotte," snapped the Raspberry. "Mosca—that's Palpitattle. Kenning—the Book of the Hours!"

In response to these orders, a red-haired boy of about eleven clambered up onto a precarious-looking stool and disappeared between the leaves of a vast leather-bound book chained to a pulpitlike stand on which it rested.

Phangavotte? Palpitattle? Sure enough, those were the Beloved under which Clent and Mosca had been born, but why this pompous interest?

"Phangavotte's names are daylight . . . just about," came the boy's thin, chirping voice from within the book. "Committee of the Hours have considered it for endarkening six times though. On grounds of Phangavotte being a patron of wile, guile, tall tales, and ruses. Acquitted on account of Phangavotte being a patron of inspiration, myth, and proud dreams." The whisper of more pages. "Palpitattle—night. Children of Palpitattle judged to be villainous, verminous, and everywhere that they're not wanted. No plans to review this judgment." The boy reappeared, and the book gave a *wumph* as it closed.

There was a long, cool silence, during which the Raspberry carefully wiped his quill before looking up at Clent with an air of pleased surprise, as if the latter had just that moment materialized most agreeably before him.

"I see. Mr. Clent, are you planning to stay long in our fair city?" The Raspberry's tone had suddenly become more civil. His pale blue eyes rested steadily on Clent, with not the slightest flicker in Mosca's direction to acknowledge her existence.

"Aah, no, alas, just passing through. . . . I have patrons in Mickbardring who will not be denied. . . ." Clent himself seemed rather confused by the sudden change in reception.

"Do you plan to stay longer than three days?" continued the Raspberry. "No? Then, sir, we shall provide you and your household with visitors' badges."

Had Mosca imagined it? The tiniest pause before the words "your household," and during that interval, the quickest, coldest flicker of a glance in her direction? No, she *had* seen it. She could feel that look stinging her cheeks like a snowball's graze. She was used to being looked on with disdain, but the Raspberry's eyes had held a contempt so deep that it was almost loathing. She looked around the room at the guards standing against the walls, and as she met the eye of each, their gaze slid off her as though she was somehow indecent.

What? she wanted to demand. *What is it?* Whatever it was, she could feel it surrounding her, like a patch of frost spreading from beneath her feet.

"Visitors are permitted to remain in the daylight city

for no more than three full days after the day of their arrival," continued the Raspberry, "and must report to the Committee of the Hours daily to have their badges renewed. After those three days, if they are still within the walls of Toll, they are issued with a resident's badge. Of course in *your* case, Mr. Clent, you would still be eligible for daylight citizenship. A man with a good name is always welcome in this city."

"Ah . . . good." Clent seemed rather baffled. "That is . . . I . . ." His eyes strayed uncertainly, almost guiltily, toward Mosca. He too had evidently noticed the slight emphasis on the word "your." Whatever daylight citizenship meant, Mosca had a strong feeling that it was not to be granted to the rest of his household.

Kenning, the youthful assistant, emerged from a side door carrying two wooden brooches. One brooch was of dark wood and had an outline of a fly carved into it. The other was of light-colored wood and featured what looked a little like a crudely carved picture of a Punch and Judy box. Both had pale blue borders. Kenning brought both badges to Clent, taking a curved circuit so that he would not pass too close to Mosca herself.

Mosca stared at Clent's badge, then at her own. It sounded rather as if Kenning's great book had a list of all the Beloved, each marked as belonging to either day or night. It was certainly true that the period of each year sacred to Palpitattle fell within the hours of darkness . . . but the same was true of Phangavotte. Why then did the Book of the Hours devote Palpitattle to night and Phangavotte to day?

"The arrival day visitors' badges have blue borders," the Raspberry explained. "Tomorrow you will be issued with yellow-rimmed badges, then the following day with green-edged badges, and the day after that, with badges bordered in red.

"Now, it is very important to keep to your Hours," he went on. "*Our* town, that is to say the town of daylight, exists from dawn until sunset. Between sunset and dawn, however, please remember that *none of us exists*, and we are expected to act accordingly. So you will be requiring these." He pushed two slips of paper across his desk toward Clent. "Hand them in at any tavern, and you will be given a room for the night. The hostel owner will claim the money from us afterward. It will not cover your food, of course, but you will be off the streets. Each day when you come to change your badges, you will be given tavern passes for that night.

"You will hear a bugle just before dawn. A little later you will hear a second bugle, and this will tell you that your doors have been unsealed from the outside, and you should feel free to unlock them, emerge onto the streets, and start existing. There will be another bugle call at sunset. This will be a signal that you have no more than a quarter of an hour to get back to your appointed residence. You must—*must*—make sure that you do so." The Raspberry leaned forward over his desk, his pale eyes agleam with meaning. "After all, Mr. Clent, no city can be expected to tolerate nonexistent people wandering around and drawing attention to themselves."

There was an icy and pregnant silence.

"Ah. Yes. I see." Clent nodded sagely, then a little less sagely, then with the cautious air of one who thinks his head might fall off. "At least . . . that is . . . no. No, actually, I do not see at all. My good sir, I mean no slight to your shining town and your eminent self, but I really do not have the *flimsiest* idea what you are talking about."

The Raspberry hesitated with a vexed and weary air, as if contemplating the prospect of a lengthy explanation, then dismissed it with a shake of his head. "Just treat it as a curfew, Mr. Clent." He dipped his quill and signed a piece of parchment, then dribbled wax onto it and sealed it with his signet ring. "Toll has its own system for keeping respectable people like yourself safe from dangerous elements, that is all." He stood and offered a small bow, his manner still crisp and footman formal, then handed Clent a piece of paper. "Nothing you need to worry about during your stay, sir. Thanks to our precautions, Toll is the safest town under the sun."

Responding to this cue, a pair of guards at the far side of the room swung open matching doors, and Mosca and Clent were ushered through. While Clent was allowed to continue down the corridor, Mosca almost immediately found Kenning by her side, beckoning her through a side door.

"Excise wants a word," he whispered.

As it turned out, the two briskly dressed women on the other side of the door wanted more than a word. They wanted to find out if Mosca was smuggling in any chocolate, coffee, Laemark lace, pepper, ginger, laudanum, silks, tobacco, or anything else that might show that she had been secretly trading with the abhorred radicals of the port town of Mandelion. They searched through their edicts with a scowl before admitting that there was nothing to forbid the import of geese. Just when Mosca was wondering if they meant to turn her upside down and shake her till the contraband fell out, they changed their tack, and Mosca found herself vigorously interrogated to see if she had any pocks, pimples, pustules, plagues, agues, aches, quakes, or queernesses that might indicate she was bringing some dire disease into the town. For a ghastly moment it seemed they might try to inspect Saracen for similar ailments, but thankfully some light in his beady black eyes deterred them from laying hands on him. Finally, just as Mosca really was feeling as if she might be some huge, disease-dripping housefly, they meaningfully read out a list of the punishments due for a range of petty thefts, and released her back into the corridor.

Clent she found in another room, where he appeared to have been given a bracing cup of hot wine and a plate of seed cakes.

"Ah, *there* you are at last, madam. Well, if you have

quite finished delaying these poor people . . ." The door at the end of the corridor was swung open for them, and Clent and Mosca emerged onto the street, Saracen muzzled at their side.

And there it was—Toll, under the sun. Mosca took in an eyeful of color and had to blink until she could see straight.

They had emerged from a building built into the side of a tower, evidently the same tower that they had entered from the bridge. From left to right ran a thronging thoroughfare, curving slightly away from them in either direction as it followed the town's perimeter wall. Opposite was a long rank of town houses some three or four stories high, bold in their milk white and butter yellow paint, their walls crisscrossed with the stripes of dark timber beams, all varnished with dew.

The street was aglitter with people, and suddenly it seemed to Mosca that for the last long month the world had been washed drab of color. And here was where the color had been hiding—the rich red of market cloaks, the green-gold of young lemons in a basket hoisted shoulder high, peacock-colored brocade spilling languorously from the door of a sedan. The people ducked through the timber archways that pocked every wall like mouseholes, leading into dark, covered alleys. They greeted one another on the finely carved wooden balconies and footbridges that crossed the gaps between the upper stories.

There was a metallic chime from above Mosca, and she turned to find that the nearby tower was adorned with a large, gleaming clock face decorated in blue and gold. Directly beneath the face was a foot-high arch in which a tiny wooden figure of Goodman Jayblister could be seen, blowing his silver trumpet. As she stared, a brief, tinny ditty issued from the belly of the clock, and Jayblister receded jerkily into the darkness, to be replaced by the Goodlady Sylphony, made unmistakable by her pink-gold wings and long honey-dipping nose. Yes, Mosca realized dizzily, this would be about the time that the hours sacred to Jayblister yielded to those devoted to Sylphony. Perhaps all the Beloved were hidden in miniature inside that great clock, waiting for their turn to waltz out and smile benignly over this sun-blessed city.

It took a moment or two for Mosca's dazzled eyes and mind to adjust and see the cracks in the stonework, the many blank and boarded windows. *Not a real city,* she reminded herself. *Not like Mandelion. Just a fat little tick of a town sucking money out of travelers and swelling up all proud.* But, she admitted grudgingly to herself, as towns went, Toll did look passing fair right there and then, under the sun.

However, her gaze was soon drawn to the badges worn by every passerby. A very few had colored visitors' badges like the ones she and Clent had been given, and a couple of these were of dark wood like hers. The vast majority, however, were plain-bordered residents' badges, and these were all of light-colored wood. The picture on every brooch was different, and she started to make guesses at what each meant. There went a sickle, representing Goodman Uzzleglean, He Who Keeps the Harvesting Tools Sharp. That was the face of a pig, standing for Goodlady Prill, Protector of Pigs. Grayglory, Syropia . . . barely a Beloved among them who was not considered auspicious.

Now at last she started to understand why Skellow's letter had spoken of his Romantic Facilitator having a name "good enough for daylight." People with day names didn't have to be born by day; they just had to be born under a "good" Beloved.

Everyone who glanced at the fly on Mosca's own badge would know in an instant that she was born under Goodman Palpitattle, the grinning godling of bitter, buzzing things. She had a bad name, in short. Or, to use Kenning's word, a night name. If she had not been a visitor, she would not have seen this street in daylight at all.

Yes, Toll was passing fair in the light of the sun, but she had a shrewd idea that for any who saw it by night, it would be anything but fair.

6

GOODLADY SYLPHONY,
QUEEN OF BUTTERFLIES

Names were important. You carried your name like a brand. You never lied about it, for fear of angering the god under which you were born.

In theory, there were no unlucky Beloved. All of them had their places in the world, and even those who munched head lice or inspired the artistry of spiders' webs were useful and to be praised. However, the fact was that some Beloved *were* seen as luckier, brighter, more trustworthy, more generous, more worthy, and so were those born under them.

As a child of Palpitattle, Mosca was used to seeing noses wrinkle and gazes chill when she admitted to her name. Palpitattle's job was to keep the flies in order and out of mischief, but this he could do because he *was* a fly, the emperor of flies. The thinly veiled loathing she was sensing now, however, was something new.

The more devoutly someone worshipped the Beloved, the more seriously they took the lore of names, and the more severe the reaction. Looking around at the Beloved faces carved into every timber beam and the painted Beloved in the clock tower, Mosca could see that the people of Toll took the Beloved very seriously indeed.

"Let's go warn this plump heiress, grab the reward, and get out of this spittle kettle," she growled.

"It is true, dispatch is of the essence," muttered Clent as he surveyed the crowds. "We are a few steps ahead of your friend Skellow for now, thanks to your ingenuity in sending his Romantic Facilitator astray. However . . . we have received repeated warnings to be off the streets by dusk. Let us strive to have our business finished by then."

After finding an inn and reserving a room by flourishing the documents given to them by the Committee of the Hours, Clent, Mosca, and Saracen set off to track down the imperiled heiress. Fortunately this proved to be relatively easy. The mere mention of "the mayor's daughter" brought gleaming smiles to the faces of the guards at the clock tower.

"Ah, you'll mean his adopted daughter, Miss Beamabeth Marlebourne! Oh, we all know of her, thank you, sir. She's the peach of Toll, the perfectest peony. Mayor Marlebourne's family live in the old Judge's lodgings, up in the castle courtyard." A vague gesture to the north. "Ask anyone as you go—they'll all know where to send you."

And indeed they did.

"Ah, you're going to speak with Miss Marlebourne? Then I envy you, sir, for she is the finest sight within Toll's walls. Seeing her, you'll think the Beloved made a person out of honeysuckle. . . ."

"Miss Beamabeth Marlebourne? Sweetest creature on ten toes. Smile like a spring day. Yes, just take this alley to the end, and you'll see the brocade curtains she's hung at her windows, bless her. . . ."

Toll, tucked tight within its walls, had solved the problem of room by building upward and cramming as much as it could into a tiny space. Shops were stacked above shops, each with a little wooden boardwalk in front of it for wares to sprawl. Some of these walkways even bridged the narrow streets, creating covered alleyways. Mosca soon got used to the creak of clogged and booted feet overhead. There was a smell too, which came as a shock after the chill, clear air of the open meadows, the stifling reek of a lot of people living close together—unwashed clothes, gin slops, last week's mutton, chamber-pot throwings.

Toll was a hill town, and all its streets knew it. They were a hodgepodge of cobbled ramps, upward zigzags, sudden flights of brick steps, and abrupt drops. By the time Clent and Mosca reached the central plaza, Mosca was out of breath again and completely, utterly out of patience with the catalog of Beamabeth Marlebourne's charms.

The name itself was a bitter pill. Mosca had been born on the cusp between Beloved, barely half an hour into the eve ruled by Palpitattle. It was an open secret that her nursemaid had suggested that her father pretend she was born a little earlier, under the deeply auspicious Goodman Boniface, He Who Sends the Sun's Rays to Bless the Earth. And if her father had listened, if he had been an ordinary man instead of a meticulous monster with a mind like a guillotine, right now Mosca would not be Mosca. She would be a child of the sun, with a name like Aurora, or Solina . . . or Beamabeth.

Every time Beamabeth's name was mentioned, faces lit up as though reflecting some distant radiance. All this love could have been *hers*. And what had Mosca's life been as a child of Palpitattle but a long string of attempts by the world to swat her? Irrationally, Mosca began to feel that this Beamabeth had stolen her name.

By the time they reached the castle grounds, the sun was dipping toward the horizon. Mosca, who had never seen a real castle before, felt some disappointment as she surveyed the ragged line of its perimeter wall and its roofless, lightless towers. The castle was certainly very large and must have been magnificent many centuries before, but it had been bested by time. The sky had found a thousand ways in, and the turrets had traded their pennants for pigeons.

In the castle's inner courtyard, a market was breaking up with some dispatch, hawkers stacking teetering
barrows with bow-headed urgency. One young chicken
escaped its crate, and to Mosca's surprise, its owner
stared after it for only the merest moment of indecision
before deciding to rattle her goods away instead of
chasing it.

The Judge's house was attached to the inside of the
castle's perimeter wall and built of the same bristling
gray flint. This was a much younger building, with high
gables, perhaps a century old, and here at least the wink
of firelight was visible through its stained-glass panes.

"At last." Clent halted at the oaken door and pulled
down the frayed hem of his waistcoat. "Now, child, let
us bring warning to this poor—"

"Rich," corrected Mosca.

"To this affluent but imperiled girl," finished Clent.
"And do try not to scowl as if you have lemon juice running through your veins, child."

Mosca settled for stony instead of bitter as Clent
rapped the knocker. A few moments later the door
opened to reveal two footmen in mustard-colored livery. Both footmen subtly craned their necks to read the
designs on Clent's name brooch before deciding how
stiffly and respectfully to hold themselves. Mosca and
the impatiently champing Saracen merited only the
briefest, most disdainful slither of a glance.

"I am Eponymous Clent," Clent declared with

aplomb, "and I need to speak with Miss Beamabeth Marlebourne or her father on a matter of the gravest urgency and gravity."

Mosca ground her teeth as both footmen went quite cross-eyed with adoration at the mention of Beamabeth, and then one of them ran inside with the message. In a few moments he returned, surprise lifting his eyebrows so high that they were lost in his wig.

"Miss Beamabeth will see you, sir."

It's just the name they're all in love with, said the bitter, stinging voice in Mosca's head. *But it'll be all right. You'll see her, and she'll have a squint, marks from the smallpox, and a voice like a peeled gull.*

The guard led them along a short hall into a comfortable-looking reception room, its tiled floor dapple lit by stained-glass windows along one wall, the stone walls concealed beneath oak paneling and cloth hangings. A young woman in a green silk dress rose from her spinet as they entered.

Beamabeth Marlebourne was about sixteen, Mosca realized. Somehow, despite the mention of suitors, she had been half expecting to see someone younger, a girl her own age, a creature who had somehow crept into her birth room and stolen *her* name day. Beamabeth had honey-colored hair that had been trained into a shimmering mass of ringlets, but she managed to look natural rather than tortured. Her skin was creamy pale, with two pretty little coffee-colored freckles just at the corner of one of her dark gold eyebrows. Her blue eyes were large and well spaced, her brow small, her nose short, and her chin daintily pointed in a fashion that made her look a bit like a kitten. She smiled, and her eyebrows rose as if the pleasure of seeing them was almost painful. Her expression was as open as a flower.

It was hopeless. She was flawless. She was a sunbeam. Mosca gave up and got on with hating her.

A moment later Mosca realized that a man in his fifties was seated in a red damask armchair near the hearth. She had not noticed him at first, because unlike Beamabeth he had not bothered to stand. A gold chain of office winked on his chest, but the eyes beneath his thick brows had the watchfulness of a hard-biting old guard dog. This, then, was Graywing Marlebourne, the mayor of Toll.

"Well, you would let them in," he told the fire irons with a slate-cold flatness. "So hear them, and have them out of here before the bugle."

"It is *very* late for visitors," said Beamabeth as she looked the new arrivals up and down, her voice soft and carrying more of the local accent than Mosca had expected from anyone in a silk dress. Her tone made her words sound more like an apology than a criticism. "Usually Father likes to have the house locked up from an hour before dusk till an hour after dawn."

"Rest assured, ma'am, when you understand the urgency—"

"Would you like to sit down?" Beamabeth interrupted Clent without apparently realizing that she was doing so. Clent and Mosca obediently sat, Mosca keeping a tight hold on Saracen's leash in case anything in this elegant room appeared edible.

"Miss Marlebourne, I must come to the point, and I hope you will forgive me if my tidings distress you. You are, I fear, the target of an odious and felonious scheme. In short, there is a plan afoot to kidnap you and force you into marriage."

Beamabeth's eyes became pools of utter surprise.

"What? But . . . I don't understand." Her eyes flew to her adopted father, who had at last raised his eyes from the fire and was staring at Clent with an aggressively interrogative eye. "I . . . that is horrible. Somebody wants to do that . . . to me?" The incomprehension in her face left no room for fear. It was the look of a kitten that has never been kicked, and merely stares at the boot speeding toward its small pink nose.

"Brand Appleton," growled the mayor. He stood, caught up the poker, and drove it into the heart of the clustered embers as if impaling a foe. "It *has* to be Appleton."

"Father, it might not be . . ." Beamabeth looked dazzled, distraught. "I cannot believe that of Brand, even now."

"All right—let's hear these people out." The mayor folded his arms, leaned against the high back of

Beamabeth's chair, and subjected Mosca, Clent, and Saracen to a withering glare. Marlebourne had over six feet of mayorness at his disposal and apparently knew how to use it to the best effect.

The tale of Skellow's conspiracy was swiftly told, though in a rather piecemeal fashion, since neither Mosca nor Clent was in any great hurry to mention debtors' prisons, counterfeit ghosts, cheated doctors, or stolen handkerchiefs. There were occasional ragged holes of silence where such things were torn out of the story, but by the end Mosca was fairly sure they had patched it up well enough. As the story continued, the mayor's eyes narrowed, and Mosca found her mouth drying under his parching gaze.

At last he turned to Clent, his face smoothing to a more civil expression. "Sir, I believe that *you* have acted in good faith here . . . but before I send half the parish's constables scurrying after this plot, I need to be sure that you have not been practiced upon. This girl says she learned of this conspiracy at an auction of the Guild of Pawnbrokers (the location of which she cannot give us) and through letters (which she does not have) and now she wishes to warn us of this Romantic Facilitator (whose name and face she does not know). Do you in fact have any evidence that is not dependent upon the word of this girl?" His gaze dropped meaningfully to Mosca's Palpitattle badge and he raised his eyebrows. "Children of Palpitattle are notorious liars, and this smacks of a taradiddle concocted in order to claim a reward."

"A taradiddle!" Mosca jerked out of her seat to land on her feet, the sheer injustice of his words stabbing into her like a spur. "What about this, then?" She held up her wrists to show the reddened marks where she had wrestled against the bonds. "Tied myself, did I? What about these?" She showed the scratches on her arms, neck, and face. "Do you think I jumped headfirst into a blackberry bush for *fun?*"

Beamabeth raised trembling fingers to cover her mouth, and the mayor's face took on a slow, seething heat.

"You might have been seized and bound by a beadle for some petty theft." The mayor's tones were as pleasant and convivial as a boot full of ice water. "You might have tangled with a bramble bush while making your escape."

Mosca could hardly breathe for rage and matched the mayor glare for glare.

"Ah . . ." Clent fluttered his plump fingers soothingly. "My young secretary is merely overwrought . . . a terrible ordeal . . . many apologies. Your excellency, I grant that this girl cannot brandish signed confessions from the brigands in question, though were she the accomplished fraud you suggest, she might well have had a few ready. Granted, we have accumulated little solid evidence, but we sped here pell-mell—"

"'Cause we thought the lady might want to know she was going to get grabbed *before* it happened instead of *after*," cut in Mosca sharply.

"And granted"—Clent snatched back the conversation once more—"this girl is a housefly, the merest and meanest of two-legged creatures, a virtuoso in the more trivial forms of vice. However, in this case I truly do believe her to be in earnest."

All was silent for a second but for the sound of Mosca's teeth grinding.

Beamabeth gestured shakily, and a servant brought in a tray with a steaming chocolate pot and several tall chocolate cups. Mosca was disappointed to discover, however, that the steam was tangy, and that the pot contained not chocolate but only hot elderberry wine.

"Nonetheless," continued Clent, "if you want proof, my lord mayor, it is easily acquired. You now have the names of two conspirators. Can you not send some bold fellows to round them up, bundle them to the county jail, and rattle a few truths out of them?"

If anything, the mayor's frown deepened, and when he spoke, his voice was heavy and hesitant. "Brand Appleton is a nightdweller, and to judge by his name, so is this Skellow. They will be . . . under the jurisdiction of Thrope Foely, the night steward. I . . . would have to write to him and request his cooperation."

Request? That seemed like a funny word to use. Surely if you were mayor you just ordered people to do things? Why should talk of arresting men at night suddenly make the mayor look so cloudy and mulish? After all, he must be in charge of the constables on duty at night as well as those on duty by day . . . surely?

Mosca's sharp ears twitched. Yes, there it was, the unmistakable sound of something not being said.

"No matter, there is a better option." Clent adjusted his badge. "Thanks to the ingenious mendacity of Miss Mye, Mr. Skellow and his Romantic Facilitator will soon be waiting in vain for each other at different meeting places . . . and we know exactly when and where. Both can be intercepted if we are wily."

The mayor's eyes took on a fierce and glimmering interest, like embers glowing in a hoary log.

"Go on," he growled.

"This Romantic Facilitator believes he will be meeting Mr. Skellow in Lower Pambrick at nine of the clock tomorrow morning," Clent explained crisply. "Send a few men out first thing tomorrow—or better still, tonight—and have them seize a man waiting by the stocks wearing a Fainsnow lily."

The response of both Marlebournes was to look appraisingly at the clock, then at each other.

"Perhaps there is time . . ." The mayor's face took on a grim and urgent resolution. "A pity that you did not come an hour ago—I might have been able to contact my High Constable before he locked up for the night. No matter. Have all the men come in here a moment!" Half a dozen footmen crowded into the room. "Now"—he deigned to glance Mosca's way—"what manner of man is the Romantic Facilitator looking for? Did you give him a description in your altered letter?"

Mosca rubbed at her nose. She had indeed written a description of Skellow, though one that owed more to spleen than charity.

"Told 'im to look out for a bony, ugly old bag o' spindles with skin like sackcloth and a grin like a sick fox," she muttered.

"Bony and ugly," the mayor murmured under his breath. "You there, Gravelip! You are the boniest and ugliest, I fancy. Smile for us—as unpleasantly as you can!"

Gravelip, a young, slight footman with a pocked nose and large ears, obediently gave a smile like a toothache. He seemed less than delighted to have outpaced his friends in the ugliness race.

"Where's my secretary?" called the mayor. "There you are. Draft a letter to the Committee of the Hours asking whether there exists such a person as Rabilan Skellow, and whether he left Toll recently. Gravelip, as soon as it is written, I want you to take it to the committee's office . . . and then set out immediately for Lower Pambrick."

Gravelip boggled and went pale. His mouth made helpless fish shapes that wanted to be a "but." His eye crept fearfully to the darkening window. Mosca could not help noticing that other servants were hurrying in and out of the room with soft-footed urgency, closing shutters, lighting candles, and in some cases moving furniture.

"Oh, Father!" Beamabeth seemed to have noticed Gravelip's plight, and her eyes were big limpid pools of sympathy. "Father, we cannot! At *this* hour?"

There it was again. Something unsaid, something too ominous to mention.

"Oh . . . very well." The mayor's tone was far gentler as he reached out to pat his adopted daughter's shoulder. "Gravelip, delivering the letter will suffice, and you may hurry back here afterward. You will have just enough time to reach Lower Pambrick if you set off immediately after bugle tomorrow morning, with three stout fellows at your back. Collar this Romantic Facilitator for us."

Gravelip looked quite weak with relief and, after the mayor had signed the letter, took it and hurried out without further ado.

"Now, Mr. Clent, I am loath to ask you to leave, but—"

"Let them stay just a little longer. Please." Beamabeth turned her face and rested her cheek against the mayor's sleeve like a younger child. "I want to hear more."

"All right." The mayor glanced at the clock again. "But quickly. We exist for only a little longer."

"My lord mayor"—Clent sipped his wine—"you mentioned a name just now. Who *is* Brand Appleton?"

There was a pause during which father and adopted

daughter exchanged glances, and something thawed and relented a little in the former's gaze.

"Brand Appleton was a friend of the family—about a year older than me." It was Beamabeth who spoke. "He was an apprentice to a physician, and well thought of, and would probably have become a full partner in a year or two. And"—she turned a little pink—"well, it all seemed a little like we might be married. But then it happened."

"What happened?" asked Clent.

"Mandelion," Beamabeth answered. "Mandelion was taken over by radicals overnight. People have explained it to me." Her brow crinkled. "Radicals are terribly dangerous, and if you don't flush them out of your town, then they eat away at everything like woodworm, and next thing you know, everything falls apart, and respectable people are hanged from the ramparts, and nobody has any coffee or chocolate." She looked a little sadly into her cup of hot elderberry. "Of course we're safer here in Toll, with the Luck to protect us, but still . . ." It took a moment before Mosca remembered the bridge guard talking of the Luck of Toll, the town's mysterious protection against all disaster.

"Anyway," continued Beamabeth, "everybody agreed that the radicals were a terrible threat. So the Committee of the Hours had to go back to their book of the Beloved and decide which of them were *radicalish*. Because we couldn't have people born under radical Beloved running around our Toll—nobody would be safe. And so lots of people were reclassified."

"Reclassified? You mean . . . they got their daylight took away from them?" asked Mosca.

"Yes—the ones with radicalish names. And that's when it all came out. Brand was born under Goodlady Sparkentress, She Who Helps Burn the Stubble to Ready the Earth for New Growth. And all these years we'd believed she was a lucky sort of Beloved—a bit hot-tempered, perhaps, but very loving and courageous. But that day we found out that Sparkentress had been reclassified. All these years we'd known him, Brand must have been a radical underneath. It was a great shock to all of us. He seemed quite surprised too."

"I bet he did," muttered Mosca. It had been bad enough walking into Toll and having everyone treat her even more like vermin than usual. She couldn't imagine what it would be like waking up one morning to discover you had gone from golden boy to public enemy without having done anything to deserve it.

"Obviously I broke off his engagement to Beamabeth." The mayor took over the story. "The mere idea of some radical night owl marrying a girl with the best name in Toll . . ."

"Not quite the best." Beamabeth corrected him with a modest little moue.

"No matter. It is a golden name, and you, my dear, are better loved than anyone else in this town. But rather than accepting my decision, Brand Appleton went utterly berserk and tried to fell me with a bust of Goodlady Syropia. My men had to roll him in a carpet before they could carry him from my house. And even now, despite being unable to walk in daylight, he has hounded my daughter by leaving gifts for her in the courtyards and gardens. He nearly blocked the western chimney by dropping rocks down it with poems wrapped around them."

From outside there came the faint sound of a bugle.

"My dear . . . *the hour*. We can delay no longer. These people must leave to seek their accommodation *immediately*." There was no denying an edge of alarm in the mayor's voice.

"Yes . . . yes, I see they must." Beamabeth stood, walked over to Clent, and held out her hands for him to take. Her smile was very simple and very sweet. "Thank you, Mr. Clent. Thank you for coming to warn me. I would be much more afraid if you were not here, if I did not know that you were investigating this to keep me safe."

"I . . ." Clent looked about him with the trapped gaze of a spider sinking into honey. "The pleasure and honor are mine, my dear Miss Marlebourne. Rest assured I shall discover more and keep you informed. Farewell for now, and good fortune to you."

Mosca kept her tongue pushed into her cheek where it could do no damage until she, Clent, and Saracen had been shown out of the house and were back in the sunset courtyard.

"So," she began when she could hold in her words no longer. "This reward, then."

"Will be ours, child, will be ours. When the mayor has his proof. But first we have a duty to that poor girl—"

"*Rich* girl."

"—to that brave little sylph to discover more about the shadowy threat—"

Something bitter that had been welling in Mosca's stomach exploded out of her.

"We did our duty! We warned her! And she's got footmen and guardians and the mayor and *half the town* looking out for her! And she just poured us a dribble of hot punch each and then packed us off to do more danger work for her! And don't tell me we offered, Mr. Clent, because we didn't. She just accepted the offer we didn't make."

"Mosca"—Clent stopped walking for a moment—"I seem to remember that coming to Toll, scotching Mr. Skellow, and warning Miss Marlebourne was *your* idea."

"Yeah." Mosca swallowed hard. "But that was b'fore I met 'er."

Clent stared at her. "Mosca, whenever I think I have the measure of your malice, I chance upon some hidden pocket of ill temper I had not suspected. In this case, it is frankly incomprehensible. If you must choose a target for your bile, why choose her? A girl who already has unseen enemies, who has treated you with nothing but kindness and civility, who is making the best of hard times. Who even let you share in her shrinking stock of elderberry wine."

"Yeah, she did," Mosca answered through her teeth. "And, Mr. Clent? If I hear any more 'bout how wonderful she is, that elderberry wine'll be back to see the light of day. I just want to be sure that once we've got that reward, we leap out of Toll like fleas off a hot rock and don't hang about *investigatin'*."

Despite herself, Mosca's voice faltered a little as she looked around the castle courtyard, which seemed to have become larger now that the shadows were longer. The busy market had been stripped away, leaving an ominous space where rutted grass was the only hint of barrows, stalls, and hobnailed boots.

The disquieting atmosphere stung a new haste into the steps of Mosca and Clent, and they first strode, then jogged back to the main streets of Toll, only to find them largely empty.

Mosca remembered the words of the Raspberry.

*There will be another bugle call at sunset. This will be a signal that you have no more than a quarter of an hour to get back to your appointed residence. You must—*must*—make sure that you do so.*

It had been ten minutes since the bugle sounded, and suddenly these words did not seem quite so comical anymore.

"Mr. Clent . . ."

"I know, madam, I know. . . ." Clent's voice had the levelness of ice-touched panic.

Door after barred door. Shuttered window after shuttered window. Wooden ladders pulled up onto boardwalks. Wells covered. Slate roofs dulling from jackdaw blue to rook black as the sun melted into the horizon . . .

In the silence the sudden bang of a shutter rang like a gunshot. Both Mosca and Clent reflexively broke into a run toward the sound. Turning the corner, they found a small inn whose door was still ajar. Outside it, a plump and perspiring woman was struggling to close a pair of stiff and rusty shutters, wide-eyed as a rabbit with a fox upwind.

"Help me!" she squeaked when she saw them, and they threw their weight against the shutters and forced them closed. Then the woman jerked upright and raised a hand for silence.

A few streets away chimed a faint, metallic sound. A rattling, musical *jingle-jangle*.

"In!" she snapped huskily, seizing Mosca's collar and Clent's arm. "What you waiting for? In! In!"

Her terror was contagious, and in an instant they gave up all thought of the inn where they had booked rooms. Instead they let themselves be bundled in through the open door, which was immediately slammed to behind them. Looking around, Mosca could see that quite a mob had been hovering by the door, waiting to throw the latches to. The same suppressed terror was obvious in every face, in the tone of the whispered exchanges.

"It's done? We're closed in? We're tight?"

"'Tis done. But that was closer than skin. Listen— here they come!"

Everyone in the tiny, cramped room hushed, and again Mosca heard the frosted metallic jingle, now much closer, gliding down the street like a sleigh bell. Then there were more ringing jingles, as if a whole company of sleighs had found a way to float down the snowless cobbles. All along the street an orchestra of strange noises began to call and answer one another. Grinding thuds. Fat clicks and thin clicks. *Skreeks* of metal on metal. *Whumps* and *whams*.

In spite of her terror, or perhaps because of it, Mosca knelt and put her eye to the inn's keyhole. She saw only a blurred impression of twilit cobbles, of a dark figure dragging something across the front of the house opposite . . . and then suddenly there was a slamming noise, and something impenetrably black cut out her view of the street.

The strange cacophony seemed to move on farther up the street, and then to the next street. Still the company in the cramped little inn remained hushed. At last another set of sounds became audible, and this time Mosca recognized them instantly.

The rhythmic clash of iron shoes on stone. The

echoing rattle of wheels on cobbles. The huffing of horse breath. Somehow in this teeter-top town of ups and downs, someone had brought a horse-drawn coach and was riding it through the crooked lanes half an hour after the signal to clear the streets.

Mosca looked at the set, tense faces around her and asked no questions. There would be no answers here.

There was a heavy silence, and then a dull booming note, the distant sound of a bugle being blown a second time.

"All right," the plump landlady said at last, "you can talk now if you do it quiet. No shouting, no banging, no existing. Changeover's done. Nighttime, gentlemen."

7

Goodman Parsley,
Soother of Painful Mornings

There were no rooms spare for Clent and Mosca, of course, but the landlady let them lie on rugs by the hearth next to her scrawny, soppy-eyed dogs. A fire was a fire, and a roof was a roof, and a rug was closer to a bed than the bracken-and-hedgehog mattresses that Mosca had known of late, so she curled up and slept with Saracen on her chest.

When she was at last woken by a young ostler politely and carefully stepping on her head in his attempts to rake out the dead coals, she found that pale daylight was painting diamond shapes across the inn's narrow, crowded room. Whatever night had brought, it had packed it up again and taken it away.

But night would be back, and as Mosca looked at her dark wood badge she felt the same chill she had experienced in the twilit streets the night before. She had been right all along. There *was* something wrong in Toll, something that nobody was willing to discuss, something more than the nervousness caused by an ordinary curfew. The landlady struggling to shut up her inn had been afraid of something more terrible than a fine or a night in the cells. And why should even the mayor be so afraid of his own curfew?

Hopefully she would never need to answer these questions. Perhaps at this very moment the mayor's men were striding back from Lower Pambrick, dragging the Romantic Facilitator. Surely that would be enough proof for the mayor? She had to hope so.

It was half past eleven when Mosca and Clent once again found themselves outside the front door of the mayor's house. They were shown into a dingy little side parlor instead of the main reception room, and immediately Mosca detected something sour in the situation, like a mouthful of bad milk.

They were left there in unexplained silence for fifteen minutes, and then the mayor strode in and subjected them to a dull, hot glare.

"I am surprised," he growled, "that you had the impudence to return here this morning."

This was not a promising start to any conversation. The fact that the greeting and the glare seemed to be reserved for Mosca alone did nothing to make her feel better.

"My lord mayor—" began Clent.

"Cast her off, Mr. Clent," the mayor interrupted without ceremony. "Wherever you found this"—he waved a hand at Mosca—"this thistle child, throw her aside before she stings you anymore. She has taken advantage of your good humor and trust, sir, and wasted the time of honest fellows in my pay. Gravelip and his companions have just returned from Lower Pambrick having encountered no sign of this so-called Romantic Facilitator."

"None at all?" Clent looked surprised, crestfallen, then speculative. "My lord mayor . . . how *exactly* did your men lie in wait for the villain?"

"There was precious little chance to lie in wait, for they only reached the marketplace at nine o'clock to the very second. I believe Gravelip stood before the stocks as described in the letter, while the others hid behind it. They waited for half an hour, and saw no sign of anybody with a Fainsnow lily."

"And small wonder, if three of them was hiding right behind the stocks!" exclaimed Mosca hotly. "The facilitator was no green shoot. I read his letter and he was sharp. He probably took one look at your boys playing peekaboo, then stuffed his lily back in his pocket and slipped away. I would have done, in his shoes."

"A glib answer." The mayor folded his arms. "Perhaps you will be as quick in explaining why the Committee of the Hours's records show that Rabilan Skellow, citizen of nighttime Toll, was *not* at large in the vales two nights ago, and has not in fact left this town in the last two years?"

There was a silence during which Mosca gaped.

"Apparently not," the mayor muttered with steely restraint. "Her river of invention appears to have run dry."

"Good sir!" Clent recovered his composure before Mosca. "This is . . . most peculiar, I grant you . . . but I still have faith in this child's story. One conspirator, alas, has had the good fortune to slip through our fingers, but the infamous Mr. Skellow will be waiting at dusk tonight in Brotherslain Walk—"

"Do you really expect me to risk honest men out on the streets at *dusk*—on nothing more than this girl's word?" snapped the mayor. "No! This is the end of the matter. Mr. Clent, my daughter has been taken ill this morning, having spent the night sleepless with anxiety over this imaginary kidnapping plot. Nonetheless, she has asked that your girl should not be dragged into the Pyepowder Court for slander and fraud, and for her sake I shall leave you to punish your own secretary. Should I hear of my daughter being troubled by any further fictions from the same source, however, Mr. Clent, I shall be a lot less lenient. Good day to you, sir—and may you have better fortune in choosing your servants in future."

They were shown out rather firmly by two footmen, one of whom Mosca recognized as Gravelip. Curiously, he looked decidedly unwell and seemed even more reluctant to meet Mosca's eye than the rest. It was only when he opened the front door, and she noticed him wincing at the daylight, that she guessed at the reason for his grayish pallor and the unsteadiness of his gait. In an instant her temper went from simmering to seething.

Face carefully bland and meek, she stopped in the doorway just as Saracen was next to Gravelip's feet and stooped to adjust her goose's muzzle. She took enough time doing this that Gravelip became impatient and tried to nudge the goose off the threshold by gentle but firm application of his boot to Saracen's white, waggling posterior.

After the screams had died down and Gravelip had been carried back into the house by his fellows, clasping a twisted ankle, Mosca looked up to find Clent regarding her with a long-suffering air.

"Madam! In what way is our situation improved by setting your homicidal familiar on members of the mayor's household?"

"Well, it made me feel a dozen yards better!" Mosca was aware that she was drawing stares from others in the castle courtyard marketplace, but she did not care. "Did you see that prancing, lug-eared ninny of a footman? Whey faced, sick as a pig, and smelling of the parsley he's been chewing to make himself feel better. I know *that* look. I'll bet my last button he was up all hours drinking last night—which is why he's as queasy as a shoe full of eels today. You saw him! Can *you* imagine him leapin' out of bed before dawn, or riding full gallop to Lower Pambrick without losing his breakfast or falling off his horse? I can't. Do you know what I think? I think him and his friends staggered out of bed too late to make it to Lower Pambrick in time . . . but they all pretended they had so they wouldn't get into trouble. No wonder he could not look me in the eye!"

"Ah." Clent appeared to reflect, then inclined his head in acknowledgment. "You might have the right of it, child."

"And if I try to tell them, nobody will believe me! Not against Gravelip, with his Goodman Juniperry name!" Mosca stamped and fumed like a muslin kettle.

"Be it even so, now is the time for calm calculation . . . and *not* for sending your web-footed apocalypse on a one-goose rampage through the house of the mayor. Mosca, rein in that viperish temperament of yours, and we shall yet have the reward. It will simply take longer than we thought."

"It's all right for you," snapped Mosca. "You can wait around for that reward long as you like. *I* got three days." Until yesterday Mosca had been trapped between two rivers, desperate to get out before winter arrived. Toll had looked like her only means of escape. Now, however, she wondered if she had traded one prison for another, a smaller prison with high walls. If she was not out of it before her allotted time as a visitor ended, then the mysterious night town with its twilight cacophony would claim her.

"Have no fear—we will be out in three days, child," Clent murmured. "By hook or by crook."

Probably by crook, thought Mosca, noting Clent's narrowed gaze.

"Something extremely peculiar is happening in this town," continued Clent, "and since we have a duty to call in at the Committee of the Hours in any case, let us begin our inquiries there. And . . . Mosca? I have a suggestion. Carry your demon fowl in your arms. It will cover your badge as we pass through the streets."

As it turned out, this strategy was only partly successful. Wearing a dark wood badge earned one suspicious and hostile glares, but so did carrying around oversized, cantankerous waterfowl with a penchant for cheerfully pecking people in the eye. With Saracen in her arms, however, Mosca did find the crowd more likely to part before her, and thus she was able to look around and observe more of the town. Once again she was struck by the way Toll's brightly painted wood and plaster contrasted with the grim, flint-ribbed cottages of the villages in the county she had just left.

Mosca was already disposed to regard Toll bitterly, and everywhere she looked she found reasons to compare it unfavorably with Mandelion. With her endless thirst for reading, she looked for posters and found almost none. *Bet nobody here can read without mouthing the words,* she thought.

"Interesting," Clent said after they had been walking for a little while. In answer to Mosca's questioning look, he flicked a glance to the nearest hanging sign, which showed a row of painted candles. "A town is like a tapestry, Mosca, a story to be read from pictures. Look at the shop signs, and tell me what they tell you."

They walked on in silence for a little longer, and Mosca obeyed, staring at the signs that swung over doors and along walkways. Some were tavern signs, some bore symbols of the various guilds of the Realm. The Stationers, the Wigmakers, the Playing Card Makers, the Watchmakers, the Goldsmiths. The powerful guilds that kept the splintered Realm from collapsing into anarchy, and who nonetheless spent their time circling one another, wary as winter wolves.

"Well?" Clent asked at last.

"Pawnbrokers." For the sixth time, Mosca had caught sight of the triple hanging bauble of the Pawnbrokers' Guild. "There's lots of Pawnbrokers."

"Indeed. No doubt many pay their way into Toll in the hope of earning or begging enough money to pay their way out again, and end up pawning everything they own. What else do you notice? What is missing?"

Mosca chewed her cheek for a moment. Then inspiration struck her.

"Coffeehouses! There are no coffeehouses!"

Back in Mandelion there had been half a dozen of them.

"No coffeehouses," agreed Clent. "No chocolate houses either. No tobacco sellers. None that are in business, anyway." He paused, dusted a grimy pane with his sleeve, and looked in through a window into an abandoned shop where pipe racks were still visible under a fine fur of dust. "And look at the stalls—can you see any silks, any Laemark lace, any loaves of sugar, any spices?"

Mosca realized that she could not.

"All the big cities and towns in the Realm, including Toll, have agreed that they will not trade with Mandelion," Clent murmured, "in the hope of starving her out. What none of them seems to have noticed is that *Mandelion is a port.* If she needs anything, she can send out ships and trade with other countries. Mandelion does not suffer greatly from the ban—but Toll does.

"Mandelion is the only major port on this part of the coast. Toll *needed* Mandelion, needed the traders who came to and fro through this town, paying in silver and loaves of Salamand sugar, gold, and Grenardile port."

"So . . . that's why they put the tolls up, then? They're running out of money here too?"

"You have the beginnings of perspicacity. Now . . . what is *not* visible in these streets? What is there here that we cannot see?"

Mosca made a number of guesses. "A way out of town" was apparently not the right answer. Neither was "any sign of that chirfugging reward."

"Think." Clent's impatience was evidently being held

at bay only by his pleasure in revealing his own cleverness an inch at a time. "What do you remember about these streets last night, just before we found sanctuary?"

"You mean apart from all the doors fastened against us, and the great big bolts, and the giant latches on the shutters, and the great big shiny locks on the . . . oh."

A penny descended with an inaudible *plink*. Mosca stood back and looked up and down the street. Nowhere did she see a sign with silver keys crossed on a black background.

"There should be 'undreds of 'em," she muttered, instinctively lowering her voice. "Toll locks itself up like a chest every night—there must be *guineas' worth* o' good locks in every street."

"Indeed." Clent cast a nervous glance over each shoulder, despite the fact that neither had spoken the word that was in both minds.

Locksmiths.

"So," whispered Mosca, "where are they? Why aren't they here?"

"Oh, they are here." Clent's words slipped out through barely open lips. "We cannot see them, but they are here in Toll. Mark my words."

They reached the Committee of the Hours just in time to avoid Clamoring Hour. All over the Realm, for one hour every other day, it was traditional for bells to be rung in worship of each and every Beloved, not only in the churches but in every house and public place. In towns and cities the sound was usually deafening, and it was a good idea to be indoors when it happened.

The Raspberry was still enthroned in full glory when they entered the office of the Committee of the Hours. As before, he managed a nod of smileless courtesy toward Clent and icily ignored Mosca. While young red-headed Kenning ran to claim their visitors' badges and replace them with second-day badges bordered in yellow, Clent took pains to engage the Raspberry.

"Good sir, I have been admiring your town's, ah, curfew arrangements." Clent's voice was careful. "An . . . intriguing system. And very logical." He flicked the briefest glance across at Mosca before moving companionably toward the Raspberry and adopting a confidential tone. "After all . . . if one knows who the bad apples will be from birth, then why mix them with the good?"

"Precisely." The Raspberrry glowed with satisfaction. "It has served us well for eighteen years, ever since Governor Marlebourne established it. All through the Civil War and the Purges we held to it, sir, which is why Toll retained order even when the rest of the Realm gave in to butchery and brouhaha. And for the last two years our system has been nigh infallible, thanks to the new measures." He mimed turning a key in a lock.

"It must present some ingenious problems, however." Clent frowned. "That is to say . . . is it not difficult for the day town to keep track of what happens at night?

For example, how can your committee keep track of those who enter or leave the town during the hours of darkness?"

"Oh, that is really quite straightforward," the red-faced clerk assured him. "The night steward's office passes our committee all details of those who are born, who die, who leave, and who arrive in the night town so that we can enter them into the town's records."

"I suppose"—Clent hesitated—"that the night steward's office never makes . . . mistakes. Have they ever left names off the records they give you?"

The Raspberry managed to redden about the neck and blanch across the cheeks at the same time. He cast a fearful glance toward his papers as though they might suddenly rebel against him.

"That," he whispered, "is unthinkable." In Mosca's experience, such statements generally meant that a thing was perfectly thinkable, but that the speaker did not want to think it.

"But, my good sir"—Clent followed up his advantage—"how exactly *are* the reliable clerks and forces of law chosen for the night town? Surely any appointed constables must have trustworthy names, so if everybody with a trustworthy name is a daydweller . . ."

Clent let the sentence trail. The Raspberry did not pick it up. It lay there on the desk between them like a stunned weasel.

"So"—Clent tried again—"the night steward and his

men control the town at night? Might I ask what manner of men can have names bad enough to be barred from daylight, yet names good enough to be placed in charge of law and order after dark?"

"There are certain kinds of cur," the Raspberry said after a long pause, "whom you would never let in the house, but who are good enough to guard the yard. Biters and barkers, but suited to the task once you have them on a leash."

It was clear that the bristling clerk would not be further drawn, so Clent sighed and changed the subject. The Raspberry appeared all too happy to seize upon a new topic of conversation.

". . . ah, yes, of course I remember that scapegrace Brand Appleton." Gradually the Raspberry was thawing again, his color mellowing to a gentle raspberry wine. "Reclassified as a nightling just a few months after his engagement to Miss Beamabeth Marlebourne. Nothing to be done about it, of course. Young Appleton made a fuss and talked of appealing or rattling our heads until our ears fell off, but what do you expect from someone born under Sparkentress? Showing his true colors at last, that is all. Miss Marlebourne had a lucky escape there. And of course her father is considering a far better match for her now—you have heard of Sir Feldroll, I trust? The young governor of Waymakem."

So the mayor planned to marry his daughter to some young noble from another city. Mosca filed the detail away for later. Waymakem was a small, thriving city on the far side of Toll, the side that she and Clent so urgently wanted to reach.

"Of course, some say that it is partly a *political* marriage," the Raspberry added in a lower tone. "Waymakem and other cities to the east have been raising an army, hoping to march on Mandelion—the radical city—and put a respectable government in charge. But they are all on the wrong side of the Langfeather. The best and nearest bridge is ours, and they do not want to be setting about a long march with winter setting in. And they cannot pass through Toll without paying tithes for every soldier, unless they win our mayor around, so Sir Feldroll came to Toll to do just that."

Mosca pricked up her ears again. It was not so surprising to hear that other cities wanted to crush Mandelion. After all, what powerful lord would want his lowly populace hearing of this radical city with its wild notions of equality, and getting ideas?

What was perhaps more surprising was the way Mosca's spirits surged to the defense of the rebel city, despite the fact that it had brought her nothing but trouble. It was too late to stop her getting ideas. Not only had she seen the fiercely joyful Mandelion reborn, she had been a tiny part of making it what it was. When its name was spoken, she felt more than affection; she felt a pride so powerful it hurt.

Fortunately it sounded as if, for the moment, most of

Mandelion's enemies could do nothing but shake their fists from across the Langfeather.

"So where is Appleton now? Is anything more known of him?" Clent had a manner of polite and engaging interest.

"Nightbound. Probably not dead—there would have been a report. Of course we regularly review all the borderline Beloved in case they need to be reclassified, but Sparkentress?" He shook his head. "Nightbound, and unlikely to change. Still, a small price to pay for a safe town."

Safe, is it? Mosca gave a small snuffle of bitter mirth. *Funny how nervous people get around dusk, then, isn't it?*

Taking advantage of this pause in the conversation, Kenning darted up like a dragonfly and dipped his head to whisper in the Raspberry's ear.

"Indeed? I see. Mr. Clent, it seems that a message has been left here for you. Apparently a lady wishes to speak with you."

Clent glanced at Mosca. She guessed that he had reached the same conclusion as herself. The only lady in Toll who might have a reason to speak to them was Beamabeth Marlebourne. Her father had described her languishing in her sickbed, but perhaps his daughter was capable of acting on her own behalf. Perhaps she was even capable of secretly slipping out of her father's house, if she had something important enough to say. Beamabeth would know that all visitors had to report to the committee each day. It was the best and easiest way to get word to them.

"And, ah . . . did she say how I might find her?"

"She said that she would be in the pleasure gardens by the Dovespit Playhouse until one of the clock, Mr. Clent."

"Then we shall thank you kindly and make our farewells. A lady should not be kept waiting." Perhaps it was Mosca's imagination, but she thought the Raspberry seemed somewhat relieved to see them go. Then again, perhaps that was just because of Saracen's muzzled but persistent attempts to eat Kenning's inkwell.

As they left, they passed a crowd of people half dragging, half carrying a small bespectacled man to the clock tower like a trophy.

"No badge!" she could hear them explaining animatedly to the guards. Sure enough, there was no wooden badge pinned to his jacket.

"I can explain!" he squeaked as he was manhandled inside. "I lost it! It . . . it must have fallen off my coat onto the grass! I tell you I am a visitor! A visitor!" The door closed behind him and his captors, cutting short his wails of dismay.

Glancing up at the clock tower again, Mosca noted with a grim satisfaction that it was showing the wrong time. Goodlady Sylphony, who should have held dominion only over yesterday's afternoon and evening, was still smiling in the arch instead of having been replaced by

Goodman Parsley, the lord of this particular day, from dawn until teatime. Up on the roof of the tower itself, she could see a shabby wooden crane, from which a rope was dangling to trail across the clock's face. Presumably it had been used to lower some unlucky artisan to work on the clock.

That clock's a lot like the town, she decided. *Looks good, sounds great, pretends to be some sort of masterpiece. But it's broken. It's rotten and broken right down inside where its heart's cogs meet. That's Toll.*

The Dovespit pleasure garden, like everything else in Toll but the castle, had clearly suffered from lack of space. It was a clenched-looking ribbon of green between two stepped slopes, each studded with shrubberies, tiny grottoes, and dwarf trees. In the doorway of a peeling pavilion littered with dead elder leaves, they saw a single white parasol leaning against the jamb.

"Look brisk, madam." Clent took the lead. "And this time try not to throw your gaze like a spear. The girl is gentle. Frightened. Well brought up. Thwark."

The last word was delivered in the same calm undertone as the rest, possibly because his brain had not caught up with the fact that a snow white parasol had just hit him in the face.

"Thwark!" he repeated as it hit him again, this time managing to deliver the word with the right tone of pain and surprise.

Beamabeth had changed, Mosca decided dizzily as she gazed up at the white-clad figure in the pavilion doorway. Changed . . . into Mistress Jennifer Bessel. Mistress Jennifer Bessel in a white muslin gown and gray shawl and kid gloves, showing no particular sign of being locked out of Toll.

Clent gave a squawk, which he somehow managed to turn into a pleased gasp of surprise, though his feet were still tending toward a rapid backward gavotte.

"My good, gay Jen!" He reached to grasp both her hands firmly, thus saving himself a parasol swipe to the midriff. "How very . . . ingenious of you to surprise us like this! Naturally we expected you to find some way into Toll, but you have surpassed yourself!"

"I'll run for a constable!" squeaked Mosca. Mistress Bessel's broad right hand snatched out, taking a firm grasp on Mosca's forearm and pulling her off balance. The next moment, quite unexpectedly, Mistress Bessel released her hold with an oath. Mosca, who had been straining against her grip with all her might, promptly fell bewildered to the ground, losing her grasp on Saracen.

Mosca had no time to wonder at her sudden release, however. As her flank hit the turf, there was a snapping sound and then an ominous silence. She lay winded for a moment, then gingerly pushed her bonnet back from where it had fallen over her eyes. She froze, belly pressed to the ground.

Somehow during her fall, the frame of Saracen's muzzle had become cracked. She was just in time to see him shake it from his face. His wings were half raised and his neck extended before him. Something had bumped and bruised him, and he was trying to work out what it was.

A second passed in which Mosca, Clent, and Mistress Bessel stared at him wordlessly; then they all moved as one. Or rather, they moved as three—three each individually bent on self-preservation. Clent swiftly slipped in through the pavilion door and climbed onto a wicker chair, the seat of which promptly gave under his weight, leaving his legs trapped within the frame. Mistress Bessel displayed remarkable agility, not to mention a pair of chocolate-and-cream striped stockings, as she hoisted her skirts and clambered into a nearby nymph-bedecked fountain. Mosca settled for wrapping both arms over her bonneted head and staying as flat and low as she could.

All were acquainted with the full destructive might of a Saracen enraged.

"Might I ask," Clent ventured at last, his tone no louder nor angrier than a summer breeze, "what has brought you down upon us like a thunderbolt?"

"That girl," murmured Mistress Bessel, her voice mellow as a cooing dove, "has ate my stew, milled my handkerchiefs, cheated the good doctor before he could buy me dinner, and forked my money. And I'll dance coin that she did so on *your* orders."

"You was going to leave us to rot in Grabely," was Mosca's muffled offering. She paused to spit out a mouthful of dandelion clock. "Anyways, got in, didn't you?"

"How does that help me?" Mistress Bessel's tone sharpened, and then, as Saracen swung his head to look at her, it once again became carefully buttery. "I *did* have enough money to get me through Toll and out the other side, before you stole from me. Now I'm scoured out." She examined Mosca and Clent keenly. "And you're no better, are you, my sweetmeats? We're all high and dry, flapping our gills and praying for rain."

"My most inestimable madam"—Clent's eyes slid from side to side, following Saracen's patrol march—"you have not brought the constables down on our heads, so I must surmise either that you have your own reasons for not wanting them involved, or that you need us for something. Or . . . perhaps both?"

"Not too tardy, my sugarplum, not bad at all." Mistress Bessel's teeth were starting to chatter, due to the fountain water soaking into her stockings and petticoats. "If you will sing to my pipe, I think I have a scheme that will garner enough for you to pay what you owe me—stolen money, shop, and all—and all three of us will still have enough to leave town."

"Sounds like your end of the bargain tastes sweeter than ours," muttered Mosca.

"Don't scorn to grab a thornbush when you're drowning," snapped Mistress Bessel. "After all, my spring pea, you're born under Palpitattle. Nightbound as owl pellets. In three days, you'll be banished to darkness."

"My dear Jenny wren, you do have a portion of a point." Clent dared to extricate one of his feet from the wicker chair. "You have our attention."

"Then listen well." The breeze obediently hushed, and even the lapping of the water around Mistress Bessel's legs seemed to grow quieter. "There's one thing in this town worth more than an elephant's weight of silver."

"And that would be . . ." Clent's gray eyes had taken on a shine that was not fear. Jackdaw eyes, Mosca thought suddenly. Steel and avarice and pin-sharp wits.

"The Luck," said Mistress Bessel.

"The . . . do you mean the Luck of Toll?" Clent's eyes widened.

"Mr. Clent." Mosca dared to tip back her hat brim a little to peer at him. "Thought you said the Luck was like to be tuppence worth of glass pot? Nuffink said 'bout silver . . ."

"Child, a thing is worth what people will pay for it. If the people of Toll believe that the Luck is the only thing keeping them from falling into the Langfeather, then it is worth more than a cataract of diamonds."

"So if they was to lose track of it . . ." Mosca voiced the unspoken thought.

". . . and somebody was kind enough to tell them where it might be found . . . ," continued Clent.

". . . then there might be a good deal of gratitude of the jingling sort," finished Mistress Bessel.

"So—the Luck—what is it, then?" asked Mosca. There was an unpromising silence. "Do you even know?"

The large woman's countenance suddenly became cloudy, cautious, and inscrutable. "I have had a muckle of trouble getting folks here to talk about it," she murmured, "but a town's Luck is commonly something small. A chalice, or a skull, or the withered core of an apple ate by a saint."

"If it's so small, what do you need us for?" Suspicion gave Mosca's neck hairs a storm-weather tingle. "It won't be too heavy for you to manage by yourself. Mr. Clent, I'll wager the only thing she wants us to carry is the blame. She's looking for someone to go to prison for her."

"Hush, child, that is hardly a courteous—"

"Actually, she is right in a way," cut in Mistress Bessel.

"What?"

"Never you mind *what* the Luck is," said Mistress Bessel, pushing away an inquisitive duck with the point of her parasol, "but I'll tell you *where* I think it is. The mayor has it tucked away in the one place with more locks than any other—the top floor of the town jail. It's up in the clock tower by the bridge."

"So . . ."

"So some ferret-faced little scrap of mischief"—

Mistress Bessel gave Mosca a pointed look—"gets hauled to the Pyepowder Court for a spot of purse plucking and thrown into the jail overnight. There this little canary bird flies out of her cell by some certain secret means. She finds the Luck, hides it in her apron, and walks out next morn when her kind friends come to clear her name and pay her fine."

"If it's so easy," snapped Mosca, "why don't *you* do that?"

"There's a spot of wriggle work involved, needs to be a child. And anyway," Mistress Bessel added quickly, "my name's too good. Jennifer—it's a bundle of good meanings, fair and smooth and bonny and white. Nobody would believe ill enough of me to throw me in the roundhouse."

"Bet they'd change their minds if you took yer gloves off!" hissed Mosca.

Mistress Bessel went deathly white. Mosca held her eye but felt a prickle in her stomach that told her she might have gone too far.

"We play things my way, my buttercups," the stout woman said at last, very quietly and evenly, "or we do not play at all."

"Then I say fie to your game, Mistress Bessel!" Mosca leaped up. "Find yourself some other playmates!"

Saracen, who had been swaggering to and fro in some uncertainty, was delighted to see Mosca on her feet and screaming at somebody. At last he knew how to choose his enemy. There was a froth of white wings, and a splash as he joined Mistress Bessel in the fountain.

For a few seconds Mistress Bessel and Saracen disappeared amid a mash of foam, muslin, feathers, and flying lily pads. Then something in a sodden bonnet scrambled out of the stone basin and made good use of a pair of stripy-stockinged legs, leaving a broken parasol floating in the fountain. After a few seconds Saracen hopped nonchalantly onto the lip of the basin, water droplets gleaming on his white plumage.

"You know"—Clent carefully emerged from the pavilion and watched the stout woman's surprisingly athletic departure—"Mistress Jennifer Bessel can be a very dangerous woman to cross."

"I reckon you're right, Mr. Clent," agreed Mosca cheerfully, plucking grass seeds from her hair. "But I'd still hazard a shilling on Saracen if he and she was matched in the pit."

"I wonder how she paid her way into Toll after you relieved her of her money," mused Clent. "Ah, but I should not speculate thus about a lady . . . particularly one who, in her day, had the most cunning fingers in the profession." The profession was, of course, the one that had left Mistress Bessel with a T for thief branded on each hand. "Alas, Jen." He sighed. "Mosca, I fear that you have the right of it. Whatever her plan was, it would probably have left the two of us in irons, your feathered friend in a cooking pot, and Jen herself plump in the pocket and on her way to Chanderind. What a work is womankind!"

He sighed again while Mosca picked up the pieces of the muzzle, knotted them into something that might hold, and persuaded Saracen to don them again.

"We are no further on," he muttered. "We have of course utterly confounded Mr. Skellow's attempts to meet with the Romantic Facilitator, who by now has almost certainly decided the whole business was a trap and fled the county. Yes, Mosca, we can congratulate ourselves on having done our duty and thrown these kidnappers into confusion . . . but self-congratulation will not pay our way past the toll gate.

"As it is, I see only one resort left to us. Madam, we are working alone . . . and we have a street to find before dusk: Brotherslain Walk."

"But . . ." Mosca felt herself dowsed on the instant by a host of midnight sensations. The memory of rain, cold steel, jagged stone, and fear. "But that's where Skellow's going to be . . . this evening!"

"Yes." Clent had a starry look. He seemed half terrified, but it was plain that some silvery idea had hooked him like a perch. He had a plan so radiant, so beautiful, that he could not resist it. "Yes, he will. He will be waiting to meet the Romantic Facilitator for the first time, tell him about his mission, and perhaps pay him some more of his fee. And it would not do for Mr. Skellow to wait in vain."

8

GOODLADY EVENAX,
MISTRESS OF THE
TWILIGHT CHIMES

Do I HAVE to come?"

Mosca found a hundred ways to ask the same question as she walked beside Clent through the tight-wound streets of Toll. And Clent found a hundred ways of saying yes. Worst of all, they were all good reasons.

She could identify Skellow and his friends by sight. Clent would need a lookout in case of a double cross, or in case the real Romantic Facilitator decided to turn up to Skellow's first suggested meeting point after all. Clent might need somebody else close by to create a distraction. And this was what she wanted, was it not? Scotching Skellow had been her plan, had it not?

"Madam, our cogs are caught in this business now. We must grind on, or we are locked here."

It was all true, but as he spoke it made Mosca feel

as if they were indeed small cogs in a great and grinding clock, being driven in ways they could not control, stifled and locked from a clear view of the sky. She had made a decision, or she had thought she was making one. She had brought them to Toll. And now events were driving her forward, to a nightmare-named alleyway where Skellow waited, knife faced, to cut off her thumbs.

Clent looked at her with a thoughtful, impenetrable pout.

"Daylight is our weapon," he remarked quietly. "Let us use it to view this rendezvous at our leisure. You will have a better stomach for this when we have half a dozen tricks and schemes in our pockets."

The first person they asked for directions was a washerwoman. She hesitated, the heavy basket of linen on her head creasing her brow into a false frown.

"Brotherslain Walk—hey, Cowslip! Do we still have Brotherslain Walk? Does it still exist here?"

"Brotherslain? Yes . . . it's duskling. It's here and it's there. It's over in the Ravens, or what's left of them."

"Here and there?" asked Clent.

But the women just gave each other the briefest glance, then launched into a long and baffling set of directions, smiled him on his way, and went about their business. Mosca snorted a laugh at their retreating backs.

"You get the feeling we just stubbed our toe 'gainst another thing nobody wants to say much about, Mr. Clent?"

"Every five minutes, Mosca, every five minutes. Whatever duskling or here and there mean, I will wager it touches on the nightbound. And asking about the nightbound appears to be an excellent way of ending conversations in Toll."

Following the directions, Mosca became aware that although they were going uphill, they were unquestionably going downtown. The streets were quieter here, the houses less well kept, and the sunlight fell to the cobbles only in stray slices.

Since Saracen kept shrugging off his broken muzzle, Clent insisted that they find a tavern as close to the Ravens as possible, book a room, and leave him in it. Saracen's displeasure at being shut away in a little chamber was soothed considerably by the sight of a large bowl of barley and dried figs. The weary, pock-faced landlady seemed startled by the arrival of a goose guest and puzzled by Clent's eloquent and repeated injunctions that she should not open the door to the chamber whatever sounds she heard, but the pressure of a coin into her palm seemed to convince her.

The Ravens proved to be a crisscross set of alleys, most barely wide enough for two to walk shoulder to shoulder. There had clearly been a fire here long ago, for the oldest houses still had singed timbers, and Mosca guessed that this coloration had given the Ravens its name. She could even see gaps where the houses on the edge of the district had been pulled down to stop the spread of fire. Given how much of the town seemed to be a collage of white plaster and dark timber work, Mosca was not surprised at the signs of fire.

"Brotherslain Walk is somewhere here—it has an old summoning bell, they did say," Clent murmured.

One alleyway was a little wider than the rest, and at the far end they found an old bell hanging from a hook, blue with corrosion and pitted as an old fruit.

"Good. Now we need to find a ferret hole for you to watch from. There's little enough life in these houses— see if the ghosts have left the doors unlatched."

Mosca obediently scurried around the nearest row of houses, retraced her steps, then stood and stared.

"Mr. Clent"—Mosca found she had hushed her voice by instinct—"I know people block up windows some- times so they won't get charged for window tax, but . . . does anywhere have a door tax?"

"A . . . I beg your pardon?" Clent's eyebrows rose.

"I been all round this row of houses . . . and they've got no doors."

There was something eerie about it, like finding a face with no nose or mouth. Upon investigation, several other rows also proved to have no doors at all.

"So . . . the doors have been blocked." Clent was clearly becoming uneasy. "Plague, possibly. Or giant rats. Or of course there was that old superstition that you could increase the life of a town by bricking up six- teen feral black cats. . . ." He was blinking rapidly, as if his eyes had noticed that his words were not improving morale and were desperately signaling to his mouth to stop moving.

In the end, it turned out that one of the doorless houses had windows, and that one window had a loose shutter that could be pried open. The shop within—an old dairy—had clearly been untenanted for some time, and even the looting it had suffered had happened a long time before.

"Well?" Clent tap-tapped at his collar and glanced up and down the street as Mosca quietly slipped in through the window. "Will it do?"

"Close enough. Least they can't see me from the street." Mosca peered at one dust-clouded pane. "And these windows give me some view of the roofs and the lanes."

"So . . ." Eponymous toyed with the chain of his long-pawned watch and glanced at the sky to judge the hour. The sun was already declining toward the horizon, and evening had come early in the narrow streets of the Ravens as the light faded out of the higher sky. "Our primary plan is . . ."

"You talk to him like you're the Romantic Facilitator," Mosca recited obediently, trying not to shiver, "and try to get your fee out of 'im or get 'im to talk about how he means to snatch the Marlebourne girl. And I keep an eye out in case he's got a couple of bravos waiting with cudgels."

"Good. Secondary plan?"

"If aught starts to look queer or chancy, I throw a stone some way off, and you talk like you're skithered of being overheard and show 'im your heels."

"And . . . tertiary plan?"

"We run like midsummer butter. Down-past-the-bell-turn-right-second-left-down-the-passage-past-the-cobbler-left-right-across-the-square-and-into-the-tavern."

A five-minute sprint. The pair of them locked eyes and nodded—a nod that said that if it came to running, neither would wait for the other. Then Mosca pulled the window shut, and Clent went to stand by the summoning bell like a magician waiting for his demon. Mosca could see Clent's face, pompous and wily, the lips moving silently as he worked through lines, his expression shifting imperceptibly as he practiced looks of surprise, pleasure, indignation.

In the midst of this silence came the distant sound of a bugle. Fifteen minutes until the mysterious changeover.

Mosca stirred her feet restlessly, hearing the mess of dropped crocks and churns crunch under her soles. Resting her fingers on the window frame, she felt something fuzz and tickle at her fingers. She looked down and saw between her fingertips the corpses of a dozen or so jet-black flies. Drawn in by the choking reek of dust and sick milk, with its lies of sweetness and warmth.

And somewhere in the shadows, the little god

Palpitattle laughed his thorny laugh at her.

Where do the flies go in winter, Mosca Mye? Where do they go?

She stared at the glossy little beads of death with their leg tangles uppermost.

Some die in the cold, and the others, they find a trap to fly into. And then they beat themselves to death inside it.

Mosca could feel her cast-off superstitions tickling at her mind, so she dug her fingernails into her palms and tried to imagine the universe free of little gods. She brandished her disbelief like a torch, but it was hard to keep it burning in the twilight with fear in her mind. And it was hardest of all to disbelieve in Palpitattle, for during her loneliest years his imagined voice had been the whisper of a secret ally.

It was dusk, and the Beloved flowed back into her head like water in the wake of a broom. She could not keep them from peopling the sky. She could not even keep them from peopling the one little alley before her view. There was a shape forming at the opposite end of Brotherslain Walk, a figure with inhumanly angular limbs.

But it was not a member of the Beloved. It was Skellow.

"Good evening." Recognition of his voice sent a shiver of fear through Mosca, and the reddened marks on her wrists stung her. "Will you give me your name, brother of the dusk?"

There was a pause, during which Clent took a deep

breath, examined his fingers' ends, and then pushed away from the bell against which he had been leaning.

"You know, I am not at all sure that I shall." Clent's tone was carefully languorous, with just a hint of steel in it. Mosca could not help admiring the way he could pull out a new voice and manner like an actor donning a wig or a fresh pair of hose. "My name is good enough that I do not like handing it out for free."

"Good enough for daylight, anyway." Skellow took some steps forward, and there was still enough light from the violet sky for Mosca to see that he was smiling his loveless smile. His dark wooden nightling badge was visible over his heart like a blot of black blood. "Just like you promised."

"That is better." Clent's voice was still elegantly frosted with suspicion. "But I would like a little more proof that you have business with me."

Mosca had forgotten that Clent could do this, become a different man. In this dusk he seemed a gentleman in control, and only she knew of the map work of stitches that held his fading waistcoat and coat together, or guessed at the scamper of his pulse as he played out his dangerous game.

Skellow's face took on an angry color.

"We do not have time for games! I am taking a chance being out here in this light!"

"As am I," replied Clent smoothly. "Sir, I am far from happy. An unknown gentleman suggests that I should meet him in this unsavory little lane, and I wrote back to change our appointment to another place and time. That gentleman did not keep this appointment, and so I was forced to traipse here against my better judgment in the hope of meeting with him and receiving his no doubt fascinating explanation."

In a flash, Mosca realized what Clent was doing. He had no guarantee that Skellow had not found someone to read the letter from the real Romantic Facilitator, or that he would not find someone to do so at some point. Clent was steering a clever route, spinning a story that would fit with the letter Skellow had actually received.

To judge by the contortions that passed through Skellow's face, however, he had *not* persuaded anyone else to read him the letter.

"I—wha—you—you changed the appointment?" he spluttered. "That . . . that sly, slither-tongued little rat! She *rooked* me! If I ever cross paths with her again . . ."

"Ah," said Clent, politely and without sympathy. "Trouble with your underlings. Someone who is in on your secret and out of your reach, yes? Will this be a danger to us? Or is the situation . . . manageable?"

"Don't you worry," growled Skellow. "We'll manage her all right." Mosca's blood ran cold.

"How reassuring." Clent did not sound reassured. "Sir, I am a busy man and much sought after . . . and not always by my friends. You have yet to convince me that you are not one of my enemies. You might start by telling me more of this job I am to undertake. But I warn you, the first moment you say something that does not accord with what I already know, I shall walk away. And if you attempt to interrupt my walk, sir, you will find that a surprisingly unpleasant experience."

"It's a snatching job," Skellow said after a pause. Yielding had clearly cost him something. "To get a girl married to a fellow who can get her no other way. The mayor's daughter, Beamabeth Marlebourne. Family will give a pretty ransom to know that she's safe, even if she has been married to our friend. You'll get the rest of your money once we have the ransom. We have settled how the money is to be paid to us—it's only the grab we need you for."

"And the gentleman whom she does not realize she is to marry?"

"Another night owl. Which is why he cannot do the job himself. But don't you worry, sir—he'll treat her well enough. Will that serve as proof for you, sir?"

"I think so. Yes, that is a good deal better, Mr. Pimplenose."

"WHAT DID YOU CALL ME?" erupted Skellow.

"Well, your letter . . . the name at the bottom was definitely Scragface Pimplenose—of course if I am mispronouncing it—"

Caution was forgotten as Skellow gave a rooklike caw of rage.

"I'll twist her into rope! I'll skin her like a fish!"

Although his hands were now barely visible in the gloom, they did seem to be clutching and contorting, miming out his threats. "My name is Skellow! Rabilan Skellow!" A few seconds, and he seemed to calm himself a little. "And you, sir, your name now if you please."

Mosca felt a tingle of panic creep over her skin. Clent's pause was long, too long. What could he say? He could not lie about his name, but giving it to Skellow had its hazards. It might allow Skellow to trace his history or track him down in the future.

The outline of Clent's throat seemed to bob a little in a dry swallow. He had maneuvered himself into a corner, and Mosca knew it. "My name . . . is Eponymous Clent."

"Thankee, sir." Skellow straightened and seemed more content. "Now, let us make good use of this meeting, for twilit times are too dangerous for us to risk such another. What plans have you made for the snatch?"

It was as though the street was a seesaw, with both men struggling to see the weight of power and fear tilting their way. Until this point, by sheer bravado Eponymous Clent had managed to keep Rabilan Skellow off-balance, but now the seesaw wavered and tilted Skellow-ward with an almost audible thud. This was not the way Mosca and Clent had planned the interview. Skellow was supposed to tell them *his* plans. He was not supposed to demand those of Clent.

"Well . . ." Clent's voice was a little higher than it needed to be, but he covered this with a cough.

"Naturally I have a few thoughts. How soon must this business be done?"

"Before the night of Saint Yacobray," Skellow answered promptly.

"Hmm. Not long. And I assume you wish the girl spirited away into the nighttime town, so that you are beyond the day mayor's reach? We shall have to make use of the half-light times, dusk and dawn. Now, I have already managed to get myself introduced to the girl, and she is a trusting soul, which is to our advantage. Her father is overprotective, which is not. She is living in a solid stone bastion of a house with guards, which is a nuisance, as is her father's habit of keeping the house locked from an hour before dusk until an hour after dawn. So, my friend, I shall be dedicating my wits to frightening her father into changing her routine, or better yet getting him out of the way for a time. Tell me—is your client one Brand Appleton?"

"Where did you get that name?" Skellow sounded startled, and Mosca sensed the seesaw tipping back in Clent's favor.

"I have heard him discussed in the mayor's household, and Miss Marlebourne clearly harbors some lasting affection and pity for him. Not enough to persuade her to defy her father and marry him . . . but enough that I might convince her to attend a meeting with him, to bid her last adieus or to beg him to turn from desperate courses."

There was a pause.

"You have the right of it," admitted Skellow sullenly. "Appleton is our man."

"Good. How many men do you have to powder, as it were?" Clent asked crisply.

"Half a dozen, including myself," answered Skellow.

"That will probably do," Clent conceded generously. "Have them ready at dawn in the castle grounds the day after tomorrow. There is a well down which they can hide in the courtyard of the keep. I shall leave a letter with full instructions just under the well's lid tomorrow evening—or a knotted handkerchief as a warning if aught has gone awry."

Skellow winced a little at the mention of a letter but did not object. Evidently he now had access to a friendly reader. "Tomorrow night? You can have all ready so soon?"

"Sir." Clent responded with frosty grandeur. "My fees are high for a reason."

Skellow gave his spectral smile, then glanced about him, noting the growing darkness. "You must go now, Mr. Clent," he rasped. "The day's in her death throes, and you'll mar all if you're caught nightling."

"Good night to you, then, Mr. Skellow." Clent gave a curt little bow and strode sharply around the corner. As prearranged, Mosca slipped to the side window of the shop, and sure enough Clent was hovering outside, glancing up and down the street. Biting her lip with concentration, she clambered out to join him.

"Wait," whispered Clent, who had peered back around the corner. "Our fellow has not departed."

Sure enough, Skellow's lean figure could be seen leaning against the bell post, still with the air of one waiting at a rendezvous. Clent and Mosca exchanged a glance. Whom could he be expecting? Another conspirator? Could they afford to wait and find out? How long had it been since the bugle had sounded? Surely they could spare a minute or two more?

The temptation was too strong. They waited and watched, feeling the seconds crackle past like sparks.

Suddenly Skellow started and half crouched, all trace of restive boredom gone. He appeared to be listening intensely. From the north came a sleigh-bell jingle. A sleigh-bell crescendo.

"Jinglers!" hissed Skellow under his breath, and he cast a panicky look around him. Then, as the noise drew closer, he broke into a long-legged sprint, directly toward the corner behind which Mosca and Clent were hiding.

As one, Mosca and Clent sprang into motion, and as two they reeled back from their collision, snatched and tugged at each other's arms, and then sprinted for the nearest alley and ran flat out. There could be no pausing to be sure whether the echo of their enemies' steps was ringing from behind them or the next street.

Then both Mosca and Clent halted abruptly as from ahead of them they heard a jingle-jangle sound, an orchestra of thuds and creaks. Whatever the Jinglers were, this route seemed to run right into them.

Mosca's legs took her on a left and a right, and a huffing at her heels told her that Clent was right behind her. But again and again she brought herself up hard, hearing the frosty metallic chiming ahead of her, and strange whams and thuds like a parliament of doors in session. Finally she almost winded herself against something that swung away from her, then hit her in the chest with a broken chink. It was the summoning bell, and she was back in Brotherslain Walk.

"Tertiary plan!" croaked Clent between wheezes.

Run like midsummer butter. Down-past-the-bell-turn-right-second-left-down-the-passage . . .

The passage was gone. Second left was gone. So was first left. There were only smooth timbers where the turnings had been. And along the opposite row, the doorless houses had sprouted doors and dull, dust-choked windows.

Mosca ran on, unable to work out how she had mistaken her route already. She weaved this way and that, trying to recover it.

. . . *past-the-cobbler* . . .

The cobbler was gone. Instead a differently placed doorway opened onto what looked like a stew or gin cellar.

She ran and twisted and zigzagged like a hare in a hunt, trusting the nose that told her that she must be heading toward the square, this must be the way to the square with the tavern. . . .

She found the square. It was no longer the same square. Passages had vanished, new walkways appeared, doors and windows had moved, buildings had become longer, shorter, taller, more angular.

There was no tavern.

Here and there. It all made sense now. Brotherslain Walk had been chosen by Skellow as his meeting place because it was both here and there; it existed in both daylight and nighttime. But somehow, with the passing of the Jinglers, the rest of daylight Toll had disappeared.

As she stood staring helplessly at the square, she once again heard the sounds of a horse's hooves and the racketing of wheels, and this time the noises filled her with an unreasoning terror. She might have stayed there, staring blankly down the cobbled street toward the sound, if Clent had not unceremoniously seized her by the collar and dragged her into the darkness of an alleyway.

A black carriage surged into view, and in an instant every sound of its approach hatched into icy, echoing clarity. Two large gray horses huffed steam into the chill air, while bells shook on their bridles. Just as the carriage passed, Mosca happened to look up at its window and caught the tiniest glimpse of the passenger who rode in state. The hand that pushed back the curtain was small and almost childlike, but the face behind was not. It was a lean face with skin like porridge and pale, incalculable eyes.

"Goshawk!"

Aramai Goshawk, thief taker and king of thieves, ghost and puppet master. Aramai Goshawk, ever sent to pull the hidden strings of teetering towns and bring them under the sway of the Locksmiths.

Mosca knew now who the mysterious and much-feared Jinglers must be. The sound she had heard had not been sleigh bells at all, but the jingle of keys at dozens of belts as their owners raced through the silent streets, locking away the day and releasing the night.

The mystery of the invisible Locksmiths was solved. Clent was right. The Locksmiths *were* in Toll. Their home was Toll-by-Night, and right now one of their most dangerous agents was riding through it as if it was his own private kingdom.

9

GOODLADY LOOMINHEARSE,
MOTHER OF NIGHT OWLS

WE'RE . . . WE'RE IN a *Locksmith town*! Mr. Clent, we're trapped in a—"

"I know it, child, I know it."

They hung back in the little alleyway, backs against the wall, not daring to talk above a whisper. Somewhere far distant came the long smoky note of a distant bugle.

Mosca swallowed and took a sidelong view of the square.

No lanterns. Silences like frozen treacle. Sounds that ran across your ear like rat feet on your skin. Scamper steps. Metal kissing metal with a hiss. The *clapper-clap* of shutters opening, doors creaking back on their hinges.

"I think the nightfolk are coming out," hissed Mosca as panic seeped up through her calves from the icy cobbles. "What do we do?"

"Try not to get caught!" whispered Clent hoarsely. He had instinctively taken hold of her collar. To comfort her, perhaps. Or so that he could push her in the way of any threat and run, perhaps. As a matter of fact, she seemed to be gripping his sleeve as well.

"We got to hide, Mr. Clent, we got to—"

"Hole up until daylight comes—yes, yes. . . ."

The fear that the dayfolk had shown at the approach of dusk made perfect sense. If the Locksmiths were the enforcers of the changeover and held free rein in the night city, no wonder not even the mayor wished to be out after curfew. Given the Locksmiths' ruthless reputation, Mosca had the distinct feeling that being caught in night Toll, when she and Clent "did not exist," would involve something worse than a night in the jail.

Run. Hide. Hide from the night? But where? In the shadows?

In the shadows that were starting to murmur, where stone flags were grinding aside and cellar doors swinging wide?

"Castle!" Suddenly Mosca's mind had filled with the green glades of the courtyard and the castle's ruined walls—as full of nooks and holes as a Jottish cheese. No houses, nobody to bother them. They could lower themselves down in a well bucket, or camp in a broken tower.

Clent gave a nod, and the pair of them peered around the edge of the wall.

All clear? All clear. Run.

Strange painted shop signs swung slowly above their heads like gallows fruit. A dagger through an apple. A bird with a broken neck. A bone. A set of keys. A set of keys. Keys, everywhere. A Locksmith town.

Dark figures looming in this street and that, forcing Mosca and Clent to weave like fish. A hand with missing fingers, reaching out through a shutter to throw some slops into the street. A slight figure sitting aloft on a gallows arm, swinging its legs.

The streets all seemed to be in different places, but Mosca knew that the castle was on the north side of the town. To reach it, they only needed to keep the dying streaks of sunset to their left. At last they reached the perimeter wall of the castle courtyard. Mosca followed Clent through the entrance arch at a sprint, only to cannon into his back as he came to a dead halt.

The castle on the other side of the courtyard was no longer barren and unlit. Reddish lantern light flickered in every arched window. Silhouetted figures spiked the parapets. At the crest of the highest tower flapped a large black flag with a set of silver keys patterned on it.

Mosca emitted a scream in miniature, a distant-sounding squeak. A similar noise seemed to have come from Clent's open mouth. They locked eyes.

"Quaternary plan!" gasped Clent. "Creative panic!"

A second later, Mosca was taking a crash course in creative panic. The most important part of it appeared to be bolting at high speed back through the narrow alleys, taking turns at random and fleeing from any alarming noise that sounded nearby. Bouncing off street corners and ripping clothes on torch brackets appeared also to be essential features. But Mosca tightened her fists and gasped the cold air and kept herself a pace behind Eponymous Clent. Right now he was running pell-mell with peril at his heels and counting on his instincts to save his skin. He had been doing that his whole life and appeared to be rather good at it.

The alleys threw all sounds this way and that, so that you could judge the direction of none. There was a sound like sleigh bells behind them. No, it was in front of them. No . . . to the right . . .

"The Jinglers—they're on all sides, Mr. Clent!"

Clent halted, clearly having reached the same conclusion. Then, unexpectedly, he lunged into an alleyway.

As he did so, Mosca realized that a little way down the alley a door had just opened a crack to admit a slight figure carrying a ewer. From within a weird clattering uproar could be heard. Before the door could shut again, Clent barged through the closing gap. Mosca barreled in after him and slammed the door behind her.

The dimly lit room in which Mosca found herself was very small, and was made all the smaller for being full of hanging laundry, tallow smoke, and confusion. From all sides came a bewildering cacophony of metallic clangs, clatters, and chimes, and yells which had grown all the more confused and high-pitched with Mosca and Clent's unceremonious arrival.

The ewer-bearing figure they had pushed in behind turned out to be a sickly-looking youth of about fourteen with white-lashed eyes and hollow cheeks. Next to the hearth, a dark-haired woman of middle years and height stopped beating two empty pans together, her jaw falling open with surprise. Another woman beside her half rose from her worn mattress and stared at Mosca and Clent with hostility and fear through the damp strings of her hair. A youngish man with a nose like squashed dough dropped the rusty handbell he had been ringing and snatched up a cudgel. Each of the four strangers had a pallid, unhealthy look, all with bruise-colored shadows under their eyes.

"Stay back!" bellowed Clent, snatching up a poker and brandishing it alarmingly. "We are not to be crossed!" And red-faced and wide-eyed as he was, he did indeed look wild enough for anything. Then again, so did the inhabitants of the room, with their inexplicable cacophony.

"You get you gone . . . you get you gone or I'll . . ." the young man was snarling, in a way that showed his teeth.

Mosca grabbed the solitary rushlight and stood with it raised close to the drab hangings that strove to hide the damp of the walls.

"Hush your cackling, all of you, or I'll burn the chirfugging house down!" she yelled.

There was a moment of silence, broken when the

woman on the mattress fell back with a whimper that rose into a full-throated wail. Mosca was filling her lungs to scream her threat again when her eye was caught by something strange about the woman's outline. Not even puffed skirts could leave someone so pear shaped. No, there was only one explanation for a great, domed belly like that. . . .

Clent appeared to have noticed as well, for he turned faintly gray and lost his grip on the collar of the pale-haired youth with the ewer, who scampered to the fireside.

"That's it!" The dark-haired woman by the fireside had scrambled to her feet, her eyes somewhat manic, rebellious hairs escaping the confines of her braided bun. "That's what we need! Again! Quickly!"

Mosca faltered under her zealous, glittering gaze. "What . . . ?"

"Scream! Quickly! You've a fine pair of lungs, let's hear you use them again! Our scaring won't work unless we get some more sound!"

The woman on the floor clenched her eyes shut and gave a small pained whimper.

"He's coming, Mistress Leap—I don't think he'll wait much longer. . . ."

"Hold your siege there, Blethemy—he's not here yet," the dark woman muttered. "We'll scare him off for that half an hour we need or burst our lungs trying. You, sir!" Clent shook himself out of his paralyzed horror just in time to catch a bouquet of bundled spoons flung at his chest. "Rattle them for all you're worth. And you, lass—come to the fireside and take these!" The rushlight was firmly and fearlessly snatched from Mosca's hands, and suddenly she was gripping the handles of two heavy, battered-looking pans. "Bang them together and scream! Tell the world you're setting fire to the house, so the little one's skithered to come out!"

"But . . ."

"What . . . ?"

"Wind and whistles! If you're going to argue," Mistress Leap snapped, settling herself down by her patient once more, "then at least do it at the tops of your voices!"

The young man launched into a bellow that startled all of them, and Clent responded with a shocked-sounding yell, and the youth pitched in with a yodeling wail to show solidarity, and Mosca released the scream she had wanted to give vent to ever since she had seen Goshawk riding past. Everyone rattled cutlery, stamped feet, banged pans, rang Clamoring Hour bells, or beat pewter plates like gongs.

Meanwhile Mistress Leap unfolded a great bundle and pulled out a slope-backed chair, a tiny metal bath, folded linen, and some small bottles. Evidently she was some form of midwife.

"I'M GOING TO BURN YOU ALL!" screamed Mosca.

"THAT'S BETTER! HOW LONG HAS SHE

HAD THE PANGS, BLIGHT?" Mistress Leap asked in a confidential screech.

"SIX HOURS!" shouted the young man, veins standing out on his face with the effort of continual bellowing. "COULD'T SEND FOR NOBODY—WE DIDN'T EXIST. . . ."

"THAT'S ALL RIGHT, BLIGHT," answered the midwife in a kindly banshee wail, patting at his hand. "NOW, BLETHEMY, I NEED YOU TO TRY TO RELAX."

The prone woman nodded feebly. Mosca could see that it was perspiration that made her hair straggle.

Now that Mosca was seated closer to the hearth, the dark midwife's features were clearer. She was probably nearer forty than thirty but had a fine-wired bone structure that gave shape and character to her face. A fan of lines creviced the corners of her eyes, the tidemark of a thousand smiles. Despite the drabness of her dress and the pallor of her skin, the brown hair under her linen cap was tied up into braided whorls bristling with pins, from which only a few spidery wisps escaped. All this could have been confidence inspiring if she had not been battering the coal scuttle with the ladle in her free hand.

"NEVER LIKE HAVING MEN IN MY BIRTHING CHAMBER," she shrieked conversationally. "CANNOT BE HELPED THOUGH. FACE THE WALL, WILL YOU, BOYS?"

Clent, the pale youth, and the young man with the

squashed nose all obediently turned to face the wall.

The midwife shouted a question at Mosca several times before it was finally audible.

"I SAID. WHAT. IS. YOUR. NAME?"

"MOSCA MYE!" The name was out before Mosca had time to think.

"CONGRATULATIONS, MOSCA MYE. YOU ARE ABOUT TO HELP DELIVER A BABY."

While the menfolk obediently yelled at the unoffending wall, Mosca helped the dark-haired Mistress Leap to guide the pregnant woman into the slope-backed birthing chair and then returned to pan banging. Mosca had just about gleaned enough to guess that the ruckus of the scaring was designed to persuade the baby that the world outside its mother was far too noisy, so that it would hold off from being born until everything was quieter.

Mosca banged the pans with her eyes closed, because there was something disturbing about looking at the stretched stomach of the pregnant woman, watching her skin glisten as she gasped for breath. And yet she could not help sneaking glances now and then, fascinated by the idea of an angry little scrap of life striving to force its way into the world. The fire was stoked to heat a kettle of water and a little crock of oil that filled the air with the smell of almonds.

The half hour passed with painful slowness, the midwife consulting her battered pocket watch again and again. At last she called for silence.

"He's coming." Her voice was hoarse from continual strain. "Everybody stop; it'll do no more good. He won't hold off any longer."

Even after the scaring had ended, the birthing took a long time. For what seemed an age, the midwife talked in a quiet calming tone like one soothing a stallion with colic. The pregnant woman's face was creased and flushed, and she gave a series of long, pained sounds of effort, like somebody trying to heave a cart off her chest.

"Take her hand," said the midwife. Mosca obeyed, and found her fingers all but crushed in the pregnant woman's grasp. Everything smelled of sweat, tallow, and almonds, and Mosca watched the face of the mother-to-be like one hypnotized. Making a new life. A new person, right here and now.

"There he comes . . . just a little more now, Blethemy . . . once more . . . and there he is. . . ."

The mother slumped back on her little chair, her face so slack that for a moment Mosca feared she had died. Her chest was still moving, however. While the midwife was busy with wet cloths and linen and her knife, Mosca hung on to the mother's hand, watching little moth-wing pulses flutter in the woman's temples and throat.

Even after the midwife had cleaned up the baby in the miniature bath, it was still a prune-faced thing with a gravy-colored splat of dark hair and a swollen purple knot on its stomach. The midwife gave it a businesslike slap, and it emitted a vibrating cry, tiny fists trembling as it was slathered in oil and swaddled in clean linen. Mosca had seen mother cows, cats, and dogs drop their young into the world like glistening parcels. This birth had been just as noisy and messy, and yet somehow it felt different. *Once upon a time that happened to me.*

The new mother's damp lashes fluttered as her eyes opened and sought out the midwife, who was cradling the child in one arm and fumbling for her pocket watch with her free hand.

"How long . . . ? Which . . . ?"

"Four minutes after the hour." Mistress Leap closed her pocket watch with a click and sat back. "Did you hear that, Blethemy? An hour sacred to Syropia. He waited just long enough. You can give your boy a daylight name."

Blethemy, the new mother, managed a smile of exhaustion and relief, and then her face unexpectedly crumpled and she started to sob.

Half an hour after the birth, the midwife had settled Blethemy back on her low bed with a cup of spiced wine and a loaf of bread. The new child, who had been swaddled into fat caterpillar proportions, lay over her heart. Mosca thought of her own mother dying in childbirth and wondered where she herself had lain on her first night of life.

"What 'bout them?" The young man nodded fiercely

toward Mosca and Clent. "They can't stay here. Least of all *him*."

Noting the direction of his pointed gaze, both Mosca and Clent made belated attempts to clutch at and conceal their visitor badges.

"No." Mistress Leap tied up her bundle again, her brow creasing as her eye rested on Clent's daylight badge. "No . . . there'll be a muckle of trouble if it's even known we've talked to them. We're done for if we harbor them."

"What? You can't throw us out onto the streets!" Mosca was shrill with outrage. "We screamed our lungs raw for you!"

"Yes, we can." Mistress Leap's tone was one of mild, brisk finality. "You've done us a good turn, so we will not report you, but now you must shift for yourselves." She heaved her great bundle onto her back and moved to the door.

"I think," Clent murmured under his breath, "that we are in some distinct danger of outstaying our welcome."

There was indeed an undeniable tension in the room again. Blight hovered protectively by Blethemy and their new child, his cudgel drooping in his hand, and the pale youth appeared to be fiddling with something sharp that gleamed in the firelight. The truce seemed to be over.

Heart in her mouth, Mosca saw the door opened again, the moonlit street looking daylight bright after the smoky murk of the room. Reluctantly she and Clent followed the midwife out onto the street.

"Madam," Clent began as soon as the door closed behind them, "if there is an ounce of compassion in you . . ."

Mistress Leap responded by placing a finger to her lips, glancing up and down the street, and beckoning them to follow her.

"You'll come home with me," she whispered, almost inaudibly. "Couldn't say so before the others, or Blight would have been down to report all three of us, quick as a half-inch wick. He's a good boy, but fear has made weasels of better men. Hold still a moment."

She took out a blackened rag and spent a moment or two daubing soot onto the badges of Mosca and Clent, just enough to dull the bright borders and darken the pale wood of Clent's brooch.

"Now hush up, and keep pace with me."

10

GOODLADY TWITTET,
FEEDER OF THE EARLY BIRD

WITH SOME TREPIDATION, they crept down the street after Mistress Leap, keeping close to the walls as she did, stopping to hearken when she did. They passed one alley in which a dozen or so shambling figures dragged their manacled feet across the cobbles, brooms and buckets in their hands, but did not pause.

"Toil gangs," Mistress Leap breathed. "Fell into debt, poor fellows. Don't stop to look at them."

After five minutes or so, the midwife stooped and slipped into a lightless covered walkway. Mosca saw her own apprehension in Clent's face, but each ducked and followed her. The tunnellike walkway proved to be part of a veritable warren, and Mosca stumbled on through darkness, one hand clutching the belt of Clent, who walked a pace ahead of her, the other trailing against the wall.

When they emerged, the moonlight was so shockingly bright that Mosca felt torchlit and exposed. The midwife led them swiftly across the street and softly knocked at a low door. A long rap, three short raps.

Somewhere locks rearranged themselves, and the door opened to show a lantern-jawed, middle-aged man with tobacco-yellow eyebrows.

"Ah, Welter." Mistress Leap patted his cheek. "Pop on some nettle tea for our guests, there's a dear."

Passing through the door, Mosca found herself in what appeared to be a cluttered hallway. A few paces in, however, she realized that the hallway did not open up into larger rooms but continued corridorlike all the way. All the business of a house, including hearth, furniture, shelves, and beds, was crammed into this windowless passage four feet in width. The farthest reaches of it even seemed to have been transformed into some kind of workshop, strewn with boxes, clock parts, and tools.

Welter's face contorted with what Mosca hoped was short-sightedness as he examined his guests. Then his watery eyes fixed on Clent's badge. He leaned forward to peer and went pale.

"Leveretia—"

"I know. Tea, Welter."

Welter turned about abruptly and hobbled away toward the meager hearth to manhandle the kettle. Mosca could only suppose that he was the midwife's husband.

"Sir, you'll sit on that stool. Miss, you'll sit on the rug." The midwife still appeared to be in bustle mode, and Mosca wondered if delivering a baby filled you with energy that took a while to wear off. It seemed impossible for Mistress Leap to be idle, and she negotiated her way to and fro across the cluttered, half-lit room with the ease of long practice, despite the fact that often this involved mountaineering over furniture or boxes.

Welter's throat was emitting a series of rasping creaks, apparently with the aim of attracting his wife's attention. Eventually the midwife took pity on him and joined him in the corner for an earnest whispering match, with many glances toward the guests. Mosca's sharp ears caught only a few words—"spot of luck," and something sounding a lot like "with the morning delivery." At last the midwife returned with a tray of chipped cups, a steaming teapot, and a bowl of what looked like desiccated droppings but which turned out to be the driest of dried figs.

"Now, sir, you will grant that you're in a bit of a spot," the midwife continued without preamble. Mosca watched her pour the dishwater-colored tea, her fingers strong but thin and worn. "You and your young friend are wandering around where you don't exist, and people take unkindly to that sort of thing round here. You need us to get back where you belong . . . and as it happens we need you too." The midwife's brow creased a little, as if her words were costing her some effort. "It . . . rubs my fur contrary to say this, sir, but . . . we are in the most desperate and urgent need of coin."

"Ah . . ." Clent's fingers fluttered over his waistcoat. "We . . . ah . . . we are not exactly well gilded at present. . . ."

"I am sorry, sir." The midwife's gaze and tone were dogged. "But you are a daylight man and will have means to come by money, means that we lack. The night of Saint Yacobray is nearly upon us, and then we will need it more than you do."

The mention of Yacobray struck a chord in Mosca's mind. When had she heard that Goodman mentioned recently? Yes, it had been Skellow earlier that evening. He had said that the kidnapping of Beamabeth Marlebourne needed to happen before the night of Yacobray.

There were few Beloved more ominous in reputation than Yacobray. He was addressed as He Who Softens the Step and Protects Those Shy of Notice, but this was mostly out of politeness. Most people associated him with death by treachery, the smiler with the knife, the hidden blade. He was the patron saint of all assassins but also their fate, patiently stalking them and waiting to claim them as they claimed others.

"What happens on the night of Yacobray, Mistress Leap?" asked Mosca.

"The Clatterhorse comes," Mistress Leap answered

simply. Her tone was almost offhand, and yet in those words Mosca sensed a wealth of menace.

Like many old traditions, the Clatterhorse was half jocular, half sinister. There were no paintings or carvings of Yacobray himself, for he was believed to be invisible. Instead it was said that all one ever saw of him was the horse he rode, which was completely skeletal. In most villages the young people celebrated the night of Yacobray by creating a Clatterhorse, a hobbyhorse with a skull for a head, and galloping astride it from house to house, rattling its loose, bony jaw and begging gifts and sweetmeats.

"What . . . ?"

"*They* send it." The midwife fixed her guests with a meaningful look, then grasped the chatelaine at her own belt and gave it a swift shake. Her keys chimed against one another, and Mosca understood. The Jinglers. The Locksmiths. "*They* send the Clatterhorse on the night of Yacobray. Not just a skull on a stick. A thing the size of a real horse, with great metal shoes that ring out like mining picks. On that night, we all hang offerings for the Clatterhorse before our door—cabbages, potatoes, squash—and then we go back indoors and we stay there. And when the darkest part of the night is past, we go out and find the offerings gone and the string bitten through."

"I beg pardon, madam, but are you saying that the Lock—forgive me, that *they* terrify the town with a giant cabbage-eating pantomime horse?" Clent looked bewildered.

"The vegetables are full of money." The midwife's hand was not quite steady as she refilled the cups. "We all pay weekly taxes to *them*, but the biggest tithe is paid on the night of Yacobray. And if we do not pay it, or do not pay enough . . . then when the horse has passed by, cabbages are not the only thing missing. This is Toll-by-Night, sir. And people disappear in these shadows very easily and very often."

"What about the night steward?" Mosca asked. "Isn't he in charge?"

"Oh, dear, no." Mistress Leap shook her head with a sad little smile. "He never really did manage to keep order in Toll-by-Night, poor fellow. Oh, the chaos there used to be! Lots of little gangs tearing each other apart, and preying on the rest of us. You could hardly step outside without being knifed for your shoes. The curfews were sloppier back then too, and occasionally the worst of the nightfolk would linger on the streets until just after dawn to rob or murder the first morning peddlers. Everything changed when the mayor brought . . . *them* . . . in to the deal with the changeover. You may say what you like about . . . *them* . . . but things are a lot more ordered now—safer even, providing you can find a way to stay on *their* good side. There is no doubt who is in charge, though. Nowanights Mr. Foely just sits in his office and scratches away with his quill, filling in papers the way *they* tell him to and pretending his title means more than breath."

"Wait a moment." Mosca narrowed her eyes, remembering Night Steward Foely's claim that Skellow had not left Toll in two years. "Do you think maybe some folks come in and out of Toll sometimes without it showing on the night steward's records?"

"Oh yes." Mistress Leap nodded. "I would certainly think so. After all, when somebody comes in or out, there is a toll paid. Every toll the Jinglers report is money that must go to the treasury . . . and every toll they do not is money they may keep themselves. Now, I do not say a word against them, for they keep order in Toll-by-Night better than anyone else could, but they always have a price. Always. And sometimes a bitter one."

"So . . . why does anyone stay here?" Mosca erupted. "Why don't they all get out?"

"Many would if they could," answered Mistress Leap, her tone brisk but her eyes still lowered. "But it is no easy matter getting out of one of *their* towns." Mosca understood. Once a town or city fell to the Locksmiths, there was precious little chance of seeing the inhabitants again, or guessing what was happening within its walls. "Paying your way out of this town at night costs twice what it does by day, and with our taxes there's no way to save the money. The walls are guarded, and even if you escape the town, they have ways of chasing you down on the moors. Some hang all their hopes on getting the

Committee of the Hours to reclassify them as dayfolk, so they can escape the night city that way, but I have never known that to happen."

"A few scratch together enough to pay the toll and leave," continued the midwife, "but for most of us there are only three ways out of Toll-by-Night: A baby can be born to a daylight Beloved and go to live in Toll-by-Day, a person can die and have their coffin dropped into the Langfeather . . . or you can join *them*. *Their* agents come and go as they please."

But Skellow got out of Toll-by-Night, reflected Mosca. *How did he get out and back in again? And . . . why did he get back in at all once he was out? Toll-by-Night does not seem like somewhere you would be if you had a choice.*

"But . . . ah . . . surely there must be other ways?" Clent sipped his tea. "If this child and I can fall into Toll-by-Night by the mere misadventure of staying out too late, why do not bright sparks do the same in reverse? Surely they may hide their badges, or steal some, or make new ones?"

"These things have been tried—of *course* they have. Sir, I do not think you realize how lucky you have already been in dodging the Jinglers this night. And you would need twice the luck to slip from night to day, for the Jinglers are twice as watchful at dawn as they are at dusk.

"Many have tried to sneak into Toll-by-Day and failed. And even those who have succeeded have all been caught sooner or later. Everybody in Toll-by-Day watches out for folks without badges, and nightlings tend to stand out in the day crowds, what with their sickly look and worn-out clothes. And of course it falls apart the moment somebody asks their name. Then when they are caught, the dayfolk hand them back to the Jinglers with the dusk, and after that we never see a hair of them again."

Clent's fingers began their dance over his waistcoat. Evidently it was dawning upon him that, however terrible all this might be for the citizens of Toll-by-Night, it might also currently be fairly terrible for Eponymous Clent. As a matter of fact, Mosca was starting to have similar uneasy suspicions about the prospects of Mosca Mye.

"What about us?" she asked curtly. "We got the right badges for daylight. What happens if we go on the streets before dawn and just wait?"

"If the Jinglers catch you out on the street between bugles, your badges won't help you" came the answer. "Nobody is allowed out then except the Jinglers themselves."

"Mistress Leap, a child has just been born under Syropia, yes?" Clent's eyes were sharply speculative. "And a babe so born is a passport, as it were, to the world of day. Could you perhaps . . . *adjust* the paperwork so that I and my young charge were listed as close relations, so that when the family passed into Toll-by-Day—"

"You do not understand, sir," the midwife interrupted firmly. "Only the babe goes to live in the daylight town. The family stays behind."

"Then that mother back in the other house . . ." For the first time Mosca understood Blethemy's tears.

"Wanted a scaring so that her son would receive all the blessings she can never have, and live under a sun that she can never see, instead of growing up wan and thin and bowlegged with rickets." The midwife drew her knuckles hard across her own cheeks, as if angry that there were no tears to wipe. "Very soon that boy will be adopted by some daylight family . . . and no doubt Blethemy will find herself nursing and bringing up some night-named child born in Toll-by-Day. That sort of exchange happens a good deal."

Mosca thought of the tremulous, furious, purple-faced baby that was so soon to be motherless, just as she had once been.

"Poor little gobbet," she muttered to herself.

Clent also looked crestfallen, but Mosca guessed that his mind was still busier with the dilemma of Eponymous Clent than the plight of the gobbet. "Mistress Leap, I can see you have an escape for us in mind, and mean to charge us toll in the place of the Lock—ah, in the place of *them*. But truly, madam, you find us without funds. Plucked. Fleeced. Bare as midwinter trees."

"So how *were* you planning to pay your way out of Toll?" The midwife folded her arms, her birdlike face a picture of skepticism.

"Ah . . ." Clent made tiny adjustments to his cravat. "We . . . ah . . . anticipate being of great service to a family of consequence and receiving our just reward. The . . . the mayor's family, in fact. . . ."

"Oh!" The midwife's face thawed instantly. "So you'll have seen young Beamabeth! How is that little peach?"

Mosca heard her cup crack as her grip became viselike.

"Hale and well, fair and blithe," Clent answered quickly, "and courted by a little lord from another town, as I hear it. But she and her family face some . . . difficulties, which they have called upon us to remedy. . . ."

"Courted by a fellow from another town, you say?" Mistress Leap's face had fallen, and suddenly she looked quite distraught. "You mean . . . she would be leaving us? Young Beamabeth Marlebourne would be leaving Toll?"

Mosca had to clench her teeth shut. Why did everyone react to Beamabeth this way?

"So . . . you will be seeing her again?" The midwife's brow cleared. "Sir, can I ask you to take a letter to her? It is a presumption, of course, for we met only once—the day I helped bring her into the world, and she will never have heard of me. But I always remembered her . . . and I believe I would like to send her a letter."

Why? How had this otherwise sensible woman who had met Beamabeth only as a screaming purple blob fallen under her spell? Or had Beamabeth slipped immaculate into the world, petal cheeked and smiling amid gleaming golden curls?

"I would be enchanted," said Clent. "But . . . ah . . . I would need to actually *reach* Toll-by-Day first. It might also help if I was alive when I did so."

Mosca sat and chewed her knuckles as Clent negotiated with Mistress Leap. There was, it appeared, a mysterious *person* who could perhaps help them back into Toll-by-Day, though at considerable risk. Mosca and Clent were to go with this *person* and would not ask any questions. When Mosca and Clent had done what they needed to do to gain their reward, they would then leave a portion of it in an agreed place for the Leaps and this *person*. There was no guarantee that Mosca and Clent would be safe with the unnamed individual, but then the Leaps had no guarantee that they could trust Mosca and Clent to leave the money. It was a deal of mutual desperation.

Mosca's eyes kept creeping to the crack-faced clock on the mantel, watching as it gnawed away the hours until dawn, a nibble at a time.

At last there came a strange rattle of raps at the door. The midwife opened it, and Mosca glimpsed a slight, youthful figure outside, dressed in a tunic, breeches, and a tight cap.

"Got parcels for me tonight, Mistress Leap?" Only as the figure stepped forward to speak did two things become clear. First, the youth outside could not be more than sixteen years old. Second, the youth was in fact a girl. A girl with a boxer's watchfulness and a pugnacious jaw, but a girl nonetheless.

"Packages of a sort" was the midwife's answer as she held the door open and glanced at Mosca and Clent by way of explanation.

The new arrival seemed loath to step into the light of the room, but she leaned forward a little to take her measure of the midwife's guests.

"So these are newborns, are they?" Her voice was gruff, almost a rasp. "Somebody must 'ave big hips."

"They need passage to Toll-by-Day. There's money in it—but they need to be in daylight to lay hands on the coin. Can you do it?"

"If they're not cacklers, and if they're not maggot pated, and if they can take orders and duck into a jague when I tell 'em . . . then 'tis possible. Risky as adder soup, but possible. If they prove slow or clatterfoot, though, I'll leave 'em in the streets to stew, mind."

This was thieves' cant. Mosca was a lover of words, and she had a sneaking liking for the grimy panache of cant and those who wore it like a ragged red cloak.

The girl raised her left hand, and for the first time Mosca saw that there were long, curved metal hooks tied to the ends of her leather-gloved fingers. With one such hook she scratched very carefully at the jut of her chin. Her other hand was bare.

"Now or never," she declared abruptly, and darted

off into the night. Half a second passed before Mosca and Clent realized that she intended them to follow and leaped for the door.

Dawn was on the way. The eastern sky looked sickly, and here and there birds made restless inquiries of one another, asking the time. The biting cold of the air seared the skin of Mosca's face and hands. The girl with the claws ran off down the street without looking back, and Mosca sprinted after her, hearing Clent huffing as he took up the rear.

A distant bugle sounded, and their nameless guide turned a corner and halted, her back flush with the wall.

"Hold here, and bleat if you see aught." The girl bent her knees and leaped, hooking her claws over the lintel of the nearest house, then found a hold with her unclawed hand, scrabbled her way up the brickwork with her feet, and hauled herself onto the roof.

The minutes dragged like hours as the girl crouched on the tiles, her head turning this way and that like a weathercock in a storm, listening to the sounds of day rousing itself. In the growing light it was now possible to see the chilblains on her wrists, the two smallpox scars on her neck. She had a fierce face and unknowingly ground her teeth as she listened.

"I hear 'em," she muttered at last. "Coming up Drake's Dirge." She dropped from the roof and set off down the lane, beckoning with her taloned hand. "It's just round— Oh, ratscraps!"

Four figures had lurched from an alley, one of them hefting what Mosca recognized as a filch, a long stick with a hook usually used for stealing from high windows but now brandished like a weapon. It swung down in an attempt to catch the girl's ankle, and she leaped it with inches to spare. The boots of a second man slithered on the icy cobbles, and he seemed to grab at Clent's coat for support. Clent reared away reflexively to the sound of rending cloth, and a slim dagger fell to the stones with a clang.

Their guide lashed out at the nearest attacker with her clawed hand, and at the last moment he decided in favor of keeping his nose and leaped back, sprawling on the ground with one of his fellows under him.

"Run!" she yelled. "Scour!"

Mosca aimed a deft kick at the nearest kneecap and took off after the older girl. Clent, whose coat was now sporting a new knife slash, also needed no encouragement. Fortunately there was no sign of pursuit.

"Jinglers," called the clawed girl over her shoulder as she slowed, by way of explanation. "Looking to catch late strays. Now, stay close—I know the path the changeover Jinglers are taking. 'Tis just a matter of staying a step behind them half the time, and a step ahead the rest. . . ."

A distant sound like sleigh bells . . . or keys jangling at belts . . .

The girl broke into a sprint, again without the slightest warning. She really did not seem to care whether or not her charges kept up with her. Unnervingly, she seemed to be running directly toward the jingling. It was with relief that they caught up with her on the second street and found she was not up to her neck in Jinglers. She did, however, appear to be doing something very strange. As she ran, she was tugging cloth pouches from her belt with her unclawed hand and hefting them, as if ready to hurl.

As they passed before what looked like a boarded pub, a casement above suddenly opened half a foot. Without breaking stride, the clawed girl deftly flung one pouch into the gap, which immediately closed behind it. Another pouch she wedged under a tree stump. A third she dropped into a hand extended through a hastily opened hatch.

At a corner where a large yew had decided to grow through the wall of an old brew house, she halted again. With her hooked hand she pulled back some of the dense, needle-filled foliage to show a narrow gap.

"In."

"What?" Clent was already wheezing with effort, and he stared at the hole with wild-eyed horror.

"They already been past here, so they'll have spiked this tree to look for skulkers. They might not do it again. Best chance you got. In." And the girl was gone again, pelting down the street without leaving any chance for protest.

However many centuries that ancient tree had stood

there, it had probably never seen anything as graceless as Mosca and Clent trying to thrash their way into it at the same time. There is little give in a yew, for it has a mesh of small, fibrous branches and thousands of bristling needles, scrubbing-brush dense. Even when they stopped trying to struggle their way farther in, it was impossible to tell whether they were invisible from the street.

"Hush!" whispered Clent. "Hold still!"

Mosca obeyed and realized that she could hear the sound of jingling nearing and slowing. There were steps on the cobbles, then a rasp of steel. Without warning, something dark and wickedly slender jabbed through the concealing foliage. Mosca heard it tear through the loose fabric of her sleeve and briefly felt the kiss of cold against her forearm before the blade withdrew. She clenched her teeth and managed not to cry out at the shock of the contact.

What easier way to check for hiders than to jab a sword idly into a few places and see whether the tree screamed and bled? She held her breath, tingling all over in expectation of the next stab, even when the jingling sound passed.

At long last, the after-dawn bugle sounded. Somewhere in the sap-scented darkness, Mosca heard Clent give a protracted, ragged sigh of relief.

"Madam, let us . . . dismount."

Clent "dismounted" fairly easily by falling out of the tree in disarray with a squawk of pain. Mosca, however, had to be dragged out by her ankles, the yew having worked itself into her hair, bonnet, and gown.

"So . . ." Clent's throat was still a little rough from gasping hurried air into his lungs. "Altogether a very successful . . . ah . . . reconnaissance outing. Very . . . ah . . . educational. . . ."

Haggard, sleep deprived, and bristling with yew needles, the pair wiped the soot from their badges and then limped down the street attempting amiable smiles at passersby, some of whom recoiled from the prospect. As they passed the stump where the clawed girl had thrust her pouch, Clent looked about him and then stooped.

"I am interested to know," he murmured in an undertone, "what *exactly* is so important that our brusque young friend was willing to brave the Jinglers in order to deliver it, and various decent citizens were willing to open their casements and hatches before bugle to receive it."

He examined the pouch, then hesitantly lowered his head to sniff at it. His eyebrows climbed, and he passed the pouch to Mosca. She followed his lead and raised it to her nose for a good sniff.

"But Mr. Clent—this smells like . . ." She stared at him.

"Yes." Clent stooped to put the pouch back in its hiding place. "Chocolate."

11

GOODMAN TRYWHY,
MASTER OF SCHEMES,
SLEIGHTS, AND STRATAGEMS

BY THE TIME the pale winter sun had put in a lackluster appearance, a slack flap of cloud smothering its face like a nightcap, Mosca and Clent had holed up in the little pleasure-garden pavilion they had found before. This provided exactly what they needed—a quiet and secluded spot for first-degree panicking.

"We're in a bleedin' Locksmith town!" Mosca had repeated this about a dozen times but had not yet worn the edge off it. "We got Mistress Bessel after our hides, that gibbet rat Skellow wants to skin me alive, and we're in a bleedin' Locksmith town! The night town's run by 'em, and I bet the day town will be as well, soon as salt, and their agents must be everywhere, and two nights from now if we're still here, they'll send me to Toll-by-Night, and I got nowhere to stay so I'll be on the streets with no money on the night of Yacobray, and the Clatterhorse'll get me. . . ."

She paused, partly for breath and partly through awareness that the latter part of her complaint had sounded a bit babyish.

"Child . . . child . . . that sinister steed shall not have you. It shall not. Mosca, you have my sincerest and unstained oath on that. Have you ever known me to break my word to you?"

Four icy seconds passed during which Mosca simply stared at Clent, her tongue pushed into her cheek, one eyebrow raised, her eyes hard black incredulous beads. Clent chose to ignore the answer hovering in the air.

"The matter is in my hands, child. The cogs of my mind whirl so fast, they might start fires. Let us settle our thoughts and analyze. At present our only plan for leaving this town is to claim a reward from the Marlebournes, and to do so we must prove to them that the damsel in distress is indeed in danger. And we still have until tomorrow evening to do so, before we lose our visitor status. Two days and one night."

Mosca said nothing. The word "damsel" rankled with her. She suddenly thought of the clawed girl from the night before, jumping the filch on an icy street. Much the same age and build as Beamabeth, and far more beleaguered. What made a girl a damsel in distress? Were they not allowed claws? Mosca had a hunch that if all damsels had claws, they would spend a lot less time in distress.

"Fortunately," Clent continued crisply, "your employer is a genius. This man Skellow and his fellows will be coming to the castle courtyard this very night to receive my written orders, counting upon me to invent a plot to kidnap that poor girl come the dawn. And I shall indeed present them with a plan of uncommon daring and ingenuity, one that cannot fail . . . unless, of course, the damsel and her family are warned in advance, and the entire enterprise is a trap for our dastardly conspirators."

"I thought the mayor said he'd hang us like washing if we warned him anymore?"

"Ye-e-es, he might have implied as much. Which is why we must persuade his charming daughter to speak to him on our behalf."

"And we do all this before tomorrow evening?"

"Inevitably. Inescapably. We concoct a plan today. We recruit the inestimable mayor and his family. We prepare our ambush. I leave a letter for our kidnappers and hook them into our cheat. At dawn we spring our trap. In a word . . . yes."

"Well, I'm glad we got a whole day to work out how to use a mayor's daughter as bait," growled Mosca. "Wouldn't want to go doing that slipshod."

After seeing Toll-by-Night, she found it impossible to look at Toll-by-Day the same way. As she walked down the street, Mosca could not help but glance this way and that, trying to work out how the whole town had transformed. Soon she found that there were clues once you knew where to look.

Most of the houses were faced with the same white plaster crisscrossed with black beams, some jutting farther forward than others. Now she suspected that some of these fronts were false, each mounted on a board and designed to swing or slide from one position to another. One position for daylight—and then at dusk it could be moved, covering one set of doors and windows and revealing another, or slid sideways to block off a passage, or flipped down to become a boardwalk or bridge. Discreet but sturdy padlocks held the whole in place.

And behind those locked boards, hundreds of human beings held their breath and sat in darkness, pretending not to exist. Hundreds who had obediently bolted and locked their doors from within, and let the Locksmiths secure and fasten their doors a second time from without, so that they could not escape even if they wished it.

She noticed other things as well as they passed through the daylit streets, and started to understand why Toll-by-Day had seemed unreal to her even at the start. The cobbles were free from litter and the walls and monuments from grime, and yet she saw nobody cleaning them. She saw no chimney sweeps, no street sweepers, no boys scooping horse dung out of the road. She remembered the shuffling hopelessness of the toil gangs they had glimpsed in the nocturnal alley and guessed when these lowly, unpleasant jobs were done.

Do the dayfolk ever wonder about that? Do they care? Or

do they just wake up to clean streets and elderberry wine and try not to think about it too hard?

Clent was scanning the town with the same eye of scrutiny, but Mosca guessed that he was riffling through ruses and sorting through stratagems, taking everything he saw as inspiration.

"Can we get Saracen while we're cogitating?" asked Mosca. Leaving the goose to grow restless was a very poor plan, and likely to result in property damage.

As it turned out, Saracen had only chewed the felt off a tabletop and had not found the breakables that Mosca had moved to the closet, so relatively little damage had been done. He tried to eat Mosca's badge by way of greeting, but she managed to fish it out of his beak before he could swallow it.

"Not a pebble, Saracen." Mosca knew that like all geese, Saracen needed to swallow small stones now and then so that they could sit in his crop, the pouch in his gullet where food was ground down. However, she had a feeling that the Committee of the Hours would not be amused if she had to explain that her badge was trapped inside a goose and likely to remain there forever.

On the way out, the sight of the tavern clock caused Clent to wince and chafe his brows.

"Ten o'clock already! These short winter days work against us. Come. We must report to the Committee of the Hours, then go to speak with Miss Marlebourne and her father."

They dutifully reported in at the Committee of

the Hours building next to the clock tower, where the Raspberry appeared not to notice their haggard and disheveled appearance, and then continued on to the castle. When they reached the ruined courtyard, Mosca could not suppress a shiver, despite the winter sunshine, as she remembered the flamelit castle of the night before, with its Locksmith banners.

Thankfully, as they approached the mayor's house, Beamabeth Marlebourne could be glimpsed on the green outside, standing at an easel, a woolen cloak about her shoulders.

"Mr. Clent! I was so sure you would come back. Have you found out anything more?" Beamabeth's gaze swept over them like a soft-haired brush, snagging briefly on the leaves in Mosca's bonnet and the large goose in her arms.

Clent tugged off his hat and nearly his wig in his enthusiasm.

"Indeed. I have with my very own eyes seen the infamous Skellow and conversed with him. . . ."

Beamabeth's eyes widened as Clent gave his account of the evening's excitement, which, Mosca noticed, dwelled somewhat unduly upon the more heroic and cunning aspects of Clent's behavior but was rather sketchy in its report of his desperate flight and intimidation of midwives.

"So . . ." A very faint crease appeared in Beamabeth's brow as she tried to push back a breeze-tugged ringlet without smearing paint on her face. "So . . . you have . . .

agreed to kidnap me?"

"After a fashion, yes. It is a snare, a mantrap, a device, if you will. A gleaming silver hook."

"With you as the worm," Mosca could not help putting in.

Both Clent and Beamabeth flinched, the latter with shock.

"Mr. Clent, I—I am not sure I like the idea of being a worm. . . ."

"Only a mean and invidious mind would make the comparison." Clent gave Mosca a look of annoyance. "I would prefer to think of you as the honey for trapping some black and malignant insect—perhaps a fly."

It was Mosca's turn to wince. She gave a small snarl in her throat. Beamabeth, meanwhile, did not seem greatly reassured by the change in metaphor. However, as they headed inside, she seemed to warm by inches to the idea of Clent's snare. Of one thing, however, she was entirely certain.

"Father will never allow it. He would never let me near the tiniest teaspoonful of danger. He says that I am his treasure chest and hold all that is valuable in his world." It was strange that Beamabeth could say such things, with the seriousness of a young child, and somehow not sound vain. "And besides, there is no stirring him once he has decided something—and I am afraid he has decided that the whole kidnapping plot is nothing but invention."

"But now it ain't just my word," cut in Mosca. "Mr. Clent talked to Mr. Skellow too, and we *both* heard 'im say Brand Appleton was in the plot up to his chops. And Mr. Clent has a daylight name."

"Yes." Beamabeth's brow gained a worried little crinkle. "I think he might have believed that yesterday . . . but then there were all those bits of your story that did not hold water, and now I am afraid, I am *horribly* afraid, that if you came back with more story, he would not believe either of you. In fact, he would probably just have to put you in prison for being out after bugle. It is really very illegal, you know."

There was a glum silence.

"I suppose . . ." Beamabeth's kitten features furrowed again with the effort of thought. "That is . . . would he absolutely have to know what we were doing?"

"The endeavor would be difficult without him. After all, we shall need help." Clent pursed his lips. "A good number of strong cudgel arms, I should say, if we are to apprehend these villains. We are hardly likely to be able to best a pack of scoundrels with only the three of us and one goose. . . ." Clent hesitated, his eyes on Saracen's blunt but determined beak. "Well, perhaps the goose would be enough at that. But it is not a force to be released lightly. No, I fear we shall have to talk to the mayor."

Beamabeth pressed her lips together very slightly and twiddled at her sleeve.

"Will Brand be there?" she asked suddenly.

"I—well . . . that is possible. I must confess that the best idea I have so far is to tell our abduction conspiracy that I have persuaded you to meet with Brand Appleton one last time, for old times' sake, at dawn outside your house tomorrow. In which case . . . yes, I rather think that that particular hare will end up in our bag, so to speak."

"Father hates him," Beamabeth remarked, rather indistinctly. "Oh, of course what he is doing is very terrible, and the way things are, any thought of marrying him is quite, quite impossible . . . but I would still be sorry if he was . . . well . . . horribly hurt during his arrest. And if Father was involved, then . . . then I am afraid that he might be." She had gone a little pink and had nearly twisted off one of her pearl buttons. "That is why I *must* be involved, if there is a . . . a snare. I need to be there to make sure he is not treated more horribly than can be helped."

"Madam," Clent said with unusual gentleness, "your compassion does you the greatest credit, but I cannot see how talking to your father is to be avoided. Even if we could find other ready hands to wrestle our brigands, the mayor is hardly likely to be blind to our preparations, or deaf to sounds of affray on his very doorstep."

Not to mention the fact that the reward would need to come from him, Mosca added silently.

"I am sure that I could find friends to help defend

me," Beamabeth insisted. "I can talk to them about it at the party this afternoon. And there's the servants, of course." She looked contemplative, then sighed. "But yes—Father will be a problem. Nowadays he never unlocks the house at dawn, you see—always a good hour or so afterward. Of course, when he is away, I am head of the household and can open the doors when I choose . . . if only he was out of town!"

"You could ply him with gin till his legs give out," Mosca suggested. "Wouldn't be so spry in the morning then."

"He never touches fiery spirits." Beamabeth looked, for the first time, decidedly offended. "Mr. Clent, can you not think of anything?"

"My dear, given more than the hours at our disposal, I could doubtless concoct some scheme to keep your father from home, but time is not on our side. Time . . ." Clent's eyes suddenly glazed over, and he eased back into his chair, beating an excited tattoo against his waistcoat with his fingertips. "I am quite, quite wrong," he said quietly after a moment. "Time is not my enemy. Time is my monkey and will dance to my tune. Miss Marlebourne, does your father have a pocket timepiece?"

"Why . . . yes." She stared at him curiously.

"You might be required to reset it by stealth. Where is he likely to spend this day?"

"Well . . . he will probably be in his study until lunchtime. Today the Pyepowder Court is not in session—I think he said that he would be in his counting house in Waggle Lane, reckoning the tolls and reading appeals to the treasury. He often tries to avoid my little gatherings, so he will stay there as long as he can. But he is bound to be back before sunset."

"And Waggle Lane is the far side of town?" Clent raised an eyebrow and received a nod in answer. "Good. You say your father touches no spirits. Does he have a taste for ale, or small beer, or anything else that might tempt him into a hostelry?"

"He never sets a foot in such places. Why?"

"Because taverns have clocks, my dear, and most other places do not. If there is a clock in this counting house, we must set it back an hour or two, and do the same to his pocket watch. If there is a chance that he will check his watch against the clocks in this house, they too must be set back. When the bugle sounds, it must come as a surprise to him—and if his distance from home is too far to cover in fifteen minutes, he will have no choice but to remain where he is."

"Then you can leave that to me, Mr. Clent." Beamabeth's brow cleared, and she fulfilled her name by beaming. "I have a copy of the key of his counting house. I can go there this morning and see to the clock. And I'll take care of the hall clock as well."

Beamabeth took her father his morning nettle tea and returned with his watch cradled in her hand, her face pink with pride and excitement, and was congratulated for her ingenuity by Clent. (Mosca tried to remember receiving such praise for any of her many thefts.) The next challenge was to lose ninety minutes from the main hall clock without the servants noticing. Clent suggested that it should be done piecemeal, turning it back ten minutes now, ten minutes then, so that it did not attract attention.

"You do remember which side we're on, don't you, Mr. Clent?" Mosca whispered while Beamabeth was out of the room. "You're playing games with the mayor now, and it's the mayor who holds the purse strings!"

"Indeed. It is a risk, I will grant you, but it is Miss Beamabeth who holds the mayor's heartstrings, and if we do not play things her way, then we shall have no means of setting our trap, nor winning the mayor round afterward." Clent gave his smallest, thinnest smile, and for a second his eyes were shards of slate. "And yes, I daresay that the mayor will be quite aggrieved when he discovers that a trick has been played on him. But he cannot help but forgive his daughter, who will have been the active party, and when he finds that he has a man he hates entirely in his power . . . I have the strangest presentiment that he will forgive us."

"You're a peach full of poison, you know that?" Mosca snapped back, but she could not quite keep a hint of admiration from her tone.

* * *

Since it would not do for the mayor to come down from his study to find his reception room full of Mosca and Clent, they spent the rest of the morning in a little-used guest room catching up on much-needed sleep. When they finally woke and rallied enough willpower to leave their beds, Clent insisted that they stroll through the market and examine the lay of the land in the castle courtyard. Within an hour, however, Mosca had almost ground her teeth to stumps.

Her dark badge was all that anybody noticed. She might as well have been covered in tar or stinging insects. Every time she passed a stall, she caught the owner pausing to count the wares on it to make sure nothing was missing. Once when she stooped to take hold of a goat's collar to stop it from munching at her skirt, it took all Clent's eloquence to prevent her being dragged to the Pyepowder Court for attempted theft. And nobody seemed to believe that she could have come by a fine plump goose honestly.

Mosca was used to the sort of invisibility that came from being beneath notice. But apparently one could be *beneath* beneath notice, and become more noticeable than ever.

"Child, you are drawing the eye like an inkblot on muslin. I daresay our patroness is back from her father's counting house by now—I propose we prevail upon her to conceal you while I make inquiries."

* * *

Waiting for Clent to return might have been tolerable if Beamabeth had not resolved to be *kind* to Mosca.

"You will want to come to the party too, won't you?" Beamabeth's eye wandered doubtfully over Mosca's tattered and mud-stained dress. "Come! I am sure we can fit you into one of my old gowns."

And so Mosca found herself in Beamabeth's room, where dried rose petals crinkled in pots, lambs frolicked across tapestries, and a red plush cushion bristled with gilded hatpins like the queen of hedgehogs. Dress after undersized dress was pulled out of an oak chest and held up to Mosca's neckline so that her hostess could scrutinize the effect.

"You are better in lemon yellow, or tansy pink, or cream. Pale is best for your age—try this one!"

Mosca found herself with an armful of cream-colored muslin and a matching lace day cap embroidered with strawberries. She was just holding the gown up to her chin to check its length when she noticed a faint scent rising from the fabric. The smell was piquant, heady, and familiar.

"Miss Marlebourne"—she lowered her head and took a deep sniff—"this dress smells of chocolate!"

Beamabeth Marlebourne's eyes crept to the oaken chest. Peering into its depths, Mosca could now see a few small boxes and bundles that had been all but concealed by the folded gowns. One of them was a tiny straw-work tea caddy. Another looked a great deal like one of the chocolate bundles the clawed girl had been throwing through windows.

Beamabeth gave Mosca a small, slightly abashed smile. "You will not tell Father, will you?" She pulled the loose fabric across to conceal them once more. "The mayor's household cannot be seen to have bought anything that might have come in through Mandelion. I just . . . I just like to have a *little* of these things. Now and then. Quietly, so that it will hurt and upset nobody. It is my secret treasure chest."

She gave Mosca a sudden, dazzling, confidential smile. "Come, put on the gown, then I shall order hot water, and you and I shall have *secret tea!*"

In spite of herself, Mosca could not help being a little touched by the offer, not least because Beamabeth seemed so delighted by the idea. As she was moving to remove her skirt, she heard a rustle in the petticoat pocket and suddenly remembered the letter that the midwife had entrusted them with.

"Here." Gruffly she pulled it out of her pocket and presented it, somewhat creased and spiky with yew needles. "Mistress Leap asked me to give you this."

Beamabeth regarded it in evident perplexity, then took it and carefully levered off the seal with an opener. Her soft blue eyes drifted down the page, and Mosca saw her color slowly seep away, leaving a look of pain and confusion.

In a moment Mosca knew why, and the real

significance of what she had already been told struck home.

Leveretia Leap the midwife had told them that *she* had delivered Beamabeth, and Leveretia Leap lived by night. This golden girl had had her beginnings in some darkened hovel in Toll-by-Night, and only her name, her radiant, peerless name, had lifted her out of the shadows and made her worthy to be adopted by the mayor. Perhaps there had even been one of those "exchanges" Mistress Leap had mentioned. Perhaps the mayor had handed over a real blood daughter for a fair-named one and never given the former another thought. Once again Mosca was confronted by the maddening fact that all that really separated Beamabeth's destiny from her own was half an hour—and their names.

Beamabeth looked up suddenly, as if Mosca's glare had burned her skin. The older girl's gaze flickered with surprise at the intensity of the black eyes watching her, then faltered and dropped.

"Didn't you know?" Mosca could not keep the question in. "Didn't you know you was born to night owls?"

"It is not something I like to think about," Beamabeth answered very faintly. Her hands shaking slightly, she laid out a pair of small lace gloves next to the dress she had chosen for Mosca. "The night—it is like a shadow at the back of my mind, cold and bleak and big . . . and I suppose . . . I suppose I am afraid that if I turn to look at it, it will come for me and steal me back."

12

Goodman Rankmabbley,
Enemy of the Winter Spider

By the time the first guests turned up for the party, Mosca's mind had reached a state of turmoil. On the one hand, the bile in her blood told her, Beamabeth was by rights a *nobody*. On the other hand, Mosca had the distinct feeling that if the older girl were snatched to Toll-by-Night, she would last about as long as a pansy in the path of a cartwheel.

Her mood was not improved by the fact that the only strategy Beamabeth had found for preventing Mosca from attracting unwanted attention was to place her against the wall like a servant, with a tray of carrot cakes held up so as to hide her infamous badge. If Mosca had not seen more than one person collared by a mob for lacking a badge, she might have been tempted to throw her own into the fire. Mosca bit her lips and tried to think demure thoughts that would keep a sneer from her face. At least her position allowed to her to view the party at leisure.

The Marlebournes had done their best to swaddle the stone walls and floor of the long, thin reception room into some semblance of warmth and elegance, but there were still low, granite-cold drafts that rubbed against your ankles like cats and teased the corners of the wall hangings. The gold-and-green paper lanterns that lit the scene stirred restlessly and shuddered against the stone.

The far end of the room was the family chapel, its ceiling a half dome painted with stars, the stone flags covered with a wooden dais for more comfortable kneeling. This dais was currently acting as a stage for two violinists, a harpist, a flautist, and a spinet player performing for the gathering. It was only when Mosca had been standing watching for some time that she realized that there was something peculiar about these musicians.

Halfway through a particularly touching little ditty, one of the violinists gave vent to a muffled sneeze, fumbled for his handkerchief, and mopped his nose. However, while he was doing so, Mosca was certain that she could still hear two violins playing, not one. And even now that his bow was busy again, it seemed to be busy in a vague kind of way that even she could tell had very little to do with the music.

Under cover of circulating to serve cakes, Mosca

took a quiet saunter across the room and took up a post nearer the musicians. Yes, she was sure of it—the sneezing violinist's bow was not even touching the strings of his instrument as he "played." The flautist was bobbing along to the music without blowing into his flute. The harpist was miming, his fingers plucking at missing strings. Only the spinet player and second violinist were really playing. Nonetheless, she could definitely hear five instruments.

Nobody else appeared to notice or care. Perhaps they all knew the trick of it, or regarded such fairylike occurrences as something to be expected in Beamabeth's presence. Perhaps Toll folk were used to that kind of thing.

Not real *gentry,* Mosca thought with a certain snobbish relish as she watched Beamabeth's guests recline and sip and confide. *Just pretty names rising to the top like bubbles in a soup. At least Mandelion had* real *nobility. Well, at least they did till we toppled 'em.*

And yet there were a few who were not just local pretty names. Mosca soon gathered that there were several guests from outside Toll, and that one, an eager-faced, dark-haired young man with a faltering lower lip, was Beamabeth's lordly suitor, Sir Feldroll of Millepoyse, the young governor of Waymakem.

As a matter of fact, he looked a little harassed. Again and again the general conversation returned to Mandelion, and everybody wanted to know the same thing—whether Waymakem, Chanderind, and the other big cities to the east would take up arms against the rebel city.

"You have left it too late to attack before spring," one of the local pretty names remarked. "It would take you a good month or two to march your troops upriver to a crossing point and then back down to Mandelion. You would never reach her before winter sets in."

"An army from Chanderind or Waymakem might reach Mandelion before winter, but only if troops were allowed to pass west through Toll without fee. But that is a matter for the mayor, and I should not really discuss it." Beyond this Sir Feldroll refused to be drawn.

Grudgingly, Mosca had to admit that Beamabeth was a gifted hostess. She noticed the way in which the older girl glided from one group to another, occasionally diverting someone to talk to Eponymous Clent. All such were gently herded into a corner to converse with each other.

There was one parlor game that was a good deal like blindman's buff, except that all the company wore blindfolds barring one person, who was unblinkered but covered in bells and had to move stealthily while the others tried to catch him. Beamabeth was particularly deft as the bell wearer, and Mosca watched with fascination as the older girl slipped between grasping hands in her satin shoes, occasionally using the opportunity to slip notes into this person's pocket or that person's hand.

The clocks had been set back to their rightful time before the arrival of the guests, and Mosca's eye kept creeping to the grandfather clock by the wall. By four o'clock, she could have drawn a chalk line down the middle of the reception room and been confident that those on one side of it were still blithely talking of quoits and the silk shortage, and that those on the other side were discussing the dawn plan with furtive intensity.

A little after four the party closed as easily and naturally as a daisy drawing in its petals. The musicians stopped playing, and a moment or two later the music ceased. Beamabeth made her farewells to each guest in exactly the same manner, except for one tiny detail.

"Thank you so much for coming!" Beamabeth told those guests who had enjoyed a pleasant but unremarkable afternoon. "Havers will see you out."

"I am so glad you could be here this afternoon," Beamabeth told those who had been brought into the secret, a meaningful look in her eye. "Mosca will look after you and show you where to find your hat."

And Mosca did not show these guests to their hats or to the door. She led them to the second parlor, where they all waited in silence until the more oblivious guests had gone. Then they all returned to the reception room.

The members of the conspiracy were a curious mix. Clent, looking a little gray around the gills. Sir Feldroll, who seemed inclined to stand behind Beamabeth's chair, gripping the back of it in a fashion that was half protective, half possessive. A few trusted servants. A number of young men, whom Mosca noticed eyeing the proprietary Sir Feldroll in a less than friendly manner. *That's all we need, a bunch of lovelorn suitors dueling in the middle of our ambush. . . .*

And last of all Mosca, setting her pewter tray down with a louder clang than she intended and wandering to squat on the hearthrug with her fists full of cake.

"First things first. There must be no prospect—no prospect at all—of Miss Marlebourne being endangered." Sir Feldroll's adamant tones were echoed in the murmurs of the company.

"Nor shall there be," Clent assured him quickly. "She is far too precious to be placed in the firing line. We are all agreed on that.

"I propose the following. I inform Mr. Skellow's happy little coterie of cutthroats that I have successfully persuaded the young lady to appear outside her house at dawn to pay one last farewell to her erstwhile fiancé. The figure that emerges to keep this appointment will not, of course, be Miss Marlebourne, but a decoy of the same build."

Mosca raised an eyebrow as several gazes crept her way, and she was suddenly very glad that she was a head shorter than Beamabeth.

"Now, as you all know, there are two morning bugles. The first warns the nightfolk that they have fifteen minutes to leave the streets, after which the Jinglers sweep through the town, locking away the night and unlocking the day. The second bugle sounds when they have finished this task. But of course the Jinglers cannot manage all this key work in an instant. Some parts of the town inevitably receive their attentions before others. Perhaps you will tell the company when you usually hear your doors being unlocked, Miss Marlebourne?"

"About halfway between the two bugles, Mr. Clent."

"Thank you, Miss Beamabeth. This house is one of the first to be unsealed from without, which, given that the, ah, Jinglers make their headquarters in the castle, is no surprise. That gives us a window, gentlemen. About seven minutes between the Jinglers unsealing our doors and windows, and the second morning bugle. The rendezvous between the counterfeit Miss Marlebourne and Brand Appleton must be set to take place within that time, when the Jinglers have swept on into the rest of the town and the coast is clear. That way Appleton and his accomplices will fancy that they still have time to flee back to the town after the abduction."

"But . . ." One young lawyer seemed to be having some trouble with the concept. "But if the second bugle has not blown, how can we go out?"

"Turning the front-door handle and pushing might be a good start," suggested Sir Feldroll.

"But . . . we will not exist yet. . . ." The lawyer was not the only person whose face showed signs of internal confusion. Most of the Toll dwellers seemed to have been hit in the midriff by a mental hurdle.

"What?" Sir Feldroll stared at them with exasperation and bewilderment. His eyebrows tended to leap and cavort when he was upset. "Are we phantoms at night? Do we lack breath or limbs? Of course we can go out! We shall simply be in large amounts of danger—go on, Mr. Clent."

"Here is the plan I intend to present to the villains." Clent unrolled a map. "I shall tell them that Miss Marlebourne has agreed to meet Appleton *here*, in this little walled courtyard, not twenty yards from her own front door. As you can see, there is a well in the courtyard. I shall suggest that they hide three or four men down within it long before dawn, so as to avoid detection by the Jinglers. The well is close to the entrance arch, so once the young lady has entered the courtyard, they can spring from their hiding place and cut off her retreat. As you can see, I have marked in charcoal an escape route for them to use in order to return to the seething bowels of the town before they are locked into daylight."

"You've thought out *their* side well enough," remarked a young goldsmith, scanning the smudged page.

"I must," declared Clent. "If the plan does not seem watertight, they will not put from port in it."

"So how do we hole it below the waterline?"

"Ah." Clent held up a finger. "I shall neglect to mention to the brotherhood of blackguards that the archway is not the *only* entrance to the walled courtyard. There is a keep in the opposite corner, once used to house castle guards—a keep in poor repair. You cannot tell from within the courtyard, but there is a hole in the outer wall some fifteen feet above the ground—an easy climb for agile young limbs. I think the scoundrels will be a little surprised to see armed men boiling out of a keep they believe to be empty. At the same time, we can have some other likely fellows creep out at the back of the house so that they are ready to make a rush and cut off escape through the arch."

From her vantage point on the rug, Mosca watched a radiance of excitement spread from face to face as Clent distributed imaginary troops like a general. After the house had been unsealed and the Jinglers had continued into the town, nearly all the guests and the servants would leave the house by the back windows of the mayor's house, out of sight of the walled courtyard, and head toward the prearranged ambush points. Beamabeth herself would stay safely indoors and survey everything from her window, taking care not to be seen. A couple of servants would be left within to guard the windows and door of the house, while Saracen would protect the landing. Mosca herself would accompany those climbing the wall at the back of the keep, since she was nimble enough to clamber up with a rope for others to climb after her.

"My friends," Clent finished, "if you can lay your hands on arms and weapons, pray do so before dusk. But remember—our plan depends upon being out of doors at a time when none but the Jinglers should be abroad. So I entreat you, discharge no firearms except in the greatest need. Our enemies will be wary of letting loose with pistols, and so should we."

The company dispersed with alacrity, and half an hour later the conspirators had returned with a peculiar collection of weapons. A few gentlemanly short swords, then a smattering of hangers, daggers, croquet mallets, fire irons, and rolling pins. In spite of Clent's warnings, Sir Feldroll had brought a brace of pistols with engraved ivory handles. One of the servants was sent to conceal Clent's letter to Skellow inside the courtyard well.

There was a general air of tension as the afternoon dragged its way toward dusk, but Mosca, Clent, and Beamabeth had their own secret reason for anxiety. There was still a chance that the mayor had noticed that his watch had been reset, and he might yet burst into the gathering red-faced, demanding to know why so many people were sitting in his house brandishing weapons. The hall clock, perhaps in revenge for the way it had been interfered with earlier in the day, decreed that the next half an hour would crawl past at a miserably slow pace.

Mosca felt herself tense as she heard the dusk bugle sound. Mouth dry, she watched the clock edge through the minutes.

Finally she heard the Jinglers fly in as though they

rode the wind bell bridled, and then there came the now-familiar sound of grinding and slams, clinks and clatters. The frail chinks of light that crept in between shutters and doors were extinguished. Sound deadened, and Mosca suddenly felt a choking sense of claustrophobia.

The house was sealed, and the mayor had not returned. There was a general hush until at last the second bugle sounded.

"Nighttime, gentlemen," Clent announced. "Our plan is in motion. Our hook is baited and trailing for our wicked fish. Dawn shall see us reel him in."

The servants were not happy. Most of the guests appeared to be blind to this fact, but Mosca was not. Their master was unexpectedly absent, there were unplanned guests, their routine had been broken, the clocks had been behaving erratically that day, and their adored young mistress seemed to be taking instructions from a stranger with a nightling accomplice.

Beamabeth was determined to pray for the success of their enterprise, so everybody was gently but firmly cleared out of the reception room and sent off to sleep in spare rooms and parlors on chairs or chaise longues. As they departed, Beamabeth could be seen kneeling on a velvet cushion, hands clasped under her chin like a much younger girl. To judge by the array of fruit and scented herbs around her, she intended to appeal to a large number of Beloved.

Mosca found Saracen in the little pantry where he had been sequestered, then curled herself around him and wrapped the hearth rug about them.

Children were told stories of the invisible winter spiders that scuttled in under doors in tides of cold and left their frost webs on the windowpanes. It was said that they would pinch and nip at the tips of fingers and toes and noses to turn them blue, and there was sickness in their bite. Goodman Rankmabbley was their enemy, and a toast to his name with a good hot posset was said to help keep them at bay. But now every time Mosca's tired mind drooped toward sleep, she seemed to see Skellow as the king of the winter spiders, his profile sharp as a guillotine, sharpening the knives held in his many hands. . . .

Remembering his threat, Mosca tucked her thumbs inside her fists to protect them and hugged her anger for warmth. *I'm the spider this time,* not *Skellow. This is* my *trap,* my *web. This is danger for* him, *not me.* And the soft thud of her heart battled the cold creak of the shutters second by second for ownership of the night, until the wind yawned and began its restive predawn murmur, and a few birdsong notes scattered the unseen dark like chalk chips.

At last there were sounds of movement in the house, so Mosca gave up on sleep and quietly levered her feet back into her clogs, wincing at the cold of the flagstones. The embers of the hearth were now squirrel-fur gray.

Out in the hallway she found the conspiracy gathering dull eyed, exchanging scant whispers and rubbing at stubbled chins. Dawn was close, and they all knew it. All ears were strained for the bugle. Sir Feldroll was particularly jumpy.

And then at last it came, one long stifled note, and the members of the conspiracy scampered to their stations, Beamabeth fleeing upstairs to her room. Mosca took a moment to lead Saracen to the stairway, where she tethered him to a banister.

"We'll protect the silly hen, won't we?" Mosca murmured as she smoothed his shoulder feathers and felt his cool beak slide against her cheek. "It's revenge on Skellow we're after, that's why we're doing this. That and the reward money to pay the toll. So I'll do my bit, and you'll stand guard—but if you got to bite her on the shin while you're guardin' her, I won't cry."

From outside came a dull thunder of running feet on turf, and the jingle of keys. *Clack. Slam. Tinkle. Crack-crick-creak. Bang.* Lost chinks of light reappeared, and drafts pierced the smoky closeness of the house. The jingling departed and was swallowed by a bellow of wind.

Clent held up a hand and frowned at the clock, face puckering as he counted out each second. Then he gave a rapid nod.

Remembering her role, Mosca scooped up a coil of rope and headed to a back pantry, where she levered open a little window. She was just about to loosen the shutters when there was a jarring jangle of metal on metal just beyond the wall. One of her fellows started so violently that he upset a stack of pans, which set the rest of her companions jumping and flinching like cat-watched starlings. Mosca's hand shook on the shutter bar. If she had pulled it back a second or two sooner, she might have found herself staring into the faces of the Jinglers. . . .

The merry sleigh-bell sounds seemed to make a circuit of the house and dawdle around the side amid creaks and thuds before racing away again. It was half a minute before Mosca clenched her teeth, fists, and will, opened the shutters, and poked out her head.

No Jinglers lurked grinning in the gray light. She clambered out and waited, hopping from one leg to another, while her five companions climbed out after her, Sir Feldroll first.

Running at a stoop, Mosca led them around the side of the house and then nimbly across the small space of the open ground to the cover of a low ruined wall. Her coterie followed her lead but tended to run into one another's backs whenever she stopped to look for danger, and then swear at each other until she hissed at them.

"Bad as a string o' ducklings," she muttered under her breath, and was almost certain that nobody but Sir Feldroll heard her.

Like a parade of hunchbacks they scuttled, until their circuitous route brought them to the outer wall of the well courtyard and the shattered back of the keep. Mosca looped her coil of rope over her own head, hitched her skirts, and started to climb, the cold of the stone making it almost too painful to grip. She reached the jagged place where the wall was breached, tethered her rope to the remains of a beam, and tossed the loose end down to her fellows, who started to climb in their turn.

If Skellow, Brand Appleton, and the rest were following Clent's plan, they would be hiding down the well already, waiting to spring out when Beamabeth entered the courtyard. They would not wait forever, of course. They were probably counting out the seconds even now, braced to clamber out and run if their prey took too long to arrive . . . or if they heard strange and suspicious sounds from the direction of the keep.

The ambush posse in the keep took up position, ready to roar down the uneven steps at a moment's notice. They heard the front door of the mayor's house open and shut. A short pause, and then those waiting in the keep could see a solitary figure in a pale blue dress and gray winter cloak stumbling carefully into view, face drowned in a kerchief and hidden by a bonnet. They all knew that this was a serving lad who had made the mistake of resembling Beamabeth in height and build.

The figure came to a halt in the middle of the courtyard, where it visibly shook in a fashion that suggested fear as much as cold. Occasionally it rubbed one foot against the opposite calf in a less than ladylike way. Beyond sight, the rest of the conspirators would be moving into position, waiting to close the trap and pounce on the kidnappers. . . .

The wind through the wall breach was bitterly cold, and Mosca saw her cohorts grimacing as their limbs cramped. At last one of them exploded in a sudden sneeze of such violence that another conspirator nearly fell backward out of the keep in shock, and Sir Feldroll came within a hair of shooting himself in the jaw. Rooks erupted from the trees and then took a circular saunter across the lightening sky, but no hordes of would-be kidnappers broke cover in affright. Mosca felt a throb of disappointment.

You're not down there at all, are you, Mr. Skellow? How did your long nose sniff out our trick?

Silence. The raw black complaints of the rooks. Then the sound of a bugle. Clent's "window" had closed.

"Can . . . can I take these off now?" asked "Beamabeth" in a quavering tone.

"Well, there is little point keeping them on now that you've wailed out in your own voice," snapped Sir Feldroll. "Come—we should at least search the well. There's a chance we might find a rat or two trapped in there."

The well did indeed seem to have a few rats, but only of the furred and whiskered sort. There were no kidnappers to be found skulking in the ruin of the round temple or in the remains of the castle buttery. When the nearby trees were shaken, nightdwellers singularly failed to tumble to the turf.

"Let us report our fortunes to the lady," Sir Feldroll sighed, disarming his pistol with blue fingers, "and see if her people can rustle up a bowl of something hot."

They entered to find a cluster of servants and overnight guests huddled at the base of the stairs with weapons gripped in their trembling fists. They were evidently planning an assault upon the stairway, where Saracen strutted with lordly confidence, head bobbing and ducking. To judge by the fresh bandages around several hands and one crown, this was not the first time they had tried.

"Stop!" Mosca pushed past them, thudded up the stairs, and curled her arms around Saracen. "He's just doin' the job I left him to do, that's all. I'll find him a bite of something and he'll be right as royalty."

Sir Feldroll was the first to muster enough courage to edge past her, followed by a long train of young men who seemed determined to pretend that they had not all been held at bay by a walking roast dinner.

Loosing Saracen's tether from the banister and prying a pair of pince-nez from the grip of his beak, Mosca could hear Sir Feldroll knocking softly at an upstairs door and calling out in polite and gentle tones. There was a pause, and then some more knocking. Then louder and more sustained knocking.

There was a clatter of steps, and Sir Feldroll appeared at the head of the stairs. His features, which had never seemed particularly happy with one another, now seemed to have fallen out completely and were leaping and jerking in the most disturbing fashion.

"Keys!" he snapped. "Keys to the lady's room! Something is amiss!"

A steward hastened up the stairs, performing an elegant pirouette to avoid a lazy jab from Saracen's beak, and found the right key on his chatelaine. The lord seized it and marched away, dragging the hapless steward behind him by his key chain.

An ominous sensation clutching at her stomach, Mosca followed with Saracen in her arms and was present when the door was opened.

A ghost of a flame quivered above the splattered wreck of a fallen candle on the dresser. One green satin shoe lay abandoned in the center of the room. The red pincushion had been knocked to the floor, its scattered pins glittering in the pale light from the open and unshuttered window.

Beamabeth was nowhere to be seen.

13

GOODLADY BATTLEMAP, RECORDER OF UNMITIGATED DISASTERS

SIR FELDROLL LEAPED across the room to lean out through the window and then gave a muffled *neep* of pain and stooped to pick the pins out of his shoes. Other conspirators followed him into the chamber and performed a search. This generally seemed to involve flinging open clothes chests, going slightly purple at the first glimpse of female lace, and hurriedly dropping the lids again.

"What's going on?" A shout from downstairs.

"She's not here!" Mosca yelled back. "Looks like somebody dragged her out the window! All her baubles are thrown about!"

"What?"

Murmurs of confusion down in the hall, and then an outcry.

"Look—look there! Stop him!"

"Don't let him get away!"

Mosca left the chamber at a run and clattered down the stairs with Sir Feldroll and the others at her heels. When she arrived in the hall, the crowd parted before her armful of goose to show her Clent struggling in the grip of a footman and two guests, his hand still tight around the front-door handle.

"He was trying to slip out through the door, my lord!" chirped one of his captors. "We scarce collared him in time!"

"Sweet singing stars, have you wits?" bellowed Clent as one of his waistcoat buttons burst under the strain. "I was not trying to escape! I was stepping out to examine the scene outside the lady's window and discover how the abduction was managed—surely you can all see that is the next logical action?"

It was a plausible story, but Mosca doubted it was true. Everybody else's mind had been busy with the obvious questions: *What has happened? Why? How?* Clent's mind, however, had skipped ahead to the more important question: *When people have recovered from shock, who will be blamed?* Evidently he had not liked the answer.

"Let us go and look outside as he suggests," instructed Sir Feldroll. "But keep a hand on the man's collar—and an eye on that girl of his."

Outside the frustrated conspirators surveyed the wall, looking for handholds in the rough stone.

"You—girl." A member of the keep ambush party

glanced Mosca's way. "You're good at climbing, aren't you? You could have climbed up to that window."

"Not at the same time as standing in a pantry with you and your friends, you pudding-faced dolt!" Mosca snapped back, her temper fraying.

"Nobody climbed the wall." Clent straightened from a stoop and with one toe pushed back the grass to reveal two deep identical ruts in the earth, about a foot apart. "These, my friends, are the imprints of a ladder."

"Steward!" The steward started fearfully in response to Sir Feldroll's bark. "Does your household own a ladder?"

"Yes, my lord—but it is usually left in the orchard."

It was not in the orchard. After a brief search it was found behind the house.

"So." Sir Feldroll scowled. "Am I to understand that a gaggle of villains ran through half the courtyard with a ladder, dodging Jinglers as they went, set it against the wall, forced their way in through the window, over-whelmed Miss Marlebournc, carried her down, then ran away with her, all without us seeing or hearing *anything*?"

A moan of the utmost melancholy emerged from Eponymous Clent.

"Alas, my unhappy comrades, we *did* hear them. We heard them circle the house, come to a halt by the window, move their ladder, and do their business. But we were too busy cowering in terror, because *they were jingling*. The second set of so-called Jinglers that ran past

229

the house a minute after the first—that must have been our kidnappers. By the time we dared to emerge and lay our own trap, the lady had been tweaked from under our noses."

"But how?" exploded Sir Feldroll. "How, without a scream or sounds of a struggle? The lady must have unfastened her window to open her shutters so that she could keep an eye upon events—but how could those dogs be sure of catching her before she fastened the windows again? There is more to this. There must be. These villains must have had an accomplice within the house." He glanced around himself fiercely. "Are we missing anybody from the mayor's household?"

Clent's eyes had been flickering out toward the town from time to time, perhaps in search of an escape route. Now his gaze seemed to lodge on something, and he deflated like a puff pie taken from the oven.

"Oh, pestilential fates," he murmured. "No, I believe we shall soon have the establishment in its entirety."

Following the line of his gaze, Mosca saw the mayor striding with rapid, purposeful steps in their direction, huffing out angry white breaths into the crisp and wintry air.

He came to a halt outside the house, and his arched white brows rose as he surveyed the rueful, tongue-tied congregation. Sir Feldroll was the first to find his courage, and he stepped forward, knotting his fingers together.

"My lord mayor . . . I hardly know how to . . . I have the worst of all possible news. The trap laid last night was not successful. And worse than that—worst of all—my lord mayor, I must ask you to brace yourself—"

"What trap?" demanded the mayor, his head turning to examine one person after another in sharp, hostile motions.

"What?" Sir Feldroll's jaw dropped, and it took several seconds for him to crank it back up again. He rounded on Clent, his face a picture of disbelief. "Am I to understand that all of this night's stratagems took place *without the mayor's knowledge or permission?*"

"Ah." Clent moved a hand to adjust his cravat but was brought up short by the tightening grip of his captors' hands on his arms. "Ah. Well . . . that is . . . ah."

The ensuing explanation ordeal that took place in the reception room bore an unpleasant resemblance to a court in session. The mayor was incandescent and strode to and fro in plum-faced fury until his boots threatened to chafe the rug into flames. He would probably have ordered everybody there to be clapped in irons, were it not for the practical difficulties of having the entire company arrest itself.

They were all imbeciles. And those who were not imbeciles were traitors. And thieves and criminals and murderers. And there was not a punishment in Toll's oldest books of litigation that the guilty parties would escape. But that would be nothing compared to what they would suffer if any harm came to his darling Beamabeth.

Interjection did not seem very wise, so nobody said anything for a long while, even when the mayor ran out of threats and strode to and fro in silence, his right fist clenched in his left hand.

"Well?" He stopped abruptly and turned upon Clent. Clent's shoulders jumped nervously, and his eyes glassed over.

"This is all your handiwork, sir," declared the magistrate. "As far as I can tell, your stratagems guaranteed that at the most dangerous time of the day I would be absent, my doors would be unlocked, and all the friends and servants who might have protected my daughter would be chasing will-o'-the-wisps across the castle green. Is there anything you can say to convince me that this was not your intention all the time? That you are not, in fact, the Romantic Facilitator of whom you pretended to warn me?"

A mottling of gasps. Self-congratulatory murmurs from the men who had "caught" Clent at the doorway.

"Hail and hellweather!" Some of Clent's color had returned to his face. "My good and gracious lord mayor, do you imagine that if I had *intended* to kidnap that child I would have done so in such a preposterous way? There are a thousand easier ways to manage the business, without hazarding my own safety and good name in this fashion."

"Oh, yes?" The mayor folded his arms, his face a picture of incredulity. "Such as . . . ?"

"Well." Clent spread his plump fingers and frowned at them. "I could of course have used the clock trick on her, instead of on your good self, and arranged some secret conference with her near the end of the day in another part of town. All I would need would be a well-muffled room in which she would not hear the bugle, and then I could have sent her on her way at dusk, not realizing that the first bugle had blown and that there was a gaggle of night owls waiting outside to ambush her.

"Or I could have drugged her food or drink, put her in a box, and hoisted her up into one of the taller trees, high enough that the Jinglers would not be looking for hiders there, and my accomplices could claim her come night.

"Or . . . well, quite simply, my good sir, I could have tried to negotiate a deal with the Locksmiths. A gamble, of course—but if it worked, then all other perils would disappear."

Clent shrugged very slightly as the mayor stared at him, his fist twitching.

"Of course, these are merely the plans that instantaneously occur to my mind," he continued. "There are many other ways I could have contrived it. Miss Marlebourne had given me her trust, and under those circumstances kidnapping her without trace would have been childishly easy. Coming up with a plan that we could sabotage so as to catch these foxes with their noses in the coop—*that* was the hard part."

The mayor was still bristling, but thoughtfulness was doing battle with rage behind his eyes, and clearly Clent's words had not been lost on him.

"So what do you claim went wrong?" he asked in a biting but more moderate tone.

"Sir Feldroll, I believe, has the matter in a nutshell," Clent responded. "There was a worm in the peach, a thistle among the good grain, a weasel in the dovecote. In short, we were betrayed."

"A fly in the ointment?" suggested the mayor, his eyes resting on Mosca with cold, hard meaning. Mosca flushed as she became aware that she was now the focus of nearly every gaze in the room.

"Don't be lookin' at me that way! I never done it!" Once again she had the feeling that she was standing in her own private patch of ice. Now she felt as if the ice beneath her feet was cracking and threatening to drop her into something infinitely worse.

"She was the only nightling involved in this plan." The mayor's tones were steely, and Mosca felt hot pins and needles flood her skin and stomach. "*She* was the one who started stories of this kidnapping in the first place and brought all of this to pass. She could easily tip off her nightling accomplices when the need arose."

Mosca could hardly breathe. Her badge was a leaden weight against her chest.

"With the greatest of respect," Sir Feldroll broke in

politely, "that makes absolutely no sense at all."

"What?" The mayor turned on him, and once again drew himself up into a quivering tower of annoyance.

"The girl certainly heard Mr. Clent's plan with the rest of us yesterday afternoon, but unlike most of us," Sir Feldroll went on, "she never left the house to fetch weapons. I have checked with the servants—she was here all the time. And overnight she was locked up with the rest of us. She did not have a *chance* to tip anyone off. The one thing she *did* have the chance to do, though, is run away, while we were all blundering around in the early morn, and if she were guilty, I cannot see a reason why she would not have done so."

Bless your twitchy little features, Sir Feldroll, thought Mosca. *You're not as stupid as you look.*

"Sir Feldroll," simmered the mayor, "use your eyes. We are seeking a betrayer in our midst. *Look* at her."

"I am not vouching for the girl's good character," answered Sir Feldroll, with the measured tones of one working hard to keep his own temper. "I very much doubt she has any. I am just saying that I do not think she can walk through walls."

"I am glad to hear it," the mayor declared, in tones as humorous as a gibbet. "Because I intend to surround her with the thickest, tallest, coldest walls we have."

Mosca had two sorts of flying dreams. The best ones were flying-as-a-fly dreams, full of weaving and soaring and walking on ceilings, her wing-whirr deafening as a drumroll. The others were mote-on-the-wind dreams, where a fickle breeze swept her up and bore her hither and thither, in spite of all her attempts to swim back down to earth. Such nightmares left her sick with vertigo, rage, and helplessness.

The blur of her departure from the mayor's house was very much like the second sort of dream. For one thing, her feet did not touch the ground, and no amount of kicking and flailing served to give her a foothold. The half dozen hands gripping her arms and shoulders might as well have been iron. She had had no choice but to leave Saracen in Clent's care, so fearful was she that he would fall foul of someone's pistol if he tried to protect her.

The market girls setting up their stalls gawped as Mosca passed, but when their eyes settled on her badge, their brows smoothed. *Ah, that explains it.* She wanted to spit in their bland, doughy faces. She wanted to pull loose for a second, long enough to frighten them. And she hated the tears that turned them into dark pillars of mist and reduced the courtyard green to a fuzzy gleam.

Unfair, unfair, unfair. They'd done for her; this rotten town had done for her; Skellow, who should have been dragged off in irons, had done for her after all.

"Where do we take her? The Pyepowder Court? Isn't that where they take visitors when they catch them breaking the law?"

Mosca wondered for a moment if daylight Toll even

had a court to try its own citizens, or whether everyone just assumed that day crimes were only ever committed by nightfolk passing through.

"The Pyepowder Court? Are you mad?" The voice of the mayor, a little behind Mosca. "This isn't some dusty-foot vagrant, or a Gypsy selling a cat as a piglet. Take her straight to the clock tower."

The peculiar procession continued through the twisting streets, followed by curious gazes and a gustful of autumn leaves.

As she was carried to the clock tower, Mosca stopped struggling and let her feet droop limply. She was in a trap within a trap within a trap. There was nowhere to run. She let her head fall back and stared up at the china blue autumn sky, speckled with birds, girded with the lean of buildings, striped by strands of her own loose hair. She filled her lungs with as much cold, searing air as she could, like a diver preparing; then she was pulled in through the heavy oak doors, and the sky was taken away from her. This time, however, they did not take her through the side door into the Committee of the Hours building but up a few stairs to a darkened antechamber.

"What's this?" A man with a red leather patch over his eye looked up from oiling a set of branding irons. A bunch of heavy iron keys clustered at his belt. "One for the clink?" His single gray eye took in Mosca in one guillotine flash.

"Yes—for a conspiracy of the darkest dye." The mayor

strode to the front, and the one-eyed man dropped a hasty bow. "The treacherous kidnapping of a young woman of birth and means. The kindest and most sweet-tempered girl in the whole . . ." The mayor's voice trembled and trailed off.

"You don't mean . . . ?" The single slate-colored eye flashed back to Mosca's face, and the seamed face in which it was set puckered with disbelief and outrage. "Not Miss Beamabeth?" Skin tingling, Mosca realized that she was about to become the most hated person in Toll.

The mayor nodded, his face ashen. "I want this girl girded about with iron and stone," he said grimly. "And watch her—she's a housefly, with a housefly's swift and sneaking ways."

The keeper nodded, giving Mosca a thunderous look. "I'll have her shackled and tossed in the Grovels, sir."

"My lord mayor!" Terror restored Mosca's powers of speech. "I'm no enemy to you or your daughter! Let me go, an' I'll find her for you, I swear it on Palpitattle's wings!" It was the worst oath she could have made; she sensed it as soon as the words were out of her mouth. Everyone looked at her and shuddered, as though she had sprouted antennae, or cleaned her hands with a long, insectile tongue.

The keeper whistled, and a pair of turnkeys came running. The viselike hands on Mosca's shoulders were traded in for other viselike hands, and she was dragged to a nearby spiral stairway. As she had feared, she was led not up but down the darkened steps, her legs shaking with fear and the seeping chill of the old stones. She smelled her prison before she reached it, a reek of sickness and rotten straw and chamber-pot perfumes and a gagging aroma of spoiled meat. At the bottom of the stairs, the keeper opened a low arched door, and the smell became overwhelming.

There were several figures in the low-ceilinged cell beyond, but as the door opened, they retreated from the light to the shadows of the walls in a way that reminded Mosca of rats, except that rats do not usually give off a metallic jangle as they move.

"Since you're new, I'll run through the charges. There's a fee for rent, o' course, but the Grovels down here is easy on the purse—you don't pay till you leave. And as a newcomer you pay a garnish—that's a bit of courtesy to the other guests." The keeper nodded toward the other figures in the cell. "Just enough to buy 'em each a tipple so they can drink to your health. You'll be wanting to pay that. If you don't, the worst of 'em will take what they're owed out of your hide. And o' course, all luxuries is extra."

"Luxuries?" Mosca stared at him. "I don't want any luxuries!"

"Yes, you do. Luxuries being, you see, things like food. And drink. And blankets. And not being clapped in irons."

"But . . . I 'aven't got any money!"

The keeper stared at her, and something changed in

his face, making his jaw heavier and his single eye hot and dull. Mosca noticed muscle meat in his arms, the cudgel at his belt, the scars around his hairline. Suddenly she felt like a doll of sticks.

"Missy, I hear that every day." The keeper grimaced and shook his head with long-suffering disgust. "And yet, somehow people find they *can* come by the coin when their backs are up against the wall—and yours *is* against the wall, make no mistake. They beg, or borrow, or call on help from friends, or find things for me to sell. And those who can't have no place coming here and trying to take advantage of a poor businessman."

The other "guests" were not slow to claim their garnish. They closed on Mosca almost as soon as the door shut behind the keeper, turned her upside down, and shook her to see what fell out. One grimy hand snatched at Mistress Bessel's handkerchief; another slyly snatched the Little Goodkin bracelet from her wrist.

The woman who tried to grab at Mosca's pipe, however, found herself with a fight on her hands. Another prisoner was sitting on Mosca's legs so that she could not kick, but she scratched and bit and wrestled until the would-be thief gave up. The others retreated to survey their finds, leaving Mosca curled in a ball around the pipe, her ribs and ears bruised from blows.

Only when she was sure that her fellow guests had lost interest in her did she dare to uncurl a little from her hedgehog pose. It was too dark for her to make out faces, but she could hear the murmur of thieves' cant, the slang of the world's underbelly. Night owls, probably. As they talked, it became clear that most of them had once been visitors with night names who had been arrested for one crime or another and had been languishing in the Grovels ever since.

Prisons swallowed men like cherry pits—she knew that much. They were arrested for this or that, and then somebody lost the papers and it never came to trial and meanwhile they starved or sickened from rotten meat or had their heads stove in by their jailers. Prison was a pit, and once you'd fallen in, you had a devil of a time climbing out again, unless you had money, a good name, or powerful friends. Mosca had none of these.

There's Mr. Clent.

Hah. He's too fond of his own neck to stick it out for me.

For a while she buried her face in her apron and shook, until the muslin was damp and her breaths were ragged.

Oh, stop sniveling, she told herself at last. *Saracen would come for you, if he was a man—he'd come with three brace of pistols at his belt. But he's a goose, and that's all there is to that. You're on your own.*

Mosca felt as if she was sharing a cave with a pack of wolves, all snarling at one another in the darkness. As runt of the pack, she guessed that her best chance of survival was to attract as little attention as possible. This, however, did not turn out to be easy.

"Oi." Somebody poked her with a shackled foot. "You

don't want to lie there. You're in Magpackin's spot."

Mosca rolled away and pulled herself up into a tight little bundle with her back to a wall.

"All right, all bleedin' right! Take your spot!" she shrilled.

There was a roar of laughter.

"Magpackin won't be taking it back just yet," said the largest of the men. "He's worm food. But that was his lying spot three good weeks before the keeper took him away. No release fee paid for him, you see."

Mosca shuddered, and her hands twitched to her shoulders and hair, eager to brush off any traces of the dead Magpackin, while the other prisoners laughed again at her discomfort.

It was during this hilarity that bolts scraped back and the door opened to show the keeper's Cyclops face, illuminated by the lantern in his hand.

"Visitor for the new girl."

Mosca's heart leaped as the keeper stepped aside. Clearly Clent, the word wizard, had somehow waltzed into the stronghold in spite of the mayor's instructions . . .

. . . or perhaps not. Not unless he had decided to infiltrate the prison by donning a white muslin dress, a lace cap, and a pair of good kid gloves.

"You poor child," declared Mistress Bessel in viper-blood tones, her sturdy figure filling most of the doorway. "I've come to bring you a little comfort."

14

Goodman Asheneye,
protector of the hearth

Mosca responded to these sweet sentiments with the short sharp scream of one who has just sat on a kettle.

"Dear good sir," continued Mistress Bessel, holding Mosca's gaze with a world of meaning in her ice blue eyes, "you see what a shrinking, timid little thing she is? Now you understand why I want a room where I can speak to her *alone*."

The keeper frowned, his patch strap making diagonal creases across his brow.

"Well, mistress, we do have some private cells, but they are generally put aside for *special* visitors. Those who can pay for the privilege—"

"Do it," Mistress Bessel interrupted crisply. "I'll buy her a new cell—the one they call Hell's Eyrie. And I want half an hour alone with her."

The prospect of being locked up with an enraged Mistress Bessel scattered Mosca's other fears like a house cat pouncing amid a congregation of pigeons. However, her second squeal of panic only seemed to convince the keeper that the visitor was right about her shy and quivering nature. He smiled indulgently at Mistress Bessel, smiled indulgently at the coins she placed in his hand, and then smiled indulgently at Mosca, somewhat to her confusion and alarm.

"This way then, ladies." Somehow the keeper's tone had become that of an obliging host showing affluent guests to the better quarters of an inn. He loosed Mosca's leg-irons and then led her from the room while the other Grovelers muttered and hissed resentfully.

The stairs coiled upward past a series of other cells, each just visible through the hatch in the door, none quite as grim as the Grovels. They passed a crammed debtors' cell where families huddled and lone figures moped and smoked, a female cell where drab-faced girls coughed into their aprons, and an all-but-lightless male cell full of fury and half-seen movement like a box of ferrets.

"Here's *your* chambers." The keeper halted outside a small oak door, dulled by years to the color of gun metal. The stairs, Mosca noticed, had not ended but continued upward. The keeper pulled back an alarming series of bolts, many of which had all but rusted into place through disuse, wrenched a couple of great keys into the splinter-edged locks, and heaved the door open.

It was a tapering room shaped like a wedge of cake, one small barred window set in the rounded wall. Near it was a narrow hearth, which curiously appeared to have been cleaned with care. No furniture, no bed. A slack iron chain, one end fixed to a ring set low on the wall, the other to a set of leg-irons.

"Best room in the house." The keeper's tone was one of real pride. "That little window'll give you a view as far as the sea on a clear day. You can even pick out the spires of Penchant's Mell. That there is the very corner slept in by Hadray Delampley, the rebel earl of Mazewood, during the Civil War."

Unlike the other cells, this one did not stink of rot and the chamber pot. Indeed, the only sign that anyone had been in the cell of late was the recently scrubbed hearth. The keeper noticed her looking at it.

"Keep ideas of that sort out of your costard," he rumbled in her ear. "You're not the first to have thought of leaving by the chimney. Not a week ago some folks showed charity to a young lad who had been caught miching, and paid for him to stay in this cell. Quick as tricks, up the chimney he goes . . . and finds there's a cast-iron grate blocking the flue. And while he's trying to shake it loose, he takes a tumble, dashes out his wits. Same thing happened three weeks ago as well. Young girl. Same luck. I get full weary of mopping that hearth. . . ."

Mosca swallowed and gave this information due consideration while Mistress Bessel bargained with the keeper for "luxuries." Yes, Mistress Bessel would pay to see Mosca free from leg-irons. No, she would not pay for her meals. Yes, she would hire a blanket for her. No, she would not buy sticks for the hearth.

"Well, I will leave you ladies to talk." In spite of the entreaty in Mosca's face, the keeper withdrew.

"You poor suffering dear," Mistress Bessel said as the door closed behind him, in tones of icy and eternal enmity. "See, I have brought you muffins." The door clicked to, and Mosca backed to the farthest extent of the cell.

"So . . . what was it you last said to me?" asked Mistress Bessel, carefully adjusting the cuffs of her gloves. "Was it not 'Fie to your game, Mistress Bessel'? Just before you set that feathered hell thing on me?"

And in a flash, Mosca remembered their last conversation, and the game that she had cried fie to. Mistress Bessel's plan. The one that required Mosca to be a prisoner in the jail of the clock tower. The one that involved her finding a way to slip out of her cell by night . . . and steal the Luck of Toll.

"I think you'll play my game now, my dumpling." Mistress Bessel's tone was still sweet. "I think you'll play it for your life."

There was a long silence; then Mosca sniffed hard and rubbed at her nose with the back of one hand.

"Those real muffins in your basket?" she asked in a small, hard voice.

Mistress Bessel's mouth tightened, then spread into her warmest smile as she recognized the unwilling consent in Mosca's tone.

"Brought up by wolves, you was, I think." The portly woman approached and crouched next to Mosca, then watched as the latter filled her mouth and apron with currant muffins. "All teeth and stomach, no manners."

Mosca could not speak but managed a few nonchalant, dry rasping noises as she munched, her cheeks and open mouth bulging with unswallowed cake.

"Now, listen well. I have word that the Luck of Toll is hid in the room above this pretty chamber of yours. Seems you can reach that room by the stairway outside . . . but there's great heavy doors barring the way, with more locks than a miser's spoon chest, and with guards who stand outside night and day. So there's no point trying that way." She nodded toward the entrance to the cell. "No—you'll have to go up the chimney."

Mosca managed to gust out a crumb-laden squeak of protest. The hearth was a miserable width, the flue likely to be more miserable still, and the keeper's darkly allusive tales had not increased her confidence.

"Don't be such a warbler—nobody will light a fire under you," Mistress Bessel continued without sympathy. "There are two chimneys out the top of this building. The one on the north side serves the guardsmen's quarters, but the other, on the south side, serves nothing but this room and maybe the one above. And I say it *does* serve the one above, because there's a trail of smoke comes out of it every day about suppertime, and *this* cell has been empty all week. Which means the flue from this room joins the flue from the hearth in the room above. Which means you can climb up the one and down the other. We know there's a grate at the top of the chimney to stop desperate snipes climbing out to freedom . . . but I'll be surprised if they've guessed that prisoners in one cell might climb the chimney to break into another one and back again."

Mosca covered her mouth and managed to swallow enough to speak.

"Well, small surprise in that!" she exploded. "Everybody who tries climbing this chimney ends up dead in the cinders! And you want me to climb *up* this chimney, *down* another . . . an' all the way back again?"

"Yes," said Mistress Bessel. And somehow, although there were a thousand protests Mosca could make, there was no real answer to that one, stony word.

"So . . . s'posing I even reached the other room, what if there's a guard inside it, lookin' after the Luck? If there's smoke from the chimney, a fire must be lit for *somebody*."

Mistress Bessel simply shrugged her motherly shoulders.

"Then you had better hope that his sleep is heavy and

your step is soft, my buttercup."

"But . . . what if I can't work out what the Luck is? Or what if it's locked away or chained to the wall?"

"If you cannot use those long, thieving fingers of yours, use your eyes." Mistress Bessel stood, her empty basket in hand. "Tomorrow I will be back with more muffins and counsel for the poor wicked children who have fallen into sin and crime. If you have a Luck to give me, then that means coin for you and Eponymous, enough to pay your way out of Toll and see out the winter. If not . . . then you had better be able to tell me every inch of that other cell so I can come up with a better plan. Either way, if you've done your part, then you'll walk out of prison with Jennifer Bessel."

"How?" This still sounded too good to be true. "I got thrown in the Grovels on the mayor's own orders. How you going to get me out when he's brimmin' with bile?"

"Have a little faith. Jennifer is a name to conjure with in this town, and if I vouch for you, the doors will fly back on their hinges so fast, the breeze will leave you breathless. As for your mayor"—a catlike smile crept across Mistress Bessel's apple-broad face—"it will not be the first time I have talked a gentleman out of a temper.

"But if I come back here tomorrow, and you are sitting here with no word of the Luck . . . then there's no more luck for you in this life, my little mulberry tree. Once you have given them your shoes and buttons to sell, the jailers here will watch you starve to death . . . and they won't even carry out your corpse unless somebody pays them to do it."

The little window was too narrow to let through much light or any hope of escape, but was just broad enough to allow in a dismal slither of a draft that chilled the whole cell. Mosca crouched and shivered on the wooden floor, wrapped in the keeper's scant blanket, warming her frozen nose tip in her apron.

If I am to do this, it had best be by night.

At night there was less likelihood of the keeper dropping into Mosca's cell to extort money from her. More hope that any guards around the Luck would be drowsy or asleep. A better chance that the suppertime fire in the upper room would have cooled so that she would not get burned or choke on the smoke.

Hours passed, and Mosca chewed her fingertips, and thought of days passing and the keeper becoming less courteous and the cudgel at his belt and nobody caring. Rat in a trap.

She heard the flues stealthily flute and boom with drafts and smelled a faint trace of smoke.

She heard the bugle and felt the taste of the air change as day became night.

She heard the second bugle.

And it was too big a decision to make, too terrifying a plan to consider. So while she was busy not considering it, Mosca carefully and silently slid off her clogs, pulled off her stockings, and tied back her hair. Then she removed her dress to reveal her chemise and the wading breeches she still wore under her skirts, even though she had long since left the waterlogged village in which she had been brought up.

She crouched down in the hearth and very carefully straightened, with the upper part of her body inside the absolute darkness of the chimney. She felt panic tighten around her chest like a corset and reflexively ducked down again, banging her head. Then she made herself straighten once more and groped around with her hands, feeling the feathery tickle as her fingertips dislodged soot.

It was chokingly narrow, and if she braced herself badly, she might stick at any moment. Climbing it would be ugly, unpleasant . . . and possible.

Grimacing, she raised one knee, found a toehold in the stonework with her bare foot, and began to climb.

Soot, Mosca decided after she had climbed three yards, was powdered evil. She could not look up without it falling into her eyes and making them burn. She had no hands free to wipe her eyes, and chafing her face against her shoulder just made things worse. Soot was on every ledge, ermine soft, tickling and trickling into her sleeves and neck and ears and mouth, catching her throat and making her cough great soot storms into life.

But while well-born children might have been brought

up with improving fables and histories, Mosca had gobbled every gallows chapbook and crime chronicle she could find. So when panic threatened to set her mind on a rat scamper, she gritted her teeth and thought of every daring jailbreak she had ever read of, Drag Minkem descending from a roof on a rope of blankets, and Swift Swathe Ferren swaggering into his favorite tavern still wearing his manacles.

Why is it that every time someone is needed to squeeze up somewhere or under somewhere or into somewhere, it ends up being me? Just as well I'm half starved, or I'd stick like a pick.

Each time she moved, loose soot and fragments of hardened tar hissed down the chute and rattled in the hearth below. As Mosca climbed, the hiss took longer and the rattle became more indistinct. Mosca braced her elbows and feet against the encroaching walls, knees tucked close to her chest, all too aware that a missed footing could send her plummeting down in exactly the same way.

You're on your own. Blackness, narrowness, walls closing in, no sky. Mosca felt her child heart calling out to the Beloved, begging for their company in the darkness. But instead she bit her lip almost to bleeding and stifled the prayers in her mind.

Then, just as she thought the flue would narrow and narrow until she was wedged like a cork in a bottle, it kinked slightly to climb at an angle. After a yard or so of this, her questing fingers discovered that a foot above her head the right-hand wall disappeared. She ascended by inches until her head was level with the gap.

A dim light was falling from above, and Mosca could see that her flue had joined another to form a larger square chute leading upward. Hauling herself up to sit on the brick ledge at the top of the division, she could see a little square of dark silver sky above, crisscrossed by stark black. Mistress Bessel had been right then—the two flues both fed into one chimney; and it was blocked off with a grille as the Cyclops had said, so that no prisoners could escape that way.

Mosca felt her stomach sink and realized that she had been hoping at the back of her mind that she might be able to make it out onto the roof. No, it seemed she would be playing things Mistress Bessel's way, like it or no.

The descent of the other flue was far more difficult than the ascent of the first. A faint haze of smoke still hung within, making Mosca gag and sneeze in spite of her terror of being heard. The bricks held a strange animal warmth, and there were sparks and feathers of hot ash lurking in ambush.

Not far now. Then grab the Luck and go. What would it be? What had Clent said?

Often a glass chalice, or an ancestral skull, or a collection of breeding peacocks . . .

"Well, I hope it's not peacocks," Mosca muttered under her breath. "Don't fancy climbing a red-hot chimney with half a dozen squawking birds under one arm."

Even as she gave words to this thought, her bare sole settled on a ledge that turned out to be harboring a family of ember-hot cinders. She swore and jerked her foot away, then dragged desperately at the sooty walls with hooked fingers as her other foot lost its grip. She tumbled down the rest of the flue, buffeted by the back wall, the air filling with soot clouds, and then a stone floor struck her in the bottom, bringing her to a halt with an agonizing jolt. For a few seconds she could only lie there, winded and mewling in pain, her legs in the air. Then she opened her eyes again, and froze.

She was in a room twice as large as the one she had just left, the walls draped with rich but faded tapestries. The floor was choked with dusty russet-colored rugs and cluttered with wooden images of the Beloved, some of whom had been arranged in lines like troops. In a corner stood a small four-poster with a chipped chamber pot beside it. A cluster of candlesticks was glued to the top of a low table by their own wax, one candle still lit and casting a slanted radiance over the whole room.

Standing directly over Mosca herself was a youth of about fifteen years, his jaw slack, his eyes popping with surprise.

His pallor reminded Mosca of the bluish wanness of the inhabitants of Toll-by-Night. His clothes, on the other hand, were lavish, although apparently designed for someone a few years younger. The sleeves of his green velvet frock coat ended several inches short of his bony wrists. His waistcoat was elaborately embroidered, but many threads had been pulled loose. No effort had been made to tie back his long dark hair. Fuzzy dark brows met over his nose.

For a moment or two Mosca was paralyzed. The stranger, however, did not call for help or move to the door but seemed, if anything, more flabbergasted and terrified by her sudden apparition than she was.

Mosca put her finger to lips and gave an intimidating hiss that turned into more of an intimidating splutter as soot caught in her throat. She struggled to her feet, soot stained and inexplicable.

"Who . . . ?" The boy's voice was a squeak.

"I am a . . . a Figure of Calamity!" hissed Mosca. "Sent by the Beloved to . . . to punish them that . . . do not pray enough."

There was a short pause in which the stranger's pale gaze wavered down Mosca's scraped and blackened form and back to her face again.

"What kind of calamity?" he whispered.

"Fire," answered Mosca promptly, her heart beating a tattoo. "And . . . hunger. And crime. And really bad moods. Now keep your ugly trap shut, or I'll blight you."

The youth stared at her, then extended one trembling hand toward Mosca's face and with great care and deliberation poked her in the eye.

She gave a short yelp and slapped his hand away. He spent a few moments staring at his sooty fingertip and then broke into a long, loud laugh. It was an embarrassing laugh, the sort of unformed yodeling noise that Mosca would have expected to hear from a toddler or a village simpleton. Mosca crouched back toward the fireplace and glanced nervously at the door, but the braying laughter summoned nobody.

"You are not a calamity," he said. "Your cheek is squashy."

There was something odd about his speech, at once childlike and formal. It reminded Mosca of a very small child reading lines for a play. He had other infantile tricks of manner too: the way he let his jaw hang open and breathed loudly through it, the way he fumbled at his own buttons and scratched himself in ways most people didn't when anyone was watching.

So. Someone *had* been left to watch the Luck. The idiot son of some high-ranking daylighter, to judge by appearances. And if he was an idiot . . . then perhaps all was not lost. Perhaps he would be too addlepated to give a good account of her if she crept back up the chimney to her own cell. Perhaps he would not even notice her scooping up the Luck . . .

Heart pounding, Mosca willed herself to think. Where *was* the Luck? Was it that silver plate heaped with dried raisins? That glass decanter with purple tidemarks left by wine? That ivory-handled candle snuffer?

The stranger was examining her again with a new, keen interest, looking in wonderment at her breeches and chemise.

"Where is your badge?"

Mosca clutched reflexively at the place where it had been, before remembering that it had been pinned to the dress she had left in her cell.

"I . . ." She swallowed. "I must have dropped it some-where—don't look at me like that!"

"But—everybody has to have a badge! Having no badge is against—" The boy broke off suddenly, and for the first time looked alarmed and cast a glance toward the door. But instead of running to it to summon help, he turned back to Mosca and put a clumsy hand over her mouth.

"Talk quietly," he said, "or they will take you away."

He took her by the arm, led her to the dark wall farthest from the door, and sat down on the rug in a jumble of angular limbs. Mosca dropped into a crouch a yard from him, all the while keeping her feet under her, in case she needed to sprint for the chimney. If his wits were twisted, could he be dangerous?

"So—what you doing up here?" she asked, as quietly and steadily as she could.

"Luck," he muttered in a distracted way. Mosca glanced at him sharply, hoping that he might betray himself with a glance toward the mysterious Luck. He did not. His angular, trembling hands were busy, shaking out a checked rug and arranging some of the wooden Beloved upon it.

"For Luck? Did your family put you in here because . . ." Mosca hesitated.

Because you were broken witted and they hoped the Luck would cure you?

"Here." The boy pushed a heap of Beloved toward Mosca. "You play this now. You have night, I have day. I want to try the new rules."

Only when her strange host started pointing out where on the rug she should place her Beloved did Mosca understand what he was doing. He had divided the statues into the Beloved that gave daylight names and the ones linked to nighttime names. Now he was laying them out like game pieces on the squares of the checked rug.

Playing games with Beloved icons? I fancy the priests would have a thing or two to say about that. . . .

He explained the rules, gabbling some parts in his excitement. Mosca watched him narrowly, cupping Palpitattle in her hands, her wits snicking against one another like sharpening knives.

"So this is a game?" Mosca chewed her cheek. "Ought to be a prize really, then, shouldn't there? Anything here worth using as a prize? What's the most valuable thing here?"

Ah! There it was at last. A small telltale gesture. Her host's hand crept up and came to rest near his own collarbone.

"What is it?" Mosca pursued her advantage. "Can I see it? Is it a locket?"

The youth shook his head, wide-eyed, then beamed and tapped at his own chest.

"What? Where? What is it? Oh." Mosca slumped and wiped her face with both hands, leaving a cage work of soot smudges across her brow. "Oh, *beechnuts*. It's you, isn't it? *You're* the Luck."

"Protector of the walls, guardian against disaster." The boy's smile was beatific. "I was born under Goodman Lilyflay, He Who Makes Things Whole and Perfect— and so I have a name full of getting-things-right and just-as-it-should-be. The finest, brightest, luckiest name in Toll."

"Might 'ave guessed," sighed Mosca bitterly. "You couldn't jus' be a glass cup, could you?" She sized up the bemused-looking Luck, peered appraisingly at the little hearth, then shook her head wearily. "I'd have had a better chance with a bunch of peacocks," she muttered. "So—what is this brilliant name of yours, Master Luck?"

"Paragon" came the answer, laced with quiet pride.

The word was slightly familiar. "Is that like a hexagon?"

"No!" He looked angry, and very confused. "Paragon is a . . . an ideal example. It's . . . perfect."

Mosca sniffed at perfection. Perfection had no pulse and no heart.

"Funny kind of a name."

"It is the best name in the town!" The Luck looked

aghast. "That is why I was chosen. My parents were night-dwellers, but I was born to higher things, born worthy of the brightest of noonday names. And . . . and now I stay here and keep the town safe, and hold off disease, and stop the bridge from falling into the Langfeather." A look of feverish eagerness came into Paragon's eyes. "You come from . . . out there, do you not? Have you seen my bridge? What do you think of it? Is it as grand and fine as they say?"

"What? Have you not seen it yourself?" Mosca stared with new eyes at the little bed, the scraped crockery. "How long have you been in here?"

"Since I was three years old, when the last Luck died. Twelve years and three months and two days."

"Twelve years!" Mosca briefly forgot to speak quietly, but fortunately the words choked in her throat.

"Night moves first." The Luck had returned his attention to the game. "Your move, soot girl." He looked up at her, face flushed and animated, undisguised entreaty in his eyes. Still stunned, Mosca picked up Goodlady Jabick, moved her to an adjoining square as he had shown her, and saw a look of utter bliss pass over her companion's face.

Twelve years. Twelve years with nothing to do but chew the ends of his hair and invent games, elaborate games of gods with rules that Mosca could barely remember from one moment to the next but which the Luck knew as well as his own fingernails. As they played, his speech became faster and sharper, explaining the mistakes she had made and helping her to find better moves.

Before long, Mosca was facing a terrible truth. The Luck was not a simpleton or a madman. He was clever, and his mind was starving.

"Do you never go out?" she could not help asking.

"No." His face drooped. "I am too precious. But . . . they send me tutors sometimes, or papers for me to make my mark on them. And when the clock is working I have charge of the Beloved images"—he waved a hand at his game pieces—"and put the right ones in the wheel each day, for I have a wondrous memory and nobody else is fit to handle them."

"But . . ." Mosca was still choking on the whole idea. "You never get to tread on grass, or see the sky, or . . . or run? This town is mad as moth soup! Nothing but a great big prison. Some of the cells are nicer than others, that's all. Precious? You're a prisoner, like everybody else here. Protect the town, do you? Save its people, do you? Then wave your wand and magic us all somewhere better."

The Luck had dropped his gaze and would not look at her, instead stroking at one of the Beloved game pieces as if it was a pet. She was shouting at the wrong person.

Mosca sighed. "Not your fault, you big moon calf." By her standards it was almost an apology. "How can you know what it's like out there, with people starving and terrified, half of them ready to sell their own souls to get out of this stinking town? But what about you?" She felt an unwilling sting of pity. "Do you never want to get out of here yourself? Run alongside streams, gaze your fill at the stars?"

The Luck's face went slack with uncertainty and longing. Perhaps the weight of the stone walls about him had not, after all, smothered his ability to dream. He was silent for a time, picking at one frayed buttonhole; then his head drooped.

"I cannot. I am *needed*. I am . . . I am the savior. Protector of the town." He clasped his hands together and squirmed his fingers. "I am *lucky*," he quavered, defiant but anguished.

Mosca looked around the windowless cell, the person-shaped dent worn into the bed's mattress, the chest full of undersized clothes.

"You don't look too blinkin' lucky to me," she muttered.

Mosca's return climb was no easier than the first, and a good deal more despondent. The Luck seemed ready to wail with anguish when she tried to leave, and the only way she could make him hush was to promise that she would return or send a friend to talk to him. She knew all too well that she would never be able to keep this promise, and was left with a bitter taste of more than soot.

By the time the dawn bugle had sounded, Mosca was back in her cell and had rubbed the worst of the soot off her face, hair, and arms. Her dress covered the dark smudges on her chemise and breeches. A quick swab around cleared up the worst of the soot and ash that had tumbled into the hearth.

Another night with no sleep, and nothing gained. Soon she would have to tell Mistress Bessel that she did not have the Luck. That the Luck was not something that could be conveniently tucked into a pocket or a sleeve. That the Luck was a desperately lonely youth a few hiccups from manhood, raised since his infant years in a room sealed from the world, a room that might as well be an oubliette.

Mistress Bessel would not like that. And Mosca was not at all sure she liked it herself.

15

GOODLADY NIZLEMANDER,
WINNOWER OF THE
CHAFF FROM THE GRAIN

MISTRESS BESSEL ARRIVED a little after breakfast time, or what would have been breakfast time if Mosca had had anything to pay the keeper.

As soon as the last bolt scraped, that stocky woman turned to Mosca with an eagerness that drew her broad face taut, her gloved hands restless with anticipation.

"Well?"

Mosca frowned and fumbled at her apron strings.

"I done everything you said. . . ." She could not stop her tone from sounding defiant.

Mistress Bessel stared at her, and then the eagerness faded and the muscles around her mouth tensed.

"You *failed*?"

"No! I shinned my way into the Luck's cell, just like you told me! And I found your precious Luck. It's not my fault I couldn't bring it back!"

"Tell me, then!" snapped her visitor. "Tell me everything you saw in that room!"

Mosca swallowed dryly. "I will—but you got to get me out of here first."

"And have you frisk off down the nearest alley as soon as you see daylight? Precious little fear of that, my dove. Tell me the truth and I'll fish you out of here, you have my promise on that, but you tell me what you know *first*. You're in no place to haggle—bear that in mind."

It was true. Mosca took a deep breath. "There's no magic skull up there, Mistress Bessel, no saint's apple core. Just a lad a few years older than me, half crazy with staring at the walls. The Luck . . . it's not an it. It's a he."

Mistress Bessel's features took on a stony cast, and it was impossible to guess her thoughts. Was she angry? Did she even believe Mosca? "Are you sure it was the right cell?"

"Sure as rock. Only one other flue off the chimney."

"What else was there in the cell apart from the boy? Tell me! Don't leave out a grain or jot!"

Mosca could only assume that Mistress Bessel was still hoping against hope that the Luck would turn out to be something else in the room, something pocket sized. Wearily Mosca set about describing every detail of the Luck's cell, right down to the wall hangings, the crockery, and the Beloved statues littering the floor, while Mistress Bessel clasped and chafed her gloved hands, her

265

face intent and inscrutable, her eyes narrowed.

"But it's no good—the Luck weren't none of those other things. It was the lad. He *told* me so."

"What?" The older woman's head rose sharply. "He spoke to you? You let him *see* you? Well, that tears the plan in two—"

"He won't tell anyone," Mosca retorted. "I know he won't. I'm his secret. I'm all he has." Mosca gave a sketchy account of their nocturnal conversation. "And the plan's torn in two anyways. Even if I could lug five foot of lumbering moon calf up the chimney, how would we smuggle him out of the prison? Under our aprons?"

There was a pause. It appeared to have brought a few friends. Apparently Mistress Bessel did not have an answer.

"Mistress Bessel, you made me a promise." Mosca could not keep a tremble out of her voice. The older woman glanced at her with features still set in a scowl, and for a terrible moment Mosca thought she might go back on her word out of spite and disappointment. "You promised!"

"Oh hush!" snapped Mistress Bessel. "One would think that nobody had trials but you! Yes, I made you a promise, and a good deal of trouble it will bring me for very little gain. But"—she sighed deeply and smoothed her apron with the air of a martyr—"I am a woman of my word, even in dealings with a rag of mischief like you." She pursed her lips speculatively for a few moments.

"So . . . tell me about his lordship the mayor. Does he have a wife? A sister? A housekeeper? Anybody of the female sort to look after him?"

Over the next five minutes Mosca found herself answering a barrage of questions about the mayor's household, temperament, likes, and dislikes. Mistress Bessel appeared to be handling her disappointment rather better than Mosca had expected, and in spite of her colossal relief Mosca could not help wondering why.

She suspected that Mistress Bessel had walked into the jail with more than one plan up her sleeve, and when one had broken, she had smoothly cast it aside in favor of the next. If so, the backup plan apparently involved ingratiating herself with the mayor. Mosca did not care a single pin providing it also ensured her liberty.

"Your mayor sounds a sore old bear," said Mistress Bessel as she took her leave, "but I've tamed fiercer beasts before today, my honeycomb. Now, all I need is a word with Eponymous. . . ."

Mosca did not trust Mistress Bessel any further than she could fly, but in spite of this her hopes once again began their battered, indomitable spider climb up the grimy flue of her soul.

After four hours of bitten nails, Mosca received another visit. She was not sure whether to be relieved or disappointed to discover that it was not Mistress Bessel but Sir Feldroll, accompanied by the portly and nervous form of Eponymous Clent.

Sir Feldroll's manner was unusually tense and curt, and Mosca soon learned why. He had spent most of the morning arguing with the mayor, leaving his fuse all but burned out.

"The mayor received a ransom note this morning," he explained, the muscles in his peaky, expressive face jumping and twitching. "In exchange for Miss Marlebourne's return, the kidnappers have demanded the Soul of Santainette."

This was a fine opportunity for Mosca to practice her blank look.

"It is an emerald of considerable renown—and no small value, if one has the right contacts. It is the size of a child's thumbnail, and cloudy, flawed you might even say, with a plume of smoky yellow coiling through the middle of it. But since it is said to have been pried out of the crown of the last king of the Realm . . ."

Mosca gave Clent the most fleeting glance and noted the feverish interest that had glossed his eyes like varnish. Apparently he had not heard this particular detail before. Battered, hungry, frightened, cold, and exhausted as Mosca was, she felt that she would cheerfully have thrown a dozen such stones into the Langfeather in exchange for a bowl of stew, a night's sleep, and an escape from Toll. The gem sounded like trouble.

"This emerald was entrusted to the care of the mayor many years ago," continued Sir Feldroll, "and I believe that he intends to hand it over to the kidnappers as instructed a few nights from now."

A memory jolted Mosca's frozen mind and forced it back into life.

"Not the night of Yacobray?"

Sir Feldroll nodded, looking somewhat surprised. "His lordship the mayor is under orders to place the gem within a radish and hang it outside the door of his counting house in town, just before the dusk changeover. A rather outlandish request."

Mosca thought it sounded far from outlandish. The night of Saint Yacobray was the one night of the year when something like that could be hung outside without attracting notice, and nobody but the Locksmiths would dare touch it. Nobody, that is, except the daring conspiracy of kidnappers.

"I have advised the mayor against this in the strongest possible terms." Sir Feldroll frowned. "This brigand Appleton is plainly obsessed with Miss Marlebourne. It is absurd to imagine that having snatched her from her family, he will meekly hand her over in exchange for mere wealth. Once he has the gem, he is far more likely to use it bribe his way out of Toll-by-Night and carry off Miss Marlebourne. To Mandelion, no doubt, for once he reaches that nest of anarchists, cutthroats, and fellow radicals, he knows all too well we shall be unable to reach him or rescue his victim. Confound it, he means to marry her!" His chin bobbed and wobbled, and his face flushed with emotion.

Mosca and Clent did not look at each other; indeed, their gaze upon Sir Feldroll's face became particularly steadfast. It did not seem a good idea to mention that they had been accomplices of many of the anarchists, cutthroats, and radicals in Mandelion, or the extent to which they had helped them take power. However, Sir Feldroll was probably right to distrust the kidnappers' promises. After all, Skellow had spoken to Clent's Romantic Facilitator of claiming the ransom even if Brand and Beamabeth were married.

"Picture it." Now Eponymous Clent met Mosca's eye with an expression at once appealing and nervous. "That poor child, captured and unfriended . . . need we say more?"

There was a long and heartfelt pause.

"Well, somebody bleedin' well better," snapped Mosca. "I don't see where you're driftin'."

"Then I shall speak more plainly," answered the knight. "I could not talk the mayor out of paying the ransom. However, four solid hours of . . . discussion with him have not been entirely in vain. My persistence and Mr. Clent's eloquence had achieved little, but by the greatest good fortune Mr. Clent happened to encounter a respectable lady of his acquaintance with an impeccable name." Evidently Mistress Bessel had acted quickly. "She added her arguments to ours, and among the three of us we finally succeeded in talking your cell door open. The hearing has been canceled. I will personally be paying your release fee."

Mosca's heart broke into a gallop, then slowed to a doubtful canter and finally a cynical trot. She crooked a black eyebrow and waited. Her short and bitter life had trained her to recognize the sound of a "but" hovering in the air.

Sir Feldroll cleared his throat.

"The argument that Mr. Clent finally brought to bear with the mayor was this: Your allotted time as a visitor comes to an end tonight. At present we have no agents in the night town, nobody at all. We have only until the night of Yacobray to find Miss Marlebourne—once Brand Appleton has the gem, I am firmly persuaded that we shall never see her again. I am asking you to help us—to help us find Miss Marlebourne, and if possible to arrange her rescue."

"So *that's* it." Mosca gave a bitter laugh and then directed a gaze of fire at Eponymous Clent. "This *your* idea, then? One of your brilliant plans? Somebody promised me I'd never have to go to the night town. Wonder who *that* was."

Clent, to do him justice, did look somewhat abashed and crestfallen.

"Child," he said quietly, "the situation was quite desperate. If I had been able to think of any other way of slipping your shackles . . ."

"Yeah. Well, thank you for gettin' me out of the

frying pan, Mr. Clent. So that's the plan, is it? Throw me into the night town, so I can rescue the mayor's daughter from a nest of cutthroats all by meself? How am I supposed to do that?"

"You will be alone only the first night," answered Sir Feldroll. "By the second I should have summoned some night-named servants from my estates. They will have the mayor's permission to enter the night town immediately, without spending three days as visitors. Your job will be merely to dig out information—my men will perform the rescue. And the reward, if you succeed, will be generous, easily enough for you and your employer to buy your way out of Toll."

Mosca scowled at nothing and nibbled soot from her fingernail while she thought.

"Child," Clent added quietly, "you and I have at least the dubious privilege of having been educated in the world. Whips and briars have been our nursemaids, kicks and cuffs our tutors. Life has whetted our wits and toughened our hides—our kind stand at least a *chance* of surviving in Toll-by-Night. Miss Marlebourne quite simply does not."

Miss Marlebourne'll survive, all right, said the bitter voice in Mosca's head. *She'll survive because she's worth something to somebody alive. They know what they can get for her; they won't so much as crush a ringlet or stain a satin shoe.* But in her mind's eye she was seeing again Beamabeth's frightened face as she talked of her fears that the night town would reclaim her.

"Oh . . ." She meshed her fingers in her ragged, abused hair and tugged it until her scalp ached. "Oh, crab-maggots. I'll do it, I suppose. Sir Feldroll, this reward—there needs to be some left over for some other folks we made promises to, and who need it as much as their necks. Oh, and my goose! Saracen comes with me."

"I do not think," Sir Feldroll remarked, with an uncharacteristic quirk of humor in the corner of his mouth, "that you will have any trouble persuading the mayor of *that* at all."

If the mayor's staff had been any happier to lose Saracen and regain their second pantry, they would probably have broken into a caper.

They were clearly less jubilant at the idea of having Mosca back within their walls once more, though it would be for only a few hours. However, there was nowhere else Sir Feldroll could take her, since he was staying at the mayor's home. The mayor himself was out, thankfully.

The smell of porridge banished all fear, anger, and thought in a moment. The mayor's footmen watched her with a mixture of fascination and distaste as Mosca demolished three bowls of it so fast that her tongue burned and her stomach cramped. As soon as she had finished, the exhaustion that she had been holding at bay refused to accept any further argument.

She did not remember drooping into sleep at the table, but a few hours later she woke to find herself in a little nest of blankets by the hearth, watched by a maid who stood against the wall, just where Mosca had been placed with her tray two nights before. Saracen slept in a basket beside her. With a sinking of the heart, she saw that the sky beyond the window was dulling to violet.

"Where's Mr. Clent? I need to speak to 'im."

Leaving Saracen to his grain-filled dreams, Mosca went to find Clent and tracked him down in the library. To her surprise, he was pacing, his wig slightly to starboard, his fingers knotted behind his back. When he saw Mosca, he came to an abrupt halt. For a few seconds his fingers fretted at the frayed ends of his cravat. Then he spread his arms in an expansive shrug and let them fall with a slap.

"It was all I could think of," he said simply. "The only plan that would tweak you out of that louse house. I dropped my bucket into the well of my invention to the rope's extent but could pull out nothing better. I am . . . truly sorry."

"Well, you chose a rosy time to run out of ideas," muttered Mosca, sitting on one of the ornate library chairs and pulling up her feet to sit cross-legged.

"Here." Clent placed a bundle on the table before Mosca and opened it. Inside lay a small purse, a knife in a leather sheath, some bread and cheese wrapped in a handkerchief, a reed pen, a bottle of ink, and a wallet full of blank writing paper. "Not much . . . but our Sir Feldroll seems loath to gild your pockets too heavily lest you pay your way out of Toll and escape into the heather. Nonetheless, *this* might be of service to you." It was a map, with the words THE FAIRE CITIE OF TOLL looping rather pompously along the top.

"This is a map of Toll-by-Day," Mosca said, scowling at the fine, spidery names that sidled down the streets.

"I know. Many of these streets will not be there come the dusk. But these will." With a careful fingertip he touched an image of a spire, a sketch of a tree, the clock tower, the castle turrets. "High points. Look for these above the roofs and you can recover your bearings. And this will not change." He drew his finger along the sweeping arc of the town wall. "Mosca, if all else fails, look for this wall and follow it until you find the house of that redoubtable midwife. She at least does not appear to be an urchin-eating ogress, and if she has tolerated you once, she might do so again. And . . . you can leave letters here"—Clent tapped the map again—"inside the mouth of the statue of Goodman Belubble that is built into the town wall. I will . . . There will be letters for you as well."

Mosca nodded, and swallowed a gulp of coarse, dry nothingness. There was a silence.

"For Beloved's sake, try to keep track of your bonnet," Clent broke out at last. He pulled Mosca's bonnet from a chair and dropped it onto her head. "Running about bareheaded like a ragamuffin . . ." His voice trailed off.

"You'll need to find somebody else to tell you when your plans are bleedin' stupid," Mosca said gruffly. "Not that you ever listen to me when I do."

"How I shall survive without the perpetual barbs of your conversation I cannot imagine," mused Clent with a little frown as he set Mosca's bonnet straight.

Just before dusk, Mosca and Clent were escorted by several of the mayor's men to the Committee of the Hours.

Day air had a smell, Mosca realized as she walked with Saracen in her arms; even chilled late-autumn afternoon air. The flowers had long since died, but the cold sun still drank dew from leaves, drew tartness from withering crab apples. Daylight cooked the sullen sludge in the roadways, the fierce green moss on old roofs. There was the nose-pinching cold smell of gleaming linen flapping itself dry on lines between the balconies.

A sunstruck spiderweb was silver embroidery against the darkened gable beyond. A robin throbbed on a hitching post, looking as if it had been dipped in tomato soup. Dead leaves flared underfoot in ginger, purple, and lemon yellow.

Mosca realized that she could not imagine never seeing the sun again. It felt a bit like going blind. She did not look at Clent's face but watched his battered boots striding alongside her, taking one pace to one and a half of hers.

The evening side of the sky was greening over and

dulling like old ham, and there a few knifepoint stars were gleaming. Soon the sky would be prickling with them.

The Raspberry looked up when they arrived in the office of the Committee of the Hours, and his eyebrows climbed and tipped a fraction.

"Ah! Yes . . ." His eyes narrowed. "We were told to expect you both. Kenning, the boxes!" Kenning obediently scampered away, returning with two boxes. One appeared to be full of light-colored badges and one full of black wooden ones, and it was into the latter that the Raspberry now peered. "Ah . . . there."

He pointed carefully into the box, and Kenning obediently fished out one badge with tongs and held it toward Mosca at arm's length as if it was hot. She gingerly took it in her hands, half expecting it to burn. It was a jet black badge with a fly carved on it, without the colored border of the visitors' badges.

The Raspberry spent a long time staring into the dark-badge box; then Kenning politely reached past him to the other box, pulled out a light wooden badge, and placed it in his master's hand. The Raspberry stared at it in some surprise, beckoned Kenning closer, and whispered into his ear. Mosca caught mere fragments.

". . . thought that under the circumstances . . . change of classification . . . after all, given his associations . . . mistake?"

Kenning's whispered return was just as indistinct.

". . . still bein' decided . . . not yet . . . might still change . . ."

Both were darting quick glances at Eponymous Clent, a fact that was not lost on Eponymous Clent. He had flushed somewhat, and his gloved fingers were beating a pitter-pat tattoo against his pocket.

So that was it. Clent had been born under Phangavotte, a Beloved who was only just considered a daylight Beloved, and after Clent's part in the terrible kidnapping of Beamabeth Marlebourne, it sounded as if Phangavotte and all those born under her were within a hair's breadth of being reclassified as nightfolk. The badge in the Raspberry's hands was a daylight badge, free from a visitors' border, but he seemed reluctant to give it to Clent.

Given his associations. That could only mean Mosca. Clent's fortunes were hanging in the balance not only because of the failed ambush plan but because he was seen to be friends with a nightling.

"Well, good riddance to you, you fat maggot!" Mosca rounded on Clent without warning. "Go ahead, suck up the daylight, what do I care? At least I won't have to deal with your whining ways anymore! All you've ever been to me is a cart out of town, and a sadder, more rickety ride I couldn't have picked. So let them tell you you're worth more than me, let them tell you that you're a good name and better off without me! It's me that's better off without you, you mincing, nettle-tongued, sorry sack of nothing!" She blinked hard and made the momentary blur of tears go away. All around, the guards were flinching with shock at her outburst.

Clent stared at her, the wind snatched from his sails, and then his face puckered into a most peculiar frown, one in which the corners of his mouth seemed in some danger of curling upward. He coughed, covered his mouth with his hand, and for a few moments seemed robbed of words.

"Dreadful child," he murmured at last, his voice rather muffled. "Ah, now the asp rises from the apple bowl to show its fangs. . . ."

"This my badge then, is it?" Mosca waved her new badge over her head. "Good!" She stripped off her visitor brooch and flung it onto the Raspberry's desk, then pinned the all-black badge to her dress. "I'll wear this with pride! Is it night yet? Can I go and find some people worth my time? Because I don't care if I never see another two-faced, toffee-nosed daylighter again!" She turned on the Raspberry. "And that goes for you too, you pompous old pustule!"

"Get her out of here!" The Raspberry's face had deepened in color almost to the point of graduating to blackberry. "Get . . . get her out of here!"

Two guards hurried over and hooked their arms under Mosca's armpits, lifting her from the floor. As she found herself receding at top speed toward the door, she locked gazes with Clent one last time.

"Yes, take her away," he said gently, his brow a curious map of crinkles, a certain softness in his expression.

"Nothing but a burr in my clothing, a cinder in my eye . . ."

"'Ope you choke on your next pie!" Mosca shrilled by way of farewell as the door closed between them.

Courtesy of the guards she flew, legs adangle, out of the room, down the corridor, and into the chamber where she had been interrogated by Excise on first arriving in Toll. There she was dropped unceremoniously onto a bench, which jumped under the three people already sitting on it.

She reeled a little as the guards left the room, and realized that she was the focus of every eye.

"I don't know what you're all staring at." She pulled her bonnet straight. "Never seen anybody with a private escort before? Made an impression on the committee, that's all."

"We *know*," came the chorus. Mosca's quick eye traveled down the line, noting the jet-black badge pinned to every chest.

"That voice of yours goes through oak doors like a bodkin through cheese," said a middle-aged woman, her threadbare scarf hiding all her hair and most of her mutilated ear. Her thin mouth was spread in a smile of genuine delight.

"Pumpus ol' pusturl," quoted a wiry young man, shoulders palsied with laughter.

"Everyone move up," said a tall, strongly built man with long, ragged black hair, cheeks rough with untended beard, and a voice that made Mosca think of chutney and gravel. "She's sitting next to me."

There was a shifting and scraping of boots, and suddenly Mosca was sandwiched among the taller bodies and festooned with glittering smiles.

"This one's a little wolf cub." The black-haired man grinned approvingly down at her. "Stay close to me when we go into the night, lass. I'll see you safe."

Mosca nodded, suddenly warm with self-consciousness.

"Let's all stick together," muttered the woman, casting a narrow glance at the darkening window. "Safety in numbers."

Little red-haired Kenning ran into the room, his mouth still hanging open with shock, a handkerchief twisted in his hands. He scuffled to a halt in front of Mosca and stared at her, entirely failing to haul up his jaw. After a few small incoherent noises, he gave a squeaky hiccup of a laugh, pushed the handkerchief into her hand, and fled the room with one fist in his mouth.

The handkerchief turned out to contain a hunk of bread and cheese. Apparently the sight of his eminent master entering apoplexy had been worth Kenning's supper.

The conversation in the little antechamber was a strange mix of the frank and the careful. Like Mosca, the other three all had nighttime names and had come to the end of their allotted time as visitors, having failed to find enough money to pay their way out the other side. Everybody gave an account of themselves, and by unspoken agreement nobody asked questions about the obvious gaps. Nobody asked why Mosca had a large goose with her either.

Jade, the thin woman in the scarf, had previously been the accomplice of a traveling "doctor." She used to come forward out of the crowd while he was proclaiming the virtues of his wares and pretend to be cured of by them. In order to enter Toll, she had needed to sell all the doctor's bottles, his alchemical scales, his hat, his stuffed crocodile, and even her own hair. (Nobody asked what had happened to the doctor or the top half of Jade's right ear.)

The leaner, younger man was Perch. His gestures were a symphony of starts and jerks, and he smelled like a crate of frightened rabbits. He had spent the last few months trudging from village to town looking for work. But as winter crept in and belts tightened, nobody wanted to spend money on having crows scared or roofs mended or firewood chopped, and he knew he had to get to the lands beyond the Langfeather. (Nobody asked Perch how he had found the money to get into Toll.)

Last was Havoc, the guttural, grinning giant of the group. He admitted to having been a "roaring boy" with a company of "blades and brave lads." He listed, with some pride, several heaths that carriages would no longer traverse for fear of meeting "the boys." He admitted that he had experience using a sword, twinned daggers, a pistol, a cudgel, and a blunderbuss. (Nobody asked him why he was no longer with "the boys.")

"So," declared Havoc when everyone had finished, "we all have something to toss in the pot. Mye here can be our sneaker, micher, and little snakesman, small enough to dodge a glance. Jade can be our face, our speak piece, particularly if we need to do a bit of coney catching. Perch here says he already has a cousin nightside who can help us get jobs if there's no other way of finding the mint. And if anyone comes to us looking for trouble, the trouble they find is me."

Mosca was relieved to hear that her companions were so well cut out for survival in Toll-by-Night, though it did occur to her that if the Committee of the Hours had been listening to that conversation, they would have heard very little to shake their belief that those born under night Beloved were destined for the shady side of the law. She knew enough thieves' cant to know that a "micher" was a sneak thief, a "little snakesman" was a slang term for a child passed in through a window to open the door of a house, and that "coney catching" had more to do with con artistry than with catching real rabbits.

"'Tis a good thing my cousin Larkin had a sharp set of wits," offered Perch in his quavering tones, his country vowels spreading like butter. "Found a way to leave me a letter 'neath a stone. Says that running loose on the streets at night is a doddypol's game and a good way to die." Remembering her brief excursion into Toll-by-Night, Mosca could not help but silently agree. "Told me to seek him out in Slake's Way, by the grand old beech, in a tavern under a yellow sign—they call it the Whip and Masty. He'll find us a place to stay."

A little before dusk the guards returned for them, now looking somewhat stony and nervous.

"You'll come with us."

Mosca and her new coterie were shown into a long, narrow stone-walled cell, which was almost entirely taken up with an enormous black iron turnstile reaching from ceiling to floor and from wall to wall.

"It's the Twilight Gate," one of the guards said curtly. "Only turns one way. Through you go."

Havoc went first, walking in among the black metal branches and pushing hard at one bough. There was a squeak, and then a long grinding note as the vast turnstile began to revolve, a jerk at a time. Havoc vanished beyond it, and Jade followed, then Perch, and finally Mosca ventured with Saracen into the forest of cold iron prongs. It took all her weight to turn it, and she found her comrades on the other side, squeezed between the stile and a small wooden door.

"Hey!" Havoc's voice echoed through the cell. "How long do we have to wait here?"

No response.

"Hey!"

"They won't hear us now," Jade said quietly. "We've passed through the stile. We're nightside. They can't admit we exist." The door beyond closed, leaving them in darkness.

There was no room to sit, so they stood in a non-existent huddle. They all sensed that silence was an enemy, so Havoc sang songs. Of a man who bludgeoned his landlady and her daughters, one, two, three, and went to the gallows without ever saying why. Of a gang of crows following Murthering Drack across the county, "For where Merry Drack has been, there the dead men lie." Havoc's voice was deep and tuneless and bleak but with a terrible jollity, and all the others held their tongues as they would during a hymn.

The sound of a bugle. Even Havoc's tune halted.

Night air had a smell too, Mosca decided, as she heard the distant music of approaching Jinglers. Night smelled the way Havoc's songs sounded. It smelled of steel and rushlights and the marsh welcoming a misstep and anger souring like old blood.

A rattle, a ring, a clatter, a clang. Bolts drawn away, a creak like a gate. Suddenly there was light through the keyhole of the nearby door. A long pause. A second bugle.

Havoc pushed at the door, and it swung open upon a silver scene, the cobbles glittering with frost stars. Once again Toll-by-Night had burst out of its captivity, like a monstrous jack from an innocent-looking box. And this time, Mosca was a part of it.

16

Goodlady Bollycoll,
spirit of solidarity

No dallying!" hissed Havoc. "But no slouching or scurrying! Walk as if you eat your enemies' hearts for breakfast." The others fell in on either side of him like a pack of mastiffs of varying sizes and tried to match his loping confidence.

Mosca knew that their group had been noticed, but their grimly determined stride seemed to afford them a certain magical protection. Their journey was full of meetings that did not quite happen. Shapes that flitted out of alleys before them, outlines of heads on roof-tops that bobbed down and were seen no more, rapid exchanges of whistles ahead of them that caused a tur-bulence in the shadows and then stillness.

Jade had noticed the "grand old beech" in Toll-by-Day and led the way, with more than a few false starts due to the changed position of the streets. Havoc insisted that they never stop, never look lost, so they continued to stride with fierce determination even when they had no idea where they were going. At last, however, they stood beneath the beech and saw opposite a cream-colored sign on which a man with a great whip was flogging a snarling but chastened-looking black dog.

Beneath the sign stood two great barrels, crude and splintered faces cut into their wood as if they were turnip lanterns. The light of the clustered candles within leered out through narrowed eyes, chipped noses, and quivering crooked grins. Between these an open archway led to a set of downward stone steps.

"I'll go first," said Havoc. "Mye—keep a pace behind me. You others follow up and keep an eye out behind."

The steps descended into what was clearly a vast old buttery cellar. Where once barrels had been stacked, however, now the proprietors had decided to cram people. From wall to discolored wall the stone-flagged floor was clustered with shabby tables, some of them no more than crates or upended butts.

There was no hearth, just a myriad of sickly candles. Everybody was breathing white vapor, and Mosca guessed that the cellar might have been as cold as the street had it not been warmed in some small measure by the press of bodies. Skinny-looking young children squeezed through the crowds with bottles or casks slung on their backs and flitted from table to table, taking money and filling tankards.

Havoc picked a table close to the wall.

"I like this one." He ran his fingernail across a rugged set of gouges in the woodwork of the tabletop, as if testing the mill of a coin. "Someone's been using a dagger on this. That's good luck, that is. Don't anybody light our candle—we want to see folks around us better than they see us."

Mosca pressed her fingers against her eyelids for six seconds, then opened her eyes and blinked hard, willing her night sight to strengthen. Having a table on the edge of the crush made sense but left her feeling as if she could be cornered. The backmost recesses of the buttery were very dark, and although she could glimpse the movement of figures, the taller ones stooping beneath the low vaulted roof, she could make out no faces. It was busy, and yet strangely quiet for a tavern, and it reminded Mosca of the times she had spent lying along one of the rafters of her uncle's mill, watching the mysterious and dusky traffic of the mice down below. All the movement was full of meaning and stealthy signals that she did not understand. A language of whisker twitches and tail flicks.

A small dark boy with great, wary fish eyes took coins from Havoc and poured what looked and smelled like dishwater into four wooden cups.

"You know what I think?" Jade whispered as the boy moved on to the next table. "I think this is where everyone comes to meet and talk—might as well be the town hall. See those down there?" She nodded toward a series of passageways leading off the main cellar. "Private rooms, I'll hazard. For making deals and talking quiet."

Hearing this, Mosca glanced about her with renewed interest. She had, after all, her mission to consider. If this was Toll-by-Night's talking shop, perhaps this would be a good place to start her investigations.

"Someone's coming our way," murmured Havoc. "Perch—is that your cousin?"

Perch looked up eagerly, and then the welcoming smile on his face faltered and faded. "No, that's not him."

The man approaching was bundled to bearlike dimensions in a greatcoat and two scarves, a large but lopsided hat perched on a small, pale, forgettable face.

"My word," he said through chattering teeth, which he showed a second later in a lifeless smile. "My word." He rubbed his gloved hands vigorously, held them palm out toward the dead candle on the table, then rubbed them again. "Havoc Gray. What a thing of wonders. You'll let me buy you a drink. Fancy meeting Havoc Gray, what a story to tell the little woman." There was something oddly colorless about his tone.

A small girl ran up and placed a cup of wine on the table before Havoc, then scuttled away, a veil of fair hair hiding her face and her chin tucked to her chest. The new arrival had not, as far as Mosca was aware, signaled to her in the slightest. The scarf-muffled man reached for a chair, pulled it over, and seated himself, still warming his hands at the imaginary flame. Or perhaps he was warming them against Havoc. It was hard to tell.

"I do not remember inviting you to join us," rumbled Havoc.

"No." The smaller man took off his hat, and his thinning hair tried to follow it in surprised-looking wisps. "But forgetfulness is quite natural so soon after arriving. Quite natural. Anyway, I really could not resist. What stories. What stories you must have to tell."

"Now, I don't want you answering this question hastily"—Havoc leaned across the table with a glitter of a grin—"but do I look like a wandering player? Somebody to caper and tell tales for you for the price of a mug of wine? You know my name. I don't know yours, nor your face. And we're waiting for somebody. And it isn't you."

"But would it not be nice if it was." The small stranger was turning his hat about and about, a slight tremble in his gloved hands. "Would it not be nice if Havoc Gray was glad to see me and if I could be of service to him. And I hope that I can be. For it is sadly true that there is no life without toil. And what makes toil bearable is our choices. Who we choose to work with."

"So . . ." Havoc moved his stool closer to that of the smaller man. "I think I can sniff out what you're about. You think now I'm here, I'll be wanting to find myself a company of steady-mettled boys, and you want to join early before I have a chance to look around, is that it?"

The hat twirler wet his lips and then cast a fleeting glance over his shoulder. Within that tiny instant, Havoc had grabbed him by the collar and tipped him back in his chair so that he was in danger of crashing to the floor.

"No," said Havoc, so quietly and deeply that his voice was almost inaudible. "No, that's not it. You looked over your shoulder when I pushed you out of the lines you had rehearsed. That means there's others behind you. They've sent you trotting in ahead like a little dog to test the ground for marsh. I have heard it all before, more times than you've been smiled at. Everywhere I go, little gangs and brotherhoods come fawning and threatening and saying that I must throw in with them. Well"— Havoc leaned forward a little, so that the smaller man was tilted at a yet more perilous angle—"I throw what I like, when I like, with whoever I like, and for no master. And if I see your face again, I'll be throwing you."

The smaller man had gone very still, perhaps trying to make himself limp and unthreatening so as not to startle Havoc into carrying out his threat. His face was frozen, almost expressionless. Great gleaming blobs of perspiration bloomed silently on his unfurrowed brow like dewdrops swelling on a leaf. It was almost beautiful.

Havoc tugged him back upright, so that the smaller man's chair righted itself with a clatter. The little man stared down into his hat and then set it back on his head with the greatest of care. He stood unsteadily and tripped off between the tables without another word.

When he was almost out of sight, Havoc got to his feet.

"Havoc!" Jade caught at his sleeve. "Where you going?"

"He has my name. And he's off to report now. Bit of business I need to deal with." He glanced around the table, then smiled at Mosca and pushed at her chin almost roughly with the ball of his thumb, as if wiping away a smudge. "You don't need to know," he said, and gave a wolf's grin. "Stay here, all of you. This won't take long." And off he strode.

"Haggard's teeth!" Jade beat the heels of her hands against the top of the table in frustration. "We said we'd stay together!"

"He can look after himself," murmured Perch.

"I know!" Jade gave a furious sigh. "It's not him I'm worried about! It's us!"

Mosca was only half listening to this exchange, her gaze following Havoc and his quarry. As Havoc's boots struck the sawdust-covered floor, the small man seemed to sense him, turned, and saw him. He froze, panic again giving his face a stillness not unlike a trance. His gloved hands, however, fluttered before his chest like frightened moths. As Havoc took a step forward, the little man took a few faltering steps backward directly away from him, into one of the nearby passages. Then he gave a half-witted twitch of the head, turned tail, and sprinted down the passage. Again Mosca felt she was up in the rafters, watching the mice. Little mouse, witless with fear. Running the wrong way. And here she was, just watching. Becoming a part of it by doing nothing.

Mosca realized that she was digging her fingernails into the tabletop and that they were full of grime and splinters. Her mind's eye was too vivid, and she could not shut it off. Little man running in terror down a dead-end passage, Havoc at his heels. Havoc with his twin daggers and the sword with the ugly bludgeonlike handle. Her new friend Havoc. She looked at Jade and Perch. Both of them were staring steadily into the foam of their cups.

"Havoc knows what he's doing." Perch took a rapid, angry gulp. "We're going to need money, aren't we?" He rubbed at his long chin. "Well, aren't we?"

"And how do we know that that little worm had any?" hissed Jade.

"Surely you heard it?" Perch gave her a sly glance. "When he was swung back in his chair. That jingle at his belt. That'll be a purse, and a full one at that, and I'll warrant Havoc heard it too—hey, what's wrong with you, Mye?"

Mosca had leaped to her feet, causing the table to totter. She hastily lashed Saracen's leash to the table leg, then scrambled and squeezed past the neighboring tables and ran toward the passage down which Havoc had disappeared.

She hesitated at the mouth of the passage, just as the little stranger had done. Then she balled her fists and sprinted into it before she could decide to do something more sensible. *It's barely been seconds,* she told herself. *It might not be too late. If I can only speak to Havoc . . .*

The passage ended at another cellar, this one still in use as a buttery. It was full of great barrels, some two yards in diameter. Most were perched on pairs of long wooden rails. One particular pair of rails, however, appeared to have tilted and tipped one great barrel off onto the floor. It had probably tried to roll all the way to the wall, but had been brought up short by the body of the man lying in its path. Somewhere under its massive weight was presumably what was left of his head.

Mosca stood on the threshold and quivered. She hoped the cask had split. She hoped the darkened pool around the cask was wine. It smelled like wine. She wondered if she would ever be able to bear the smell of wine again.

There's something I want to tell you, Mr. Havoc Gray. It's about the man you're following. It's the little details, you see— only makes sense when you got all of them.

A jingle at the belt. Well-made gloves. An offer of work.

Not a frightened little mouse. Not a mouse at all. Cat. Locksmith.

Whoever the nameless, nervous little man in the hat had been, he was now nowhere to be seen. The corpse on the floor was that of Havoc Gray.

There was a step behind Mosca, a very deliberate step. She almost turned, but some instinct screamed at her not to do so.

"What in the world are you doing here, little miss?" The voice was unfamiliar, reasonably educated, and so close that it was almost in her ear.

Boom, sounded Mosca's heart. *Boom.*

"I'm . . ." She took a deep breath. "I'm just standin' here. And not turnin' round." *So I haven't seen your face, whoever you are.*

"You came down here at quite a run. Looking for someone?"

Mosca shook her head slowly. "Not anymore."

"That man down there—he wouldn't happen to be a friend of yours, would he?"

Mosca forced herself to breathe evenly and shook her head again.

"Face don't look familiar," she whispered.

She felt a warm gust of breath as the person behind her gave vent to a small burst of laughter.

"Oh, that's quite good. What a sensible head you have on your shoulders. And what a good place for it that is. Little miss, do you know how to play hide-and-seek? You stay exactly where you are without turning round, and you count. You count all your fingers ten times. But when you are done . . . you do not play seek. You walk out of here very slowly and calmly and you never say one single word about any of this as long as you live. Do you think you can play that game?"

Mosca nodded.

"Good." The steps moved away, more softly now, punctuated by the occasional faint jingle of metal on metal.

Mosca stared down at her own shaking hands and counted her fingers. And counted them again. And again. If she took her eyes off them, she might look up or over her shoulder. She counted them, eleven times, twelve times before she realized what she was doing. Then she turned very carefully and walked on trembling legs back to the main cellar.

When she reached her group's table, she found Saracen casually overturning stools and Jade sitting alone, her cup gripped fiercely in both hands. She looked up as Mosca approached, and her thin mouth grew thinner still.

"Where's Havoc?"

Mosca sank onto a stool and opened her mouth, but as soon as she did so, she seemed to feel a presence floating ghostly just behind her, a calm and pleasant voice a few inches from her ear. Her throat tightened and would let no words out. She bit her knuckle hard and slowly shook her head.

There was a long pause before Mosca found words again.

"Where's Perch?"

Jade quivered, and her eyes suddenly became dark and alarming.

"Do I look like his mother?" she snapped with sudden savagery.

Mosca simply stared at her.

"Stupid, addlepated gull!" Jade thumped the table. "Him and his cousin. His precious cousin who was going to sort everything out for us. Well, his cousin has debts, see. He's in what they call the toil gangs, trying to work off what he owes. And seems he's rid himself of a heap of his debt by telling 'em Perch will take it on instead. That's why he told Perch to come here, so the toil gang could grab him and drag him off."

"But . . . where did they take him? What's going to happen to him?"

Jade said nothing but continued staring into her nearly empty cup.

"You didn't ask, did you?" Mosca felt a wave of warmth sweep up from her socks to her crown. "You didn't say a thing! You just let them take him! I thought you said we were supposed to stay together!"

"Well, what do you expect?" muttered Jade sourly. "I was born under Goodlady Gofflemire, She Who Helps Those Who Help Themselves. I'm not made to stick my neck out for anyone but myself."

"Is that it?" Mosca exploded. "The Committee of the Hours—are they right about us? We nightfolk, are we just a bunch of cheats and bawdy baskets and sheep steal-ers, all just waiting to stick a knife in each other's backs?"

Jade's head snapped up, and Mosca found herself

bathed in a glare of infinite loathing and contempt.

"Oh, yes, you're loud enough when it's safe, when you're surrounded by daylighters who will only tut and get vexed. But you'd have held your tongue just like I did. And you know it."

Mosca could say nothing. She thought of herself carefully and obediently counting her own fingers with Havoc's murderer a pace behind her.

A heavyset man appeared by the side of the table.

"You ready, mistress?" The question was evidently directed at Jade. "He don't like waiting."

"I'm ready." Jade stood.

"No connections, you said." The new arrival was examining Mosca speculatively. "This girl with you?"

Jade shook her head without looking Mosca's way. "Who's with anyone?" she snapped, with a bitterness that was almost despair. Mosca could only watch, stunned, as the last of her new allies walked away without a backward look.

Mosca remained frozen in her seat, cold beads tracing their way down her back. She did not look around to see who was noticing her, a flimsily built young girl with a tasty-looking goose, sitting alone and undefended. But there would be eyes on her, she knew it.

The minutes dragged. Time and again she tried to chafe her cold wits and muster the spark of a plan, but every time, she saw Havoc spread-eagled in the dark cellar and the bleak and horrible glare of hatred in Jade's eyes.

Got to get out of here, buzzed Palpitattle in Mosca's head. *Now. Right now.* Gingerly Mosca got to her feet, wincing as her stool scraped and the table rattled.

She stooped and gathered Saracen in her arms. A big, hearty-looking goose, white plumage gleaming in the murk. A succulent roast dinner on webbed feet. A poster inviting every cutthroat to waylay her in an alleyway.

Mosca stroked a trembling hand over Saracen's furled wing feathers, feeling their strange rough softness. "Me and you," she whispered against his neck. "Me and you 'gainst 'em all, right?"

Legs shaking, she edged through the crowd, squeezing past seated forms. Her neck prickled as behind her there was a stealthy, deliberate scrape of wood on wood as somebody else pushed back a chair. She pretended not to notice and made her way toward the exit, both arms around Saracen, hearing faint sounds of disturbance behind her, as if another figure was pushing his way along the same route.

She reached the edge of the tables and set off as calmly as she could across the cellar floor. Her instincts screamed that she was being followed—she could smell the menace, feel it like the dry crackle before a storm. She reached the base of the steps that led up from the cellar . . . then raced up them like a kicked cat.

By the time she reached the street, gasping icy night air, there was a clattering of steps behind her that was not an echo. With a gasp of effort, she kicked one of the carved-face barrel lanterns onto its side before the archway, then booted it down the steps. Off it rolled and bounded, spitting wax and dropping candles, and Mosca heard it recede with a *bangitty-bangitty-bangitty-bangitty-YEEEAARGH-thubbitty-bangitty-bangitty-WAAAH-bangitty*.

She did not wait for Messrs. Yeeeaargh or Waaah, since she doubted they were in a mood to talk. Even if they had not intended her any harm before, they probably would now. So instead she set about showing the Whip and Masty a set of heels. Not clean ones, perhaps, but certainly very rapid.

There was only one place in Toll-by-Night that might be a sanctuary: the house of the midwife and her husband. And it looked as if Mosca would be searching for it at high speed, with murder half a step behind her.

17

GOODMAN LARCHLEY,
HOARDER OF PENNIES

A<small>T A CORNER</small> Mosca stopped, and hopped, and hooked off her clogs, then ran again. The cobbles bruised her feet but did so silently. Behind her, she could hear other footsteps ring out, then muffle as they headed down the wrong street.

Her only hope of finding the Leaps' house was to reach the town wall and follow it until she saw somewhere she recognized. As she ran, her quick black eyes caught one scene after another.

A line of skinny men and women mending the town wall, a long chain linking their leg-irons—perhaps one of the toil gangs Jade had mentioned. Two youths squatting on either side of a prone and motionless man and wiping something dark off his pocket watch. A ragged little alley unexpectedly full of a surging throng, wrestling one another for meager bundles of firewood.

Everywhere Mosca went, she felt more spider-thread gazes adhere to her, as quickly as she could throw off the old. There were footsteps behind her again now. Perhaps they were Yeeeaargh and Waaah, perhaps not. It did not matter.

There! She recognized the Leaps' narrow house, the scribble of creepers against the wall. The door was half open, Mistress Leap emerging from it cautiously with her bundle on her back. She was speaking in furtive, urgent whispers to a young man who held a dark lantern in one hand and kept the other tucked under his armpit out of the cold, all the while shifting with nervous impatience from one foot to the other.

". . . nearly ready to burst with the baby . . ." A few of his murmured words were just audible.

"Mistress Leap!" screamed Mosca, hearing pursuing steps gaining behind her. The two figures at the door froze, and Mistress Leap took a startled pace backward through the still-open door, pulling the young man after her. Horrified, Mosca realized that she was in danger of finding herself pounding on a closed and bolted door.

She put on a fresh spurt, the cobbles biting into her soles. The door was not shut yet, she might be able to hurl herself in at the same time as the young man, by ducking low and squeaking past his legs. . . .

This plan might have worked perfectly if the young man had not turned in the doorway to stare out into the darkness with bemusement. As she streaked into his pool of lantern light, Mosca saw his thin, pocked face grow taut with surprise and apprehension. She almost fancied that she could see herself and Saracen reflected in miniature in each of his widening eyes.

"Tway!" she screamed. It was a lot shorter than "out of the way" but unfortunately was not a real word, and so the young man did not step to one side, or backward, or anything useful. Thus when Mosca doubled up and dived forward, she did not slide past him. Instead she planted her head firmly in the middle of his stomach with great force.

He made a *thyuck!* noise, and there was a tinkle as something metallic fell to the ground. The lantern smashed on the cobblestones at the same time, plunging the street into darkness. Saracen exploded from Mosca's arms in a lather of wings, and she tumbled headlong past the stranger and in through the door. There were more muffled noises as other people collided in the dark outside and sounded surprised about it. Somebody standing just inside the threshold made two or three panic-stricken attempts to close the door on Mosca's ankles. She pulled in her feet, and the door slammed shut, completing the darkness. There followed the guillotine *thunk thunk thunk* of bolt after bolt being driven home.

A *click, click, fizz* of a tinderbox, and Welter Leap's nose and eyebrows appeared amid the gloom, spectrally lit from below. As Mosca's eyes adjusted to the meager radiance, she realized that his shaky hand was holding a dim and slender rushlight. He blew on it, and it reluctantly flared. Behind her husband Mistress Leap became visible, determinedly clutching a pair of needlework scissors, evidently ready to trim and hem any assailant.

"What . . . ?" Mistress Leap seemed profoundly nonplussed at discovering her twelve-year-old intruder. "But . . . who is this? Welter, that young man! Where is he? Surely he is not still—"

"Where's Saracen?" The room that met Mosca's eye was chillingly gooseless. "Didn't he come in with me?"

Before further questions could be asked or answered, a furious hubbub broke out beyond the bolted door. A scuffle, a sound of rending cloth, a flapping sound like wind-whipped washing, and occasionally an unmistakable honking.

"He's outside! My goose is out there! You got to open the door!"

"Welter, you *must* open it, that poor man, that young father-to-be . . ."

Welter Leap, however, hung on to the uppermost bolt, resistant to all his wife's urgent tugging and Mosca's attempts to mountaineer up him using his knees and pockets as rungs.

Only when the sounds of scuffles ceased, running footsteps receded, and silence settled did Welter relinquish his hold on the bolt and his position against the door. Mosca and the midwife pulled back the locks and flung the door open, so that a rush of cold air slapped at their faces.

The dark and narrow street was all but empty, except for one solitary figure two yards from the door, a figure that was only visible because of the gleaming whiteness of its plumage. It was unmistakably the pale outline of a goose, but Mosca's stomach plummeted as she noticed that the gleaming outline appeared to have no head.

The next moment the apparition shook itself with a doleful rattle, and Mosca realized what she was looking at. It was not a headless goose, still eerily upright. It was a goose with its head stuck in the remains of a dark lantern.

She stepped forward and stooped to pull off the lantern. Saracen seemed unconcerned by the removal of his new battle helm and continued champing at a piece of cloth caught in his bill.

"Oh . . . where *is* that young man?" Mistress Leap was casting concerned glances up and down the street. "Something has happened to him, it must have. His wife is in labor; he came all the way from the other side of town to find me—where can he possibly have gone?"

Mosca pulled the piece of cloth from Saracen's beak. It was brown and looked uncomfortably like a piece of the sack cloak the young man had been wearing. *Saracen, you didn't* eat *him or anything, did you?*

She hid the piece of cloth in her hand and glanced nervously up at the Leaps to see whether they had noticed. At that same time the midwife's gaze fell on Mosca's face and froze with recognition.

"You! It's you!"

Evidently the midwife had not recognized her in the half-light of the house, but now the moon was on Mosca's face. All of Mosca's instincts balled into a fist. When people recognized you at the top of their voice like that, it usually meant beadles, bellowing, or slammed doors. Right now the slammed door seemed like the worst possibility of the three.

The Leaps sprang aside in confusion as Mosca hurled herself past them into the house with her arms full of goose. She disappeared into the darkened room beyond with a melody made of thuds, clangs, clatters, and scrapes, and finally a dull metallic clang.

The midwife and her husband picked their careful way over a fallen army of spoons, a tipped stool, and an avalanche of potatoes to where their metal bath lay overturned like a turtle shell. A little muslin and a single bonnet ribbon trailed from under the bath's brim. On top of it perched a large white goose, resplendent as a general surveying his troops from a convenient hill.

"You can't make me go!" shouted the bath, its voice metallic and echoing. "You can't throw me back on the streets! Don't touch me! You can't make me!"

Welter advanced, dropped to a squat, and reached toward the bath. He gave it a few experimental rattles, then made a disconsolate noise and shuffled away from it again.

"Leveretia," he called in notes of great solemnity, "I cannot throw this child out into the street."

"Well said, Welter," responded his wife in tones of quiet pride.

"No . . . I mean that I *cannot*. I would dearly like to, but whenever I try to grip the bath, the goose pecks my ear and the child nips my fingers with our sugar cutters."

"Oh, Welter! Of course we cannot throw her out—did you not see who it was? That visitor girl who was locked out after dusk by accident! She came back! I told you they would not forget us! There must have been some trouble with the drop point, that is all. And after this poor girl has risked coming back to the night town again just to keep her promise to us, you want to throw her out? Well, that would be fine thanks. I'll talk to her, Welter. You be a sugarplum and keep watch at the door for that poor young father-to-be."

Skulking in the darkness of the overturned bath, Mosca felt a weightlessness in the pit of her stomach. This conversation was unlikely to go well.

"I think we still have some . . . yes, here we are." *Step, step,* the rustle of Mistress Leap's skirts settling as she sat next to the bath. "Here we are—look! Nettle and blackberry cake."

A damp, sweet foody smell reached Mosca's pointed nose, and although she knew she was being tempted and tamed with food like a feral puppy, still she could not resist tipping up the edge of the bath until she could see Mistress Leap's thin, worn hand waving what looked like a hunk of ancient mold. It smelled like food, however, and once she had snatched it and pushed it into her mouth, it tasted like food.

"That's better." There was another rustle, and Mosca could just see the edge of Mistress Leap's face as the midwife laid her cheek against the floorboards and tried to peer under the bath. To judge by her frown, she could not see much. "You're the girl who helped us deliver Blethemy's boy, aren't you?"

Cake was clinging to the roof of Mosca's mouth, so she could only nod. Then, remembering that her head was invisible, she wobbled the bath in a nodding motion.

"So. Do you have it?" There was an undeniable edge of desperation in the midwife's voice.

Have what? Oh. The reward money. The money we promised them.

Mosca dryly swallowed her cake, then took the bath's weight on her hands and very slowly waggled it to and fro in a head-shaking motion. The midwife's face disappeared from her crack of vision, and there were more clothy noises as if she had sat back. A long moment of morguelike silence followed.

Mosca's stomach squirmed sideways. The Leaps clearly still had no other money to pay the Locksmiths' tithe on the night of Saint Yacobray.

"I believe I said she would be back without the money," murmured the midwife's husband with a relentless and dolorous complacency. "Back with no money but wanting our help again. She will burst into our house, I said, and her goose will eat our furniture." There was a faint grinding sound as of a determined, roughened beak gnawing on a stool leg.

"Well, that was very clever of you, wasn't it, Welter?" His wife's tone was brisk, with no sarcasm and only the slightest tremble. Another long silence. "Well . . . it changes nothing. Come on out now, lass. Nobody is going to throw you onto the street."

Gingerly Mosca tipped back the bath.

"That's better. Not so terrible out here, is it?" Mosca bit her lip as she saw the midwife's thin, pained, resolute smile. "Not much in the way of hobs and cutthroats, is there? Nothing to worry about."

"Ahhm." After this rather cryptic pronouncement, Welter Leap returned from the door, his movements slow, his head bowed over an object he held in his hand. "Leveretia?"

He held it out, and the struggling rushlights gilded a blade edge, a leather-bound hilt. "On the doorstep," he explained.

"That man in your doorway!" exclaimed Mosca. "I think he dropped it when I run into him, same time as the lantern. I heard something metal go *ping* off the cobbles."

"So did I." The midwife reached up a trembling hand and took the dagger out of her husband's hand. "He . . . He kept one hand tucked in his armpit all the time, as if his fingers were cold," she added, numbly. "Oh, it's one thing to carry a knife in your belt so you can defend yourself. But carrying one hidden in your hand means . . . something else. It means . . . that there was no waiting wife. No baby. Just an ambush in an alley so he could sell everything in my bundle." She gave an unsteady, wondering little laugh.

"It should not surprise me. But it does. Every time." Mistress Leap shook herself. "I think we all require a little gin, would you not say?"

The beautiful sound of bolts being driven home and shutting out the night streets. The click of cups, and a bottle telling out a scale in glugs as it poured. And then, finally, the dreaded question.

"So—what happened?"

Well, it's like this, Mistress Leap. We had this brilliant plan to stop a gang of would-be kidnappers from snatching Beamabeth Marlebourne by catching them in the attempt, so that we could claim a reward from her father. Only our brilliant trap didn't work. In fact, it got her kidnapped. So now we have no money and everybody in the day town hates us and Beamabeth is trapped in Toll-by-Night somewhere and so am I.

There are no good ways to tell a story like that, and Mosca's tremors and stammering did not make it any better.

The midwife listened with admirable self-restraint, sipping her gin with the composure of a queen and the aplomb of a veteran. She had blinked herself brisk again and lost the bewildered, exhausted look that had afflicted her after the discovery of the dagger. Her replacement smile was a bit *too* brisk and made her look a little mad.

And in answer to her questions Mosca found herself recounting the whole haggard tale of her encounters with the would-be kidnappers, the mysterious notes exchanged at the Pawnbrokers' Auction, the journey to Toll, the twilit interview with Skellow, the failed trap laid by Eponymous Clent, and her own adventures in the night town. She skimmed over those times when she or Clent had broken or twisted the laws, of course—and she could not bring herself to speak of the discovery of Havoc's body. The back of her neck still tingled with the memory of the calm voice that told her never to speak of it. She did, however, tell the Leaps of the gem ransom and Sir Feldroll's fears that Beamabeth would not be returned if it was paid.

"Oh, dear," Mistress Leap said at last when the tale was done. "Beloved above, poor Miss Marlebourne!" The midwife raised her hands to her mouth and looked first pensive, then resolute. "That cannot be allowed. Oh, dear. Oh, dear—there is no help for it. We must report this to . . . to *them*. Once they have hunted down these kidnappers—"

"No!" It was exactly the response Mosca had feared. "No, please . . . please, Mistress Leap, we cannot go to the Locksmiths!"

The midwife's calm, generous face underwent something of a transformation. Suddenly she looked wan and evasive.

"You have to understand," she said, her tone rather weary, "that the Locksmiths really are the best people to deal with this kind of mischief . . . and they do not take kindly to people hiding things from them. If it ever came out that we had held back something like this—"

"Mistress Leap, if *any* of this comes out any which way, we're done up like partridges for a pie! For all we know, the Locksmiths are part of this whole plot! That Skellow showed up to the Pawnbrokers' Auction with a fat old purse—fatter than the likes of 'im should have had. Maybe the money came from Brand Appleton, but it don't seem likely. And Skellow left Toll without it showing in the records. Maybe it's like you said and they jus' leave out names sometimes and pocket the toll—or maybe the Locksmiths covered up for him."

"Perhaps . . ." The midwife looked uncertain, but Mosca's words had clearly penetrated.

"An' supposing this kidnap isn't a Locksmith lay?" continued Mosca. "Then we'd be telling 'em where to find a gem worth more than a wagonful of pearls and the most precious heiress in Toll to boot. Which means that there will be a ransom paid, right enough, and a reward too, I'll bet, but they won't come nowhere near us. And like as not the Locksmiths would have to shut us up permanent so nobody knows it was them that grabbed the ransom. Mistress Leap . . . we can't tell the Locksmiths. Or we're supper for the Langfeather, whatever happens."

The midwife's face was still creased with conflict. Mosca suspected that the Locksmiths probably rewarded those who turned informant, as well as punishing those who did not.

"Oh, dear . . . no, I fear that does make a good deal of sense." Mistress Leap bit her lip. "But then . . . what are we to do?" She glanced at Mosca, then gave a warm sigh and reached out to swab at Mosca's grime- and perspiration-stained cheeks with her handkerchief. "Well . . . do not fret about any of this tonight. I suppose none of it can be helped. You and your goose will have to stay here for now, and . . ." The midwife let out a breath and shook her head. "Oh . . . between us we will come up with something."

"We" was such a comforting word. "We" meant weathering things together. Camaraderie. Safety in numbers. All the things that Havoc and Jade and Perch had talked about. And yet Mosca had seen all these things collapse within an hour of the dusk bugle.

This was Toll-by-Night, and here alliances were bridges made of eggshell. Mistress Leap seemed kind—*was* kind—but kindness could be eaten away by fear, desperation, and soul weariness, just like everything else.

"Who's with anyone?" Jade had snarled.

Oh, scallops to it, thought Mosca.

"Mistress Leap?" Mosca beckoned. The midwife

drew near, and Mosca continued in a whisper. "There's a thread o' hope. It's not enough to stitch a sail, but it's all we have—you, me, Mr. Clent, the mayor's daughter, any of us. Beamabeth Marlebourne's here in the night town somewhere, and I know the names of some of the men who snatched her. And there's a reward for them that can rescue her. A big enough reward to pay your tithes—and our toll out of Toll.

"There's help coming to Toll-by-Night tomorrow night. Friends of Beamabeth, all set to rescue her. But it won't do a spot of good if they don't know where she is. That's why I am here ahead of them, Mistress Leap. I need your help and you need mine, and the mayor's daughter needs both of us.

"We got till the night of Saint Yacobray to find out where Beamabeth Marlebourne is being held."

There were, Mistress Leap informed Mosca, a good number of problems.

"The first is that I know *exactly* the person to bring into our plans. Somebody who knows everybody and has eyes and ears so sharp, you'd fancy her mother was a hare. And yet we absolutely *cannot* involve her, or even have her know what we are about."

"What? Who? Why?"

"Laylow. Do you recall Laylow? The girl who helped you escape the night town last time?" There was no danger of Mosca forgetting the clawed girl who had led them at a devil's pace through the dawn town. "She would be the perfect person to help us find these villains . . . if she were not a friend of Brand Appleton. Oh, yes, I have heard of him. Quite the most dreadful radical, so they say, spreading all sorts of barn-burning ideas. But for some reason Laylow has struck up a friendship with him."

"You think she's one of 'em? The kidnappers?"

"Probably not . . . but she is a difficult creature to read. And sharp as a bodkin. Best keep you out of her sight, or there will be a world of awkward questions to answer."

Mosca thought of the claw-handed girl with a sting of admiration and apprehension. She would have liked to have her as an ally, she admitted to herself, and did not much fancy the idea of being her opponent.

"Sometimes I fancy that *they* are just looking for the right moment to recruit her," Mistress Leap added, giving "they" the hushed tone she always used when talking about the Locksmiths. "They have never yet caught her on one of her 'dawn runs,' but I suspect they know about them. A trickle of black-market goods like chocolate comes through Toll-by-Night on their way east, you see—with 'custom fees' paid to *them*. Hardly anybody nightside can afford them, but there are some folk in Toll-by-Day who will pay high prices. Most of the day-side black marketeers are in league with *them*, and charge the very earth, I hear. Only Laylow is bold enough to take the risk of making her own deliveries."

Mosca bit her lip. If the young chocolate smuggler had already gained the attention of the Locksmiths, then avoiding her sounded like an even better idea.

"But you know of Brand Appleton?" she asked. "You know where we can find him?"

"I have a notion. They say he is found at the Bludgeon Court whenever it is held. But if we go there to look for him . . . we strike against the second problem. The court is run by the local beadles—if I take you there, I shall have to bring you before them to let them know that you are staying with me, and in their 'parish.'"

"The . . . beadles?" Mosca was a little surprised to hear that the ominous neighborhood had law enforcers other than the Locksmiths.

"Yes. The Sapler's Yard Beadles, to be precise. They look after this part of town, from Dreg Lane to Muller's Square. On behalf of . . . *them*. They . . . well, they keep the streets 'clean' and collect . . . donations for them. They're in charge of the census as well."

"There's them 'mongst the Locksmiths might recognize my name if it was given to 'em," Mosca muttered a little grimly, thinking of Goshawk. Would he remember her name? Would the king of the ghosts really recall a thin and weaselly twelve-year-old girl of no account? But she had looked him in the face, and Aramai Goshawk had unforgetting eyes. "I'm not so keen to be handing my name out to their pets—and I can scarce give 'em a false one, can I?"

"No, that is rather what I thought." The midwife busied herself pulling down boxes from her highest shelves. "The third problem is that your dreadful Mr. Skellow knows you by sight. We need to disguise you. Fortunately"—she smiled—"I think I have a ruse that will solve all three problems."

The midwife had a very soothing smile and an extremely persuasive manner. That was the only way Mosca could explain the fact that five minutes later she found herself bathing in what looked and felt a lot like warm gravy.

It was, Mistress Leap explained, a dye made from a mixture of different lichens and leaves, with a few dried blackberries for good measure.

"Really we should pop some embers under the bath," muttered the midwife as she dabbed some of the dye sediment onto Mosca's face and neck. "It always helps to simmer the mix when I'm dyeing wool—"

"Mistress Leap, I don't want to be simmered!" Mosca already felt a lot like the prime ingredient for orphan stew, and the little blackberries bobbing against her knees did not lessen this impression.

"Oh, as you please. We can paste it on, and you should come out a lovely oak color. I think we might say you are from . . . one of those wild distant places where they wear sequined boots and eat camel brains? The Peccadilloes? Or the islands of Seisia? If they think you speak only foreign babblish, then nobody can expect you to give your name."

When Mistress Leap was satisfied that Mosca was as dyed as she was going to be, she made her stand behind a screen to dry. Then the creation of the Seisian costume began. After a quarter of an hour of experimentation, Mosca stood awaiting Mistress Leap's judgment, trying to see herself reflected in the other's expression.

"Well . . . now that we've covered it with the cravat," the midwife began slowly, "I think the willow basket works quite well as a headdress. Particularly with the feathers. And the shawl looks much more exotic with those beads sewn to it. The main problem is that your face is a little . . . well, I was aiming for an oaken color. It's just a bit more . . . oak *leaf* than I expected."

"I'm green?" Mosca gasped.

"Oh, only a little bit. And Seisians might be green, mightn't they? I have never met any. Let us hope nobody else has either. Now, those shoes. Should we replace them with something more soft and floppy?"

"I reckon I'll keep these," Mosca answered grimly. "Sounds like I might need to do a lot of running."

Welter listened to his wife's account of their plan with the air of a man regarding a waiting gallows. "Remember later that I said it would all come to disaster," he muttered, and shambled off to his workshop.

"Do not mind him," whispered his wife. "He has

a fine mind, that is all, and needs challenges—being cooped up with me all day and most of the night was bound to wear out his temper. I did so hope that when they started mending the tower clock, they would call on him, since he is the best clock worker in town, but the Locksmiths brought people in from outside instead, and the poor dear has been sulking ever since."

Mosca could not help feeling that the poor dear might have a point about the likelihood of disaster. Having tasted Toll-by-Night's moonlit stew of murder, menace, treachery, and pursuit, she had fallen wildly in love with the six shabby bolts that held the door shut and the danger out. Her new regalia did not make her feel any better about venturing out either. There was no help for it, however. Time was not on their side, and unlike Mistress Leap, she could at least recognize Skellow.

"Tsk, nothing to worry about," Mistress Leap said vaguely as she put on her shawl. "Murderers get bored terribly easily, I hear, so I am sure the ones chasing us have run off to be murderous somewhere else now. Besides, if I worried about *that* kind of thing, then I would never go out at all."

"My goose . . ." Mosca hesitated at the door. "If I leave him here . . . nobody will sell 'im or eat 'im, will they?"

"What, after he guarded our doorstep from cut-throats?" Mistress Leap tutted. "Certainly not!"

18

Goodman Varple,
drinking partner of the thief and vagabond

Stars were now scattered across the sky, as if the white-faced moon had grown bored waiting for something to happen and started spitting gleaming fruit pits.

The streets no longer had the same desolate emptiness. Although the lanes did not throng the way they did by day, muffled figures could be seen hurrying about their business, some with baskets over their arms.

"This is the busiest time of night," murmured Mistress Leap. "The first hour or two after dusk is dangerous—most ordinary folks stay inside to avoid running into the Jinglers or those who prey on newcomers. But now and for a couple of hours, everybody scurries about their business quick as they can, before the worst of the cold sets in. Now, keep a tight hold on the knot of my apron with both hands—that way nobody can pluck you away without me knowing."

This was more necessary than it sounded, for Mosca's guide proved to be capable of a fearsomely brisk turn of speed. And, Mosca could not help noticing, people did seem to get out of Mistress Leap's way. Furthermore, they seemed to do so ungrudgingly. A few even gave her a glance and a nod—a curt, quick nod like a sparrow pecking apart a cherry, but a nod nonetheless. The midwife appeared to be a recognized figure.

However, the crowds all the while maintained their mouse-tense hush, their air of urgency. Fear. There was a reek of it everywhere, Mosca realized, in every guarded glance or falsely friendly back slap. A clammy smell, like rotten leaves. And everybody went about their lives in spite of it, because fear was part of their lives.

Flying out behind the midwife like a set of coattails, Mosca was dragged through slick, clenched alleys, then roofed passages where she briefly exchanged a black-and-silver world for one of rusty shadows and the murky, flickering gold of spitting rushlights and lanterns. At last they came to a halt in the street so suddenly that Mosca flattened her long nose on the midwife's muslin-clad back, leaving a dark green smudge.

Ahead the street widened to make space for three bare trees, around the base of which were arranged makeshift tents, so that the trees looked like gangly, stiff-backed women with voluminous canvas skirts. Drawing closer, Mosca could see that the tent cloths were a tattered patchwork of scraps and rags, sailcloth and burlap and leather and linen and blankets, many sporting water marks and mold rosettes. In one tent she saw a rail of dead rooks, tethered upside down by their feet; in another, drab heaps of Grabely wool.

It was a sort of market, and Mosca experienced a throb of relief at the sense of familiarity. Here at least the dreadful hush was less absolute, and there were even raised voices, cries of wares.

"Owl soup!" To one side a weedy fire bowed beneath the breeze as it struggled to do service to a dozen pots and cauldrons, which rattled their lids and chuckled steam. "Robin and beechnut!"

"Moss!" came another call. "Dry as a miser's eye!" And yes, there did indeed seem to be a great heap of dried moss, brown and tousled like spaniel hair. More surprisingly, a small crowd had gathered around it. Others were paying to fill their bags and crocks with scoops of dead leaves from a great barrel. Only when she witnessed a scuffle over a meager bundle of kindling did Mosca guess the reason for the hushed, bright-eyed earnestness of the crowds.

Toll-by-Night was readying itself for a long and bitter battle against a single enemy: winter. There was precious little timber to be seen, and so the busiest stalls sold gorse bundles, withered grass, twigs, kindling, biscuits of dry animal dung, anything that could be burned. Toll's trees had not been chopped down for firewood, however, and this told Mosca something else. For all its murky appearance of anarchy, Toll-by-Night clearly had rules, and one of those rules prohibited felling trees.

Several women gripped bouquets of meager rush-lights and were doing a roaring trade. Only one stall sold real candles, and its shriveled-looking little owner was flanked on one side by a hulking, cudgel-wielding bear of a man who watched the inquisitive fingers of everyone who passed by as if the sticks were fashioned of white gold instead of tallow. On the other side stood a gray-haired man who made a note of every candle sold. The stallholder was clearly miserably afraid of him.

"Tax man," whispered Mistress Leap with a meaning-ful glance toward the notetaker.

Mosca wondered what kind of person would intro-duce a candle tax for a people who lived in darkness. Somebody with a chatelaine of keys at his belt, she suspected.

But Mistress Leap was pushing on past the skirted trees to a set of weathered wooden steps that almost spanned the width of the strange thoroughfare. Mosca followed her up the steps and found herself looking into an arena.

The area was long and thin and flanked by two high brick walls. Makeshift box balconies hung from these walls by chains, each containing four or five fig-ures, most leaning over the front of the box with avid attention. The space between was filled with a series of shabby wooden stages raised on narrow legs. The stages were stepped and linked by various tilting planks and splintered bridges, as if a dozen carpenters had spontaneously gone insane. Every inch of every stage was thronged with people. Children crowded the very top of the walls like starlings.

Two stubby plum trees pushed their way up between the stages and spread their leafless branches above the crowd. A stiff, slender bridge ran between them, each of its ends bound firmly to a bough. On the bridge stood two figures, each carrying a rough cudgel. Each time one swung his weapon at the other's head, there was a wave-crash roar from the crowd. The combatants' swings were uncoordinated and drunken, their footwork stuttering and uncertain, and as she drew closer Mosca realized that both were wearing blindfolds.

Here and there between makeshift stages, the moonlight fell on tousled grass. Nonetheless, Mosca did not realize where she was until a brazier on the right-hand side caught her eye. By its light she could make out behind it a shape of splintered lattice with a white pointed roof. It was the pavilion where Mistress Bessel had confronted her not two days before. Somewhere beneath the shadowy scaffolding and ragged crowds of the Bludgeon Court lay the prim rockeries and trimmed lawns of Toll-by-Day's pleasure garden.

"Mother Midnight." The whetstone rasp of a voice came from directly behind them. "Beadle wants to see you." The voice's owner was a lean man with bristling black hair and a sickle-shaped scar that tugged a kink in his upper lip.

Mistress Leap jumped disproportionately and clasped her hands nervously. Mother Midnight was an irreverent term for a midwife.

"Oh! Yes—I . . . I was just coming to see him, in fact. . . ." She placed a reassuring arm around Mosca's shoulders, and they followed the man across an obstacle course of plank and plinth, on a twisting route toward the pavilion.

At one point Mosca's foot slithered on the worn and frosty planks, and she almost toppled from a beam to the lawn below. The stranger caught at her arm and righted her at the last moment.

"Stay off the grass!" he hissed.

And of course that was what this whole wooden wonderland and its inhabitants were doing. Staying off the grass. The lawns needed to be lush and pristine for the daylighters, not trodden to mud by chilblained feet and battered boots. No doubt the night owls were forbidden to chop down trees for much the same reason.

The pavilion was transformed. The brazier's light flushed it peach, and it hung in the smoke like a genie's mirage. Bent sequins glittered on the cloths that shrouded its sides. Within it, a broad-bellied man sat enthroned, lolling aloft like a sultan in his palanquin.

Adopting the meekest manner she could, Mosca

followed Mistress Leap to stand before the pavilion. Her skin stung and tingled with the sudden warmth of the brazier, and though she kept her eyes lowered, the brilliant firelight seared orange through her lids.

The message proclaimed by the blazing, uncovered brazier was almost deafening. *I am a man who can afford to be wonderfully, wastefully warm on this wretched winter night,* it said. *I am a man whose favor is worth winning.*

"Master Beadle." Mistress Leap's voice was still brisk, but it was the voice of a brisk but asthmatic vole.

"Ah, Mistress Leap." The man whose favor was worth winning had a voice that was half whinny, half gasp. A pair of bellows with a whistling hole. Mosca could not see his face. "Always a pleasure, isn't it?"

Mistress Leap made an obliging, high-pitched noise that was not exactly a word.

"That friend of yours, Mistress Leap. A problem. What's to be done about it?"

Mosca stiffened and tightened her fists so that her arms and shoulders didn't tremble. *Friend. Is that me? Is he looking at me?*

"Yes, you know the one," the beadle continued. "The mother whose kinchin went dayside. Blethemy Crace. Been acting the zany and making all manner of hubbub. Clinging to the wall of a daylighter's house, saying she can hear her babe crying on the other side. Over in Spikepock's parish. He wants to know what we plan to do about it."

Mosca imagined a mother pressed against a cold stone wall, listening to the cries of a baby who did not understand that it was not supposed to exist at that hour. *Poor little gobbet.*

"I . . . I will speak to her about it," breathed Mistress Leap hurriedly.

"Of course you will." A pause. "Now, what's this shred of life clinging to your skirts?"

Mistress Leap's arm tightened slightly around Mosca's shoulders. "I was . . . just bringing her to you. To register. A little foreigner—from Seisia, we think. She'll be staying with me—I've needed an apprentice for a long time and she seems a keen, hardworking sort of a child. . . ."

"Name?" wheezed the beadle.

"We do not know," Mistress Leap said quickly. "I have tried to get sense out of her, but she does nothing except chatter like a chicken coop in her foreign tongue."

"Bring her to me."

Guided forward by Mistress Leap, Mosca gingerly made her way past the brazier to the beadle's side, hoping against hope he would not see that her nationality was painted on. She tried to make her face as bland and mild as possible.

The beadle's face was pinkly discolored and pitted like a crab shell. His eyes, peering sleepily between the folds of his lids, also put Mosca in mind of a crab. The mind behind them was a crusted, scuttling thing, used to thinking sideways.

"You sure she's not just simple?" asked the beadle. Mosca realized that in her attempts to look wide-eyed and innocent, she might have overshot and hit half-witted. The beadle leaned forward and prodded her in the ribs with a fat finger.

"Go on, then," he said. "Jabber for us. What's your name?"

Mosca licked her lips dryly and let fly a stream of babble. A few real words like "hobble" and "wisteria" got mixed in somehow, but she hoped nobody would notice.

"Huh. Open wide, there." A thick finger tapped her on the chin. She opened her mouth and held as still as she could while the beadle stared intently inside. "Yes—that's a foreign tongue all right. Pale and blue and too pointy at the end. Nothing you can do about it." The meaty hand patted Mosca's shoulder twice. "Keep her nose clean and her feet off the grass."

Mosca was just turning to go, her stomach turbulent with relief, when the beadle's next words caught her attention.

"Grib, how's Appleton doing?"

The question was answered by the sickle-mouthed man.

"Took a couple of blows to the costard, but he's keeping his feet, Master Beadle."

Mosca tried not to stare at them as Mistress Leap dragged her away.

"Did you hear that?" she hissed when they were out

of earshot, moving her lips as little as she could. "Sounds like the beadle knows where Brand Appleton is!"

"I am quite sure he does," the midwife responded quietly, staring out into the center of the arena. Mosca followed the line of Mistress Leap's gaze to the two cudgelers on the precarious plank walk. "And so do I, and so does everybody else here. You see the young fellow up there with the red hair?"

Peering, Mosca could see that one of the combatants did indeed have red hair. His motions were more reckless and clumsy than those of his opponent. He lunged where his enemy edged, and swung his cudgel wildly to find his enemy instead of hunching down to listen for his steps. Mosca thought he seemed younger than his opponent, perhaps seventeen or eighteen years old.

"He's here every time they hold a Bludgeon Court." Mistress Leap sighed. "All the folks in the boxes and big stands pay a trifle to come and watch, but the prize the contestants fight for isn't money. It's hard-to-come-bys, luxuries—a bottle of Vantian sherry, a roll of chocolate, spices—and tonight it's candied violets. He enters the contest every time. I suppose he still has daylighter ways—maybe he'd sooner die than go without his silks and coffee." There was a cold edge of disdain in Mistress Leap's usually kindly voice, and Mosca could hear the mutual distrust of day and night grinding together like a giant's teeth.

"I don't think so," Mosca murmured. "Gifts for a

lady, I think." She could picture Brand Appleton limping home each night with cinnamon and sweetmeats, like a disgraced dog dragging in a mangled game bird and hoping to be loved for it. "Let's get closer."

Through time-honored use of the elbows, Mosca and Mistress Leap found standing room on a stage near the battle bridge, and Mosca's suspicions were confirmed— Appleton was not doing well. His opponent was a few inches shorter, but strongly, squatly built. Both were stripped to their shirts, but only Appleton's was marred by dark splotches that Mosca guessed must be blood. Furthermore, he did not seem to be a favorite of the crowd. Time and again a piece of fruit peel or a small stone pattered off his shoulder or clipped his ear.

The shorter man darted a blow that fell short, but his foot slapped the boards loudly, and Appleton launched himself toward the sound with a wild, crane-fly flailing of his limbs. Instead of retreating, his opponent stepped neatly forward and aimed a deft lateral lash that caught Appleton on the temple and unbalanced him. He slipped off the bridge, grabbing at its edge at the last moment and banging his chin and chest against the boards. There he hung, winded, while his enemy edged cautiously toward him, one step, two . . . and then a third, which rested the weight of his boot on the fingers of Appleton's right hand.

The crowd dissolved into a maelstrom of noise. Some were clearly trying to shout to Appleton's opponent, to tell him what it was that he was standing on, but their words were lost in the general cacophony. Appleton's face was screwed tight, but he made no sound or motion for the ten long seconds it took for his enemy to move his boot, advance, and unwittingly step over Appleton's other sprawled arm. The shorter man continued to advance, occasionally darting questing jabs with his cudgel in search of his foe, and Appleton was free to wriggle his way painfully back onto the bridge, his legs waggling froggishly until he could get a knee back onto the planks.

Then he stood, blood from his injured ear soaking into his collar, his face locked in a grimace, and limped quietly after his oblivious enemy. At the last moment the shorter man seemed to hear him and whirled around, but the motion caused the board beneath him to creak, and Appleton swung his cudgel with all his ungainly force. The roar of the crowd drowned the sound of wood on skull, but the shorter man spun about, tilted his head vaguely as if looking for something, then dropped to his knees and sprawled softly to the boards.

A bell rang, and Appleton pulled off his blindfold, wiped his face with it, and hobbled to the end of the bridge, examining his wounded fingers. He clambered down a ladder to stage level and hobbled to the pavilion, where Mosca could see him nodding, bobbing small bows, and accepting a bag, presumably of candied violets. There were new contestants climbing the trees to the battle bridge now, and he was largely ignored as he reclaimed a bundle from one of the attendants and staggered away, his red hair just visible above shorter nightdwellers.

"Well, there's no chance of following him in this crowd," murmured Mistress Leap. "Perhaps we can talk to people later and find out where he went. . . ." She turned, and her sentence trailed away, hanging like smoke in the empty space that an instant before had been occupied by her greenish companion.

It had been the work of a moment for Mosca to stoop and pretend to adjust her clog. The newest combatants were waving to the crowd, and suddenly all heads were up, all eyes on the bridge. Nobody noticed a mysterious foreigner with a bell-shaped basket for a hat ducking down in the crevice between two stages, dropping to the sacred, untouchable grass, then running, crouched beneath the creaking, thundering structure.

When she found Brand Appleton, he was sitting alone on a set of wooden steps built into the side of the stage, his back to her. His head had been clumsily bandaged with a long kerchief. Peering at a slight angle, Mosca could just make out the little bag of violets in his lap. With trembling, tender fingers he was trying to wipe a spot of blood from the linen of the bag.

Some higher steps creaked above Mosca's head.

"You're the radical, aren't you?" A voice like someone sandpapering a cello. Mosca tried to imagine its owner, and every time he came out seven feet tall with fists like melons. "Go on, say something radical."

Brand Appleton turned his head, allowing Mosca to see his split lip. He blinked, and Mosca could almost hear his temper clicking into readiness like a pistol hammer. But then his eyes fell to the bag in his lap, and his hands stealthily moved to cradle it against his stomach. When the man farther up the stairs took another step toward him, he wrapped both arms protectively around the bag and ducked his head down.

"Er . . . the . . ." He shook himself to gather his battered wits. "The . . . An end to all kings and we . . . their crowns should be beaten into plows and . . . for every man that is born a . . . in the sheds and stables and fields as much as in the . . . er . . . have a right to, um, a right as sacred as the air or . . . or sunlight . . ." He bowed his head and swallowed.

A heavy boot placed itself gently but firmly between his shoulder blades and gave him a contemptuous shove. The creaks were apparently satisfied and took themselves away.

Mosca watched Appleton's shoulders shake with suppressed emotion, and her own feelings were thrown into confusion. Was this the ruthless, crazed kidnapper she had been led to expect? This half-stunned man hugging a bag of sweets?

Then Appleton turned his head to look about him, perhaps to make sure that his persecutor had gone, and

Mosca saw his face properly, with its dark trails of blood down the left cheek and jawline. A young face, perhaps only a year or two older than Beamabeth. There was no disguise to his expression, and Mosca found herself flinching as if an oven door had been left open.

In his wide eyes she saw pain, and mortification, and exhaustion, but also a fierce and haggard stillness. And behind that stillness, a roar like a forest fire, a driving fervor that would eat all the air and shrivel whole trees with a hiss. His gaze seemed to burn through the world and every obstacle in his path to rest on something distant and desired, something that reflected in his eyes with a steady white light. This was a man who might do anything. He might not do it well, but he would do it until it worked.

He turned back, gently placed the bag down by his side, and busied himself with fastening a sword belt about him. Two pistols were dusted off and checked for powder, then tucked away. Apparently he had put aside his weapons for the fight.

Very slowly and carefully, Mosca drew out the little knife she had been given for self-defense. If she could only make a hole in the bag, perhaps when he left, sugar and violets would trickle out to leave a trail for her and help her find his lair. But Appleton was maddeningly protective of his little prize. He kept reaching out to pat it, just when her knifepoint was an inch away, or moving it to the other side of him. Finally he shifted it back into his lap again, out of Mosca's reach. Soon he would put it in a pocket, stand, and walk away among the crowds.

Mosca pulled back her knife hand, a rash and terrible impulse gnawing away at her mind. The worst thing about Appleton's gabbled radicalish was that he had clearly once heard a fragment of *something*. Some forbidden text hidden in cabbage barrows and badly copied and learned by rote and misremembered and half forgotten until it washed up in fragments on his tongue like so much meaningless sand. Somewhere a book was screaming.

She bit her tongue hard, but somehow the sentence slipped out anyway.

"You got the words wrong, Mr. Appleton."

He froze and turned his head a few degrees.

"What?"

"That radical speak of yours. You got the words wrong."

A long, long second of silence.

"You know the right words to the *Solace for the Thousands*?"

"No, but those weren't them. I been to Mandelion. I *know* radicals. They make a load more sense than that."

Her words seemed to poke Appleton into alertness, and his posture noticeably straightened.

"When I got here, I heard you were this terrible radical, so I come to find you." Mosca took a deep breath, then threw what was left of her caution to the winds like so much chaff. "And you know what? You're more than terrible. You're bleedin' useless. Don't turn round!" This last was delivered in an urgent hiss since Appleton seemed in some danger of twisting about to remonstrate with the steps. She had gone too far. She must have gone too far.

"Funnily enough," Appleton answered through clenched teeth, "my childhood tutors failed to ground me properly in the basics of revolutionary thought. And when I reached manhood, I wasted my time studying books of anatomy in the mistaken impression that I would become a physician as planned. Back then, nobody told me I was a radical!"

"Well, you don't sound like much of one," muttered Mosca.

"The Committee of the Hours is never wrong," intoned Appleton. The words rang hollowly, as if he had recited them to himself too many times and worn the heart out of them. "If they say I am . . . then I am. I can . . . I can face that. But—"

"But nobody told you how to be one—am I right?" Above all, Mosca had to keep Appleton interested, inquisitive. "Could help you there, maybe. Might have some radical teachings off by heart. And words right from the mouths of the *real* radicals, in Mandelion."

Brand Appleton sat motionless, his head at a considering tilt. Mosca stared at the back of his neck and tried to guess his expression. A brand was a fiery torch. She hoped that she was holding it by the right end. Either way, she was certainly playing with fire.

"These teachings—are they wild and subversive?" he whispered at last.

"Frothing," Mosca reassured him quickly. "Mad as a melon cannon."

"And . . . you come from Mandelion? You know the place well? The people in power?" He had the hesitant tone of one tiptoeing around a new plan for fear of smudging it.

Somewhere the tower clock struck a tinny chime, and Appleton's head twitched.

"I have to go. Listen, whoever you are—meet me at Harass and Quail's tomorrow night at two of the clock. It's in Cooper's Dark—do you know it? Opposite the old stone trough."

"I'll find it," hissed Mosca, marveling at the success of her strange gambit, "and I'll be there. Bring a notebook. We'll have you lopping kings' 'eads off before you can say fraternity."

At long last Appleton ventured a swift glance behind him, and then twitched his narrow head about, looking for his fellow interlocutor. Mosca pulled back so the moonlight would not fall on her face.

"Hey—are you under *there*? *On the grass*?"

"Just between you and me," Mosca whispered, "radicalism is *all about* walkin' on the grass."

19

Goodlady Adwein,
Wielder of the Pestle of Fate

Watch him. He's standing up. Walking away . . . after him! Now!

Mosca had made an appointment with Appleton for the morrow, but there might still be some small chance of following him. She clambered out from under the scaffolding, as unobtrusively as anybody with a basket on her head possibly could, and hastily climbed up onto one of the plank walkways so that nobody would know she had been on the grass. Unfortunately, much as she had suspected, Brand Appleton was gone by the time she had extricated herself.

When she felt a light touch on her shoulder, she jumped a foot in the air and would have fallen off the walkway if Mistress Leap had not grabbed her arm.

"Did you see him, Mistress Leap? Did you see where he went?"

But the midwife had not witnessed Brand Appleton's departure. The streets of Toll-by-Night had swallowed him once more.

"My dear, we really should be heading home soon." Mistress Leap's voice was muted but urgent. "There is a frost falling. Have you noticed?" It was true, Mosca realized. The chill of the night was becoming more bitter, and there was a subdued sparkle to the cobbles. "It is getting cold, and from now on the night can only get . . . colder."

Mosca understood. Cold meant fewer people. It meant the people who were still on the streets had either nowhere to go or the wrong sort of reason to be out. Besides, this was not her last chance to track Appleton down. He had promised to meet her the following night.

"All right, Mistress Leap. But before we go back to your house, I got one more place to go. I got a letter to write."

The route to the location where Mosca had agreed to leave letters for her daylight allies took Mosca and Mistress Leap past the clock tower. Looking up at the clock, Mosca could see that the wooden Beloved sentry above the clock face had changed again. Paragon had clearly done his duty. And now it was Goodlady Adwein gazing forgivingly out across the town, her pestle and mortar in her hands.

All this will pass, she seemed to say. *Everything that seems so large and inescapable now, I will grind down in my pestle, and in a century it will be a fine powder that nobody will notice. There is no crime you have committed, no pain you have felt, that I cannot grind to nothing so that the world forgets it, in the fullness of time.*

This was no comfort to Mosca at all. In fact, she reflected, she didn't much like the idea of a fine, powdery world where nothing really mattered in the long run. She preferred her world painful, and lumpy, and full of chaff.

One such human piece of chaff was clearly on clock-mending duty. A basket was suspended from the crane on the tower roof, and a man in overalls could be seen standing precariously inside it. The clock face had been levered open, and he was leaning over with some long-handled tool to tweak reverently at its metal innards. All the while Goodlady Adwein smiled and smiled, caring nothing for him.

Mosca scuttled past the tower to the agreed place in the town wall. Out of her pocket she drew a letter written hastily by moonlight, dropped a single eyelash in among the folds, and squeezed it into a crevice between two bricks as arranged. This was her lifeline, the only rope that might stop her from plummeting to disaster. She had no choice but to cling to it, even if the other end was held by Eponymous Clent.

After Mosca Mye had returned to the house of the Leaps, the night air took on a more determined chill.

Eventually the sky paled, and nature began its own changing of the guard, the owls retreating to their crofts and rafters to huddle like tufted urns. Those rooks and crows that had not been grabbed overnight by hungry boys with slingshots and bags took to the air, knowing by some instinct that a generous breakfast previously known as Havoc Gray was making his way toward the sea on the back of the Langfeather.

And below them, Toll-by-Night set about folding itself away, like a stilt-legged monster into a closet. Its inhabitants crept back into the unwanted places, the crannies and cellars and forgotten attics, and locked themselves in.

A bugle blew. A silver jingling swept through the town, sealing away all bad reputations and bitter-tasting names.

Another bugle sounded. And day swept in like a landlord, not knowing that it was only a guest in night's town.

Being locked away at night with the dayfolk had been claustrophobic, but at least there had been something familiar about it. After all, who had not seen an inn-keeper drop a heavy bolt against the predations of the night?

It was a very different matter sitting in the Leaps' strange narrow room, lit only by a few rushlights, and hearing the dawn chorus offering tentative chips of sound outside. In spite of the darkness and chill of the room, one could tell it was day, one could feel it in one's bones.

Then came footsteps, sounding recklessly clear after all the hushed bustle of the night, criers calling the hour, hawkers bold with their wares. Mosca realized that she had been thinking of Toll-by-Day as impossibly remote from her, and it was weird to realize that the barrier between them was less than a hand's span thick.

Her back was to the door, and she nearly leaped out of her skin when a rubbery bang reverberated just behind her. Only when it occurred again did she realize that it was the sound of a ball being bounced against the door, or more likely against a panel concealing the door. Her hand tightened into a fist, and it was all she could do not to knock out a response. But she restrained herself. She was a phantom in a house that did not exist.

The days were shortening, so Mosca made herself a nest of rugs by the cooling hearth, knowing that she would need all the sleep she could get. But the raucous sounds and raw alertness of day seemed to seep in under the door and down the chimney, and to sting her mind awake. The Leaps were no help at all. They appeared to have no interest in sleeping. Again and again she was jolted by the creak of a spinning wheel, or a *flip-flip-flip* of pages turning, or the groan of furniture and boxes as the Leaps clambered over them with balletic ease, or clicks and squeaks as Welter fiddled with some contraption in his workshop.

They barely spoke, but every few minutes Mistress Leap would knock a double tap on the nearest piece of furniture in order to get her husband's attention and then perform a series of rapid mimes that completely baffled Mosca's eye. Welter responded to these silent gambits by jumping at each *rap-rap* as if stung, turning a gaze of icy weariness upon his wife, then looking away with the bleak countenance of a long-term prisoner.

Saracen did not help either, since he was in a mood to clamber damply across Mosca's face. He was restless, very wet, and, Mosca was concerned to notice, green. Evidently the dye bath had not been thrown out after Mosca's dip, and Saracen had made delighted use of his new miniature pond.

Mosca's conversation with Brand Appleton spun around and around in her head like a carriage wheel, jolting into the potholes of her surmises and fears. Tomorrow she would see him again, and this time there would be no way to stop him from seeing her. What if he brought Skellow with him? Was her disguise good enough? Would the promised reinforcements from Sir Feldroll be sufficient for an ambush?

And as her mind crowded with night worries, night plans, she ceased to hear the rumble of barrows and hand-clap songs outside. It was background music, nothing more. Already the day world was starting to seem just a little less real.

Although most did not know it, little pieces of night were abroad in Toll-by-Day. Who would suspect them? They all had good names. And in such a cold month, who would remark upon the fact that they all wore gloves, or guess that the right-hand glove of each hid a key-shaped brand? Even now the gloves were abroad, all busy in the same cause.

One pair quietly closing the door to the mayor's study, then picking delicately through his letters. Ah, a letter from the mayor of Waymakem. That looked interesting. The left glove held the letter prisoner while the right pried away the seal. "Honored sir, we call upon you once again to join us in Cutting Out the Malign Growth that is Radical Enthusiasm and allowing our Troops Passage through your Town so that we may Drive these Usurpers out of Mandelion." Fascinating. The letter was returned deftly to its envelope, the sealing wax softened in a flame and pressed back into place.

In the Committee of the Hours, another pair of gloves dropped a few coins into the waiting hand of young Kenning, who obligingly found something very important to do in a back room while the gloves turned the pages of a book of admissions to the daylight town, a forefinger running down the column of names and coming to a halt on a pair of entries.

A third set of gloves tap-a-tapped a table in an inn, a table that offered an excellent view of a particular stretch of town wall. The tap-a-tapping only faltered when a certain plump poet known to his friends, admirers, enemies, and creditors as Eponymous Clent strolled into view and came to a halt against exactly that portion of wall. His hands were behind him as if to cushion his back, while he gazed with apparent poetic rapture at the porridgy massing of the clouds above. His reverie over, Clent was on the move again, tucking something into his waistcoat pocket.

The gloves threw a coin down onto the table, then off they went in pursuit, the left glove slapping a hat onto a balding head, the right swinging a cane jauntily in time with the stride of a couple of well-brushed shoes. Nobody could suspect that anybody who walked so boldly and breezily could be a spy following a mark.

Clent himself walked in a leisurely fashion, as if strolling alongside his muse, occasionally offering small bows to any passing ladies. Only his tendency to extend the same courtesy to small trees, empty sedan chairs, and tethered whippets hinted at some distraction of mind. And after him went the gloves, the hat, the cane, the well-brushed shoes.

Clent took sudden turns through narrow passages, and the gloves took shortcuts and quietly appeared behind him in the next street. Clent dallied to listen to a traveling orator, who was holding forth on the dangers of malignant radicals to a relatively warm reception. The gloves waited in the crowd, applauding politely from time to time. Clent frowned at his watch, sped around the nearest corner . . . and the gloves rounded the turn after him, only to run headfirst into a substantial helping of Eponymous Clent.

A jolt of bodies. Near loss of balance. Each reaching out instinctively to steady the other, a recovery of equilibrium.

"Ah—a thousand apologies!"

"No, no, the fault is all mine—"

"I have not ruffled your—"

"No, see, all is well."

The gloves had no choice but to continue past the poet at the same steady, jaunty pace until they were quite out of view. At the nearest corner, however, they halted so that their owner could peer back into the street, blunt moleskin fingers tap-a-tapping against the bricks.

Too late. The street that had held Eponymous Clent did so no longer. Somehow the portly poet had slithered through that gap of a few seconds and vanished into the crowd. The gloves tightened into fists of frustration, to a background harmony of sotto-voce swearing.

A few streets away, Eponymous Clent strolled on in his ponderous fashion, his eyes skittering from one side of the road to the other in search of pursuers, his heart pattering like rain. During his collision, he had steadied his pursuer with a firm hand at belt level and had felt the shape of a chatelaine beneath the cloth. He had been followed by a Locksmith. Worse still, he had left that Locksmith feeling foolish.

"Ah—Mr. Clent!" The footman had barely opened the door to Clent's knock when Sir Feldroll pushed past him, dapperly dressed in a scarlet redingote that brought out the redness in the lids of his sleep-starved eyes. "Mr. Clent, what word? Your girl . . . the drop . . . is there word?" His mouth quivered through a thousand nervous little shapes, while his eyes made high-speed reconnaissance missions across Clent's countenance and aspect, noting the latter's breathlessness and disheveled air.

Clent gave a ruffled nod. "Ah, yes—news indeed, my lord, but a closed-door matter, methinks." He cast a small, significant glance at the footman, who was doing his best to veil his interest in the exchange. "Not words that we should let the wind catch."

He was shown into the breakfast room, where he offered a somewhat distracted bow to the mayor. However, Clent might as well have capered in jester's weeds for all the attention his courtesy earned. As soon as he pulled a letter from his pocket, nobody had eyes or thoughts for anything else.

The mayor seized it first, and read it aloud with a deepening frown.

"Have found Lodgings with those persons we spoke of. BA well known hereabouts for getting Knocked Silly so he can win Candied Violets & Preserv'd Cherries & like Fripperies for You Know Which Lady. I have spoke with him and will meet with him tomorrow when it would be well to have some Strong Arms to heft Cudgels so those Friends of our Friend needed Soon as Possible. Also think my Landlords might be a bit pixillated."

"Does anybody have the faintest idea what this means?" The mayor's eyebrows shot up interrogatively into two gray steel arches, and he thrust the missive into the eager hand of Sir Feldroll.

The younger man read it with an expression very like pain, tracing the lines with his fingertip again and again in his determination to absorb their meaning.

"She's alive," he murmured at last. "The sweetmeats—it must be for Miss Marlebourne. So she is definitely alive. And"—the page quivered in his hand, and he smoothed it with his fingers as if trying to calm it—"at least . . . at least this ruffian Appleton seems to be taking some pains to see her treated well."

"Naturally, naturally," Clent cut in soothingly. "Dark as their hearts might be, those villains would as soon bowl with their own heads as harm that child. She is worth a fortune to most of them, and the very world to one of them, is she not?"

Sir Feldroll dropped into a chair. One sleepless night had evidently allowed him all too much leisure to imagine dark and terrible events befalling the mayor's daughter.

"And it would seem"—Clent tapped the letter—"that our young spy has convinced Appleton to meet with her. BA can only be Brand Appleton."

"But why does she not describe the place where they are to meet?" The mayor tweaked the letter back into his own grasp and tried to stare it into submission. "And these people with whom she is staying—who are they? Where are they? Why is she so damnably cryptic?"

Clent paused, drawing in a breath through pursed lips, and examined the mayor's boots as if trying to guess their price.

"Ah, yes," he answered pleasantly. "A curious string of obfuscations . . . but not, I think, inexplicable ones. Recall that she is a fly child, fostered and fed all her life long on mistrust. Naturally she has a darkling mind and habits of secrecy. It is in her nature. It is in her name. And in this case . . . it is a very good thing. A very good thing indeed."

"What? What do you mean?" asked Sir Feldroll.

"I mean that if Mosca Mye had included the names of her hosts and the location of their dwelling in that letter I would not give *this*"—he snapped his fingers—"for her life right now." Eponymous Clent drew himself up, his native sense of theater overwhelming him for a second. "Gentlemen, someone has smelled us out. We are detected, decoded, discovered. Somebody was watching the letter drop."

He left a dramatic pause, which his companions obligingly filled with consternation and exclamation.

"With some degree of ingenuity," he continued, "I succeeded in losing the man who sought to follow me back here, but not before I had made good view of him. A Locksmith—I would stake my wits on it. The Locksmiths have doubtless read this letter, but they left it where they found it so that we would suspect nothing and send a response, allowing them to learn more. So let us all spare a moment to thank Goodman Palpitattle for the tricky habits of mind that made young Mosca loath to include her own name—or anybody else's—in her letter."

"But . . ." Light was dawning in Sir Feldroll's gaze. "What are we to do about this? If we cannot send Miss Mye letters through this drop . . ."

". . . then we cannot even warn her that the drop is compromised," continued Clent, clasping his hands and examining their interweaving. "Our young delver into the night town is herself in considerable danger. If we leave a note for her, it will be read. If we leave no note, they will know that *we* know that the drop is compromised. Mosca will become their only lead. They will follow her . . . or, more likely, wait to ambush her at the drop."

Sir Feldroll creased his narrow, tufted brows. "Half a dozen of my men will arrive later today—men with night names. His lordship the mayor is willing to make arrangements with the Committee of the Hours, so that they can be let through the Twilight Gate tonight. Miss Mye is expecting them—if she has good sense, she will be waiting at the Gate to meet them. They can warn her about the drop then. And she can lead them to ambush this man Appleton at her next meeting with him."

"Assuming, of course," the mayor muttered dangerously, "that it is not the girl herself that has betrayed the location of the drop in exchange for her own freedom."

A maid came in to clear the breakfast table, but the mayor continued speaking. Clent winced, and his hands made tiny involuntary motions, as if patting some restive child back to sleep. *Hush, hush.*

"Indeed," continued the mayor, apparently oblivious to Clent's concern, "if it were not for the testimony of Mistress Jennifer Bessel, I would have considerable doubts about placing my reliance this far on *you*, Mr. Clent. However, given that you have managed to earn the respect of a lady of such elevated sensibilities and decency . . ."

A couple of expressions pulled Clent's face to and fro between them like puppies trying to fight their way out of a bag.

"Ah, yes—an admirable, ah, admirable creature. With boundless . . . qualities, and unfathomable . . . talent."

"I cannot imagine where this household would have been without her this last day or so." A gentle expression wandered onto the mayor's angular features, where it looked rather out of place. "But then, I suppose she discovered an inner strength and courage after the death of her husband."

"The death of her—ha, hmm, of course." After a brief convulsion Clent's face took on the kindly expression of a pitying cherub. "So tragic. And . . . extremely unexpected."

The maid departed again, tray in hand. Clent waited until the door closed behind her, eyes raised as if assessing the thread by which his good graces hung.

"My lord mayor, I know that you have grave doubts about my secretary." He paused, then sighed. "Gentlemen, let me be perfectly candid with you. Before we came to Toll, Miss Mye and I had some . . . encounters with the Locksmiths—with Aramai Goshawk specifically. We did not precisely make an enemy of the gentleman, as you can see by the fact that we are both still above ground, but we most certainly did not make a friend.

"Miss Mye knows all too well that crossing his path again would probably have fatal consequences. She *cannot* betray us to the Locksmiths without risking her own neck. If I might be blunt, you can place your trust in her because you are still her best . . . her *only* chance of weathering these disasters without being undone entirely."

Neither of his listeners looked approving, but his words appeared to have sunk home.

"Very well." The mayor settled back in his chair. "Then we had better contrive some letter to leave in the chink—something that will tell the Locksmiths nothing."

"And let us pray to the Little Goodkin that she goes to the Twilight Gate before the drop," murmured Sir Feldroll.

20

GOODMAN SNATCHAVOC,
THE VOICE IN THE GAMBLER'S EAR

LIKE A GOOD housewife eking out her store of dried fruits, Eponymous Clent knew how to make a little truth go a long way. It was a matter of theater, like everything else. You sighed, as if you had given up all pretense, as if your listeners had been too shrewd for you. You spread your arms or your hands, as if flinging wide the doors of your treasury of secrets. And then, in tones of weary resignation, you said something like "Gentlemen, let me be perfectly candid with you. . . ."

In short, you let your audience examine your pockets so that they did not think to look up your sleeves. Eponymous Clent was sometimes candid. But he was never *perfectly* candid.

For example, his mind was currently full of thoughts that he had no intention of sharing with the mayor or

Sir Feldroll at all. The letter drop had been discovered. How? Had Mosca betrayed them, or been clumsy and let herself be followed? Both were . . . possible. And yet he thought both unlikely.

Somewhere our secrets are spilling out of the sack and into the hands of the Locksmiths, he mused silently as his feet led him away from the mayor's abode. *And I will wager my wits the hole is in the mayor's own house. If I were Aramai Goshawk, I would have placed a spy in the mayor's household as soon as I arrived in Toll—before my horses' flanks had even dried. And the mayor speaks of covert matters before his servants as if they had no more ears than a hatstand.*

So. The Locksmiths have an agent in the mayor's household, and so, I suspect, do the kidnappers. Are they one and the same? Are the Locksmiths and the kidnappers working together? Pray heavens they are not, or we shall have the devil's own time rescuing the mayor's daughter.

One thing was certain. Another means of contacting the night town was needed. And Clent's daylight allies could not be trusted with knowledge of it.

An hour later in a very different part of the town, a wooden door was flung abruptly open, so that daylight flooded into the scruffy little room beyond. The two figures within started and gaped, the fingers of one halting on the keys of his spinet, the other ceasing to drag his bow across the strings of his violin. In spite of their startled paralysis, music could still be clearly heard, and amid it the quavering of an invisible flute and the silvery glissando of an unseen harp. This phantom melody limped on for a few confused bars until the spinet player beat out a panic-stricken tattoo on the back wall with his fist, at which point the sound stumbled to a halt.

"Sir!" The violinist was the first to recover. "I . . . We are busy rehearsing, sir!"

"Oh yes." The portly intruder offered him a beatific smile and invited himself into the room. "I was rather counting on that." He settled himself down on a battered chair and beamed. "I hope you will pardon me for running you to ground in this irregular fashion, but I have a lifelong passion for the arts. I myself am a poet, but music—ah, music! Without it my soul has no wings. Oh, that I could only understand the way in which talented spirits like yourselves can pluck the very notes from the air. . . ." He stared about in ecstasy, as though untamed notes were flitting around him like fish.

The spinet player attempted a confused, seated half bow, and the violinist managed a wan smile. Both were making a point of not glancing back at the wall from which the mysterious music had issued.

"Though I must confess," continued the plump intruder in a lower tone, "I would be considerably more interested to know how one violin and a spinet can produce five instruments' worth of melody."

Both musicians promptly stammered and went crimson, which was more and at the same time less eloquent than they evidently intended.

"Yes, I saw you perform at the mayor's house a couple of nights ago. I daresay that in the better circles it is terribly bad form to notice that you two gentlemen are the only members of your troupe actually playing . . . and yet somehow managing to sound like a five-piece orchestra. Talking of manners, I have quite forgotten mine." The stranger pulled off his glove and held out his hand so that his unbranded right palm was clearly visible. "Eponymous Clent."

Recovering a little, the musicians each shook Clent's hand, still regarding him warily.

"I can guess how it happened." Clent's narrowed eyes gleamed like parings from a silver coin. "The whole orchestra was made up of dayfolk, am I right? And then over time some of you were reclassified and sent into the night? And since then you have been rehearsing and performing in places where the walls are thin enough that your nightling brethren's instruments can be heard as well as your own?" He looked meaningfully toward the back wall, the one against which the spinet player had knocked his signal. From somewhere beyond it there was a stifled sneeze, and a muffled hush.

The two musicians glanced at each other. Then the violinist gave a small and rueful nod.

"So you pay some day friends a few pennies to pose with instruments when you perform," continued Clent, "and most people do not notice, and the few who do turn a blind eye to it. Of course they do. If they did not, then they would have to go without decent music. Now, I am sorry to breach etiquette in this fashion, but the moment I thought about your position properly, I realized one important thing." Clent leaned forward and dropped his voice. "The whole orchestra simply had to meet up from time to time, in a place where you could hear one another? How else would you rehearse, or discuss where you would be performing next? And . . ." He raised his voice a little, glancing toward the back wall. "If I could only interrupt such a rehearsal, I would have a way of getting a message to somebody in the night town. This is something I must do—as soon as possible.

"Trust is always a gamble, is it not, my dear fellows? Particularly with a stranger. Can you trust me? Can I trust you? It seems I must. This is a matter of life, death, and . . . remuneration."

This last word brought a glimmer of light to the musicians' eyes, and the violinist recovered the use of his voice. "Re . . . remuneration? What kind of remuneration?"

"Well." Clent spread his hands. "I fear I have no *actual* money, but nonetheless I suggest we go and visit some of the town's better shops. Strangely enough, since it became known that I was staying with the mayor, I have had no trouble acquiring credit throughout town. My dear fellow, money is no substitute for the *right kind of friend*."

* * *

358

There was one more conversation that Clent needed to have, but before he sought it out, he took certain pains. He obtained the services of a barber, "borrowed" a cloth rose from a milliner by claiming he wished to compare it for color to his new waistcoat, and pounded some of the dust out of his coat. Hence when he met with Mistress Bessel in the pleasure garden, he had all the extra dapperness that haste, eloquence, and no money could apply.

She smiled at his flower, with the even smile of one who knows where her purse and wits are, thank you very much, and does not intend to be distracted into losing track of either.

"I gather that your inestimable qualities have made a considerable impression on a certain esteemed gentleman," Clent remarked pleasantly. "I should doubtless shoot myself through brokenheartedness, or perhaps shoot him—I am yet to decide which would have greater romantic flourish."

Mistress Bessel's smile thinned and her eyebrows raised.

"Yes . . . I gather he is particularly impressed by your courage in the face of bereavement," Clent continued, finding fascination in his own fingertips. "Out of interest, what did your husband die of this time?"

Mistress Bessel bristled like a fat ginger cat with a trodden tail. "Eponymous Clent! Have you said anything to the mayor to sour the jam?"

"No. No, Jen, I would not dream of spoiling any tale of yours." Clent gave her a brief glance in which there was enough affection that the spoonful of sadness was almost lost in the mix. "Ah, winter is coming, and we cold birds must all feather our nests as best we can, must we not, Jenny Wren?"

The nickname won a small smile from his companion, and something crumpled in her face, making her look both younger and older.

"And there are few enough feathers to go round," she admitted. "The mayor says he might need a housekeeper. And take that look off your face, Eponymous Clent! I said a *housekeeper*."

"If you say so, then be it so. And . . . if in time the mayor should decide to marry his housekeeper . . ."

"Then what would you have her do?" Mistress Bessel demanded crisply. "Spit in his eye?"

There was a long pause, during which Clent twirled his false flower between his fingers. "No," he said at last, placing the flower in her hand. "No. You should take everything fine that can be squeezed out of this bitter little life. And I will aid you any way I can. Friends scratch one another's backs, do they not?"

"Hold hard—are those the words of a man with an itchy back?" Mistress Bessel's brow darkened. "I knew it! You want something from me!"

"A trifle, a morsel, a mere nothing." Clent's hands danced before him, pinching the air into minuscule gobbets. "But, ah, an important nothing. You, my dear, are currently a light in the mayor's darkness, the warm hearth to which he gratefully creeps after the cruelties of life. And if he values you as he seems to, doubtless he takes you into his confidence and gives you the run of the house. . . ." He trailed off and gave a small shrug. "He trusts you, you trust me, and the world is richer for the benison of trust."

"Ha!" Mistress Bessel gave a scornful laugh, though her gaze was less barbed than her tone as she pinned the flower to her dress. "'Richer,' is it? So is that your pretty way of asking where the mayor keeps his silver? You are a scheming black-hearted dog, Eponymous."

"No, dear Jen, not this time." Clent's tone was unusually serious. "Believe it or not, I have good reasons for asking this of you. There is a spy in the mayor's household, and you are better placed to track him down than I. But for the Beloved's sake, be wary—we are playing a game of secrets against very dangerous opponents."

The sun sank in blood, and all over Toll shadows stretched like waking cats. A bugle sounded. Night swept through Toll on chimes of silver. A second bugle sounded. The last true daylight departed the sky, leaving only a bruise of luminosity over the west. The doors of Toll-by-Night opened.

Since an hour before dusk Mosca had been awake. In fact, "awake" was too weak a term. She felt as if she was full of ingrowing spikes of apprehension, like an inside-out hedgehog.

It made her restless, and restless was a very bad idea in a corridor room as narrow and cluttered as that in which the Leaps lived. Mistress Leap had told her to stay still and touch nothing, and she thought she *was* staying still and touching nothing, but somehow she managed to fidget a warming pan off a wall hook and a stack of fire irons onto the floor. She even elicited a small hiss from Saracen, who had contrarily chosen this time to settle down to sleep.

The sound of the bugle filled her with terror and relief.

"Mistress Leap! We got to go—the men I told you of, they'll be waiting by the Twilight Gate! And if we don't find 'em, then five to one somebody else will." Unable to bear inactivity anymore, Mosca was on her feet, pulling on her basket hat and clogs.

"One moment. Just let me make sure the coast is clear." Mistress Leap opened the door a crack, peered out, then gave Mosca a smile over her shoulder. "It all looks safe enough," she whispered. And with that she stepped out through the door onto the step, stiffened, and toppled sideways out of sight.

When Mosca scampered out to join her, she found the midwife slumped against the doorjamb nursing her temple, her bonnet knocked askew. The culprit was clearly visible, a chunk of masonry that lay shattered on the step. Mosca glanced upward in case more of the house threatened to fall on their heads, but the midwife shook her head.

"No, it was thrown from down there." She pointed down the street.

Mosca peered into the darkness but could see no sign of any lurking assailants. Feeling exposed, she quickly helped the wobbly midwife indoors. A bleary, half-asleep Welter blundered over just in time to help his stunned wife into her chair and then set about rummaging through boxes for some ointment to smear on the injury. Mosca peered suspiciously at the older woman's head and found a rosy swelling bump, but thankfully nothing worse.

"Did you see who it was?"

"No, just a blur at the street corner. Probably some lads throwing rocks for sport, without realizing that I was about to open the door." The midwife glanced up at Mosca's doubtful face and patted her hand reassuringly. "My dear, do not worry, I will be all right. Go! Find those friends of yours at the Twilight Gate! After all, if you do not, then we will have no tithe for Saint Yacobray, and we will *all* be lost."

Mosca hesitated, concerned at the prospect of leaving Mistress Leap so soon after her injury. However, the midwife had her husband to attend to her, and time was running out.

"All right, but keep Saracen here to guard you. And . . . you better lock the door behind me."

Rocks thrown for sport? Mosca was not a great believer in innocent explanations, and that went double in Toll-by-Night. But why would anybody hurl rocks at a kindly midwife and then run away? Just for a moment, Mosca wondered if perhaps the mysterious attacker had not seen his victim's face but just a bonneted head peering around a particular door. Was it possible that the missile had been meant for the skull of Mosca Mye?

There was no such thing as a safe street in Toll-by-Night, but at least after walking with Mistress Leap Mosca could hazard a guess at some of the *safer* streets. The day map in her skirt pocket was now crisscrossed with her own additions—names scribbled out and others added, new walls or highways drawn in. However, it was still early in the evening, and early meant danger.

After her sojourn in nonexistence, the fading twilight seemed curiously bright, and she wondered if the bugles might have been mistimed, until she realized that the wheeling shapes she could see against the sky were not birds but bats.

By now she knew what sort of person would be lurking by the Twilight Gate, like cats around a mouse hole. Cutthroats looking for some plump victim loaded down with all his earthly possessions, eyes still dazzled with the darkness of his new world. "Landlords" with crocodile smiles who would welcome strangers in for the night and then smother them or sell them to the toil gangs.

Pickpockets. Scissor women, waiting to steal the hair of children and young girls. She would need to weave her way past them like a perch past pikes.

I'll take the route along the town wall, she decided. And then, with a leap of the heart, *Yes, that way I can look in at the letter chink first. See if Mr. Clent has left a message for me.*

The moon was low enough to be sallow, and everything cast shadows that might have been made for the Mosca Myes of the world.

There were patrols along the top of the wall, of course, making sure that nobody tried to scale it, but it was their task to look for rash souls rearing up in silhouette on the wall's crest. They did not notice the slight figure that ran from one patch of shadow to the next, a pint-sized attic creature hastily fashioned from jumble and rags.

Even in the dim light Mosca could make out the stone faces of the Beloved carved into the wall. At last she glimpsed the curmudgeonly features of Goodman Belubble, He Who Snuffs the Last Candle Before Sleep. *There. Goodman Belubble's surly slit of a mouth. That's where the letter will be.* She crouched, scanned the wall for patrols, and counted the seconds till her moment by instinct, like a housecat watching blackbirds.

Two seconds. One second. Now.

And then the darkness reached out a hand and gave her a polite prod between the shoulder blades.

"I really would not do that if I were you."

* * *

Meanwhile, unbeknownst to Mosca, another darkling meeting was taking place.

The little door that led to the Twilight Gate creaked open, and six men emerged into the night town, breathing steam and staying close to one another.

Their leader cast a glance up and down the street and felt not disappointment but a grim resignation. If the girl Sir Feldroll had told them to expect was there to meet them, she was doing an excellent impression of a cobblestone.

"Blades take it, the little mort's probably already been caught," he muttered. "All right, everyone, we'll wait for her awhile, but not here in the bold of the moon. This is wolf country. If we huddle and bleat where everyone can see us, we deserve to be mutton."

Briefed by both Sir Feldroll and the mayor, he knew something of the town into which he was stepping. His birth under Goodman Snatchavoc the Gambler thirty years ago that very night had given him a "night name" in the opinion of the Committee of the Hours, who as a result considered him to be a fiend of card and dice, reckless, undisciplined, lavish in vice, and certainly unsuited to daylight. Perhaps the Committee had really believed that he would be more at home in the nocturnal town, but right now he could feel the enmity of Toll-by-Night tickle his neck hairs as if his collar was full of spiders.

Accompanied by his five colleagues, he slipped into the shadow beside the clock tower and waited. The hands of the clock above them moved, but it appeared to have lost an hour or two somewhere, and he could not tell how truly it told the minutes as they crawled by. It seemed that a winter's worth of nights passed before they finally saw a short figure tripping determinedly toward them, keeping close to the wall and muffling its footsteps as much as possible.

It was definitely not a twelve-year-old girl. However, neither was it particularly intimidating. It was a man. A short man alone, his small, pale, forgettable face just visible between his large, lopsided hat and the whorls of his two great scarves. Despite the new arrivals' attempts to hide themselves, he made his way directly toward them, gloved hands slightly raised in a gesture of harmlessness and timid appeal.

"My word. How good it is to find you." There was something odd and drab in his tone. Perhaps it was caused by fear, or a desire to keep his voice low. "Stout fellows capable of swinging a cudgel, just as promised." He paused and seemed to notice for the first time that he was surrounded by suspicious gazes and tense pistol hands. "Friend of Mosca Mye," he offered in the same limp voice.

"Describe her, then," hissed the leader.

"Stands this high." The little man made a flat of his hand and let it droop in the air before him. "Black eyes, black hair, ferrety features." The new arrivals glanced at one another, exchanged nods, and relaxed a little. "Ran into some trouble at the letter drop. Somebody was waiting for her. She got away. Injured though and terrified. Poor child asked me to come in her place." The little man could not seem to keep his head still but kept turning it to look this way and that, eyes luminous and watchful. "And it is a pleasure to speak with you gentlemen, but here there is a danger of interruption. If you will permit me to show you somewhere more relaxing."

He's terrified, concluded the leader. *Well, what do we do? The girl is not here. If we do not trust him, what else can we do and where else can we go?*

In his pocket, his fingertips stroked the knucklebone dice sacred to the Beloved who had given him his name. He chewed his cheek and took a gamble.

The voice that had sounded behind Mosca was adult and male, but crisp and light toned. It sounded as if it might sidestep deeper, gruffer voices without difficulty and deftly jab a pointed remark under their guards.

Mosca leaped away from the sound and spun round, braced to flee into the night. The shape in the doorway behind her, however, made no attempt to lunge for her but remained flattened against the panels of the door, in a strip of darkness that had concealed it from Mosca's notice. She could make out little more than the subdued gleam of a cream waistcoat and the pallor of a face.

"If you are looking for sentries, my dear, you are looking at the wrong wall. There is a fellow who has been sitting in the eaves just across the road from your letter drop ever since quarter past bugle."

"How . . . ?" Mosca trailed off and left the word to fend for itself. There were so many questions it could begin. *How do you know about the letter drop? How did you know I was going there? How did you happen to be here at all? How did you spot the spy?* But all these questions paled in comparison to one other: *How do I know I can trust you?* It was this unasked question that the stranger chose to answer.

"Eponymous Clent sends his greetings to you and your winged war zone." Staring into the darkness, Mosca could now just make out two large eyes, the dark line of a mustache, and neatly cropped sideburns. "I *do* hope that means more to you than it does to me."

It did. "Winged war zone" was just one of Clent's many tender terms for Saracen, usually uttered in a tone of long-suffering despair. It was not a phrase that many would use.

"Might do," she admitted.

"Delighted to hear it. Your friend Mr. Clent wanted us to warn you that the letter drop was compromised— betrayed, in fact. He believes that somebody in the mayor's household is spying for the . . ." He glanced about him before mouthing the last word of the sentence. *Locksmiths.* "Now, can I suggest we go somewhere else, and quickly? If we loiter about on a night like this, we are likely to catch our death. Worse . . . our death might catch us."

21

GOODLADY QUINNET,
FRIEND OF THE WILLING PUPIL

MOSCA FOLLOWED HER new guide back along the wall but kept a distance of three paces between them. She had learned to look every gift horse in the mouth. After all, it was amazing how many of them bit.

When they crossed moon splashes, she took advantage of the instant to examine her companion. He was slightly below average height, deft gestured and dapper, despite the fact that his tailcoat was more of a collage than a garment: patches of dark wool, leather, linen, and curtain fabric nestling in bewildered proximity. Two large, expressive dark eyes kept a watch on the rooftops and corners.

"Hey!" She risked a whisper. "I got to go to the Twilight Gate. There's—"

She halted, her mouth still poised to shape the next

word. A sound had grazed her ear, a distant croaking cry, so muffled that it could almost have been a raven call or cough. But the ravens were all abed, and no cough could have traveled that far, even through the eerily silent streets.

"Ah." Somehow Mosca's mysterious friend managed to put a wealth of meaning into that one light sound.

"That came from the clock tower!" hissed Mosca. "They're in trouble! People waiting there for me!"

"No, I think not," came the clipped response. "Not by now, anyway. Trust me. Let us simply withdraw while we have the chance . . . or . . . instead . . . you could run pell-mell toward the sound of the death cry. Wonderful." He gave a resigned sigh as Mosca's sprinting figure disappeared around a distant corner. "Yes, let us do that instead."

To do him credit, the patchwork stranger succeeded in catching up with Mosca a couple of streets later, only slightly out of breath. Mosca was pressed against a corner from which she could gaze out at the clock tower, which looked back with all its shadowy bulk, as unruffled as a whale suffering the scrutiny of a damselfish.

Nothing remarkable or bloody appeared to be taking place in the street before the tower. Indeed, it was entirely empty and would have looked serene to anybody who did not know that six men should have been standing there. To Mosca, that omission was as glaring as the ragged remains of a ripped-out page.

"They got to be here!" Mosca gnawed at her fist, fighting down a sickness in her stomach. "They got to be here! Nothing works if they're not! Nothing . . . they have to . . ." She trailed off, gasping.

She jumped when her patchwork guide placed a hand on her shoulder. "Listen, my dear, we did promise to warn you of your danger, but nothing was said about joining you in suicidal gallops. Your letter drop was betrayed, as it would seem were your reinforcements.

"Now, this promenade has been charming and exhilarating, but I fear I must go and practice for a recital tomorrow night. So I shall make my adieus. Steady . . . steady—can I recommend that you try breathing?" He patted her arm, then squinted down the street, where one of the shadows had briefly showed signs of movement. "A-a-and perhaps running. Yes, my dear. Definitely time for some running."

Sprinting for ten minutes did nothing to help Mosca recover her breath. She continued running even when she realized that her new guide was no longer at her side. She ran until her legs seemed to become butter and gave out under her, leaving her gulping and shaking against a wall, the feathers on her basket hat aquiver. Then Mosca's mind, which had held together while she needed to remember how to put one foot in front of another, set about unraveling.

The disaster was absolute. The invisible silver lifeline

that had linked her to the bright, safe world of day had snapped. The ambush she had planned for Brand Appleton later that night was impossible, for she had no reinforcements. There was nobody to compel him to reveal the kidnappers' lair. And, she realized with a lurch of the heart, there was no money to pay the tithe for the night of Saint Yacobray.

The very next night, there would be nothing to stop the kidnappers from claiming the ransom, and Brand Appleton would spirit his unwilling bride-to-be out of Toll. Then the dreaded Clatterhorse would ride through the streets, and the Leaps would not be ready for it . . . and so Mosca and the Leaps would be lost.

And she could tell none of this to her day allies because the letter drop was compromised. Did that mean that Clent and his friends were also in danger? Desperately she tried to remember what she had put in her own letter. Had she been cryptic enough? She hoped so.

Mosca closed her eyes, and swallowed, and set about gathering her wits. Reinforcements vanished like smoke. Probably taken by Locksmiths. Probably dead. She muttered a prayer for them under her breath but could not muster much real feeling. To her the lost men were as faceless as eggs, and there was nothing she could do about that. The crushing sense of dread and panic pushed out everything else. She tried to think of Beamabeth's kitten-faced plight but could not help feeling that her own situation was probably worse than that of the mayor's daughter.

For one thing, Beamabeth was the last person in the world Brand Appleton would ever hurt. Mosca Mye, on the other hand, had no such guarantee, and she had an appointment with him that she would have to keep alone.

Cooper's Dark, where Mosca had promised to meet Appleton, turned out to be a nightling version of Cooper's Lane. A series of upper-floor facings had folded down to form a new walkway that roofed the street and turned it into a tunnel. The upper walkway was Cooper's Perch; the lane below, Cooper's Dark. Fortunately a couple of cloaked figures were being led into the darkness by a lantern-wielding link boy, and Mosca was able to follow a few paces behind them in less than total pitch.

Appleton had told her to meet him at Harass and Quail's, opposite the stone trough. Mosca was unsurprised to discover that it was a gin shop.

Mosca's hands were shaking, but she could not pause, even to calm her breathing. Hesitation was weakness, fox blood on the heather that hounds would smell out in an instant.

All right, Mosca Mye, we're going to play a game, she told herself. *A game where Sir Feldroll's reinforcements came through safe and everything's fine and there's six men just waiting in the dark by the wall for your signal. Six men all pistoled up to the teeth, with shoulders broad as a barn. Walk like you got an army in your pocket.*

She pushed open the door. Within, like most of

the nightside buildings, the gin shop was narrow and clenched, stools of varying heights clustering throughout like a mushroom epidemic. Given her preposterous appearance, she was glad to see that the lanterns were dim and low placed, making a great deal of the customers' chins and nose hair and pouches beneath their eyes, but a lot less of their brows and upper cheeks.

Brand Appleton was seated by a wall, beneath a mildewed tapestry of a cavalry charge from the Civil War. Even in the murk, Mosca could see that Appleton's bruises had reached their full plummy glory. He had taken off his gloves and was busy twisting and torturing them in a fit of frowning impatience. To her relief, he appeared to be alone.

She cleared her throat, and he released the gloves, looking up at her suspiciously. She recalled that he had never seen her face before.

"Mr. Appleton," she said, and watched recognition, realization, surprise, and eagerness canter across his features. Usually it made Mosca feel safer when she met somebody whose expression she could read so easily, but somehow with Appleton it was different. The very helplessness with which his emotions escaped him made her feel uneasy. He was open, like a lion-cage door. He was unguarded, like a pistol at full cock.

"Sit down," he said, and winced as the spread of his smile reopened a cut on his lower lip. "I *thought* you sounded young." He looked her strange Seisian regalia up and down, and suspicion came out on a black hobbyhorse to join the caper of other emotions. "So . . . you say you're from *Mandelion?*"

"Not *from*." Mosca scrambled up on a tall stool that left her clogs dangling. "I said I *been* there. The ship I was on had to land somewhere, didn't it?" Mandelion was the area's biggest port, and it seemed the best explanation for the presence of a mysterious foreigner in the town.

"Ship from where?" Suspicion's canter seemed to have slowed to a trot, but Appleton's brows were still furrowed.

Mosca wet her lips, tempted for a second to fling open the sluice gates of her invention and flood Appleton with tales of an exotic eastern past. But she was not Eponymous Clent, so she gave a mental grimace and pushed the images away.

"Not somewhere I'll ever be returning," she muttered sourly. "Not somewhere I'm in a hurry to think about neither. So don't go dwelling on that. Mandelion is all you need to know about." A grim little mystery was better than a tall tale. Less likely to fall on its face, anyway.

She could read Appleton's countenance like an open diary. He had been ready to bargain with some urchin who knew Mandelion, but strange green foreignness had confused everything. He was comparing her outlandish dress with her commonplace accent. He was wondering whether she was an impostor. And the possibility that she might actually *be* a heathen from the distant east had sent his small-town mind hunkering down in its kennel and growling suspiciously.

Mosca chewed her cheek, testing the edge of the situation with her mind, and then took a gamble. She let herself down from her stool.

"I see how it is," she snapped. "You're no different from all the others. One glimpse of a green face, and you're climbing up the curtains like there's a tiger in the room. Well, worry not, the tiger is leaving. You can stew in your own juice, Mr. Not-So-Radical Appleton."

She made a small and hopefully Seisian-looking gesture with the entwined middle fingers of her right hand and then strode sulkily toward the door. Push something in someone's face, and they will shove it away reflexively. Threaten to snatch it away from them, and sometimes they become convinced that it is what they want.

But Appleton had not called her back. She reached the door. Her fingers brushed the handle.

"Er, no—wait! Wait!"

Without turning, the mysterious foreigner allowed herself a small green smile.

"Come back—come, sit down. No more questions about your homeland. I promise."

Mosca had to wrestle the grin off her face before she could turn around. In the end she managed this by reminding herself that, yes, she had persuaded the fish to bite down on the hook, but that she was armed with a small and fragile rod and faced by a large, dangerous, and unpredictable catch. With a grudging air she trailed back to the table and seated herself with all the regality of a shrunken empress.

"So you want to know how to be a radical."

"Yes—and I wanted to know—what did you mean about walking on the grass?"

"I meant . . ." Mosca took a moment to think of all the radicals she had met. "The heart of being a radical isn't knowing all the right books, it isn't about kings over the sea or the parliament over in the capital. It's . . . looking at the world *around* you and seeing the things that make you sick to the stomach with anger. The things there's no point making a fuss about because that's just the way the world is, and always was and always will be. And then it means getting good and angry about it anyway, and kickin' up a hurricane. Because nothing is writ across the sky to say the world must be this way. A tree can grow two hundred years, and look like it'll last a thousand more—but when the lightning strikes at last, it *burns*, Mr. Appleton."

Brand Appleton's gaze was unblinkingly intense, and he seemed to be memorizing her every word.

"Toll," he said under his breath. "A thousand injustices, bound up in one set of town walls . . ."

"A rotten, stinking gin trap of a town," agreed Mosca. "I can teach you all about seeing things the radical way. It will take lessons, though."

"Yes, yes!" Brand Appleton entwined both his hands into a giant fist and bounced it off the surface of the table. "I have given this thought. A good deal of lessons.

So it is best if you teach me on the way."

Mosca suddenly had the feeling that her great fish had just jerked at her line. She had formed plans for Brand Appleton's lessons, and the words "on the way" had not been involved.

"On the . . . On the way to where?"

"Mandelion." Brand Appleton glanced up at her, surprised and a bit impatient. Perhaps he expected her to have kept up with his unspoken thought processes. "Mandelion, obviously. You are clearly a traveler—you cannot be too fond of Toll-by-Night, surely? I will need you to come with me when I leave tomorrow night, that is very plain. I need a guide who knows the best way to Mandelion. Someone to explain radicalism en route. Somebody to make introductions when I get there. You need money. You *must* need money, or you would not be here."

Beneath her thinly painted nationality, Mosca went pale. Brand Appleton was planning to leave the very next night—immediately after the hours of Saint Yacobray. He must already have a buyer for the jewel. Just as Sir Feldroll had suspected, Appleton would seize the ransom, sell it, and leave with his captive "fiancée" before anybody could act. And now he wanted to take Mosca with him, back through the county she had tried so hard to escape, maybe in company with Skellow and his minions, to a town that she had been forbidden to reenter.

"How much money?" she croaked.

The sum he named was large enough that Mosca's

hands crept down to the stool top to steady herself. "Not all at once, though. I'll pay your way out of Toll first. The rest when we reach Mandelion."

Mosca's plan was going either really really well or really really badly. She could not quite work out which. The fish was still hooked, but it appeared to be pulling her tiny rowboat out to sea.

"All right, Mr. Appleton. Tomorrow, then. Tomorrow night. When and where?"

"Two of the clock in Chaff's Dryppe."

For the second time, Mosca let herself down from the stool. She could only hope that her shivering would be blamed upon the bitter cold.

"Wait." She tensed, but turned to find that Appleton was smiling. "I forgot to ask your name. This night-bound hellhole has destroyed my manners."

It was a question that Mosca should have anticipated, the one question she could not answer falsely and could not afford to answer truthfully, for "Mosca" was hardly likely to be mistaken for a Seisian name. But there are always ways of not answering a question at all.

"You better call me Teacher. I got a real name, but"— Mosca remembered the beadle in the white pavilion—"but in this country nobody's tongues are pointy enough to say it properly. Till tomorrow, Mr. Appleton." And a mysterious green stranger walked out of the gin house, hoping that she could come up with a very cunning plan in the twenty-four hours before their next meeting.

22

GOODMAN CLUTTERPICK,
LORD OF THE JUMBLE

MORTAL TERROR, LIKE most things, is relative. Mosca was right in thinking that the majority of people in Toll-by-Night lived in fear, but some lived with more of it than others. And at that moment one man was living with about as much of it as a person could stand without shaking himself into pieces.

A short while ago, this unfortunate individual had been the leader of half a dozen men sent by Sir Feldroll to find Beamabeth Marlebourne. Now he was just a terrified, two-legged jelly. His mind was full of the ferocity of the wind that buffeted and swayed him and the prickle of sweat droplets as they traced a course along his back and neck, then out of his collar and up into his hair. Or, to put it more accurately, *down* into his hair, since that was currently the lowermost thing about him.

When ambushed and captured, he had prayed to the Beloved with all his might and main that he would live long enough to find himself outside the walls of Toll. Being dangled upside down from one of the coffin chutes in the western wall above the precipitous Langfeather gorge had not been exactly what he had meant.

His knucklebone dice fell out of his pocket and bounced off the underside of his chin, and he could only watch as his luck and the favor of his Beloved plunged toward the half-visible roar that was the Langfeather. Wind-bitten scraps of a conversation above him reached his ears.

"What *are* you doing?" A rasping voice like pumice that he had not heard before.

"One of the spies, master guildsman." A matter-of-fact sparrow-chatter voice, belonging to the man who had fastened the rope about the captive's ankles. "Weren't too talkative, so I thought maybe something was stuck in his throat. If you turn 'em upside down and shake 'em, all sorts of things fall out."

"We have no time for this kind of game." The first voice again, impatient, cold. "One of his fellows has already told us more than enough of their mission. This man is an unnecessary waste of our time. You had better . . . let him go."

The spirits of the suspended man soared skyward, and just as quickly yo-yoed back down again as it occurred to him that right now the last thing he wanted was for somebody to "let him go." Worse still, he could feel hands busy with the ropes around his ankles, confirming his worst fears. This could be his last moment.

"Wait! Stop! I can tell you more than the others! I was the one who received our orders from Sir Feldroll! Please! Stop!"

A short pause, and then the captive felt himself being hauled back up the chute, an inch at a time. Tears of relief and humiliation flooded his eyes and ran up his forehead.

Ten minutes later Aramai Goshawk knew everything the terrified man could tell him. As a matter of fact, he had known most of it already, since the other five captives had been subjected to exactly the same ordeal and offhand-sounding conversation and had cracked with equal speed.

When it became clear that there would be nothing more from this prisoner but sobbing and expressions of his wish to see his family again, Goshawk had him locked up. It was, after all, still just possible that a use might be found for him and his fellows. Goshawk was not surprised that he had broken—like most desperate men, he had leaped for the only chink of hope he could see. The important thing, Goshawk knew, was to make sure that there *was* a chink of hope. Men who despaired, who were *truly* desperate, became dangerous. The night of Saint Yacobray, for example, was a carefully judged exercise in fear. Most people would manage to pay the tithe, and only a tiny minority would fail—and these could serve as warnings to the others.

To look into the pale eyes of Aramai Goshawk was to peer into a winter forest. Stark, wakeful, birdless, colorless, all its paths hidden beneath a smothering of white. You could stagger through it for leagues until you gave up hope, and your every footstep would be remembered, preserved, and analyzed by the unforgiving snow.

He understood fear too well to allow it a foothold in his mind. If you had pointed a pistol at his head, he would have looked at it with interest, noting every visible detail of its construction, because he knew that everything around him, even the weapons of his enemies, was a tool waiting for him to use it. It was almost impossible to frighten him, but with a little work it was possible to annoy him.

Right now he was downright irritated. In the world according to Goshawk, if somebody wanted something stolen, they should come to him. And if they wanted to recover something that had been stolen, they should come to him.

He mulled over what he had learned from his prisoners, from the two cryptic letters that had been found in the secret drop in the town wall, from the reports of his spy placed close to the mayor. A set of amateurs in Toll-by-Night, *his* town, had set their minds on the theft of a valuable young heiress, and they had not come to him, nor to the Locksmiths at all. Instead they had managed the matter themselves without as much offering the Locksmiths a cut or tithe.

Worse still, the mayor had not approached the Locksmiths about recovering his daughter. Nor had he told the Locksmiths that he was sending in armed men to rescue her. That was worse than rude, that was *trespassing*.

Last but not least, two familiar names had been brought to his attention. For some reason the charlatan poet Eponymous Clent and his girl, Mye, had become involved in the mayor's business. Was Clent still spying for the Stationers' Company as he had been in Mandelion, or was he working on his own agenda? If Clent did have his own scheme, Goshawk suspected that it would be small-minded, selfish, and poorly planned, but he had noticed that Clent had a tiresome talent for entangling himself in more important matters. Eponymous Clent would need to be watched.

So—how could the whole situation be turned to his advantage? It seemed from his captives' whimpering that a ransom was soon to be paid, though they could not say exactly what, when, or where. Well, let it be paid. Even with the money the kidnappers could not leave the night town without his permission. If they did not offer the Locksmiths a suitably tempting deal, then why not capture them *and* their ransom, then bargain with the mayor for a reward for finding the girl?

Nobody but the Locksmiths, therefore, should be

allowed to return the heiress to her father. The immediate threat had been defeated with the ambush of Sir Feldroll's men. The child Mye had not appeared at the rendezvous point and had thus escaped capture, but that did not worry Goshawk greatly. If she was not already dead, then she had undoubtedly been scared into going to ground. She would be alone, unaided and incapable of receiving further orders from her scheming employer, so Goshawk could not imagine that she would cause further trouble.

However annoying this amateur kidnapping was, however, Goshawk had larger fish to fry. He could not afford to be distracted from the imminent culmination of his own plans.

The mayor suspects nothing, he reflected, *and by this time tomorrow night the mayor should be ready to do whatever I say.*

"Mistress Leap! Let me in!"

The front door opened a crack, allowing a greenish foreigner, a groggy midwife, and an emerald goose a sliver view of each other, and then was opened properly so that Mosca could enter.

"You still don't look too well, Mistress Leap."

"Oh, no, no, it's nothing serious." The midwife gave a slightly cross-eyed smile and dropped into her favorite chair. "Nothing that a little rest won't fix."

This answer was not as reassuring as it was clearly

meant to be, and Mosca insisted in finding a cup of kill-grief for her hostess before sitting down.

"Mistress Leap," she began at last, "we're in a lot of trouble. The men who were going to help us were snatched by the Locksmiths right by the Twilight Gate. So we got no money and no reinforcements . . . and I can't get word to my dayside friends. We're . . ."

Plucked, stuffed, and spitted, Palpitattle helpfully suggested in Mosca's head.

"We're . . . going to have to think of something else," Mosca said instead. "Really really fast."

Unfortunately, Mosca and the Leaps were not alone in their desperation. Everybody in Toll-by-Night had a wild and panicky look, as if they could hear the Clatterhorse snapping its dry teeth an inch behind their necks. Nobody was in the mood to give or lend. A few parents with newborns dug out coins for Mistress Leap through gratitude, but it was a tiny fraction of the amount needed.

An hour later, therefore, Mosca and Welter Leap were shoving their way through the unusually crowded streets, loaded down with every rickety, moth-eaten stick of furniture that could be spared.

An outing with the morose and quietly bitter Welter Leap was not a prospect that filled Mosca with joy, but carrying the furniture clearly required two people, and she was fairly certain that Mistress Leap should not be

on her feet right now. In the end she had left Saracen
behind to guard the midwife again.

Mosca had a bad feeling about their odds of selling
their furniture as soon as she noticed the throngs around
the Pawnbrokers, hefting everything from fire irons to
mattresses. They pushed their way into the shop and
found it in uproar. The woman at the front of the queue
was gripping the counter, gasping as if she had been
dowsed with water.

"You cannot offer so little! A table like this one . . . no
worm, good joinery . . ."

"'Tis a buyer's market this night, madam," the fat
little man behind the counter told her, his jewel glass
bulging in his eye. "Everybody selling, nobody buying. I
tell you, you will get no better for it in all Toll. Now take
the money, or make way for those who will."

The woman's face crumpled like a rose and her
eyes brimmed, but she snatched up the paltry collection of coins on the counter and shoved her way out to
the street. Her place in the throng was filled instantly,
fists thrust across the counter gripping bead necklaces,
battered skillets, mats woven from grass, embroidered
napkins.

As the crowd surged forward, Mosca was forced
against the wall, nobody paying her the slightest heed
as the antlers of someone's mounted stag head scraped
past her face. Her mind filled with rage, but it was not
rage toward the frenzied crowd in danger of trampling

her. It was anger at all the smug little men like the one behind the counter, who had reckoned the odds and realized that they could squeeze this panicking throng for everything they had. She could not blame the crowd's desperation. She understood it too well.

Desperation is a millstone. It wears away at the very soul, grinding away pity, kindness, humanity, and courage. But sometimes it whets the mind to a sharpened point and creates moments of true brilliance. And as she stood there, nose tickled by the dusty hide of the stuffed deer head, such a moment visited Mosca Mye.

With difficulty she fought her way out to the street, dragging Welter after her. He did not resist but regarded her with the quiet loathing usually shown toward scabs or cold sores.

"It's hopeless," Mosca said when she had recovered her breath. "If they're only payin' half a sneeze for that table, then what we got here won't raise more than a sniffle. Even if we sell it all, and our hair and teeth thrown in, we'll never get enough on *this* night."

A gentle, melancholy smile eased its way onto Welter Leap's face. He seemed to be settling into despair as into a particularly comfortable armchair.

"But we're not done yet," Mosca snarled under her breath. "How much money we got right now, Mr. Leap? Hmm. Well, it's not much—but it might do. That chubby little leech got it right—this is a night for buyers, not sellers. So we're not going to sell. We're going to buy."

* * *

Mistress Leap opened the door to them with a cold cloth clamped to her wounded temple. Her expression, initially a free-for-all skirmish between hope, apprehension, and relief, froze slightly as she realized that Mosca and her husband had returned carrying, if anything, more than when they had left the house.

"What . . . ?" It was the stuffed stag head in Mosca's arms that finally seemed to fracture the midwife's mind. Welter Leap, on the other hand, had a soft moony glow in his eyes, a tender eagerness as he carried his boxes of new acquisitions into his workshop.

"I—what—where did you get these?"

"They was all going for a pittance, Mistress Leap."

"You—you went bargain hunting?" whispered the woman faintly as Mosca saw to the bolts. She sank into a seat, her eyes filling with tears, and regarded Mosca with a look of weary disappointment and betrayal. "You *spent* the few coins I managed to scrape together? Then . . ." She shook her head, closed her eyes, and let her head droop.

"There was no help for it, Mistress Leap." Mosca felt a sting of compassion, but she had already cast the die for all three of them. "It's the only chance we got. Listen! We could have run down every street with your goods on our backs and got nothing for them but spit and a wink. All *this*"—Mosca set down a box of ropes, dry bones, and coils of wire—"is nothing now, but thanks to your husband's making ways and cunning hands, it'll be a miracle by the next dusk bugle."

"A miracle. Yes, we will need a miracle." Mistress Leap sighed.

"I'll tell you what kind of miracle, as well," Mosca persisted, her eyes black and steady as a coal face. "A miracle that will get us our tithe, easy as yawning. Because tomorrow night all the money we need will be right there to be grabbed—just hanging outside everybody's doors! So we go out and we take it. And nobody will stop us, because if they look out their windows they'll see just what they expect to see. A Clatterhorse taking the vegetables from outside the houses. Your husband's going to make us our *own* Clatterhorse, Mistress Leap."

"But . . ." Mistress Leap sat bolt upright. "But . . . we cannot! The Locksmiths would—"

"If we cannot find the chink in time, mistress, the Locksmiths will see us river fodder anyway," Mosca pointed out.

"But . . . if we take others' tithes, then other households will suffer, other families, nobody deserves—"

"Nobody? What if we take a tithe from outside a pawnbroker's?" There was grit and venom in Mosca's grin. "Locksmiths might not trip over 'emselves to attack another guild. And even if those potbellied, bloodsucking leeches *do* end up being chased up and down a few streets by a horse made of bone, *I* won't be weeping out my heart's juice."

391

"If anybody sees us . . ." Mistress Leap had her hands pressed to her temples as if her thoughts were trying to fight their way out. "If the Locksmiths ever found out . . . If *anybody* ever finds out . . ."

"The urchin is right," called Welter from his workshop, over a rasp of earnest sawing. "It is our only chance, Leveretia."

"And not just ours," added Mosca. "In a few hours the mayor will look for a letter to say his daughter has been rescued. If it is not there, then come dusk he will hang the ransom outside his counting house. Then Skellow and Appleton and those other fine boys will dance out and snatch it. And by dawn they'll be out of Toll and halfway to Mandelion, with Miss Marlebourne slung over one shoulder like a rug.

"And the only way we can stop them is to prevent them getting the ransom. Gallop there ahead of them. Steal it first."

The sky paled relentlessly. From black to charcoal, to a greasy gray, to apple-flesh white. Then the Jinglers swept the town, and the nightfolk were sealed away, with nothing more they could do to prepare for the tithe except tear up floorboards and shake furniture in search of stray coins. The day doors opened, the colors came out to play, and the people of Toll-by-Day emerged to complain about the cold and the price of pepper.

By midmorning, unbeknownst to the populace, a blazing row was taking place at the mayor's house. Sir Feldroll was doing most of the blazing.

Until now he had taken a good deal of care to be polite and deferential in the mayor's house. However, he was growing increasingly tired of pretending that he was not the heir to a full-blown and powerful city, visiting the petty official of a self-important provincial town. Toll's power was its position, and its position was starting to drive him steadily insane.

"My lord mayor, listen to me! No message has been left by the men I sent into the night. None! And no word from Clent's girl. Nothing! My men are gone, and the girl is probably dead too. They have failed. Are you still determined to leave out that ransom?"

"Would you have me do otherwise?" flared the mayor. "What is a jewel compared to my daughter?" The mayor had a groggy, punch-drunk air, though the only blows he had received were loss of his daughter, lack of sleep, and the incessant battering ram of his guest's conversation.

"Then the kidnappers will flee with both the jewel and Miss Marlebourne as soon as they can. My lord mayor, you *must* allow me to bring troops through Toll this very day, so that they can be waiting to catch them on the western side! Appleton is a radical—where would he flee but to Mandelion?"

"If I do this, without charging toll for your troops, then Toll will be declaring war on Mandelion! Your army will march on and lay siege to her, do not deny it! We have always, *always* remained neutral—"

"My lord mayor, with the *greatest* of respect, neutrality is a luxury you can no longer afford! Mandelion must be crushed, or other radicals like Appleton will be inflamed and inspired! Radicals cannot be wiped out if they have a whole city to flee to whenever they wish to escape the consequences of their crimes!"

The mayor gazed out through his window toward the clock tower, now partly hidden by scaffolding for the repairs of the clock, and Sir Feldroll could guess all too well what was in his mind. It was the Luck, the infernal Luck of Toll. They all acted this way, the people of Toll, gazing like trusting children toward the clock tower where the Luck was held, knowing in their hearts that nothing *too* terrible could happen, because the Luck would not permit it.

Sir Feldroll had no faith in the Luck's ability to hold up the bridge, protect Toll from attack, or extract Beamabeth Marlebourne from the clutches of her captors. In fact he was starting to wonder if the clock tower would have to be burned to the ground before he could get a sensible conversation out of anybody.

"Sir Feldroll, no troops will pass through the town this day. But if with the next dawn my daughter is not returned to me in exchange for the ransom . . . I shall give permission for your men to march through Toll without payment."

An army of arguments massed in Sir Feldroll's mind, but he held them back and bade them build camp until they were needed. The mayor's promise would do. It would have to do.

"Very well. I shall send orders for our troops to approach Toll, ready to pass through once we have your permission."

The sun slid lazily downward, ignoring all those who prayed for it to stay longer in the sky. The low moon brightened, and the town went through its dusk ritual of shudder, rattle, and shift.

In the alcove below the clock face on the clock tower, the figure of a little goodman receded joltily. With a mechanical clatter like tin hooves, a shape with a skeletal horse's head replaced it. The night of Saint Yacobray had arrived, and now nothing could prevent his deathly canter.

23

SAINT YACOBRAY,
RIDER OF THE HORSE OF BONE

THE SIGHT OF a Clatterhorse should chill one to the bone. Sure enough, when Mosca surveyed the result of Welter Leap's day of manic construction, she was struck dumb with a sense of acute dread and foreboding. However, this was not because it was an image of Death in a bridle.

"You sure it'll even hold together?" Mistress Leap prodded it doubtfully. Its jaw promptly fell open and then off, just to prove a point. The stuffed stag head had been painted in flour paste and charcoal to give it a skeletal look, and its horns had been sawed away, but this had not been enough. It needed a jaw to snap, or nobody would mistake it for a Clatterhorse. So Welter had cunningly crafted hinged jaws of wood that clapped open and shut when you pulled a string. Sadly, despite all his skill, it looked very little like a skeletal horse, and more like a deer that had gotten its head stuck in a xylophone. The bulging glass bottle-top eyes might have been a mistake as well, in hindsight.

"It'll look better in the moonlight," declared Mosca with more certainty than she felt. Welter gave his wife a baleful glare as he set about nailing the jaw back into place.

The body of the horse was a series of curved frames over which was thrown a mass of coal-stained blankets, sewn together by Mistress Leap and studded with dry chicken and mutton bones. There was just enough room for three people to hide inside the main section, in single file. The rearmost portion of the horse was a separate cavity, and within this a large sack hung from the frame, so that stolen goods and tools for hasty repairs could be carried in it.

"And what if we meet the real . . . ?" Mistress Leap could not muster the courage to complete the question.

"We won't." Mosca hoped she was right. "We'll only be out on the streets a little while. B'sides, the Clatterhorse clatters as it goes, don't it? We hear it coming, we skedaddle." The midwife seemed a good deal recovered but was still a little pale and fragile, so Mosca thought it best to sound as cheerful as possible.

As the first bugle sounded, Mosca looked for Saracen to wish him farewell—a temporary farewell, she hoped. But during the night he had vanished into the farthest recesses of the room in search of new and inconvenient places to sleep, and despite a tug at her heart she knew there was no time to make a thorough search for him.

"Hssst!" Welter grimaced them all into silence. There came a silver jingle outside, then the slam and click of the false house facing being swung away and locked into its nighttime position. All three of them held their breath, frozen into the hunch-shouldered, guilty posture reserved exclusively for those who are about to launch into forbidden streets with a fake spectral horse.

The jingling faded, and Mosca unlocked and unbolted the door, and opened it just enough to peer up and down the street.

"Now!" she mouthed. Her accomplices ducked into the horse through special flaps in the cloth cover, and Mosca threw the door wide. The newborn Clatterhorse shuddered, lifted slightly, whispered to itself furiously, then wobbled forward two feet and head-butted the doorjamb.

"Oh, pig on a spit! Left a bit! No, left! Here—this way!" The dread Clatterhorse was guided out into the brilliantly moonlit street through tugs to the muzzle. Then its green stable girl locked the front door behind it and crept back inside its belly.

Even somebody watching the Clatterhorse's jolting progress would not have guessed at the full extent of the confusion inside it. Welter had had the foresight to cut eyeholes in the cloth covering, but they were scattered at odd heights and let in very little light. Mistress Leap was foremost, holding up the front of the horse's body frame, while her husband supported the back, so that the whole thing was raised from the ground and could be carried around. Mosca, in the middle, was on clattering duty. She turned a wooden handle that somehow created a clicketing noise not completely unlike the galloping of bone hooves. Mistress Leap quickly proved a somewhat skittish horse head, given to stopping or veering sideways without warning. In short, they were all trapped in a darkness full of trodden toes, sudden elbows, squawks, whispers, and the smell of moldy blanket.

Clicket-a-clicket-a-clicket. The rattle dinted the icy, motionless air. At the sound, householders who had stepped outside to tie up their tithe vegetables scurried back inside again. Doors were slammed and shutters fastened by the time the Clatterhorse jogged unsteadily into view, deer head gently bobbing, its glass goggle eyes little mirrors of the perfect moon overhead.

It came to an uneasy halt just in front of a pawnbroker's shop. Two small green hands emerged from a slit in its side just long enough to yank a hanging turnip from its string. The horse then wheeled about and lurched off back the way it came.

"Here it is . . . stop . . . Ow! Stop!" The horse halted by committee, and the green hands emerged again, this time to tie the turnip outside the Leaps' front door. "Now—the counting house!"

Clicket-a-clicket-a-clicket. Every street was aglitter, sugared with frost as if some master chef had fashioned an entire candied town for the Clatterhorse's snapping jaws. From the porticoes and icicle-fanged eaves hung beets and potatoes, cabbages and carrots. The Clatterhorse was evidently in two minds about these juicy trophies, and kept veering toward them, only to lurch away from them again.

Within the dread beast's flanks, an ardent but whispered argument was taking place.

"No!" The horse's head was adamant. "We cannot steal our neighbors' vegetables! It would be no better than murder!"

"I think we can," murmured the animal's rear. "I am almost certain it would be quite possible."

"Hush!" hissed the horse's stomach. "Listen! You hear that?" She halted her handle cranking, and for the first time the sound that had been drowned by their own clattering and whispering became audible to all of them.

Clacket-a-clack. Clacket-a-clack. A sound like Death drumming his fingers.

"Oh no," breathed Mistress Leap. "It's the *real* Clatterhorse! The Locksmiths!"

"Quick!" growled Welter. "Down that alley!" The deer-headed Clatterhorse hoisted its skirts and sprinted. It reached the darkness of the alley with mere seconds to spare before another apparition turned the corner.

A shape lurched and twisted into view, its motion

grotesquely playful despite its bulk. Moonlight creamed over the sheep's skull at the crest of its long willow-pole neck. The red ribbons that fluttered from its eye sockets gave it a festive ghastliness. The body was a shaggy mass of fluttering rags, patches, and ribbons that trailed right down to the ground.

The skull turned this way and that on its stick neck, as if the horse was eyelessly scanning the icy street for prey. A slender rod tugged at its jaw so that it snapped with a *clacket-a-clack*, and Mosca had the uncomfortable feeling that it was tasting the air and would catch the flavor of their fear.

Everybody in the deer horse held their breath. And then, just as it seemed they would escape detection, Welter released his breath in a wordless cry of anguish. Mosca turned and found that a spectral green-white something, curved like the spine of a harp, had risen out of the tool sack at the back of the horse, in which it had presumably been sleeping, and had seized Welter by the nose.

"Aaag! Ged de blarmuggin bird off by nose!"

"Saracen!"

There is an ideal time and a place for everything, particularly the discovery of unexpected homicidal geese. This moment of necessary stealth was not that time, and the confines of a fake horse not that place.

Clacket-a-clack. The sheep skull's jaw snap-snapped as it turned to gaze sightlessly toward their hiding place.

"It's heard us!" commented Mosca, proving it was possible to screech under one's breath. The next moment she was nearly knocked from her feet. Mistress Leap had taken to her heels down the alley, hauling the rest of the horse with her. They took a high-speed left, bouncing slightly off the corner as they went, and then another.

"Is it chasin' us, Mr. Leap?"

Gargling noises behind her suggested that Welter was still suffering from a goose-related speech impediment. Mosca could feel the rasp of busy wing feathers against the back of her neck. It was virtually impossible to see out now, the eyeholes jogging up and down too much to be useful. As they slowed for a second corner, Mosca pushed the entrance flap open a slit and dared a glance down the alley behind them. It was empty.

"Mistress Leap, I don't think it's—*aaarghh!*"

In speaking to the midwife, she had turned her head to face forward again. Thus, when they turned the corner, she had an immediate eyeful of the solitary figure waiting ahead of them. It was the very monster they had just fled, standing squarely in their path, dark ribbons aflutter. Mosca's shrill shriek of surprise was matched by that of Mistress Leap, who brought the deer-head Clatterhorse to a jarring halt.

"Back! Back!" Mistress Leap yanked her end of the frame widdershins, so that the whole deer-horse was dragged head-about-tail to face the other way, and set off at an impressive gallop. Just as the entrance flap fell back into place and cut off her view of the street, Mosca had the strange impression that the other horse was also whirling around to depart in the opposite direction. Perhaps it was playing with them, slipping away to head them off again until they ran themselves into exhaustion.

Running, however, still seemed an excellent idea. After sprinting down several streets without pursuit, it became clear that Mistress Leap, true to her horsey role, had panicked, lost her wits, and bolted, taking the rest of them with her.

"They saw us" was all she would say when Mosca finally calmed her and persuaded her to slow. "They-sawustheysawustheysawus . . ." Even Mistress Leap, who would dare murderer-infested streets every moonlit night, could apparently be reduced to twittering help-lessness by fear of the Locksmiths.

"We got unlucky." Mosca stifled the superstitious whispers in her own mind and was glad that nobody could see her face in the darkness. "We rolled black dice, mistress, that's all—but no matter, we got to roll those dice again. We got to go back for that gem. If we don't grab it, somebody else will—maybe Skellow's boys, maybe the Locksmiths, maybe both if they're hand in glove. We got to race them all to that ransom, or we can say good-bye to Beamabeth Marlebourne and our own escape."

By day, the mayor's counting house was in a broad and fresh-faced street, favored for promenades despite its steepness. By night it turned treacherous, bristling with sudden alleys, its slope snared with unseen ice.

A head gingerly emerged from one such alley and tilted to peer uphill toward the counting house. It was a smudgily painted deer's head with no horns.

"The radish is still there!" came the word from Mistress Leap. "I can see it hanging from the lintel of the counting house!"

Mosca felt her spirits rocket. "Quick! Let's grab it and—"

Clacket-a-clacket-a-clack.

Without warning, a shaggy shape barreled up the street past their alleyway hiding place, paying them not the slightest notice. There was no mistaking the spindly neck, the sheep's skull rattling at its crest. The other Clatterhorse was making a beeline for the counting house and its precious radish, ignoring all the other vegetables arrayed to tempt it.

"Oh, frog spawn!"

"What do we do?"

There was no time to do anything, or even to answer the question. It was scarcely out of Mistress Leap's mouth before they heard another sound, this time from the uphill end of the street beyond the counting house.

Click. Clickclickclick. Clickclick.

Near the top of the street, something black had stepped out of the shadows with macabre grace. Something with the figure of a man, its arms and legs of

404

spidery slenderness. Rising above its shoulders gleamed a ghastly hobbyhorse head, its eye sockets hollow and its grimace charnel white. From its shoulders hung a mantle of willow sticks, which dangled like finger bones and clicked against one another as it moved. It stirred up every nightmare of beast-headed men who ate the hearts of children. It was a third Clatterhorse, and this one carried two long knives in its hands.

This did not, however, daunt the sheep-skull-headed horse, which continued its uphill charge toward the counting house even when the shadowy two-legged horse broke into a sprint to meet it. Sheep-skull reached the counting house first, and Mosca saw its skeletal jaw close about the radish, biting clean through the string. Instead of making its own snatch at the prize, however, the shadowy man horse flung itself at the main body of the sheep-skull horse. Its clenched fists plunged deep into the sheep-skull's ragged coat, driving in its daggers with all the force of its charge.

There was a rough, tearing cry of pain and surprise. The sheep-skull horse kept its feet but reeled. Its skeletal jaw fell open, spilling the radish onto the street. The man horse aimed a snatch at the falling vegetable, but it rebounded off his knuckles and skipped away down the sloping street, slave to every quirk of the cobbles.

The occupants of the deer-headed Clatterhorse watched openmouthed as the radish danced past their hiding place, then, without need for discussion, set off in pursuit.

The radish liked the central drainage ditch. Then it jolted off a boundary stone and found it liked the nearby breakneck flight of steps even better. Down and away it bounced, dwindling into darkness, its flourish of greenery trailing like a plume. After it scrambled the deer horse, glass eyes agoggle, then the man horse, and finally the tottering sheep skull.

Certainty of disaster filled Mosca's head from the moment the ground gave out under her and she realized she was running down steps. She could barely see her own feet, and these steps had been worn into slapdash slopes by centuries of soles. It was too fast, then it was faster, and then the frame she was gripping lurched and tilted around her, throwing her off balance. Her falling foot caught a step edge, and the next caught nothing. A wall clobbered her in the flank; then, with a ghastly inevitability, the deer horse tipped headlong amid snapping and splintering, and the stone angles came up to bite.

Mosca lay in a heap of pain, smothered by the "horsehide" blankets. Mistress Leap had broken part of her fall, but she had broken part of Welter's fall, and her role as the filling in a Leap sandwich was crushing the breath out of her.

She wriggled her head and torso free and shook the blankets from her face so that she could breathe. The first thing she saw was the man horse leaping over her head, his boot sole nearly grazing her nose, and landing on the cobbles beyond.

The second thing she saw, looking back up the steps, was the ragged mass of the sheep skull tearing down toward her with a haste born of lost balance. She was too terrified even to scream, but fortunately the sheep skull's occupants seemed to be devoting a fair bit of lung power to that themselves.

Then the sheep skull was upon them, plunging them into darkness filled with the thunder of unhorselike boots. Mosca took a kick to the shoulder and felt a foot fall not an inch from her head. Damp ribbons and greasy wool trailed across her face. A moment later she had the moonlight back and was gasping air into her lungs. She prodded and tugged at the blanket around her until a head-and-shoulder–shaped bulge rose up on either side of her. With whimpers and sobs of pain, the deer horse staggered unsteadily to its feet again, its wooden ribs jutting and its head quizzically tilted.

The radish, the radish! Nothing mattered but the radish.

The man horse was running up and down the alley at a stoop, scanning every gutter, its lean body quivering with agitation. The sheep skull was also stumbling about the lane, no longer capering, twisting this way and that in search. The radish was nowhere to be seen.

And then the arctic silence of that realization was broken by a clear, crisp sound, like a mirror shattered by a bone knife.

Clatter-clack. Clatter-clack. Clatter-clatter-clack.

A clean, loud, hard sound that might chip the walls as it echoed off them. A sound the very hills would hear, and pull their forests about them for comfort. Suddenly the "horses" in the street became figures in a play, carnival games with a deer's head and a child's hobbyhorse and a sheep skull found by the roadside.

The clatter hushed for an instant as if somewhere a black theater curtain was being drawn back, and then the real Clatterhorse rode into view, flames burning in the depths of its bone-rimmed eyes.

24

GOODMAN HOBBLEROOT,
NURSE OF THE BITTER WOUND

THERE WAS A moment of utter paralysis, a cool droplet of moon madness. Large as a real horse, the Clatterhorse stood in the street, white winter steam huffing from flank and muzzle. Like a knight's horse it wore armor, but there was no knight and the armor was bone. Frills, and spikes, and scales of bone, rough and sallow as old wood, and bone blades jutting from its black wheels.

The night could hold its breath no longer. A breeze rose, and the candle flames deep in the monster's eye sockets flared. A chorus of whetstone swishes, and suddenly its flanks were bristling with swords. The man horse took only half a second of quivering contemplation before spinning about and taking to his heels.

"RUN!" shrilled Mosca with all the power of her lungs. But her legs were tangled and unsteady, her companions still rising. Worse still, as she watched, the front half of the sheep-skull horse staggered and slumped, bringing the whole creation crashing down at the base of the steps to block Mosca's own escape route.

However, terror is the most calming thing in the world. Nothing makes life simpler. Suddenly nothing mattered but escaping the Clatterhorse as it glided closer. Now the phantomlike sheep-skull horse, with its bloodred ribbons, was just something in the way.

"Run! Runrunrunrun!"

Everything was frenzy and yet had the numb, painful slowness of a dream chase. Still draped in their splintered horse, Mosca and the Leaps lurched to their feet and scrambled over the prone sheep-skull beast in a bid to reach the street. Blanket-cloaked limbs stirred and squirmed under the weight of Mosca's knees and elbows. Without warning, a black-gloved hand shot out of the sheep skull's ragged trappings, raking wildly at the deer head's blanket hide. Mosca glimpsed a gleam of metal and felt the hooked fingers draw lines of cold across her knee.

A second later she was past the sprawl. Her clogs found the cobbles, and before she knew it she was running. Her spirits returned to her in a rush as she found the Leaps keeping pace, the little cloth horse galloping along around her. At the same time there was the warming, sickening, shameful relief that the sheep skull had stumbled, that it would probably draw the attention of the Clatterhorse just long enough for Mosca and her friends to escape.

Mosca ran as if the Clatterhorse behind her was no beast of strings and stitchwork, as if there were no gloved and pitiless hands holding its dozen gleaming blades. At that moment it might as well have been the bone-scaled beast of legend with invisible Yacobray straddling its back.

By the time the deer-head horse had holed up in the pleasure garden, panting with the force of six exhausted lungs, it became clear that Mosca and the Leaps had successfully shaken off all the monstrous and dangerous creatures besetting them. This included the real Clatterhorse, the sheep-skull Clatterhorse, and the man Clatterhorse. Unfortunately this also included Saracen.

Mosca was frantic and might have run back to look for him if he had not suddenly appeared at the park entrance in all his cabbage-hued glory, swinging his paunch with particular self-importance. Scooping him up, Mosca spotted a few threads dangling from his beak and had an uneasy feeling that some tithe vegetables had ended up as goose dinner. There was nothing she could do about it, however, so she put it out of mind.

Three pairs of feet set a new record in their sprint for the Leaps' house. Once inside, three pairs of hands made short work of driving home the bolts. Then, at long last, three intrepid Clatterhorsemen could fall into chairs and contemplate fully the events of the night.

There was a silence, punctuated by panting.

". . . ah . . . hah . . . heugh?" Mistress Leap asked eventually, pointing an unsteady finger toward the door, beyond which lay the incomprehensible horse-infested streets.

Mosca shook her head helplessly and managed a tiny, breathy tittle of sound by way of explanation.

"Graargh," creaked Welter Leap in agreement, and let his shoulders slump. For a little while there did not seem to be much else to say.

They were, however, all still alive. After a while they noticed this fact and began a quiet inventory of their limbs to make sure that none were missing. Everybody was bruised and scraped, Welter Leap had lost a tooth on the steps, and Mosca had three shallow but sheer cuts across her knee that looked as if they had been scored by razors. However, their little league had survived the hours of Saint Yacobray. The true Clatterhorse had evidently taken the turnip tithe from their door and passed by peacefully.

But why had there been so many Clatterhorses on the streets? If the last arrival had been the *real* Locksmith Clatterhorse, then who had been inside the other two imposter horses? One explanation immediately sprang to mind, of course. Beamabeth's kidnappers must have come up with just the same cunning plan as Mosca. They had realized that if they disguised themselves as a Clatterhorse, they could romp through the streets, collect the mayor's radish ransom, and be gone before anybody knew any better.

But that explained the presence of only one of the other false Clatterhorses. Why had there been two of them, both ready to seize the ransom? Their terror at the arrival of the real Clatterhorse made one thing very plain—neither of them had been working with the Locksmiths.

So who *had* ended up with the world's most valuable radish? With a feeling of deathly apprehension, Mosca realized she had one way of trying to find out.

One scant hour after the reign of Yacobray had ended and the people of Toll-by-Night dared to open their doors, a greenish foreigner with badly scratched stockings and a basketlike hat could be seen making her way to Chaff's Dryppe, a low-eaved, ill-smelling alley on the edge of the Chutes district, where moss-dyed wools hung from hooks and stained the walls like lichen.

Mosca found a dark arch and pulled herself into it so that she could watch the street unseen. Brand Appleton had said that he would meet her there at two of the clock. She would risk talking to him if he came alone, but if he did not, she would stay in hiding and then follow him back to his lair. It was her only plan. If Brand Appleton *had* seized the ransom jewel, then by now he probably had the money he needed to flee the town and disappear into the night. This might be Mosca's last chance to find out where Beamabeth Marlebourne was being held prisoner.

She listened to the distant chimes of the tower clock. Two o'clock came and went, and nobody approached down Chaff's Dryppe.

As a matter of fact, somebody *had* come to attend the appointment, but it took Mosca ten minutes to realize it, for the simple reason that they were doing exactly the same thing she was. In the end she became aware of the other person at the same moment that the other became aware of her. One of her legs cramped, so that she moved it hastily, causing her clog to click against the stony ground. In response, there was a tiny startled movement on the roof opposite, and Mosca saw a solitary figure crouching behind the stumpy chimney.

It was not Brand Appleton. It was not Skellow. It was Laylow, the crop-headed girl with the clawed glove.

"Fffsst!" The girl cast a glance up and down the street, and then ventured to the edge of the roof to peer down at Mosca. "Below there! Teacher!" It took a moment for Mosca to remember that this was what she had told Brand Appleton to call her. "Wait down there!"

What to do now? The last time Mosca had met Laylow, the older girl had helped her escape back to Toll-by-Day, but now everything was different. If Laylow was running errands for Appleton, perhaps *she* was in the kidnapping conspiracy too. And Laylow had met her as

Mosca Mye, might recognize her. . . . Could she outrun the older girl? Mosca doubted it.

Think Seisian, Mosca told herself as the older girl let herself down from the roof and advanced. *Think spices and silks and people eating birds' nests and monkey fingers.*

As she got close, Mosca realized that the older girl looked as nervous as she did. Laylow seemed to be much more interested in staring up and down the alley than in examining her green companion in great detail.

"Come on." Laylow's unclawed hand gripped Mosca's arm with painful urgency, pulling her down the alley. "Brand's a-waiting for you."

"He said he'd meet me here!" squeaked "Teacher" as she found herself being propelled down the lane. "Him, and nobody else! I'm not a piglet to be dragged off by the nose!"

Without warning Laylow grabbed Mosca by the shoulders and shook her roughly.

"You come with me." Only now that their faces were close could Mosca see the desperation and frustration contorting Laylow's features. At the corner of her mouth a new cut was drying, and a swelling above her eyebrow had ambitions to become a bruise. "You hear me? No bleating. No running. No fun. Or I'll hush you." Laylow was shaking, and Mosca could feel the hard points of the claws trembling against her shoulder blade, not quite piercing her clothes.

It was the bristling, dangerous desperation of a fox

in a trap, and Mosca knew better than to argue with it. She let herself be pulled like a mannequin down lane after lane, all the while watching her captor with hard, black eyes, ready to pull free and run should the other girl's grip slacken for a second. But Laylow's grasp did not weaken, and before Mosca could form another plan, Laylow was fumbling a key in a lock, then dragging her into a narrow, reeking room.

The air was clogged with fumes of different sorts: smoke from the dulling fire spitting fat on the rush-lights, vinegar, and the acrid, stormy smell of injury. There were no windows, and the room was narrow enough that the straw mattress at the far end reached from wall to wall. The blankets draped over the figure on the bed were too short. They reached only halfway up his chest, and his feet and shins in their blotchy stockings jutted out below them. His pallid skin was now ghastly against his red hair.

Mosca did not need to be a physician to see that Brand Appleton was far from well. Indeed, if his eyelids had not kept up a feverish, moth-wing tremble, she might have thought that he had escaped Toll-by-Night by leaving both the world and his body.

A dig in Mosca's back. She turned to find Laylow staring past her at the prone kidnapper.

"Can you . . . ?" Laylow swallowed awkwardly and grimaced, as if her throat were dry or the rising words knobbly. "Can you physick him then?"

"What, me?" Mosca stared in horror at the greasy pallor of his face and the hand clutching at the folds of blanket.

"You're from the spice islands. Seisian or something, he said." Laylow was breathing quickly, and her claw tips were gingerly, furtively tracing lines across the callused palm of her ungloved hand. "Can you not . . . put him right with spices? Nutmeg or the like? Or . . . or rub him with tiger spit or unicorn powder—something to put the claret back in him?"

Drawing closer, Mosca could see that Brand Appleton's ribs were clumsily wrapped in yellowing bandages through which something dark red was painting rosettes. They looked sodden, and Mosca guessed they were soaked in vinegar. She pulled back, clamping a hand against a sympathetic tingle in her own side as if she was the one who had been bleeding. Prickles flowed up her face, and her head felt light, the smells stifling and sickening her.

"So what put that hole in him?" she snapped, unable to keep a creak of fear from her voice. "Moths?" Even as she spoke, however, she guessed the answer. She remembered the collision between the sheep skull and the man horse, and the man horse driving his knives into the forequarters of the sheep skull. So Brand Appleton must have been inside the sheep-skull horse, at the front. But that had been a two-man horse. Who had been his partner?

Another easy question. Mosca remembered the gloved hand that had lashed out as she scrambled over the fallen sheep-skull horse, a hand that had slashed three parallel grooves through blanket and cloth and skin. A glove with claws. For whatever reason, Laylow had been playing horse's tail during the grim Clatterhorse gavotte.

"He thought you would help," intoned Laylow numbly, watching Brand Appleton. His breaths were audible. They rose, fell, and whistled to their own private rhythm. "Told me to fetch you. Thought you would help."

"You need a proper sawbones, you do." Mosca clenched her fists and stared at the wall. She had a sudden sick horror that the wounded man might shudder and die right in front of her. "What would you have me do? Slap on a cobweb and tell him to mend?"

Laylow shook her head. Her face was numbly crumpled as she stared at the patient, her lips in motion like a child struggling to read. Perhaps the Locksmiths kept track of all the doctors.

As if her gaze had grazed his skin, Appleton's breath briefly halted in its murmuring meander, and his eyes opened a straw's breadth. His exposed hand stirred on the blanket, then the fingers curled and twitched in a feeble, clutching beckon. With some trepidation, Mosca drew closer and crouched beside the invalid's bed, lowering her ear to hear his whispering.

"Need . . . get me out of here . . . that girl over there . . .

damned harridan . . . keeping me locked up here . . ." His eyes were cloudy and unfocused, but there was still that blazing, bewildered stubbornness, like firelight behind a misted pane. Mosca could not stop her hand flinching away when his trembling fingers moved to grasp it. His breath smelled of some searing back-room brandy brewed from beetles and dregs. "I must get back . . . nobody to protect her . . . cannot leave her in their hands if I am not there. . . ."

He was trying to sit up. Laylow sprang forward and shoved him back roughly.

"Doddypol!" she spat, sounding almost tearful. "Ninny! What are your wits worth? Lie down and stay there, or I'll break your pate!" Mosca could not help feeling that Laylow's bedside manner lacked a little polish. Appleton fell back with a thump, and a groan of pain and frustration.

"Witch kitten!" Appleton sounded not far from tears himself. "You infernal haglet! If you had an ounce of heart . . ." His eyelids drooped shut again, and his breath returned to its feverish murmuring.

Laylow gave Mosca another knuckle nudge in the ribs and drew her away from the bed, to a distance where their whispers would not disturb the sleeper.

"No doctors." Laylow's eyes rested fully on Mosca's face for the first time, and for an instant Mosca thought she saw a wrinkle of perplexity, a shade of recognition. But it passed. After all, how could a green foreigner possibly look slightly familiar? "There's no trusting the doctors in this town. But once he's outside Toll . . . can you get him out, by magic or such? A sailor told me a story of a Seisian who had a flying carpet—"

Mosca groaned and rubbed at her temples with her knuckles. "Look, miss—do you think I would still be here in this dreg pot of a town if I could fly?" She chewed her cheek, watching to gauge the older girl's reaction. "Why don't you pay his way out? He . . . he said there would be money."

"There will be!" Laylow's boxer jaw jutted. "It's just . . . not in our fambles yet."

Fambles. Another word lodged in a grimy reach of Mosca's mind, the part that had read every criminal chapbook and hangman's history to fall into her hands. It was the part of her mind that she had long since given Palpitattle's name and voice. As she remembered her thieves' cant, it was Palpitattle's rasping, sarcastic voice she seemed to hear.

Fambles is hands. Not in our hands yet, is what she is saying. So she and Appleton ain't got the jewel, have they?

"Listen!" Laylow went on. "I do not know all the twists of it, but Brand come to me yester eve and told me that he needed help with a lay. Said he was in deep with some parties but did not trust them not to take the ribbin and run if they found it within their grasp. So tonight we was out to fetch the gilt, but a gang of scapegallows was waiting for us and set us about on all sides, and one of them stuck Brand through with a blade. They must have took the money—I went back after and searched half the streets in town, but it was gone. So somebody made a pair of calf lollies out of us, but I will find them, and then Dark Gentleman take me if I do not beat the chink out of them."

What she means, rasped Palpitattle helpfully, *is that Brand was scared of a double cross. So when he went to get the reward, he didn't trust the folks he was in league with and asked* this *wildcat to come with him instead. And she don't know what's going on, but she thinks he was betrayed by his comrades, and that the parties what stabbed Mr. Not-So-Radical Appleton took the money too. And she wants to get it back.*

"Did he mention any names?" Mosca kept a sly watch on Laylow's face. "Names of the folks in his gang he didn't trust?"

Slow nod. "Said there was one fellow with a hang-gallows look and a snakish way about him. Name of Skellow."

Had Brand been right? Had Skellow been waiting for a chance to double-cross him? Could Skellow have been the lean and capering man horse who had stabbed Brand? He was tall and slight enough. Yes. It could have been him.

"And now Brand wants to go back to his cronies, to their blasted lair!" muttered Laylow, glancing across at Brand. "Cleft-pate gull! Walking in to let them finish their handiwork—that's a plan and a half!"

"He . . ." Mosca hesitated, wondering if she dared go on. "He said something about a girl waiting there, one he had to protect—"

The effect was instantaneous and explosive.

"Blight take her and every last ringlet! What right does she have—oh, that moping, cow-eyed, dunder-headed gull! I should throw him to the Jinglers! Like a bullock in love with the butcher's knife! I will, I swear I will, that'll be a lesson—I *knew* it, *knew* she was in Toll-by-Night somehow, *knew* it—kites and kettles, I'll . . . why is the sun not enough for her? Well, plague on the pair of them! I do not care, do not need—but not even her *scraps*, her *cast-offs*—she never wanted— *Why do you look at me like that?*"

Mosca was goggling at her openmouthed. "You're in love with him!" she exclaimed accusingly as Laylow's tirade ended. "You must be—you've stopped making any sense!" Even thieves' cant was more comprehensible than that.

"Go kiss a cat," snarled Laylow. Which was not, Mosca reflected, exactly a no.

Mosca thought about trying to tell a hysterical, love-lorn, claw-handed renegade that her dear Brand had actually kidnapped another woman so as to force her to marry him, but she thought that might go down like a lead chaffinch.

"I offered to go back there in his place—look to the

lay of the land," Laylow went on. "But he would have none of it. Would not trust me. Or tell me where to find those blackguards' stop hole." She glared at Mosca with a sudden flare of suspicion. "So what did he want with you, if you've no medicine nor tricks to help him? What are *you* for?"

"I—I'm a *teacher*!" squeaked Mosca quickly, eyes on her companion's sharp claw tips. "Ask him yourself! Teaching him radical matters, telling him how to get to Mandelion—"

As soon as the words were out, she could have bitten her tongue. Laylow gasped as if the air had been knocked out of her.

"Mandelion? He is . . . leaving? Never told me—never told me he was *leaving*. . . ."

Brand Appleton was stirring again, but Laylow seemed too stunned to notice, and Mosca scrambled to his side unhindered, glad to be out of reach of the claws.

"Teacher!" He took hold of her wrist with furtive urgency. "Talk quietly, don't let her hear us—she has a heart of flint, that one, won't let me leave. I think she spikes the possets to keep me dizzy—"

"That's no spiked posset, Mr. Appleton," Mosca whispered, feeling a reluctant sting of pity. "Look at you—you're all leaked away, limp as an empty wine bladder. I could help you till my face turned blue—but I would never get you on your feet—not with you like that."

Appleton sagged with disappointment and frustration; then his grip on her wrist tightened again.

"*You* could go! You could go and see how she is, tell her . . . tell her that I will make all right and she shall be sorry for none of this in the end. And tell the others that if they hurt her, if they frighten her, then I'll . . . I'll . . . make their hearts into . . . purses. Or tell them I'll go to the Jinglers and turn evidence. Tell them I am well and strong and the knife missed me." His eyes drifted to Laylow. "That scratch cat! You see how she is—I cannot send her—she would not understand—she hates . . . but *you, you'll* go." Large, eager blue eyes met hers, open as summer, mad as hare hopscotch.

Mosca took three deep breaths, one after the other, like a diver preparing to plunge.

"Yeah," she whispered softly. "I *will* go for you. For three shilling extra. Paid when you got the rest of the money." She could not afford to seem too eager. She would let him think that her face was brightening at the thought of money. "So . . . where do I go?"

Mosca had to stoop to hear the kidnapper's whispered words, and straightened with her eyes full of black mischief and wonder and suppressed excitement. She hardly dared meet Laylow's gaze as she edged back toward her.

"Your friend there—he has a notion that he will start to mend if he drinks a posset made of . . . whey and thistle wine. I told him I would find some, and it settled him down. For now, anyway."

"Whey and thistle wine." Laylow's brow creased again. "Will that help him?"

"Maybe. It cannot hurt." The door was six feet away. All Mosca had to do was talk her way outside it. "I can find you thistle wine for him, and honey, and . . . and blood sausage to help his strength, but I'll want paying for it when you find that chink of yours."

Laylow rubbed the back of her head, the calluses rasping against the wiry, cropped fuzz of her hair.

"Well then—go! Come back when you have them—and tell nobody what you seen or heard here."

"Of course not! I'm not a . . ." Mosca remembered one of Laylow's own choice words for idiot. "I'm not a doddypol."

A lock turned. A door opened. And then Mosca was out on the frozen streets again, quivering with the shock and disbelief of a fisherman who has trailed his rod for a particular large and dangerous fish, only to see it unexpectedly leap into the belly of his boat.

At long last she knew where Beamabeth Marlebourne was being held prisoner.

25

GOODLADY UNDLESOFT,
DWELLER WITH THINGS BURIED

STARING SKYWARD, MOSCA noticed some smudges of pallor to the east and heard the warbles of the first robins. The night was waning, and she gave a *tsk* of annoyance. She barely realized that she had already started to think of the night as the true day.

Mosca pulled out her pipe, gnawed on the stem, and willed herself to think clearly.

Everything had changed. Brand Appleton, the so-called chief kidnapper, was desperate and pitiable and wrongheaded and possibly dying. She had felt scared of him . . . but she had felt *sorry* for him too. Beamabeth was no longer safe. Brand Appleton would do anything to protect her, but right now Brand Appleton was in no condition to protect even himself. The mayor's daughter was at the mercy of Skellow, and Skellow was not well supplied with mercy. Once he had the ransom or had to cover his tracks, Mosca would not give a bent pin for Beamabeth's chances of survival. Mosca could only pray that neither of these circumstances had occurred yet, but it was only a matter of time.

Mosca needed reinforcements to rescue Beamabeth before the worst could happen. However, if her dayside allies heard nothing from Mosca or Sir Feldroll's men, they were hardly likely to send more. She needed to get word to Toll-by-Day.

But even her daylight allies could not be trusted. The more she chewed at her pipe and thought, the more it seemed that there must be *two* spies among them. One spy for the kidnappers, who had warned them about the ambush and helped them capture Beamabeth. One spy for the Locksmiths, who had betrayed the location of the letter drop and the arrival of Sir Feldroll's men. Of one thing Mosca was now fairly sure: The kidnappers and the Locksmiths were not working together.

No, Mosca needed to get word to the person in Toll who she knew best and trusted most, and the sorry truth was that that individual was Eponymous Clent. Contacting him in the ways they had arranged was impossible, but he had managed to send word to *her*, and that would do as a start. She had to track down the man who had given her warning in the alleyway, and she had only one clue to work on. It was a single word that he had uttered before disappearing.

Recital.

As the dawn chorus was engaging in their ancient but uncoordinated musical efforts, another more elegantly trained group of musicians was making its way back through the streets to its lodgings. It had been a long night, and now their nerves were as threadbare as their carefully patched gowns and waistcoats.

Performing for the Locksmiths at the castle was never calming, but since the former were willing to accept such performances instead of a Yacobray tithe, the three musicians were inclined to bear it with a good grace.

The grace was becoming less good, though, as they struggled their way home from their ruined venue, sensing the approach of the dangerous dawn, hampered at every step by the barrow that carried their group's harp case. The wheel had been carefully wrapped in rags to soften its progress, but even so occasional jolts stirred a musical thrum from hidden strings, and the guardian of the cart insisted on choosing each cobble with care, more like a mother afraid of waking a sleeping infant than a barrowman.

"Oh, Quince, for Peachbucket's sake!" A tall woman carrying a flute case turned and twitched, the flaws and blots in her face powder starting to show in the unforgiving predawn light. "My nerves are in flakes! Will you try to keep pace! Is it not enough that I have to hear that infernal instrument without having to die for it?"

The harp's attendant seemed not a jot discomposed. "My sweet, given that you yourself have no art worth dying for, you should be grateful to me for letting you perish in the name of something worthwhile."

"Er . . . friends?" The group's gangly, gray-haired violinist was peering down the alley. "Does anybody know anyone really short . . . and oddly appareled . . . and . . . green? It is just that, er, there seems to be one such creature watching us from the corner. And, er, waving a little green hand."

Quince lowered the handles of his barrow.

"Ah," he said.

"Recital" had meant music. Asking around, Mosca had learned that there was only one orchestra in Toll-by-Night, and that on this night it would be entertaining at the castle. So she had set out to intercept the musicians as they returned.

Mosca had no trouble recognizing Quince as the man who had warned her away from the letter drop so mysteriously, and she was not entirely surprised to see him with a harp in his custody, though she was a little taken aback to see that the cloth enclosing it was of decidedly better quality than that he had used to clothe himself.

"Is *that* what you were risking your neck to rescue, Quince?" The tall woman surveyed Mosca from head to foot through a lorgnette that did not appear to contain any actual glass. "It looks like a ferret in jester's weeds!"

"Ignore the silly besom," Quince advised Mosca crisply. "Listen, my dear, it is delightful to see you intact, but if you will excuse us—"

"Wait!" Mosca caught hold of his sleeve. "You're in contact with Mr. Clent! Please, you got to get a message to him. He's staying in the mayor's house. Tell him . . ." She hesitated, gaped guppylike for the right words, and found herself shaking. "Tell him the old plan's turned to slush. That someone was waitin' for the reinforcements, and now everything's gone to the devil in a battered old basket . . . and the radish is lost, and Brand Appleton ain't got it . . . but I know where to find the lady—"

"Slow, slow! Look, I *do* hate to interrupt while you are being so splendidly cryptic, but this will have to wait—"

"It cannot!" Mosca almost screamed. "If I cannot get word to him *now*, then the lady's as good as dead . . ."

From the distance came the unmistakable sound of a bugle. The other two musicians stiffened like hares. But Mosca did not release the harpist's sleeve. Her eyes were mad and adamant.

Quince seemed to spend a brief second weighing his chances of pushing a harp at high speed down the road with a twelve-year-old clinging to his arm, then came to a decision.

"Your friend is living in the mayor's house? Then you can speak to him yourself. This way!" To Mosca's bewilderment, he abandoned his barrow and tugged her back toward the castle grounds. Just outside the perimeter walls he stooped, reached deep into a mass of ivy, and knocked against something that resounded like wood.

"There!" Before Mosca could protest, he had taken off down the street after his friends. "Pull the frog! Mind the drop!" he called over his shoulder. "Follow the smells! And not a word to anyone!"

Mosca stared at the ivy-covered wall, then pulled back the curtain of creeper and stared at the little door hidden behind it. The door itself was carved to resemble the surface of a pond, complete with ripples, the snout of a surfacing fish, and a lily pad with a chipped and blackened frog crouching upon it. Even as she stared at it, her ear caught the sound of a faint but approaching musical jingle.

"Pull the frog," whispered Mosca, mouth dry, and curled her fingers around the frog's lily pad. She tugged, then heaved in growing panic, and the hidden door swung wide, offering an inviting darkness. As the Jinglers drew close to her street, Mosca flung herself forward into the waiting tunnel, only to find that she had thrown herself full length onto something that was not exactly a floor.

Mind the drop.

Swearing and wincing at the bottom of a three-foot shaft, Mosca decided that she minded the drop quite a lot. Even as she was gingerly sitting up and twisting around to examine what remained of her bruised knees, her small, painful, oblong slice of world abruptly darkened. Through the ivy-fringed arch above her, where the secret door had opened, she could see a pair of boots. Then the little vista vanished, leaving her in pitch blackness, and she could hear the *crang* and *clink* of bolts and locks being fastened.

Her immediate response was unreasoning panic. She had been tricked into a trap by the harpist—she would never see the light of the moon again, let alone the sun. She would perish alone, and centuries would pass before anyone found a diminutive skeleton with a basket perched on its skull. If she had been less winded, she might even have screamed for help.

Fortunately she recovered her common sense before her breath. The man who had darkened her door had been a Jingler about his dawnly duties, locking away the nightbound areas and unlocking the daybound. In fact, he had probably just moved a piece of wooden wall facing and fastened it without even noticing the tiny, ivy-shrouded doorway he was sealing into darkness. At worst, she would be trapped only until dusk, when the Jinglers came past again. At best, there might actually be some meaning in the harpist's cryptic instructions.

Pull the frog. Mind the drop. Follow the smells. And not a word to anyone.

Mosca was not entirely alone, she realized. Besides the dank, moldering oubliette reeks there were comforting living smells. Baking-bread fragrance, warm as a hug. The vinegary aroma of preserved meat. The sooty scent of cracked peppercorns.

She had not fallen into a sealed cell, then. This shaft must lead to somewhere, somewhere with cooking. Her groping hands told her that to either side the walls were close, but ahead her fingers met no brickwork. Tentatively she started to crawl away from the door and toward the beckoning smells.

She appeared to be crawling through a low and rough-cut tunnel, the roof of which had apparently been carved so as to jab into the shoulders and back of an intruder as painfully as possible. Only the dark gold smell of buttered toast kept her going.

At last the tunnel started to brighten just a little, and then opened out into a musty little fox den of a cellar. There was no other exit from the cellar, but it was dimly lit by little holes that polka-dotted its ceiling and let in slanting fingers of light. The stone floor was strewn with malodorous rugs. The sooty gauze of ancient cobwebs adorned the walls, draping like veils before a set of little apertures in the grimy brickwork, each filled with a tiny wooden Beloved idol.

Funny place for a shrine, thought Mosca.

The ceiling was just high enough for Mosca to stand, so she did so and pressed her eye to one of its holes. Directly above her she saw sky, but it was not the great cold sky that spread its wings over the world. Rather, it was a smaller, more modest mimic of the heavens, and one that she had seen before. The inside of a deep blue dome, adorned with painted silver stars . . . yes! She was staring up at the chapel end of the reception room in which she had first seen Beamabeth Marlebourne. With a rush of excitement, she realized that she must be under the mayor's house. So *that* was what the musician had meant when he said she could talk to Clent herself!

Far distant, the second dawn bugle sounded to announce the start of day. Somewhere in the room above, a door clicked shut, and overhead, shoe leather slapped on tiles.

Voices.

"Open the doors!" It was Sir Feldroll in the room above, she was sure of it. "If the Beloved have heard our prayers, if the kidnappers have received the ransom, then Miss Marlebourne might be waiting outside even now! And if not . . . your master will be back from the counting house soon enough to give us word." The pitch of the knight's voice was higher than usual, and Mosca thought of harp strings drawn taut.

So the mayor had slept at the counting house. Mosca guessed that he had not wanted to trust the handling of the precious ransom gem to anybody else. She heard footfalls moving to and fro along the hallway, followed by the muffled sounds of bolts being drawn and locks being turned. A door creaked, and the air flowing through the little hole onto Mosca's cheek became very slightly colder.

"Nobody there, sir" came the call from down the hall.

"I feared as much," Sir Feldroll muttered. Pace, pace, pace. The little spots of light above Mosca winked one by one as somebody strode over her head. Then, more curtly, "How can you eat breakfast at a moment like this?"

"My noble sir, I am gripped with anxiety and palpitation as you are; it simply takes me differently. You pace and give orders, I turn to toast for solace." The voice of Eponymous Clent, unmistakably Eponymous Clent. To judge by the faint crunching, Mosca thought he was probably just a few yards out of view, seated at the breakfast table.

"Then I shall leave you to your solace, sir," muttered Sir Feldroll, through clenched teeth by the sound of it. "You fellows—come with me and we shall see whether Miss Marlebourne has been left on the grounds. It might be that she is too weak—that perhaps she has swooned— or if she has been left tied up . . ."

There was then a good deal of clipping and clopping around, and Mosca couldn't keep track of all the steps. She thought Sir Feldroll had left through the front door with at least two people, but she could not be sure who was still in the room above. For a long time she remained at the hole, staring up at the penny's worth of painted ceiling and listening to the steady *crunch, crunch, crunch* of Clent's toast and the scrape of his cutlery.

If there really were spies in the mayor's household, then she needed to speak with Clent alone. The last thing she wanted was a Locksmith spy knowing where she was and what she was doing. She very much doubted that the Locksmiths knew about this secret passage, for if they had, they would surely have kept it locked to stop others from wandering in.

Was anyone else with Clent in the room above? She could not tell. But she had to take a risk, before the mayor returned and threw the house into turmoil.

"Hssst!" she hissed. "Mr. Clent! Over here!"

Somewhere above, a knife halted midsqueak. A pause, and then a chair ground its feet against the tiles above. Slow, careful steps. Silence.

"Mr. Clent!"

Some more steps, and then Mosca's peephole went dark. She pulled out one of her hairpins and poked it up through the hole to prod at the foot resting on it.

"Down *here*, Mr. Clent! Under the floor!"

The foot was twitched away with a noise of alarm, and Mosca withdrew the pin. Peering up, she could just about see Clent's face gazing down, his chin made enormous by the strange angle.

"Mosca?" he whispered. A light powder of mortar and beetle grit fell to dust her cheeks as he dropped to his knees and lowered his head to a few inches above her peephole. She could make out no more than a patch of face, one eye wide and startled, brow contracted as if in pain.

"Yes, Mr. Clent, it's me! It's me! Are you alone?"

"Yes—yes, for the moment. But probably not for long. Child, are you . . . ?" He trailed off and shook his head. It felt strange to see Eponymous Clent run out of words. "Little Mosca Mye," he said instead, inconsequentially, and laughed incredulously under his breath.

"I got all my limbs," Mosca answered quickly. "I been knocked and scraped and chased about, but my heart's still beating inside my hide. And I'm hungry, Mr. Clent, I'm hungry as a winter fox."

Clent's face vanished. Steps retreating. Steps returning. A crumb fell in Mosca's eye, and then a crust was pushed down through the peephole, doused in honey, followed by another and another. She took them and crammed them into her mouth.

"If only I could pull up this floor!" muttered Clent. "But it seems we are divided by six good inches of timber and stone. What has happened to you, child?"

"E'ryfing wen' wrog," Mosca explained through a mouthful of crusts, then swallowed. "There was folks waitin' to ambush Sir Feldroll's men outside the Twilight Gate, Locksmiths like as not, but the kidnappers ain't working with the Locksmiths, and I think Skellow betrayed Brand Appleton and stuck him with a knife so he could grab the ransom, and the radish bounced off halfway cross the town with everyone chasing it and strike me blind if I know who's got it now. Brand Appleton ain't got it, and he ain't got Beamabeth neither; all he got is a fever and a hole in his side the size of your pocket. But *I did it*, Mr. Clent! I found out where the mayor's daughter is being held! I did it!"

"You found her? How? No—tell me later. *Where* is she?"

"Top floor of a cooper's shop in the Chutes, right near the holes where they drop the coffins into the Langfeather. Jus' opposite a broken-down old stew called the Owl's Head. But there's no windows to Beamabeth's room, and no way in but through the front door and five bravos. Sir Feldroll needs to send more men, because this is fist-and-cudgel work, if I know it. So I come here to tell you." As Clent listened, Mosca poured out the tale of the many Clatterhorses and her last strange interview with Brand Appleton.

Clent exhaled slowly as he absorbed the news, eyes closed. "But . . . but how did you get here? Are you daylight side, child?"

"No—I don't exist! The musicians—they told me where to find the secret way in. I'm in some kind of cellar, with rugs, an' little Beloved figures all set up like a shrine—"

"A salvation hole!" interrupted Clent. "I knew it! I had heard of such things—many rich houses had them built during the Civil War, to hide relatives or servants in danger of arrest. Under the chapel, no doubt, so that the unfortunates concealed could listen in on services and prayer. That answers the mystery of the orchestra! Two dayside musicians playing on the stage, and the rest making up the melody down in the salvation hole. Quite ingenious. . . ." Clent faltered and blinked hard. "Songs of the celestial, child, are you saying that you came into that hole *unhindered*? That there is a nightside entrance to this very house, and there is nothing to stop anyone from *simply wandering in*?"

"Nothing, unless they're uncommon portly or fond of the skin of their knees," growled Mosca. "Any nightling who knows where to find the door could wander right in."

"So." Clent released his words carefully and slowly, as if they were pebbles to be dropped without rippling his thoughts. "All the while we were engaged in our secret conference in this room, plotting the manner in which we would lay an ambush for our kidnappers . . ."

". . . one of 'em could have been skulking down here, hearing every word!" It gave Mosca a chill to think of it. "So they never needed a spy in the household after all!"

"No wonder our ambush failed so abysmally," rejoined Clent, "if they knew all our plans and had a hiding place ready so close at hand. I suppose they were hidden in the passage before dawn, emerged to abduct the young lady, and then retreated back underground."

Mosca felt a reluctant sting of compassion as she imagined Beamabeth, bound and gagged in the salvation hole for a whole day, able to hear her desperate would-be rescuers searching for her but unable to call out to them.

"Well," murmured Clent, "I think now we know why

secrets leak out of this house with such ease."

Mosca frowned. "No," she muttered. "That ain't it—not all of it, anyways. Maybe this creep hole tells us how Skellow's boys dodged our ambush and whisked away Beamabeth Marlebourne, but it don't explain how the Locksmiths found our letter drop, or were ready and waiting for Sir Feldroll's men. We did not plan *everything* in this room, Mr. Clent! Weave it how you will, there's a Locksmith spy in among us."

"I fear you are right. In fact I fear the mayor has trusted too many people with our secrets already. His steward, the head clerk of the Committee of the Hours, and the high constable are all in his confidence. Worse still, *I* am not. I would be quite in the dark if I had not persuaded Mistress Bessel to look into it. She—she might show an unladylike ferocity of temper at times," Clent continued, in tones of quiet admiration, "but when it comes to finding things out, that woman is sharper than lemon. And thank the Beloved, she has managed to win the mayor's trust where I have failed. Just yesterday evening he remarked that she was the finest—"

But Mosca was not to learn what Mistress Bessel was the finest example of, for at that moment the front door crashed open and through her tiny scope Mosca saw Clent scramble onto his knees so that he seemed to kneel in prayer in the little chapel. However, it soon became clear that the new arrivals had no attention to spare for Eponymous Clent.

"Help him—help him!" Sir Feldroll was shouting. "And close the doors behind us, man—we do not want the whole world agog! My lord mayor, will you sit—fetch him a chair!"

Confusion ensued, with a lot of people running around to show that they were eager and concerned.

"Send for a physician!" shouted Sir Feldroll. "Tell him his lordship has received a great shock and is suffering palsies of the limbs. Mistress Bessel, call for laudanum!"

"A shock?" Clent had risen to his feet again. "Simpering stars, has there been ill news of Miss Marlebourne?"

A terrible croak of a voice interrupted. It was hardly recognizable as that of the mayor. "No—worse! Worse!"

"Worse?" Sir Feldroll sounded outraged. "How can anything be worse?"

There was a sound of coughing and ragged breaths before the mayor spoke again.

"The Luck . . . the Luck! The Luck of Toll has been stolen!"

26

GOODLADY BLATCHETT,
LIFTER OF THE STONE FROM THE TOAD

AFTER THIS ANNOUNCEMENT, nobody was any use for about five minutes. A young maidservant running in with the requested laudanum had by chance overheard the mayor's words, and promptly went into such violent hysterics that she had to be dosed with it herself. She seemed convinced that Toll was about to pitch off the cliff into the Langfeather, like a tilted hat with its crucial pin removed. Worse still, the mayor seemed much of the same opinion.

Maddeningly, everybody wanted to rush about so that Mosca could not keep track of them, and nobody wanted to stand where she could see them through her little peepholes.

"Send that girl to bed, and close that door!" shouted Sir Feldroll at last. "Nobody leaves this house! If the common people find out that the Luck is stolen, half the town will be thrown into fits!"

"Oh, probably a good deal more than *half*," Clent opined helpfully, and was ignored. Sir Feldroll, however, was not, and after a while things got a lot quieter.

"Steady yourself, my lord mayor," came Mistress Bessel's warm, motherly tones. Evidently she had entered with the rest. "How in the world did somebody come to steal the Luck?" Remembering that Mistress Bessel had had her own ill-fated plans for stealing the Luck, Mosca suspected that she was probably a little aggrieved that somebody else had managed it.

"Through the clock face!" The mayor had the breathless, rasping tones of one who has just been punched in the stomach. The kidnapping of his daughter had left him towering and wrathful, but the loss of the Luck had apparently broken him. "They took advantage of the repairs to come in through the clock face on the front of the tower! I did not even know that was possible!"

Mosca realized that she at least *should* have guessed that it was possible. Paragon had told her that he was in charge of adding the little wooden Beloved figures to the clock mechanism as required. Therefore there must have been some way of accessing the clock's works from his cell. Under cover of repairing the clock, the thieves must have stealthily removed the cogs until they found the hatch into his private chamber.

"So . . . you are saying that the Luck of Toll is an actual

object?" Sir Feldroll was keeping the situation under control very well but was clearly a few pages behind when it came to understanding it. "I always assumed it was a figure of speech!"

"Not an object . . . a *person*," answered the mayor. "A . . . a boy. The Luck of Toll is the person born under a more auspicious Beloved than anybody else in town, and thus granted the best and most fortunate name. The Luck is shut away from the world, close to the bridge so that his luck seeps into it and keeps it aloft . . . and holds the cliff steady under us. . . ."

"A *boy*? Locked up inside a clock . . . so that his luck . . ." Sir Feldroll cut short his sentence, perhaps realizing that it could go nowhere tactful. "Well, as far as I am aware the town has *not* noticeably fallen into the river, so if everybody could please recover their senses—"

"Not yet, but the power of the Luck only holds while he or she is within the walls of the town," intoned the mayor. "Should they ever stray outside, then Toll's good fortune leaves with them once and forever, and all is calamity. Then we shall see agues and poxes sweeping through Toll, and the wells filling with poison, and foes storming our gates unopposed, and the ground crumbling beneath us. . . ." Somewhere on the far side of the room, the youngest footman started to whimper.

"My lord mayor, you are not helping!" exploded Sir Feldroll. "This is mere superstition! And besides, if the Luck is the fellow born under the brightest Beloved and gifted with the best name, then surely it is a simple thing to replace him? Who has the second-best name?" There was a long pause, during which everyone singularly failed to sound as cheered as Sir Feldroll had evidently expected.

"The second-best name in Toll," explained the mayor coldly, "is possessed by my daughter, Beamabeth. Who you have told us is *also* in danger of being spirited out of Toll. And besides, the title of Luck only passes on to the next-best name when the current Luck *dies*. If the Luck is taken outside Toll while still alive, then disaster and catastrophe—"

"Yes, yes," Sir Feldroll interrupted hastily. "I believe I have grasped the point."

Mosca wondered if she was the only person who remembered that Paragon was a person in his own right, regardless of whether he was lucky or not, and right now possibly a frightened and ill-treated person. Then again, given that he had lived under lock and key for nearly all his life, perhaps his existence actually had been improved by being kidnapped. It would certainly have made it less monotonous.

"Well," Sir Feldroll pronounced grimly, "surely *everybody* must now agree that things have gone far too far, and the strongest action is required. As I predicted, the ransom has been taken by the kidnappers, and Miss Marlebourne has not been returned to us. And now this further outrage! My lord mayor, *surely* you cannot still doubt the wisdom of striking at these radicals with all the might we can muster—striking at the very root and fountainhead!"

"Ah . . ." Clent's cautious tones edged gingerly into the ensuing silence. "I hate to interrupt any eloquent and ardent speech . . . but do we have the slightest reason to believe that Miss Marlebourne and the Luck have been stolen away by the same party?"

"The slightest reason?" If Sir Feldroll had been an ordinary man, his tone might have been described as "shrill." But he was a knight, so Mosca assumed he was probably just "impassioned." "These blackguards Skellow and Appleton are *kidnappers*. They kidnap your girl Mye from Grabely, they kidnap Miss Marlebourne, and now, hey presto, we have another audacious kidnapping of a young and defenseless victim! The *slightest reason*? How stocky do you require your reasons to be, Mr. Clent? Make no mistake, this *is* the handiwork of the same monsters. Appleton has undoubtedly fled with Miss Marlebourne, and now his men have taken the Luck to throw us into confusion, so that we lack the coordination to pursue Appleton and act against his radical allies."

This was agony. Mosca had to bite down hard on her own knuckles to stop herself calling out. What Sir Feldroll had said made perfect sense, but he was so completely *wrong*! Brand Appleton had *not* left Toll, and neither had Beamabeth. Furthermore, from what Mosca had seen, Beamabeth Marlebourne's kidnappers had been far too busy running around stabbing one another to kidnap anybody new.

"Sir Feldroll is right," declared the mayor wearily. "I have given up as ransom a valuable item entrusted into my care as mayor . . . and all that has done is convince these villains that they may acquire anything they want through abduction. Sir Feldroll, I owe you an apology. You have been right all along, and I should have heeded you. You there—Pratewill! Run down to the Committee of the Hours and tell the chief clerk to come here immediately, with all the paperwork needed to grant a large number of men passage through Toll. A *very* large number of men. We strike—as you recommended from the start, Sir Feldroll—at the fountainhead! At Mandelion!"

"*What?*" mouthed Mosca in her nocturnal cellar.

Her mind was beset by a flurry of images as she remembered those she knew from the rebel government of Mandelion. A gentle-eyed idealist named Hopewood Pertellis, risking his life to run a secret school for the poorer children. A stiff-backed manageress named Miss Kitely, defending her floating coffeehouse from attack with the sangfroid of an admiral. A gruff-voiced highwayman named Captain Blythe, fighting a rooftop duel midriver because it was the only way to save his people. And she remembered the city's convulsions of happiness after the overthrow of the Duke, the festival flags, the carnival crowds. . . .

"My lord mayor," spluttered Clent, "good sir knight—are we not being a little hasty?"

"No," Sir Feldroll replied promptly. "Appleton and his gang are *radicals*. None of these crimes would have occurred if they did not have the backing of Mandelion. I came to Toll two months ago with one purpose: to help the mayor see what we of the other cities had already seen—the necessity of marching upon this rebel city, arresting its so-called government of felons, and putting a *respectable* ruler in charge instead. Our armies are ready, sir—they have been ready since Mandelion's revolution. All we need is your permission for them to pass through your town without paying a toll for every single foot soldier."

Down below, Mosca yanked at fistfuls of her own hair, stifled a cry in her throat, and jumped up and down in a fit of silent, impotent rage, nearly banging her head. *You ninny!* she snarled voicelessly at Sir Feldroll. *You pudding-witted, pompous poltroon! Mandelion's got nothing to do with any of this! Brand Appleton's not even a real radical! And Mr. Pertellis and the rest would never want anything to do with kidnapping or forcing people to marry people! You just want a reason to attack them!*

Why don't you say something, Mr. Clent?

But of course he could not. There was still a snake in the grass, a spy in the inner circle, perhaps in that very room. Any plan he suggested in front of the spy would probably be doomed from the outset. Worse still, if Clent hinted at what he knew, people might want to know where his information came from, and those were questions he could not answer without endangering Mosca.

The Locksmith spy! Who was the spy? Mosca gave the question one last angry kick, just as she might have kicked a recalcitrant old travel chest. To her surprise, however, the imaginary catch clicked and the lid swung wide. She knew—quite suddenly and without any doubt—who had been spying on them all this time. Hastily she rummaged for her pin and poked it up toward Clent's foot to get his attention . . . just as he stepped forward and off the stage to join the crowd in the center of the room. Mosca's pin was left to waggle uselessly, unnoticed.

By the time the chief clerk of the Committee of the Hours arrived, Mistress Bessel had asked Clent three times whether he had a headache and commented that he seemed uncommonly pale. In short, he was finding discretion every bit as agonizing as Mosca was. Being unable to speak was bad. Being able to speak but unable to explain anything of importance was, if anything, worse.

The raspberry-faced chief clerk was even more rubicund than usual, puffing self-importantly under the weight of a huge valise of parchments. Little redheaded Kenning came after him, bent backward under a writing slope and a stack of boxes. Within five minutes the papers within would bear the mayor's signature and seal, and the die would be cast.

"Discretion above all," the mayor insisted. "If anybody hears that the Luck is missing and people start to wonder if it has been taken outside Toll, then *nobody* will be willing to use that bridge. And I think that will include the men in your armies, Sir Feldroll, whatever you might think."

It was at this point that a crisp knock sounded at the door. The footman opened it, then leaned forward to peer, then stepped outside altogether. After an interval he returned, a wax-sealed letter in his hand.

"Nobody there, my lord mayor," he explained apologetically, "but this letter left on the step."

The mayor eyed it with raised brow, then broke the seal. He read it with increasing palpitations of face and limb.

At last he looked up, and wordlessly gestured all of his servants from the room. When his only companions were Eponymous Clent, Jennifer Bessel, Sir Feldroll, the Raspberry, and Kenning, he lowered his eyes and read the letter aloud, in a voice that shook like a loose sail.

"To Graywing Marlebourne, Lord Mayor of Toll,
 "Lest you think you had been robbed in the night, I thought I should write and inform you that the Luck of Toll is quite safe. It came to our attention during the

repair of the mechanisms in the clock tower that the location used for the Luck's protection was very far from secure, and I believe the ease with which it was removed proves our point admirably. Therefore, for the sake of the town that we both hold dear, we have moved it to a far safer sanctuary, and we are more than happy to take over the duty of keeping it secure on behalf of Toll.

"My next priority shall be the recovery of your adopted daughter. I believe I might claim jurisdiction here, and must ask you not to take any steps of your own in this matter. I am a little surprised at having learned of this affair through sources other than your lordship, but I daresay that your missive simply failed to reach me. You and I both know all too well how easily letters can go astray and fall into unexpected hands.

"Your respectful servant,
"Aramai Goshawk"

"What?" Sir Feldroll strode up and peered over the mayor's shoulder almost as though he suspected the other man had been inventing the contents. "The Locksmiths? The *Locksmiths* stole the Luck?"

"This," the mayor said heavily, folding the letter, "changes everything. There is no question now of attacking Mandelion. The Locksmiths state explicitly that we must take no steps of our own, and the Locksmiths have the Luck. My friends—I fear we must leave the matter of my daughter in the Locksmiths' hands—"

"Pardon me," interrupted Sir Feldroll, his voice icy and his face scarlet, "but I do not see that at all!" His veneer of deference had all but frayed away, and he could be seen clearly now as the lord of a large city nearly out of patience with the mayor of a country town—a country town, furthermore, that was standing in his way. A storm was evidently in the offing.

At long last Eponymous Clent managed to catch Mistress Bessel's eye. "These gentlemen seem to have . . . ah . . . a great deal to discuss. Perhaps, my dear Jen, you would join me for a moment in the chapel to . . . pray for the rescue of poor Miss Beamabeth?"

Come back, Mr. Clent, I need to talk to you. Come back over here, Mr. Clent. . . .

How could Mosca get his attention? Rustle? Honk like a goose? But she could hear steps—he *was* coming back! She ran from peephole to peephole and finally found a view of him. He was returning to the chapel, but not alone. Mistress Bessel was with him. They knelt side by side on the stage, Clent's face in a pious pout, Mistress Bessel glancing narrowly at him from time to time.

"What game is this, Eponymous?" muttered Mistress Bessel eventually out of the corner of her mouth, her tone its usual mix of butter and bite. "If you've become gods-fearing, then I am a dandelion."

"Dear Jen," whispered Clent eventually, his lips scarcely moving, "there is something you must know and—*aaaagh!* Prattle and pique, would you maim me?"

Mosca's frantic thrusts with her pin had evidently made contact at last.

"Eponymous! What means this yowling and writhing?" demanded Mistress Bessel.

In the darkness below the stage, Mosca breathed hard and clenched both her fists, willing Clent to read her mind. The army of her thoughts was marching, and her heart was their battle drum.

"A spasm of . . . spiritual anguish," answered Clent through his teeth. Mosca could just make out his fingers clutching at his newly injured knee. "Would you excuse me for a moment of . . . private prayer?"

An impatient sigh, and soft steps withdrew.

"Your explanation will doubtless astonish and delight me," Clent hissed down toward Mosca's chink.

"You were going to tell her about me being here!" hissed Mosca. "She *hates* me! She'll betray me in a second!"

"Child, if I ask the mayor to send reinforcements to Toll-by-Night without explanation, he will glare me to dust. But Mistress Bessel has a way with him. We *need* her in our stratagems, child."

Mosca held still a few moments, breathing great lungfuls of the musty air, her thoughts whirring as fiercely as spiked chariot wheels. "All right," she said. "You *are* right, we *do* need her help. Listen, Mr. Clent! I think I know who the spy is! And Mistress Bessel can help us uncover 'em. But before you tell her about me being here, first you got to make her promise not to tell anyone. Make her promise *properly*, the way the farmers trade oaths in the marketplace. You got to clasp her right hand, firm as you can, look her in the eye, and make her swear by the Beloved. *Just* like that, Mr. Clent. Please."

"Oh . . . fates have mercy. Very well." Clent's face disappeared again as he rose to his feet. "Jen," he called aloud, "will you humor an old friend? If I might take you by the—"

His words were cut short by a screech that sounded more like a scalded vixen than any human sound. All other conversation in the room was killed in an instant. There was a shocked silence; then feet thundered from the room and down the passage to the front door, which banged open. A patter of steps receded into the drowsy noises of the winter morning.

"Clent!" bellowed the mayor. Mosca had the feeling that he had leaped to his feet. "What did you do to her, you devil!"

"I . . . took her by the hand," faltered Clent, sounding stunned and incredulous. "All I did was . . . take her by the hand."

"But that scream! And the way she looked at you before she ran—as if you were something venomous!"

A long pause, then a soft but drawn-out sigh.

"Jen." There was no obvious emotion in the word, and

if Mosca had known Clent less well, it might almost have sounded offhand. "Oh, Jen." Mosca found a peephole through which she could see the back of his head. He was still staring at the door by which his oldest friend had departed with so little warning.

Yes, Mr. Clent. You understand it now. She leaped away and looked poison at you because you gripped her right hand. The hand she's been protecting since the night of the Pawnbrokers' Auction, where she sold her services for good and all. It's why she couldn't carry her own bags and boxes, why she couldn't grab hold of me properly that day in the pleasure garden. It's her palm, Mr. Clent; it hasn't had time to heal since the Locksmiths put their brand on it.

She's a Locksmith, Mr. Clent. It's how she got into Toll after I stole her money. It's why she changed her lace gloves for kid, so nobody could see the brand. It's the reason she asked me to go after the Luck—the Luck that the Locksmiths wanted. She probably knew the Luck was a person and that I couldn't steal it—all she really wanted was a description of the room so she'd know if there was a way in . . . and I told her everything the Locksmiths needed to know.

"I would not bother going after her," Clent remarked, as calmly as if he was recommending trout over tripe. "They will have given her very specific orders, you see, concerning where she is to run if she is, ah, *unmasked*. Preparations will have been made. By now she is gone, and I do not think we shall be seeing the lady again. She will be sent elsewhere—wherever the Locksmiths need her next."

"The Locksm— What? Impossible!" The mayor sounded as if he might explode.

"Far from impossible, I fear." Clent sighed. "Has anybody here seen her take off her gloves, even when sewing indoors?" Silence. "My lord mayor, cast your mind back to your conversations with her. Did you, by any chance, confide in her the location of Mosca's letter drop, or the imminent arrival of Sir Feldroll's men the night before last?"

"Do you mean to say that all this while she has been—that duplicitous adventuress!"

"No, no." Clent's tone was wistful and gentle. "Just a sorry autumn soul. The tide of one's years and fortunes goes out, and one is left on the beach to scramble for a living as best one can. And the things one resolved never to do are suddenly a way of surviving long enough to see next year's snowdrops. Ah, poor Jenny-Wren."

The mayor made a squashed noise. "Wren? No, vixen! Harpy! Yes, she tricked me into speaking of the letter drop and Sir Feldroll's men! And all this last night, when she and I and my steward were locked in the counting house, her crocodile sympathy . . . coaxing me to tell her more of my daughter's kidnapping! The names of the kidnappers—the circumstances of her disappearance—the nature of the ransom itself!"

"And . . . how much did you tell her?"

Silence.

Everything, thought Mosca. *You told the old tabby cat everything.*

"Ah. I see. But this does at least mean, gentlemen," Clent went on, "that I can at last unbind my tongue. For the last two days I have suspected that we had a spy in our midst, and could not speak freely without danger. But now . . . I believe that it is about time I told you all a story. A tale of a radish, a midnight horse race, and a ferret-featured child with the devil's own wits."

And a tale he told, of Mosca Mye, with much flash and flourish, a tale that took all dangers and made them magnificent as djinn, a tale that gilded each sickening gamble with a dashing nonchalance. A pair of coal black eyes watched him from the dank cellar below, widening as their grubby, battered owner heard herself become a heroine for the span of his story. A story that ended triumphantly with an account of that daring heroine's infiltration of the salvation hole.

"But . . ." The mayor seemed to be piecing things together. "Does that not mean that right now the child is—"

"Over 'ere under the floor, yer lordship!" Mosca called out. There was a host of small scuffles and thuds, suggesting that several people had jumped out of their skins.

"Precisely." Clent sounded a little smug. "Forgive us our reticence, but it did not seem prudent to mention Miss Mye's masterful intrusion before the Locksmith spy had been driven from our midst."

"My lord mayor—can the floor not be raised?" asked Sir Feldroll.

The mayor gave orders, and tools were brought by mystified servants, but a few experiments with pick and saw quickly revealed that under the chapel's tiles lay solid stone slabs on timber beams, sealed into place with mortar. There was no way to break through to Mosca's cell and haul her up into the day.

Clent waited until the servants had left once more before continuing.

"Gentlemen, thanks to our intrepid miniature agent below, we know where Miss Beamabeth is, and the Locksmiths at present do not. But mark my words, if they mean to find her, then they *will*. And when they have her, what are they likely to do? To hand her back to her friends with a doff of the cap? Or will they perhaps tell you, my lord mayor, that they are better able to arrange her safety than yourself, just as they did with the Luck? Will they perhaps choose to keep her in night, like the old folktale about the Princess of Butterflies who married the Lord of the Dead? Or will they ask a second ransom, one that you can ill afford now that the first is gone?

"If we wish to recover her, then it must be done with the greatest of haste. Rescuing her from the scurrilous Skellow and his coterie of cutthroats is likely to be hazardous . . . but I would not give half a fig for our chances of snatching her from the clutches of the Locksmiths once they have her. And if the nefarious Skellow *does* have the ransom, it might, I fear, bode badly for the lady's future unless we can slip in before, shall we say, the fall of the blade."

"The Locksmiths' letter . . . the Luck . . . my hands are tied." Such a short time ago the mayor had seemed like a cliff of granite, towering, harsh, and capable of weathering anything. But the recent succession of shocks seemed to have broken him apart. Now others could scoop him up by the handful like gravel, and the Locksmiths currently had the largest scoop.

"Yes, my lord mayor," Clent hastened to agree. "Yes . . . your hands are tied." There was the tiniest hint of stress on the word "your."

"But mine are not," responded Sir Feldroll promptly. "And you, my lord mayor, are not responsible for anything I do. Perhaps, Mr. Clent, you would be so good as to tell us what you have in mind?"

27

Goodman Garotten,
red-handed bringer of
retribution

There were a lot of questions Aramai Goshawk wanted answered. Why, on the night of Saint Yacobray, had his men stumbled upon a come-as-a-Clatterhorse party? How had Mistress Bessel been detected as his spy in the mayor's household? But at the moment the most pressing question was: Where is Beamabeth Marlebourne? And the woman before him apparently could not answer it.

"So what *do* you know?" he asked without looking up.

Mistress Bessel was perched on the edge of her seat, under the gaze of two dozen golden eyes. Stuffed owls regarded her from bench and shelf with frozen, predatory astonishment, as though she was a novelty mouse.

"Only what the mayor himself told me before Eponymous tumbled to my secret—but that was a good deal. The names of the kidnappers' ringleaders—Rabilan

Skellow and Brand Appleton."

"Appleton," repeated Goshawk, with such relish that the word might indeed have been an apple to be polished on his mind's sleeve.

He prided himself on noting curiosities and inconsistencies, because they were so often important. Hence he had noticed that of late a well-brought-up young man by the name of Appleton had been exposing himself to the hazards of the Bludgeon Court to win sweetmeats and little luxuries. Now Goshawk was experiencing the exquisite satisfaction of one who has preserved half a broken cup just long enough to find the other half. "So *that* is why he had such a need of candied violets—he had the tastes of a little captive princess to pamper. How gentlemanly.

"Now what in the world," Goshawk murmured, raising his eyes to stare at Mistress Bessel, "should I do with you?"

His colorless gaze covered her face like a cold, damp cloth, just long enough for her autumnal ruddiness to wane and pale under his scrutiny.

"I think your talents will serve us best in Dogmalton for a while, until we can discover how far news of your . . . allegiance has spread." She read his dismissive gesture correctly, and gratefully fled his presence.

As a matter of fact, Aramai Goshawk was fairly well pleased with Mistress Jennifer Bessel, particularly for helping him with his long-term plan to seize the Luck, but he had no intention of telling her so. Such as she were often most useful when kept slightly uneasy and off-balance. He cleared his throat, and by the time he looked around, two men were at his side, gloved hands neatly clasped before their bellies.

"Brand Appleton," Goshawk said aloud. "He has lodgings in Preck Street, and he might be just stupid enough to be found there. If not, hunt down the girl known as Laylow. If she is suiting her actions to her name, seek out every rat cranny she has ever used as a bolt hole. Tell her that we are looking to take Appleton, and if she helps us find him, we might choose to take him in one piece."

Ah, the difficulties of *balance*. If one wished to control, the balance of fear had to be just right. You could not allow people to become desperate, or they lost all fear and did wild and unpredictable things. And yet you could not let them become complacent, or they became impudent and rash. These kidnappers, for example. Daring to set up their own little scheme in Goshawk's town without consulting him.

The daughter, if she could be recovered, would be valuable, for it seemed that most of Toll-by-Day was within half a hop of falling in love with her. However, he doubted that she was still alive, now the ransom had been paid. The jewel, however, was of considerably more interest. If he gave the kidnappers time to catch their breaths, they would find eager buyers among the Pawnbrokers, and if that happened, the gem would slip through his fingers and out of Toll.

"Abject lessons are in order, I think." His tiny, child-like hands interleaved, forming a toy church and steeple. "These kidnappers must be dead by dawn. Find this ransom, and silence anybody who sees you taking it. Have a couple of men watching the Twilight Gate entrance in case the mayor or this Sir Feldroll have sent any more clodhopping oafs to rescue Miss Marlebourne. If any such do appear . . . follow them and arrange for them all to be personally introduced to the Langfeather."

His oyster-pale eyes narrowed for a second.

"If the mayor heeds my letter and sends nobody, we might even ransom his daughter back to him, if we can recover her alive. But if he does send more marauders into our streets . . . then I suppose poor Beamabeth Marlebourne will have 'died during a botched raid by the mayor's men.' A lesson in the dangers of taking things into one's own hands instead of leaving it to the professionals. She is useful to us but, now that we have the Luck, not essential."

The finger church unfolded itself, and Goshawk thoughtfully fiddled with his blotter before speaking again.

"If you can . . . try to keep that headstrong urchin girl alive."

"The urchin—do you mean Eponymous Clent's girl, sir? The one he sent nightside a couple of nights ago?"

"Mmm? Oh. No, actually I meant Laylow. As for Clent's girl . . . yes, I suppose it is *possible* that she is still alive after three nights. If so . . . she is just another messy detail. Dispose of her."

In the heart of the clock tower, cog fought cog in darkness, each biting with all the force of its metal teeth, never guessing that they were part of one great, relentless machine. Somewhere on the walls of the town a bugle blew, and the clock answered with a tinny ditty of its own. Across Toll, the day retreated indoors, and at the same time the little model of Goodlady Blatchett, with her bright eyes and sack of toads, retreated into the darkness of the clock archway. As the second bugle sounded and night prepared to advance, Goodman Garotten emerged to take the Goodlady's place with his sickle and scales. His painted eyes were yellow as yolk, his tiny teeth clenched and bared.

Without knowing it, Mosca Mye was at that very moment imitating his expression exactly, not twenty yards away, her stomach knotting itself with apprehension. As soon as the locks on the false wooden wall covering the secret frog door had been unfastened and the sound of jingling faded, she had emerged and sprinted for the Twilight Gate. Now she sat watching from the farthest reaches of the street. The plan that she had contrived that afternoon with Clent and Sir Feldroll was about to be put into action.

As she watched, the little door to the Twilight Gate opened and five figures emerged. Without a moment's hesitation they scattered, each taking their own pre-planned route. If there were spies watching for new arrivals, it was unlikely that they would be able to pursue *all* of them.

Mosca grinned with relief as she saw the plan being followed, then turned about and ran toward the agreed rendezvous. The scraps she had tied about her clogs turned her feet into fat, ragged mop heads, but they did not ring out against the cobbles.

The reinforcements would be a medley of all the cooperative night names that could be mustered in desperation at a few hours' notice. One ex-soldier attached to Sir Feldroll, one man with a visitor's pass who had consented to join the rescue in exchange for the toll out of Toll . . . and three prisoners from the Grovels, the grisly cell into which Mosca had been thrown a couple of nights before. All three had leaped at the first chance of pardon and freedom they had seen in several long years.

The rendezvous point was a darkened archway that Mosca had chosen because the slanting light of the early evening moon did not touch the neighboring alleys, and because it could be reached at a run without stepping into the light. She was the first to arrive, and tucked herself away into the recess, hugging her ribs and forcing her breathing to slow. At last she heard footsteps and panting breaths approach.

"Prattler's Jack!" she whispered, tensed to run again if the right password was not given.

"Sangrin's Tumble!" came the answer. Both were the names of dice games. "Is that Mye?"

"Every inch. Tuck yourself in here with me—we wait five minutes for the others and then we wait no more."

Three more figures arrived to whisper the right password within the next two minutes. Mosca clenched her fists and counted her heartbeats until five minutes had passed without any sign of their last comrade.

There would be no more waiting. The plan had been quite specific on that point. *If any of you thinks you are being followed, then do not go to the rendezvous. If you cannot lose your shadow, then lose yourself in Toll, and pray that you are not lost in good earnest.*

"We're in your hands, Mye." Mosca thought it was probably Sir Feldroll's man speaking. "Where now?"

"The Chutes," whispered Mosca. "Undertaker district. Stay close, and keep your steps soft."

In your hands. The hands in question were shaking, and not just with the cold. Fear of the Locksmiths and Skellow's thumb-cutting knife flooded Mosca but did not fill her. Somehow there was room in her core for an angry little knot of excitement, tight and fierce as a pike's grin.

Being a Locksmith meant never having to kick down a door. A flick, a click, and there you were in the hallway.

Sometimes there were screams, but usually the breath people drew in to bellow at you leaked out in little whimpers once they realized what you were. Sometimes the truth hit them like a fist to the belly, and they literally crumpled to the floor. Something had brought the Locksmiths to their door, and they would do anything, say anything, sell anyone to make them go away again.

"Yes, Laylow does stay here sometimes—but she has not been here this last week! Here—let me show you the room she uses! And this is where she hides her packages, under the floorboard! Yes, I can give you the names of her friends. . . ."

Search the room, picking up her few belongings. Gather up the chocolate-scented, muslin-wrapped packages from their hole in the wainscot. Snatch up a chicken leg from the landlady's table on the way out.

Being a Locksmith meant never having to say sorry.

"Nobody told me you were a *foreigner*." Sir Feldroll's ex-soldier sounded disgruntled and suspicious. The little rescue party's steps had taken them now into more open streets, and when they crossed a patch of moonlight, Mosca's outlandish garb and greenish skin had become visible.

"Well, nobody told me *you* were a slack-bellied noddy with a busy jaw," Mosca retorted sharply. "I guess we both got cause to complain."

"Just show us the Chutes, you peppery little minx!" the other snapped.

It was not just the fact that she was green, Mosca

suspected, that was causing her new comrade's sudden hostility. Perhaps he had not realized until now how young she was. Perhaps now he felt absurd at having placed himself under her captaincy. The giddy, terrifying sense that she was in control of a unit of a men started to slip away from her, like a giant's boot falling absurdly off her narrow foot.

"How would you like a new grin for a necktie?" came a sudden snarl from behind Mosca. She turned to find that one of the ex-prisoners from the Grovels was glaring at the soldier hot eyed. His face seemed to have been used as a whetstone, and a mesh of scars folded his forehead and left his eyebrows as dotted lines. "Leave the little mort be, or I'll tie your tongue to the railings!"

The threat, implausible as it was, served to silence the other man. Perhaps he reflected that even a failed attempt to execute it was likely to be very, very painful. Or perhaps he had noticed the way in which the other two ex-convicts had moved supportively to Mosca's side.

"Pratin' popinjay," one of them whispered in her ear. "Bold enough in the street, ain't he? But if *he* was dropped into the spring-ankle warehouse, he'd be keening like a kitten."

Mosca understood, and turned her head to give the speaker a nasty little grin of agreement, which he answered with a wink. "Spring-ankle warehouse" was a cant term for prison. Somehow, in spite of her disguise, the Grovelers had recognized her as their former cell mate—perhaps because they had met her in darkness and known her only through her voice and temper. In the Grovels she had been their prey, but now they were part of the same fraternity—at least while there was a chance to gang up on somebody who had never known leg-irons. Belatedly, it seemed, Mosca was getting her garnish's worth.

"Any more gabble? No? Then come this way." She hoped she was sounding confident. The rescue party's odds were poor enough without them fighting among themselves.

"Laylow? Yes, came in here for a dram o' gin two nights ago with that young radical cove, the firebrand with the mad eyes. No, I never listen in, but the Beloved put ears on our heads, and mine pull in sound something fearsome. So . . . I hear him asking her for help, saying he don't trust some folks . . . something about a horse.

"No, I do not know where she lays her head. Perhaps you ask her radical friend? What? No, not as such, but I have often seen him awalkin' off toward the Chutes. . . ."

It was in the Chutes, of course, that the plans became shaky, for Mosca had never even been in this district before. There were a few wrong turns in the glistening streets, and Mosca's hairs rose at the thought of her followers losing confidence in her. On either side of the streets were ominous stacks of person-size boxes. Some were cracked and battered wood, and she slipped past them as fast as she could, fearful of glimpsing a dead eye or pallid hand through a crevice. Here and there in tiny shrines models of Goodman Postrophe stood sentinel, ready to squirt mellowberry juice into the eyes of any dead who decided to climb out of their boxes. His presence was only slightly reassuring.

There were sounds as well, from deep in the icy, intestinal tangle of streets. A stutter of wood being dragged across cobbles. A shriek of a metal winch. A clatter of hatches. A weightless handful of silent seconds, then a smash far below, softened by echo, so that it was little more than a cough in the Langfeather's throat.

"There." It was exactly as Brand Appleton had described, a cooper's shop opposite an abandoned alehouse with a broken door. It stood on the corner, a small cask swaying from a chain over the door. It was a mean, narrow little shop with one small shuttered window at the front and two floors above it.

"How many inside?" asked the soldier.

"Five," answered Mosca. "Maybe six. And the lady."

"Then we'll have to move fast—knock down anyone in the shop, then run upstairs, kick in the door, and cover all within with our pistols before they can hurt the lady. . . ." The soldier trailed off, realizing that nobody was actually listening to him. Mosca and the other ex-Grovelers had formed a huddle and gone into muffled conference.

". . . milled a ken like this when I was nine," one was saying. "No point in puffing our way up the stairs and expecting to catch 'em winking—these old wooden steps ring out underfoot like a regiment of drums."

"Roof, maybe?" Another ex-convict leaned back. "Boggarts take it, I can see no holes. Pity we cannot whip in at a glaze—and the chimney looks too narrow, even for Mye—"

"No—the trick is to sneak up there, or bring those bullies *down* the stairs, one at a time," interrupted the first again, the man with the whetstone face. "We need a lay to hook 'em in."

"Well, however we gull 'em, it had better be sweet and swift," whispered Mosca. "Or we shall have the Jinglers snappin' at our heels!"

She glanced up at Sir Feldroll's man and felt a bittersweet flush of malicious satisfaction. Perhaps she felt out of place in Toll-by-Night, but it was plain that this was nothing compared to the plight of the soldier. His eyes looked fearful, dazzled by the unfamiliar mosaic of murk and moonlight. The thieves' cant terms that were starting to roll off her tongue so glibly had bounced off his ears like pebbles.

Mosca was a fast learner, and after three nights she was starting to think and speak as a nightling. She was learning to see in the dark. At another time, this might have worried her.

* * *

A tall Locksmith came out of a gin shop's back room, pulling off his gloves. He tucked them in a pocket and replaced them with clean ones.

"The cooper in the Chutes" was all he said to his companions. Without another word they rose and followed him out through the front door. They left it ajar, letting the wind play over the broken furniture within.

The cooper looked up from the splayed staves of a half-fashioned firkin when the door of his shop swung open. Two men had entered, both of them strangers, rolling in a heavy-looking hogshead barrel over three feet high.

"Hey, cooper!" called one of them. "We've a barrel that's split and starting to spill—can you take a look and tell us if you can mend the crack without taking out all the grain? We're in a hurry."

"Not likely." Whistling under his breath, the cooper strolled toward his customers, a hammer dangling from one strong, callused hand. "But let us have a look at it." He pried away the lid of the cask and froze.

Holding her breath inside the barrel, Mosca saw the rounded roof of her cramped world tugged away abruptly and replaced by the face of a startled young man. He was not handsome, having a bunched sort of nose that wanted to be a fist. His lumpy, good-humored mouth was pursed with whistling, but as he saw the pistol gripped tightly in her hands, the whistle died and was replaced by a breathy little thread of sound.

Mosca could hardly breathe. Her knees were tucked tight against her chest. The metal of the pistol was very cold, and her two fingers tucked around the trigger shook uncontrollably. The cooper had wide, light-colored eyes. She thought they might be green.

"Keep whistling," whispered the Groveler with the whetstone face, "and put down your hammer."

The cooper wet his lips and managed a husky warbled note. He stooped and obediently laid down his hammer.

"Clever lad," murmured Whetstone Face approvingly. "Keep your wits this way, and you'll live long enough to bounce grandchildren on your knees."

While one of the Grovelers took up the cooper's whistle, mimicking the tune perfectly, the cooper obeyed the orders muttered by Whetstone Face. He sat down on a barrel and let his hands be tied behind his back. He answered questions about the rooms upstairs, the number of people, the stations of the guards. Mosca listened, her stomach curdling. Everything was going according to plan, but somehow she did not feel like a rescuer anymore. She felt like a robber. It was the fearful eye whites of the cooper and the fierce, oily smell of the pistol.

"Come on, Mye," said one of her comrades, tipping her barrel so that she tumbled out of it and dropped her gun with a clatter.

One Groveler listened at the door behind the counter, then very carefully turned a key from the cooper's belt in its lock and opened it. The cooper was bound and gagged, and left in the care of the increasingly perplexed and disdainful ex-soldier. Two of the Grovelers slipped through the door and onto the stairway beyond, Mosca and the third Groveler just a few paces behind. The man in front of Mosca took the greatest care to step along the edges of the stairs so they did not creak, and Mosca copied him.

They had just reached the door at the top of the stairs when there was a crash from the shop below, and a hoarse cry. Instantly the door before them was flung open and two men hurled themselves out of it. To judge by their expressions, they only realized midhurl that they were flying past four flabbergasted strangers who had just flattened themselves against the wall to let them pass. With remarkable presence of mind, Whetstone Face stuck out a leg to hook the ankle of the foremost, and the pair went tumbling down the stairs, using their bellies and faces as toboggans.

Still pressed back against the wall, Mosca saw the Grovelers bound through the door into the open room. She wondered whether she was supposed to be holding the fallen men prisoner with her little pistol. But she could not bring herself to point it at them, for in her mind's eye she could so easily imagine hiccuping with fear and sending a little bead of death through somebody's forehead. In any case, they did not seem ready to get up yet.

From the room into which the Grovelers had rushed

there came two pistol cracks, then a lot of crashes, oaths, moans, scuffles, and floorboard creaks. Then, quite suddenly, about four people shouting at once.

"Easy, easy—"

"Halt—put your pistol—"

"Get back! Back, or I'll—"

Mosca entered the room and found it in a state of stalemate. Two men lay motionless on the floor, and she could not tell if they were alive or dead. One she recognized as one of Skellow's men from the bastle house. Another lay amid the wreckage of a broken table and had a thin, pocked face that also looked faintly familiar. All three of the Grovelers had weapons drawn, though one had a hand clasped to his side. All were currently bow tense, their attention focused upon a tall, angular, sickle-faced figure. It was Rabilan Skellow, and he had a pistol held to the head of Beamabeth Marlebourne.

Skellow was backing slowly away with his captive, his breath coming raggedly through his teeth. His eye flickered over Mosca and lodged there, and she could see him grappling with frayed shreds of recognition.

"*You!*"

For a moment, Mosca was afraid he would turn the pistol on her instead, but he kept it against Beamabeth's temple and reached behind him with his free hand to open a door. He backed slowly through it, dragging the mayor's daughter along with him. Her eyes were kitten wide, her face pale and wondering, and one of her satin shoes was missing. Her hands were tied behind her back.

A few seconds later the Grovelers forced their way through the same door, Mosca just behind them, and found themselves in an apparently empty room. Just as they were spinning this way and that looking for the vanished pair, there was an earsplitting shriek.

It appeared to come from behind the wall. Whetstone Face kicked at the plaster, which tore before his boot, proving to be no more than a dingy canvas panel concealing a passage beyond. One good yank slid the panel aside, and beyond could be seen a narrow corridor, illuminated by a side window. In the middle of the passage Beamabeth was kneeling, Skellow standing over her with a knife in his hand, the blade almost touching her limp ringlets. He looked up as the canvas tore, and it seemed to Mosca that he looked directly at her, his teeth bared in a parody of his horrible smile. Then there was a deafening crack, and Skellow gave a sort of backward nod, drew himself unsteadily up on tiptoe, and then collapsed.

Something seemed to jump in Mosca's chest, and her nose filled with the smell of the old wine cellar where Havoc Gray had met his end. For a moment she wondered wildly whether it was her gun that had fired. But hers was still cold and still in her hand. Smoke was drifting from Whetstone Face's pistol.

Beamabeth still sat quivering, but quivering was better than no motion at all. She raised her head, and blue eyes peered out at Mosca without recognition or much in the way of wits. Whetstone Face strode forward and pulled her to her feet.

"All right, lass. We're here to take you home to your father." It was said kindly enough. Apparently Beamabeth's magic was working even here.

From behind there came the thunderous noise of many boots on the stairs. A sound as loud as a battle drum, just as the Grovelers had said. One pair of boots might have been their comrade, the ex-soldier. A whole gang of boots could only mean trouble.

There was no going back the way they had come. They could only go forward, down the corridor that Skellow had hoped would provide him with escape. Whetstone Face scooped up Beamabeth.

"Come on!" he rasped, then turned and ran down the passage. The others followed.

In spite of the thunder of her own blood, Mosca could not help wavering an instant as she passed the fallen body of Skellow, the man she had come to Toll to undo. There was a spreading darkness on his chest. She knew that he must be dead. And then he spoke.

"Little witch" was all he said before his lizard-hiss breath stilled. His long fingers released the knife in his hand. Mosca felt as though she had killed him, and she was filled with too many emotions at once to know whether it made her happy or not.

"Quickly!" A Groveler grabbed her arm and dragged

her away. One corridor, two doors, and a rope ladder later, they were out on the open streets.

Mistress Leap coped very well with the sudden and unannounced arrival of Mosca, Beamabeth Marlebourne, and three of the most disreputable, gibbet-worthy strangers she had ever seen. She remained upright, indeed rigidly so, though for a couple of minutes she could manage nothing but a string of broken vowels.

"Sorry, Mistress Leap! I had no chance to tell you the new plan! This is Beamabeth Marlebourne, I think she might have had the sense scared out of her—"

"You poor little violet!" Mistress Leap recovered her voice and enfolded Beamabeth in a motherly embrace that seemed to rumple the mayor's daughter even more. "You *are* beautiful—every bit as beautiful as they always said! I knew you would be, even when I delivered you!"

In Beamabeth's cornflower blue eyes, realization appeared amid confusion, like a butterfly reeling out of a dust cloud.

"You are . . . the midwife lady? The one who sent me the letter?"

"Yes! Oh, you read it! Then you know . . . it must have been a shock, of course, but I am sure you always knew you were special. . . . Ah, how I wish I could introduce you to your real parents, but they passed away of influenza ten years ago, the poor dears. . . ."

Mosca had snatched off her basket hat and was

halfway out of her Seisian regalia.

"Mistress Leap! We got to hurry because the Locksmiths are huntin' Miss Beamabeth! I think we shook them all off, but we got to get her disguised. And then we need your help! We need you to take us to the Committee of the Hours."

"But their doors will be shut!" protested Mistress Leap. "The only part still open will be . . . oh."

Mosca nodded grimly as she splashed water onto her face from a bowl and began rubbing the greenishness from her skin. "The hatch where you put in the babies born with daylight names, along with their papers. The committee members are waiting there to pull us through the chute. Then they'll drop down money for you—and for them." She gave a nod toward the Grovelers.

The midwife cast an uncertain glance over Beamabeth's figure. "Are you *quite* sure that Miss Beamabeth will fit through?"

"The mayor's people measured it yesterday, and took measurements from her brocade dress."

"Brocade—the *green* brocade?" faltered Beamabeth. "It is just that . . . of late I have had some trouble with the buttons. . . ."

Mosca hesitated for a moment. Perhaps Beamabeth's figure was not quite as slight and delicate as she had thought. "Well, you might have to wriggle a bit," she admitted. "But with us pushing and the other side pulling like fury, we will wrench you through somehow.

Now, Mistress Leap, can you give Miss Beamabeth some clothes that make her look less like a princess?"

The Locksmiths made a thorough search of the rooms upstairs, then came back to the cooper's shop. The ex-soldier had put up a decent fight when the Locksmiths burst in, and that had been his worst and last mistake. The cooper still sat stiff shouldered on his barrel, having worked out that clenching his eyes shut and saying nothing was his best chance of survival.

"No sign of the Marlebourne girl."

"Keep searching for the ransom—and check the kitchen for radishes. Any of the kidnappers alive up there?"

There were a few heartbeats' silence.

"You wanted 'em *alive?*"

A long-drawn-out sigh, then the sound of gloved fingers irritably scratching at stubble.

"We were told to hush them—but after they told us where to find the ransom, not before. Do you want to explain that to Mr. Goshawk?"

The population of Toll-by-Night was just starting to emerge onto the streets when a dowdy threesome set out for the Committee of the Hours. There were many nods for Mistress Leap, and nobody paid any attention to the two girls who followed behind her, the eldest clutching a baby-shaped bundle to her chest, the younger carrying a large box. Many nightfolk were accustomed to seeing the midwife taking a baby to the committee, so nobody was particularly surprised. Some even jokingly asked the baby to remember them with a groat or two when it became a rich daylighter.

Right now, however, the older girl looked as cowed and fearful as Mosca could possibly have wished on her bitterest day. Each glance shook her like a cowslip in the breeze. She had every reason to be afraid. Mosca had, with some glee, helped smear grime over Beamabeth's perfect nose and chin, and the golden ringlets had been damped down and tucked under a stained cloth bonnet, but there was still a risk that somebody would notice the fineness of her hands or the lack of Toll-by-Night pallor, and ask her to lower her "baby" so that they could see her badge.

Perhaps a greater danger was the restless stirring that Mosca could feel inside the box she carried. To judge by the soft hisses within, the contents were a few short minutes from an explosion of goosely impatience.

"Oh, thank the Beloved—here we are!"

Mistress Leap had led them to a small building not far from the clock tower. Set in the wall was a square wooden door a foot and a half wide. Mistress Leap took a key from her pocket, unlocked the door, and opened it. Beyond was a tiny cavity like the inside of an oven, but with a shaft leading upward.

"Usually they lower a bucket for the baby and its paperwork," whispered Mistress Leap. She leaned forward. "Hello?" she called tentatively. "This is Leveretia Leap!"

A bubble of eager conversation floated down the chute. "Do you have Miss Marlebourne there?" came the whisper.

"Yes! Are you ready for her?"

"Ready!"

The threesome glanced about to make sure the street was clear; then Beamabeth handed over the bundle of dishcloths that had served as her "baby." With obvious trepidation she stooped and peered up the chute. Hands reached down toward her and took hold of her forearms.

"Pull!"

Beamabeth gave a faint squeak and started to disappear up into the chute, hauled by the hands above. Her torso vanished, then her hips, until there was nothing visible but her feet and petticoats, kicking and scrabbling at the sides of the chute. There were indecorous sounds of scuffling and whimpers of discomfort.

"Too many candied violets," Mosca muttered heartlessly, once Beamabeth's feet and skirts had vanished. After a short pause a bucket was lowered, containing six pouches.

"Money," explained Mosca urgently as she pushed the pouches into Mistress Leap's hands and loaded Saracen's box into the bucket. "Three for those men in your house—but the rest's all yours." Mistress Leap seemed overwhelmed, and Mosca thought she might be fighting back tears as she hid the money in her apron. "And if I was you, mistress, I'd take it home *right now*, and pack up, and get out of Toll *tonight*. Before the Locksmiths can work out you had any part in all of this."

"Believe me, my dear, I mean to be out within the *hour*." As Saracen's box was hauled up the chute, the midwife cupped Mosca's face in her worn hands and gave her a gentle peck on the forehead. "Good luck!"

"See you under the sun."

They exchanged a last smile before the midwife hurried off and disappeared into the alleyways.

"This is Mosca Mye!" she hissed up the chute. "You ready to pull me up?"

"Hey!" The call came from across the square, from a group of three men who had just turned a corner. Three men in gloves. Three men who had just noticed a young girl leaning into a chute for which she should not have had the key.

"Pull me up!" shrieked Mosca, ducking and maneuvering her head and shoulders into the chute as Beamabeth had done. "Quick, or I'm done for!" She could see a square of light above, with heads and shoulders silhouetted against it. Hands came down and grabbed her reaching arms, and she was rudely dragged upward.

In the street there were further cries and sounds of running steps. She felt a strong hand grab at her ankle and gave a squawk as she briefly became the rope in a tug-of-war. She kicked, and kicked, and then her shoe flew off and hit somebody, to judge by the sound, and the grip on her ankle was released. Then the half dozen hands on her arms dragged her upward and into the light.

28

GOODLADY MELNIECK,
CONCEALER OF THE THORN
WITHIN THE ROSE

OF COURSE MOST of the welcome waiting in the lighted room above was for Beamabeth. Her father was there, along with Sir Feldroll and the family physician, to make sure she had contracted nothing too dreadful. Her fears had now caught up with her, and her ensuing fit of faintness had the whole coterie running to and fro with cut-glass bottles. However, in the midst of this frenzy people did find time to whisper, "Well done!" in Mosca's ear.

"Fissure!" barked the mayor, who seemed to have recovered a little of his grit and bristle. "Tend to Miss Mye next!" Mosca watched numbly as the mayor's physician came over and examined her bruises and scratches and the reddened marks on her wrists left by her bonds during her imprisonment at the bastle house, days before. Beamabeth had managed to avoid all such marks—apparently the rich even got a better class of kidnapping.

The candlelight seemed very bright, and Mosca was too dazzled for a little while to realize that Eponymous Clent had quietly sat down next to her.

"Hello, Mr. Clent. We . . . did it, didn't we?"

He nodded. "We shall be free to leave Toll tomorrow. It is *done*."

Mosca drooped her head against Clent's arm, suddenly exhausted.

"Technically," Clent continued with a twinkle, "you will be under arrest when the sun rises, as a nightling trespassing in Toll-by-Day. But I have been assured that your 'custody' will involve a good deal of actual custard—not to mention rabbit pie, dumplings, and preserved pears. Tomorrow you can expect to be 'evicted' from Toll, alongside myself, through a gate of our choice. In the meantime, however, you will be sentenced to a long, deep sleep in a nice soft bed."

Mosca did indeed wake up in a very comfortable bed.

She had only the dimmest recollection of nodding off against Clent's arm and hearing the conversation around her dull to a drone. Somebody must have carried her to a bed, removed her remaining shoe, stockings, and bonnet, and tucked her under cotton sheets and three soft woolen blankets that smelled of lavender. She opened her eyes and saw peach-colored curtains around her bed.

She closed her eyes again, and there was a warm and weightless sense of comfort, and the cool of a clean pillow against her cheek.

It was after an hour of such drowsing that Mosca roused herself enough to sit up. She drew back the curtain and stood, squeezing at the chocolate-colored rug with her toes. The shutters of the little bedroom had been thrown back, and through the window she could see the ice-pale sun in a sky of eggshell blue. Mosca's eyes hurt, but she realized they were watering from more than the light. Until this moment, in the deep, cold roots of her being, she had not believed that she would see the sun again. Walking to the window, she discovered that it looked out upon the green castle courtyard and realized that she must be in the mayor's house.

For a little while she sat in a small wicker chair, watching golden dust motes chase one another slowly and futilely in the shafts of sunlight, and the birds string themselves like beads along the roofs of Toll-by-Day. Then she looked at herself in the mirror on the dresser, noting the dirt and bruises she had not noticed in the netherworld of cut-price rushlights. She splashed water on her face, cleaning the last hints of green crusting from her cheeks and eyebrows. There was no doubt about it—she was paler than she had been before entering the town, and there was a touch of shadow under each eye. Four nights in Toll-by-Night had, in keeping with the name, taken their toll.

I'm going to get out. Her spirits lurched unsteadily into the air like a wounded pigeon. *I'm going to get out of this worm pit of a town. And I will never, never come back here again.*

As she found out before long, a lot of other people had similar plans.

Shortly after a maid had brought Mosca a tray with a bowl of hot rabbit soup and a golden-crusted loaf of fresh bread, Eponymous Clent arrived with news of the town.

"Stories of Miss Beamabeth's daring escape from her captors are all over town, of course, and the citizens of Toll-by-Day are itching to see Brand Appleton aloft on a gallows." Clent stood by the window, peering down into the castle grounds market, plump fingers tap-tapping impatiently at his waistcoat pocket. Evidently he was eager to shake the dust of Toll from his shoes and write something curt and cryptic about it in his little black book of never-come-back. "However, it would seem that word of the missing Luck has gotten out . . . and now a number of notables are *also* trying to get out. The guilds, mostly."

"The guilds?" Mosca halted her attempts to cram as much bread into her mouth as possible without her cheeks exploding.

"The Stationers left first thing this morning. All of them. The Playing Card Makers were half a step behind them, and I notice that all the Goldsmiths seem to have shut up shop."

"What? Surely the *guilds* do not believe that Toll will fall in the river if the Luck is took from the town?" Mosca boggled.

"I am sure not all of them believe that . . . but they see the way the wind sits. I think there is little doubt now that Toll-by-Day will fall to the Locksmiths, just as Toll-by-Night did before it. The mayor's spirit is broken. He is terrified that if the Locksmiths are angered, they will take the Luck away, and that Toll will suddenly fall off the cliff like a pie off a sill. And so he has taken on new advisers—Locksmith advisers. From this day forth, I do not think he will be seen without them."

Mosca's blood ran cold. Toll was now a sinking ship, and she could hardly blame the Guilds for their ratlike scamper away from it. The subdued urgency in Clent's manner was starting to make more sense too.

"How long we got, Mr. Clent? B'fore the Locksmiths take over?"

"I, ah, have no idea. None at all. It might not happen for a fortnight or, ah, for all I know, by dusk today. . . ."

"Today?"

By now Aramai Goshawk would know that Beamabeth Marlebourne had been snatched from under his nose, and since Mistress Bessel was spying for him, he might have a shrewd idea that Mosca and Clent were responsible. If they were still in Toll-by-Day when Goshawk took control of it, she had a feeling their future careers would be limited to a very long drop followed by a brief and lethal swim.

"Precisely," answered Clent. "And since it is currently such fine weather for traveling, I, ah, thought I should drop by and find out how quickly you were recovering."

Mosca jumped up. "I jus' got a lot better. Where's my blinkin' bonnet? And where's Saracen?"

Over the next ten minutes Mosca made short work of her lunch, scrambled into the lilac gown that had been laid out for her, then flung herself into hurried packing and goose retrieval, after which Mosca and Clent were almost ready to make their hasty adieus.

"Typical," muttered Mosca as she fitted Saracen's muzzle. "After all the trouble we went to, rescuing Beamabeth from one Locksmith town, now she'll be trapped in another."

"I think not." Clent remarked wryly. "In all probability she will leave and marry Sir Feldroll—a gentleman who stormed out of Toll in the highest dudgeon this morning, by the way. The mayor, on the recommendation of his new advisers, has said that even fewer people will be let in and out of the town from now on, and all tolls will be raised from tomorrow. So poor Sir Feldroll will *not* be marching his army through Toll after all, it seems. Mandelion is safe from *that* quarter, at least." Clent regarded Mosca with a gleam of amusement. "Yes, I rather thought that would please you."

Brave, jubilant Mandelion and its intrepid radical

government were safe for now. Yes, that *did* make Mosca happy. So why did she still feel a strange uneasiness of spirit? Her steps slowed unwillingly and she halted by a window, biting her lip almost to bleeding point.

"Child! More haste! We are done here. You have even avenged yourself upon the detestable Skellow, who was bent on your destruction—he is no more, I gather? Killed while on the brink of shooting Miss Beamabeth."

"Stabbing. But . . . yes." Mosca thought of the last breath hissing out of Skellow's lean profile and felt queasy.

"Stabbing, shooting, it is all the same." Clent gave a dismissive wave of his hand. "Caught on the verge of committing dire damselicide. The point is, your nemesis is defeated. There is nothing more for us to do here." Clent was squinting eastward, his mind already on the road.

But Mosca was no longer listening. Looking down through the window into the castle courtyard, she could see a young woman walking to and fro beside her vegetable stall, trying in vain to calm a squalling baby. There was something about its tremble-fisted frenzy that reminded her of Blethemy's baby, the gobbet. She thought of Mistress Leap with a hundred desperate mothers, all struggling to have their babies born in a lucky hour so that they could live a better life, all clutching at that one gleaming strand of hope. That strand was about to snap. Soon Toll-by-Day would fall to the

Locksmiths as Toll-by-Night had done before it, and the town would shut up like a clam. Nightfolk and dayfolk alike would be trapped under the fearful rule of the Locksmiths, and escape for either would become all but impossible.

"Oh . . . oh, rat pellets!" exploded Mosca. "It's their last chance! Wait here a few breaths, Mr. Clent!" She stamped away down the hall. "I have to talk to Miss Beamabeth. If anybody can make the mayor listen, it will be her! And she *must* listen to me, Mr. Clent! Drizzle an' dregs, I hauled her out of Toll-by-Night by her hair! That has to be worth more than spittle!"

Mosca found Beamabeth in the long reception room where they had first met a few interminable days and nights ago. The mayor's adopted daughter was sitting at a sampler frame. From Mosca's side, she could only see the back of the design, a tangle of cream and fuchsia threads. Beamabeth was, Mosca noticed with relief, entirely alone.

"How lovely to see you looking so well, Miss Mye!" There it was again—the utterly disarming kitten smile. "That dress of mine becomes you very well. You must take it with you when you go. I can give you a shawl to match it." Beamabeth's hair was back in ringlets, and their color had come out like the sun. "You do not mind if I do not stand? My nerves are still so weak after everything that has happened."

"Miss Beamabeth . . . I wanted to talk to you about Toll. About the things the Locksmiths want the mayor to do. You got your father's ear—"

"Oh, dear." Beamabeth made a pained little moue. "Sir Feldroll was talking to me about that sort of thing this morning, and I really cannot bear to hear any more right now. It gives me a horrible headache."

"But . . . your town is running out of time! When your father signs papers with the Locksmiths, then everything goes into the night! Toll-by-Night, but all night and all day! Listen—there is still time to let people out first so they don't get trapped inside the town! The mayor could do it—he could let folks out without paying toll—"

"But Father already is making sure the important people can leave—I am certain he said so."

"But it's not just important people here! There's . . . there's the nightfolk. He could save some of them. Reclassify lots of 'em really fast, bring 'em into the day and let them out too before it's too late."

"And have all the nightlings running around loose?" Beamabeth looked appalled and astonished.

Mosca swallowed her annoyance with difficulty. "Toll is a sinkin' ship, miss, and those left in her will drown."

"Yes, it *is* very sad." Beamabeth's brow puckered as she pushed her needle into the web of threads. "That is why Sir Feldroll says we should live at his estates in Waymakem when we marry, instead of Toll." She gave a long, heartfelt sigh. "It really is very difficult to leave somewhere, though, when you have lived there all your life. But it has been getting harder and harder here over the last two months, thanks to the loss of Mandelion trade, and we have been running out of all the essentials one by one—chocolate, coffee, sugar, tea, nutmeg. Of course such things are scarce in Waymakem too, but at least there are not so many rules—"

"Hard for *you* to leave, is it?" interrupted Mosca, forgetting her determination to match Beamabeth's courteous manners. "'Tis a bleedin' sight harder for those as *cannot* leave for lack of coin! Toll-by-Day might be running out of nutmeg, but Toll-by-Night is even running out of *rats*! They been putting owls and robins in the cooking pots!"

Beamabeth pulled her face back, small crinkles appearing in her perfect nose. Now she was a kitten that had smelled something distasteful, or burned itself on something hot. It was a signal to Mosca that she had gone too far and should change her tone and the subject. But she had gone too far indeed, too far to stop.

"Everybody loves you—everybody's been risking their *lives* for you! And now you want to abandon them all to Goshawk's crew and waltz off to Waymakem with Sir Fidgety-Face Feldroll so you can keep your tea caddy full?"

"They will all be happy as long as I am happy," Beamabeth said simply. And smiled, as if she was saying something self-evident. "The town *wants* me to be safe. I shall be doing it for them as much as myself."

Mosca's mouth fell open. The surge of bitterness she had felt when she first met Beamabeth was back, and now there was no damming it.

"You spoiled, selfish, soft-headed hoity! I thought you were supposed to be some kind of angel! Just because everybody talks to you like you're the most precious thing in Toll, that doesn't mean it's *true*! You're not the only person who bleeds when they're cut, or bruises when they're struck. But nothing ever *does* bruise you, does it?"

Outside, the birds hushed and the market noises seemed to recede. Toll itself seemed to have halted in shock. The impossible had happened. Something more incredible than horses of bone or green-skinned foreigners. Somebody had shouted at Beamabeth Marlebourne.

Beamabeth's face froze, and she lost a little of her sunny rosiness. For a moment Mosca thought that the older girl might faint outright, but there was no tremor in her small pink mouth. Instead, Beamabeth's big blue eyes just stared and stared between their dark gold lashes, not even seeming to blink. At last she spoke, still in the same gentle, lilting tone.

"You really are a horrible little thing, do you know that? The way you look, the way you talk. No wonder you disgust everybody. You have no place here. The sooner you are gone, the better."

Mosca stood there stupidly in her borrowed dress, stunned and winded. She had been ready for tears or flight, perhaps outrage, an attack of nerves or a call for assistance, but not this strange calm venom—not from the girl she had rescued from Toll-by-Night by the skin of her teeth.

Mosca had been so busy working the oars of her little plan that she had failed to see the iceberg upon which it was doomed to founder. And now here it was in front of her, a towering glacial mountain of selfishness, and she could not understand how she could have missed it. How vast was it? How far beneath the surface did it go?

"No. Nothing *ever* touches you, does it?" Mosca whispered. "Look at you—not a scratch, not a bruise. Not even marks on your wrists where they were tied." She rubbed at the bruise lines around her own wrists. "If you struggled—the way *I* struggled when they tied me— there *would* have been some. Why weren't your wrists marked when we rescued you?"

Some instinct stilled Mosca's tongue, but her last sentences hung in the air like smoke, curling and forming misty shapes.

Beamabeth's hands had been tied behind her back when Skellow had held her hostage to cover his escape. As the image danced before Mosca's eye again, she recalled what Clent had said about Skellow.

. . . killed while on the brink of shooting Miss Beamabeth . . . Stabbing, shooting, it is all the same.

But stabbing and shooting were *not* the same. Skellow had been holding Beamabeth at pistol point, but then, when surprised in the hidden passage, he had been holding a knife. For some reason, midflight, he had tucked his pistol away and pulled out a blade, despite knowing that his pursuers were armed with pistols. A knife was certainly quieter if he had murder in mind . . . but why *had* he decided to kill Beamabeth right there and then?

Mosca shook her head slowly. "Makes no sense," she whispered. "Skellow was a viperous, flint-hearted old villain, but he weren't *stupid*. You were the only thing keepin' him alive! Why would he try to kill you before he got to safety?"

Two pairs of eyes remained locked in a stare, one pair black as gunpowder, the other as blue as a summer morning. And yet it was in the black eyes that there came a dawn of realization and fear.

We got it all wrong, thought Mosca. *We got it all topsy-turvy.*

"No marks on your wrists," Mosca said slowly, "because . . . before we got there to rescue you . . . *your hands weren't tied.*"

Nothing. Not a flinch, nor a flutter of lashes. Just wide, blue eyes, as warm and pitiless as a drought.

"But Skellow heard a cry from downstairs in the cooper shop, so quick as stitch he must have slipped a rope round your wrists and given it a quick knot. Then *we* burst in, so he held you hostage and pulled you through a secret door. And then he got his knife out." Mosca swallowed. "But not to kill you. *To cut through your ropes.* So the pair of you could run faster.

"But you didn't run. You waited till he had a knife in his hand, then you dropped to your knees and screamed—so we'd come burstin' in through the wall and find him like that, looking like he was about to cut your throat. So that we'd shoot him down like a dog before he could get a word out. So that he'd never have the chance to tell any of us the truth. 'Little witch.' That's what he said as he died. And maybe he said it to me. But he wasn't talkin' *about* me, was he?"

Mosca was breathing quickly now. Her anger was returning, filling her ears with a furnace roar. She could not hold back the rush of words.

"Money. Everything's all about money in Toll, ain't it? Everyone thinks about it all the time—most of them because they want to get out of the town, or pay their tithes, or eat this week. But maybe *some* people decide they need more money because they're runnin' out of chocolate and tea and silk handkerchiefs, and they can't imagine the world without them, and getting things like that on the black market costs a *lot*.

"And you could have just married in the first place and gone off to be Lady Feldroll, but in Waymakem you might not be everybody's golden girl, everybody's special angel. No, why would you do that when you could stay here, with Sir Feldroll and everyone else courtin' you and lettin' you string 'em along? You wanted to keep your cake and eat it . . . and eat everybody else's too.

"And I bet it was easy, setting up your own kidnapping, what with Brand Appleton being half mad in love with you. I bet he was pleased as a pig in slurry when you told him you wanted to elope with him using the money from the ransom. Bringing Skellow into the plan must have been your idea too—Appleton never liked him, never trusted him. Who was Skellow then? Your black-market man? You must have been thick as thieves with him all along, plottin' to double-cross Appleton when he'd served your turn and take the ransom for yourselves, so you'd be right for the rest of your lives. But they were both nightside, weren't they? You needed somebody dayside to make the kidnapping *happen*. So you gave Skellow some money for tolls and sent him out to hire the Romantic Facilitator at the Pawnbrokers' Auction. Only . . . what you got instead was us.

"But you put us to good use, didn't you?" Mosca could feel all the parts of the truth tumbling into place one after another like dominoes. "We got your father out of the way for you, and afterward, that night, you went off to pray in the chapel—I remember. So when Skellow crept into the salvation hole to report in to you, you was kneeling, ready to talk to him. It was *you* who told him we were imposters, *you* who told him about the trap we were laying.

"*You* threw your trinkets and pins around your room,

so it looked like there had been a struggle. Then you just climbed out your window and down Skellow's ladder and away. And when we found your window open and you gone that morning, we all guessed there must have been a traitor in the mix . . . but none of us thought it might be *you*."

All was quiet, but for the tutting of the clock and a scattering of bird notes like china splinters. *One of the two of us,* thought Mosca, *is in a lot of trouble right now. I wonder which of us it is. She isn't turning pale or plucking at her handkerchief. Oh, draggles, I think it's me.*

"Some people get a mad sickness from reading," Beamabeth said at last, her voice still calm. "If I say that your reading has driven you mad, everybody will believe me. If I say that you were in league with my kidnappers all along, everybody will believe me. If I say you came and threatened me just now, everybody will believe me." It was true. Mosca could feel it in her bones. Everyone would succumb to Beamabeth's charm like beetles drowning in marmalade. At long last Beamabeth lowered her eyes and returned her gaze to her sewing. "Now I want you out of my sight. And by dusk I want you out of my town."

"You're nothing but a name!" Mosca clenched her fists. She knew everything, and it was unbearable to know that her knowledge was useless. "Without it, you would be nothing! All they love is your name!"

"Oh?" Up went the dark gold eyebrows. Out came the dimples and dainty little teeth. "And do you imagine that if you had *my* name, you could ever be like me?"

"No," snarled Mosca, tingling from toe to crown. "Not in a hundred thousand years." The cups on the breakfast table rattled as Mosca stamped out of the room and slammed the door.

"Mr. Clent! We been hoodwinked! By a shuffling, wheedle-cutting shurk of a—"

"Child, child!" Clent raised his eyes to heaven. "Four nights in Toll-by-Night, and thus she returns to me," he muttered under his breath. "Mosca, I wish sometimes that you did not pick up words *quite* so swiftly."

However, as Clent listened to Mosca's high-volume explanation, she saw his expression pass through indulgence, incredulity, astonishment, and outrage, making its final stop at a grayish shade of mauve.

"Gambling fates . . . and we have been risking gizzard and gullet for this precocious piece of perfidy and perniciousness!"

"That's exactly what I said at the time!" agreed Mosca eagerly. "Only . . . with not quite the same words."

"Such treachery behind such a sweet . . . er, one moment. Did you say 'said'? You have *spoken* of this? To whom? Not to *her*?"

Mosca looked mulish. "There are words I can swallow and words I cannot, Mr. Clent! Not without them turning to poison in my belly. 'Twas all I could do not to take her nose between my knuckles and twist it till the

500

freckles turned blue *ow OW!* Mr. Clent, you are pulling off my arm!"

"Madam, we are leaving!" Clent had, with the dexterity of custom, snatched up his coat, Mosca's arm, and a bowl of dried fruit, taking only a moment to empty said bowl into his pockets. "May I point out that the last person to pose a threat to Miss Beamabeth's secrets took a bullet through the vitals last night? For the moment she will be taken aback and out of step, but it will not be long before she realizes that the best way to blunt your blade is to blacken our names before we can tarnish hers. If we are to leave this accursed town, it must be NOW, before the wind changes and we find ourselves under the hatches again."

"But . . . that smirking spit gobbet! She will get away with it all! We must show everyone what she is—"

"Child, our credit stands on the shakiest ground— nobody will believe us! *Nobody.* Yes, yes, by all means expose her—but perhaps by letter?" Clent, gripped by his new momentum, had already dragged Mosca halfway across the room, and it was all she could do to pull free and run to collect Saracen. "Once we have put some town walls and several leagues between us? Revenge is a dish best served unexpectedly and from a distance—like a thrown trifle. Come!"

Mosca, Clent, and Saracen took no leave of the mayor, for that would only have caused delays. Instead they strode purposefully through the curiously quiet and nervous town to the eastern gate, Clent with his best veneer of dapper confidence, Mosca with her arms full of goose, taking only one footman to show that Mosca was in "custody" and the paperwork to show that she was being "evicted."

The daylit streets looked peculiar to Mosca now. She kept glancing around for shortcuts she had learned over the last four nights, or seeing half-familiar corners gilded with sunlight. Could that gentle road full of glovers really be where she had seen the Clatterhorses clash? Could that homey lane full of drapers really lead into the Chutes? And could Toll-by-Day really turn on Mosca and Clent a second time, after all they had done?

Yes, probably.

At the eastern gates they requested passage out and presented the toll they had taken so many risks to acquire. The guards were suspicious and made a point of examining their papers thoroughly and counting the money with care. The presence of a footman in the mayor's livery, however, seemed to be a point in the favor of the would-be travelers.

The guards brought out a ponderous ring of keys and unlocked a small door set in one of the gates. A rush of cold, moor-scented air hit Mosca in the face, and she almost panicked. She had grown so used to Toll's reek of closeness, its trapped-animal smell, that she had forgotten how the air of freedom tasted. It was too good, it was too close, it would be taken away from her. The door opened to show a craggy rise shivering with weather-bleached grass. . . .

"Hey! You!" One of the guards caught her by the arm as she was stepping through the door. Saracen's neck rose into an ominous curve. "Hand it over!"

Mosca stared at the guard in incomprehension until she realized where he was glaring. With an incredulous snort, she pulled off her badge and dropped it in his hand.

"This? Did you think I was planning to *steal* it? Do you think I ever want to see that—or your stinking old pit of a town—again?" She pulled loose from his grasp, staggered out through the gate, and then broke into a run. She ran into the very throat of the wind, so her bonnet ribbons whipped against her ears and deafened her, and her lilac skirts were blown back against her legs.

She gave a banshee shriek of sheer glee and whirled about, Saracen erupting from her arms, wings spread for his own little victory glide. There they were, the high walls of Toll, dull and rugged as stale cake, and she was *outside* them.

Ignoring Clent's look of entreaty, Mosca caught up a small rock and threw it at Toll with all her might. It rebounded off the stonework above the gate with a *pick* noise, startling a family of jackdaws above.

"Good-bye, Toll, you old maggot barrel! Hope you fall off yer perch!" The town's arrow slits seemed to stretch in astonishment as they peered down at her tiny impudence. She scampered a little farther away, snatched up another missile, and flung it after the first. "Hope all your chimneys clog!" Thrown stone. "And your clock falls off!" Thrown stone. "And your . . ." Her voice trailed away.

Her pursuit of better stones to throw had led her in a backward scramble up the rise. Now, twisting around to stoop for yet another stone, she at last saw what lay beyond the rise.

Looking down across the declining plain of wind-whipped moss, she could see a long road twisting between the gorse-strewn shoulders of the crags, all the way down into the leveling moors. Up this road, in the direction of Toll, surged a river of people. Hundreds of men, trudging in columns with pikes along their shoulders. Great wagons, laden with sacks and barrels. The stubby black muzzles of mortars, twitching as they were hauled up the uneven path. And behind them, a few full-blown cannons, dragged by teams of horses. To judge by the different standards fluttering in the breeze, the three nearest cities had massed their forces to march on Mandelion after all, and it seemed the march had already started, even without Toll's permission.

Perhaps, like Mosca, Sir Feldroll had lost patience with Toll and decided to throw stones at its walls. However, it looked as if his stones were bigger than hers.

29

GOODMAN GIDDERSING,
GUIDE IN HIGH AND
TREACHEROUS PLACES

MOSCA'S GLEE BURNED itself out in a second. She dropped down to sit on a boulder like a lilac-colored imp. All these troops and weapons were meant for Mandelion, for people she knew. And so she could only stare at the soldiers raising tan-colored campaign tents, the riflemen cleaning their guns, Eponymous Clent handing a paper over to Sir Feldroll in exchange for a small purse of money. . . .

Clent did not look around as Mosca ran to join him but continued pointing out details on the map in his hand with a tone of airy pride, as if everything it showed belonged to him.

"And as you can see, it was originally a map of Toll-by-Day, but some of the nighttime alterations have been added in ink, should your men find themselves fighting their way through the streets after dark. And I have marked in a few murder holes I noticed above the gates for dropping hot sand or pitch on invaders—"

"Hopefully this will not be needed," responded Sir Feldroll, whose face had now settled into a steady crimson twitch gavotte. The close attention he was paying to the map rather suggested that he thought it would be needed. "My thanks, Mr. Clent, Miss Mye. You at least have been as good as your words throughout this bitter business. I am glad to see that the pair of you are leaving, before everything becomes . . . difficult." He halted, clenched his jaw, and regarded the walls of Toll with a resentful but appraising eye.

"This is our last chance to strike against Mandelion before winter settles in," he added through his teeth. "If not now, then the radicals of Mandelion will have months—months!—to strengthen their position and find their feet. I have given the mayor an ultimatum. If he does not keep his promise and arrange for the troops to have passage through Toll by noon . . . then perhaps a carcass over his walls will serve as a warning, and show him how serious I am."

Mosca boggled. A "carcass" was a term for a bomb of burning gunpowder and sulfur hurled out of a cannon.

Sir Feldroll the mild-mannered, attentive fop had vanished. This was a nobleman who was not used to being opposed, and who was reaching an impressive powder keg of temper at the end of a two-month fuse. Perhaps he still cared about winning Beamabeth's goodwill, but evidently not enough to stop him bombarding her town.

"But Sir Feldroll—"

Mosca's outrage was clipped before it could fly by Clent grabbing her arm and dragging her away, directing a warm and engaging smile over his shoulder at Sir Feldroll as he did so.

"Mr. Clent!" squeaked Mosca. "You sold him my map!"

"And why not?" answered Clent in an undertone, still guiding her from the simmering knight. "We have no further need of it, and *that* gentleman might. What we *do* need at this time is traveling expenses . . . with which we are now supplied."

"You got no more soul than a toadstone, Mr. Clent!" spat Mosca, yanking her wrist free. She screwed her features into a scowl and looked away, so that he would not see the tears prickling into her eyes.

"Do you really imagine that your scrawl of a map has just sealed the fate of Toll and Mandelion?" Clent asked quietly but coolly. "Madam, it will make no real difference. *We are simply not that important.* We are ants watching the clash of dragons and trying not to get cooked to a crisp by creatures that have barely noticed us."

"We *did* make a difference once." Mosca dug her nails into her hands. "We made a difference in Mandelion."

"Perhaps." Clent gave a long sigh. "Yes, in a small way we helped Mandelion to revolt. And even that—what good has it done? We have seen the whole area between the rivers plunged into a state of near famine, Toll collapsing from within and turning to the Locksmiths, and now the armies of the other cities marching in against the 'radical threat.' And if Mandelion does not fall now, more armies will march next year, and there will be yet more bloodshed. Bold actions have *consequences*, child."

Mosca felt a tear threatening to tip out of one of her eyes, and she wiped it angrily away with her knuckle.

"I ain't sorry." She glared at him. "Even with all that has gone wrong since, it was right. We made a *good* difference!" *And maybe that is the only thing either of us will ever do that was worth anything. And if Sir Feldroll's army gets there, it will have been for nothing.*

"Well . . . put your mind at peace. The mayor is unlikely to give in to Sir Feldroll, even when he does start pelting the town with burning debris. He will count on the Luck to stop Sir Feldroll from invading successfully. So instead the mayor will turn to the Locksmiths and sign papers with them all the faster, a couple of unlucky people will be cooked in their houses, and Toll will become a Locksmith town by nightfall. There will be a siege until Sir Feldroll gets bored, some people will starve . . . and Mandelion will be safe a little longer."

"But that . . ." That was not much better. "There has to be a way—"

Clent's expression had set up camp somewhere between amusement and pain. "Sometimes I forget that your small size is the result of youth, not pickling. You are . . . young, Mosca.

"To be young is to be powerless, but to have delusions of power. To believe that one can really change things, make the world better and simpler in good and simple ways. To grow old is to realize that nobody is ever good, nothing is ever simple. That truth is cruel at first, but finally comforting."

"But . . . ," Mosca broke in, then halted. Clent was right—she knew that he was. And yet her bones screamed that he was also wrong, utterly wrong. "But sometimes things *are* simple. Just now and then. Just like now and then people *are* good."

"Yes." Clent gave a deep sigh. "Yes, I know. Innocent people force one to remember that. For you see, there is a cruelty in all innocence."

Mosca remained silent for a few moments, daunted by the colossal sadness in his voice. "I'll never understand you, Mr. Clent," she said at last.

"Mosca," he replied simply, "I truly hope you never do."

They might have spent another few minutes in pensive silence if down by the road Saracen had not decided to begin the war on his own.

To be fair, he had been provoked. Two soldiers who had already pitched camp had broken open a loaf without any thought for the hunger of waterfowl in the vicinity.

The soldiers in question were now hiding on the far side of one of the provisions wagons, and one had sneezed gunpowder over his arm and shoulder while trying to load his pistol in too much haste.

"Don't shoot!" Mosca sprinted toward Saracen's enraged green-and-white form. Nonetheless she might have been too late, had another figure not run in to place a restraining hand on the soldier's arm.

"No, please, I *know* this goose, it belongs to a friend of mine—"

"Mistress Leap!" It was indeed the midwife, with her bundle of goods on her back and her husband in tow, who had interceded on Saracen's behalf. "You got out of Toll!" Mosca was genuinely relieved, for she had been worried that the Locksmiths might have guessed at the Leaps' involvement in Beamabeth's escape and stopped them leaving.

The soldier with the pistol very reluctantly lowered it, all the while meeting the gaze of Saracen's fearless, unblinking black button eyes. The man did not seem reassured, but there was little he could do with a happy reunion taking place between him and his enemy in plumage.

Mistress Leap pulled Mosca into a hug, and then the pair of them held each other at arm's length and studied their faces by daylight for the first time. Despite the overcast sky, the midwife was having to squint against the light, but her spirits seemed to be giddily high. Her husband stood nearby and had the look of a rabbit that has just realized the pen door is open and is staring at everything beyond it with rapt terror. He seemed particularly afraid of gorse.

"Look at you!" Mistress Leap beamed, and Mosca could see how dingily pale and hollow her cheeks were and had probably always been. "Your eyes really *are* jet-black! I thought they were. I am so glad you managed to escape as well! We have been waiting out here for you since we left town last night—and I was worried, but then I saw your goose, so I knew you must be nearby.

"Oh, and Mr. Clent safe as well!" Mistress Leap beamed at Clent as he approached, walking carefully around Saracen's animated dissection of the bread loaf. "Glad to see you well, sir. Why do we not all travel to Waymakem together?"

"A fine idea," Clent agreed with unnecessary haste. "Before, ah . . ." He glanced at the army.

"Oh, these troops?" Mistress Leap cast an unconcerned glance at them. "Yes, I was worried myself when I came out and saw an army massing outside Toll. But I have talked to some of the young men over there, and they swear they are just passing through so they can march on Mandelion. Apparently the mayor gave his permission days ago."

"Ye-e-es," Clent answered gingerly, as if the word might give under his weight. "But then he . . . ungave it again. I fear that the Locksmiths now hold the keys to

Toll-by-Day and the mayor's own strings, and he can give no permission without their say-so. You see, madam"—his voice dropped to a whisper—"they have seized the Luck."

"The Luck?" Mistress Leap clapped a hand to her mouth, her large eyes aghast and mortified. "Paragon? Are you telling me that they have seized poor little Paragon Collymoddle because they think he is the Luck?"

"Alas, that is exactly . . ." Clent halted as realization came knocking belatedly. "Pardon? What precisely do you mean, *think* he is the Luck?"

"Oh, this is all my fault!" Mistress Leap's fingers trembled as they covered her mouth. "But he was so small, so very small and weak, he would never have survived in Toll-by-Night. I wanted to save him—I never imagined that I would be sending him to a different kind of danger, I—"

"My good lady," interrupted Clent, "are you telling me that he is *not* the Luck? That you have in some way obfuscated the chronology of his nativity?"

Seconds passed. A beetle flew into Mistress Leap's hair while she stared at Clent; then it struggled free and flew off again.

"Did you lie about when he was born?" translated Mosca.

Mistress Leap dropped her gaze. "He was so close to being born under Goodman Lilyflay instead of Goodlady Habjackle, so close to having a really beautiful daylight name instead of the worst sort of night name.

We scared as long as we could, but he just would come out at the wrong time, and there was no dissuading him. Two minutes! Just two minutes more and he would have been a daylight name. So . . . when nobody was looking I reset my pocket watch and told his mother that she had a daylight son. I . . . have never lied about the paperwork before or since. My conscience has never been easy about that one time, but at least I could think of that poor little boy living in the light of the sun—"

"But he never did!" exploded Mosca. "He ain't *been* in the sunlight! They locked him away in a little room in a tower, with no windows or company, and left him to go half crazy! And now he's been stolen like a necklace or a sovereign, and all anyone cares about is what he's worth!" She was shouting at the wrong person, of course, but Paragon's treatment had been eating away at her for days.

"What? Oh, the poor little thing!" The midwife's eyes were dazed pools of horror. "I . . . I knew he would be living in the clock tower, but I never thought he would be locked in there all the time!"

Mosca put her hands on either side of her head. Her thoughts had been kicked over like a cup of water, and now they were spilling off in all directions. "Anybody else know that he ain't the Luck, mistress?"

"No, of course not." Mistress Leap shuddered. "Can you imagine the scandal? Nobody knows. Except Welter, of course. Oh, and Miss Beamabeth. As soon as I heard that she was thinking of leaving Toll to marry Sir

Feldroll, I *had* to tell her. That's why I asked you to give her that letter. Can you imagine how terrible that would have been—the Luck leaving the walls of Toll because she did not realize she *was* the Luck?"

Of course. Beamabeth Marlebourne had the second-best name in Toll. If Paragon did not really deserve his name, then the real Luck of Toll was . . . Beamabeth Marlebourne.

Mosca remembered Beamabeth's reaction to Mistress Leap's letter, the sudden pallor and trembling that she had explained away as a fear of the night town. . . .

"That letter of yours must have put a terror in her." Mosca snickered. "You did not know that the Luck was kept locked away from the light o' day, but *she* did. I am surprised she did not try to—oh!" Mosca broke off, and jumped up and down on the spot, trying to jog her thoughts into order. "What noddies we all are! Mistress Leap—somebody has been trying to kill you! More than once!"

"What?" Mistress Leap stared at her aghast. Even Welter abandoned his usual glower of weary misanthropy for a look of real outrage and concern.

"Twice, I think," continued Mosca. "That man with the dagger and the pimply face, who tried to trick you into walking off into the night with him. I seen him since, in the top room of a cooper's shop—with Skellow's men. I *knew* he looked familiar. Then . . . there was that rock that flew out of nowhere and hit you in the head, mistress."

"But why would Skellow's people try to murder

Leveretia?" asked Welter, still goggling watery eyed at the very idea.

"Because Beamabeth Marlebourne told them to," answered Mosca promptly. "Because if you ever told what you knew about Paragon, there was a speck of a chance that the mayor would lock *her* up in the clock tower 'stead of him."

Not for the first time Mosca had to listen to a stuttered list of Beamabeth's virtues and the reasons why she would never do anything so vile.

"She'd do a dozen worse things before breakfast, then complain if the toast was cold!" retorted Mosca. "Oh, the stories I could tell you of *her*! No, *no*! I'll be spitted before I let her win, after everything she's done and tried to do!"

Mosca spread her arms like an enraged lilac gull.

"She uses *everybody*. And when they're bleedin' at her feet, off she trips before she can get her satin shoes stained. Skellow served her like her own right hand, and she tricked him into taking a bullet. Oh, and that blockhead Brand Appleton is *innocent*! Innocent of kidnapping, anyway—innocent of aught but being a half-wit over a girl who cares nothing for him, and doing whatever she says. And now the whole city is after his blood, so even if he don't die of fever, they'll find him and drag him to the gallows, and probably Laylow with him if she is still trying to protect him.

"The whole rotten town is full of folks ready to die for Beamabeth Marlebourne, and she would *let them*.

She *saw* Toll-by-Night, she *knows* what will happen to this town. And now that her plans have gone wrong, all she thinks about is gettin' away and living comfortable. She doesn't care a pip if Toll goes to the devil and the Locksmiths, or if Sir Feldroll burns it to the ground, so long as she can prance off to Waymakem and *eat chocolate*." It was not the best speech in the world, but the heartfelt ones never are, and it was at least loud. "She used us! She made *us* a part of her games, and I . . ." She waved her arms helplessly. "We have to do *something*! Something about her . . . something about Mandelion . . . something about Toll. . . ."

"Mosca, child." Clent shook his head and counted out slowly on his fingers. "One—if we denounce the Marlebourne creature, nobody will believe us, and we will probably find ourselves decorating a pillory.

"Two—Toll and Mandelion are a cleft stick, for they cannot both be saved. If Toll-by-Day is snatched from the grasp of the Locksmiths, then these troops march on Mandelion. The only thing stopping Sir Feldroll's army from threatening Mandelion right now is the Locksmiths' new grip on Toll-by-Day. You should be delighted at Toll's fate—particularly since you have shown nothing but loathing for the town since setting foot in it."

"But what if Sir Feldroll burns half the town and marches through anyway?"

"Three"—Clent ignored Mosca's question and

continued—"even were there the tiniest thing we could do about any of this, we could not do it out here. The gates have closed behind us. We are out. They are in. Our part in this play is over."

Mosca turned about, breathing heavily, glaring up at the dingy walls' machicolations and arrow slits. Mistress Leap looked distraught. Welter looked bemused.

"Child, after all the trouble it has cost us to leave this accursed town, are you seriously considering reentering?" Clent shook his head. "How, precisely? Do you plan to glare the walls down? Or climb into a mortar and wait to be fired over the walls, perhaps? Or will you be asking Aramai Goshawk nicely, in the hope that he is in a forgiving mood?"

Mosca's only answer was silence. Clent's first mistake was assuming that this was a sign of defeat. His second was taking his eye off her five minutes later.

In the end, Mosca found the lair by following the carriage tracks.

Most of the visible wheel tracks stuck to the road that led to Waymakem, but Mosca hunted and hunted, and at last found some that etched their own path cross-country. Once she had found them, she followed them doggedly despite an uncanny sense that sound was dying around her. It was not just that the noises of the town and army camp were fading as the rugged land blocked them from view. Even the birdsong seemed to be dwindling.

She realized why when she saw the first owl. It perched with dark, stooped malignity at the top of a pole, its angular head and blunt ears silhouetted against the sky. Mosca peered up at it, then walked over and shook the pole. No flurry of feathers, no reproachful orange glare. Instead the owl wobbled with the pole. It was made of wood. A little farther down the path she saw another, then another.

The owl lollipops were comical in a way, but they did make one feel uneasy, watched . . . mouselike. Certainly their fearsome outlines seemed to have frightened away the ordinary birds, resulting in an eerie silence.

"I've eaten owl stew," Mosca told them, conversationally.

Here and there the wheel ruts were clearer, slicing through bright moss and leaving fresh gashes of mud that smelled of cold greenness. A few red hawthorn berries had been tumbled and crushed. And then she fought through a shielding wall of heather and found the carriage.

There it was, real as rent day in its gleaming black paint, the carriage that she had seen tearing through the streets of Toll-by-Night. It was just as she suspected. If the carriage had been kept locked up in the town during the day, everybody would have heard frustrated whinnies from behind locked doors, and the horses themselves would quickly have become sickly and fretful. The carriage and horses had to be let in and out each night.

The carriage was empty. Two black horses tethered nearby cropped at the thick, wind-shivered grass with their grayish, clever mouths, quite unperturbed by Mosca's presence. The whole scene had the weirdness of a fairy tale. Mosca stroked the neck of one of the horses, then reached up to feel the wood of the driver's seat. It was very slightly warm.

"Hoy!" Her voice came out more squeaky than she intended. The only response was the wind, rattling the dry husks of seed pods so they buzzed like insect wings. She took a deep breath, gathered her courage, and tried again. "I know I ain't alone! I come here to talk to Aramai Goshawk!"

The silence lasted just long enough to make her feel stupid, disappointed, and relieved, and then the response came.

"Name?" It was a rough, guttural voice, knobbly with the local accent. Mosca spun around but could not see its owner, nor could she be sure where the voice had come from.

"Mosca Mye!" she shouted, then realized that her name would probably mean nothing to most people. "Secretary to Eponymous Clent, who Mr. Goshawk knew in Mandelion!" It seemed safer than mentioning anything they had done in Toll. "I come 'ere to talk to him 'bout the Luck of Toll!"

Whisper, whisper.

"Stay there," ordered the voice, "and do not move the tiniest muscle." There was a damp sound of steps crushing grass as they slouched away. Mosca stayed rigidly where she was, her mind performing panicky whirligigs.

A horseshoe of heather bushes surrounded the clearing where she stood beside the carriage, and she felt watched on all sides. She was a mouse in owl country once again, frozen amid the twitching grass. When a broad-shouldered stranger finally lurched without warning from the undergrowth, she could not help starting.

"This way." He gave a jerk of his head, and Mosca fell in behind him, wondering whether she would ever get the chance to retrace her steps, or whether this strange landscape would swallow her whole.

Her taciturn guide took her along a path down a hidden ditch, flanked on both sides by hawthorn hedges. It ended at a cairn of heaped boulders, probably raised centuries before to Goodman Giddersing, Who Guides the Careless Step in High and Treacherous Places. At ditch level there was an entrance into the cairn, framed by three long stones arranged as doorposts and lintel.

Her guide stood aside and waved her through, and Mosca walked on, ducking beneath the low stone doorway.

The cave beyond was a lot less dark than she had expected, for there were six lanterns hung from chains attached to the ceiling. Their light was, furthermore, reflected in about two dozen steady, unblinking orange and golden eyes. Barn owls, snowy owls, tawny owls, all rigidly examining Mosca's every move as if preparing to tear her apart with their cruel little hooks of beaks. It reassured her somewhat to see the dust on their claws and realize that they were stuffed, but they still had the look of things enchanted, awaiting an order from their master.

Amid this tawny parliament sat Aramai Goshawk in a finely carved chair, his tiny gloved hands picking through a sheaf of scrawled letters, his pocked and pitted face expressionless. He looked up at Mosca with eyes as cold and colorless as midwinter slush.

Mosca had come armed with a rich pack of lies, ready to pick whichever seemed to suit Goshawk's mood best. Under the wintry draft of his gaze, however, she felt most of them wither away in her hands. Her mouth dried. He would see through her. What had she been thinking, coming to this place?

"'Mosca Mye, secretary to Eponymous Clent, whom I knew in Mandelion,'" quoted Goshawk, in a pensive grindstone rasp. "Yes. I do remember. I remember the events in Mandelion very clearly." Perhaps raising the subject of Mandelion had not been such a good idea either. "Elaborate interference appears to be a hobby of your employer. It is not a healthy pastime. His meddling in Toll has been clumsy and . . . unappreciated."

Mosca racked her brain quickly. How much was Goshawk likely to know? He probably knew that she and Clent had been involved in the rescue of Beamabeth. She could only hope that he did not know about any of her curfew breaks, or her part in the cavorting of the world's least convincing Clatterhorse.

"As a matter of fact, I was thinking of extending an . . . invitation to Mr. Clent and yourself, so that we could discuss his recent activities and the whereabouts of a certain ransom gem." There was something in his tone that gave Mosca the clammy impression that the invitation would be hard to refuse, and the discussion would be hard to survive. "But . . . here you are. Walking into my study of your own accord."

"I don't know nothing about where the ransom went!" exclaimed Mosca in alarm. "We ain't got it!" Perhaps Goshawk had only let her walk in alive because he wanted to know where the ransom was. Perhaps his men were waiting to draw secrets out of her with hot irons and screws.

"Do you know, I actually believe you." Goshawk gave what might have been a smile. "If you had it, you would be putting leagues between yourself and Toll right now. But your willingness to approach me was sufficiently interesting that I was willing to spare you a minute or two. Do not let me find that you have wasted my time. You wished to speak of the Luck?"

"Yes."

"I cannot see there is much to discuss. The Luck is in our care."

"That is the grit of the matter, Mr. Goshawk." Mosca

wet her lips with the tip of her pointed tongue. "You do *not* have the Luck."

The owls stared. Goshawk stared. The drafts grew colder.

"What?"

"Paragon Collymoddle got given the wrong name. He was born the murky side of the cusp 'tween Lilyflay and Habjackle, but the midwife had her watch set a few minutes wrong, and by the time she found out, all the paperwork was done and the baby was dayside. She was too ashamed to tell anyone." It was not quite the truth, but it was a close relative of the truth that might get Mistress Leap into less trouble.

Goshawk's face went completely dead as his thoughts retreated into their inner recess like a soft gray snail pulling back into its pitted shell.

"Do you have proof of this?" he asked.

"We got the midwife." Mosca's knees were shaking. If she had been on dangerous territory before, it was nothing compared to the ground she was now treading. After all, she was all but blackmailing a lord among Locksmiths, by telling him that she had it in her power to make his greatest bargaining chip for control over Toll completely worthless. "She will testify if we ask her. And you will not find her in Toll no more."

"Who else knows about this?"

"Mr. Clent, me, the midwife, and one other who will stay mum if we wish it." Mosca took a deep breath. "But if I don't come back alive, then Mr. Clent will—"

"Yes, yes." Goshawk waved one hand dismissively. "Mr. Clent will spread the story far and wide, et cetera. Hmm. I suppose you are expecting to be paid for your silence?"

Mosca shook her head. "We do not want to queer your play, Mr. Goshawk." *Here it is at last. Time to throw down dice and see how they tumble.* "Everything is caught in a cleft stick. One of two towns must fall. Either Toll falls to your folk, or Mandelion falls to Sir Feldroll and his army. The way I hear it told, you will not let Sir Feldroll's armies through Toll. And that is all I need to know. I—we—have made up our minds.

"Mandelion must be saved. You can have Toll. It's a rotten two-faced swill tub of a town anyway." Mosca heard her own voice become stark and hard. "We will *help* you get it. All I want—all *we* want—is to be let back inside the walls to get revenge on somebody who deserves it. Beamabeth Marlebourne. The second-best name in Toll. If your people happened to capture her, then you *would* have the Luck, after all. Wouldn't you?"

"And supposing I even wanted to do so, why would I need the help of Mr. Clent and yourself?"

"Because the mayor has his daughter watched even closer than she ever was, and you lost your spy in his house," Mosca answered promptly. "His household trusts me now—and there's naught to link you and me if it goes wrong."

There was a long silence, during which Goshawk

pensively clasped and unclasped his tiny hands. "So—after setting up an elaborate trap that resulted in Miss Marlebourne getting kidnapped, and going to tiresome lengths to rescue her, you are now proposing to have her abducted again?"

Mosca met his gaze with eyes like black stones. "It would be right crooked of me to even suggest such a thing, Mr. Goshawk."

The very corners of Goshawk's mouth deepened into pits for an amused second. "The symmetry is pleasing, I suppose." Every motion of his little hands was perfectly delicate. Mosca thought they were probably smaller than hers. "If you have won Miss Marlebourne's trust, then . . . I can think of ways that such a thing could be managed. Very well. You will follow the man outside. I shall make some arrangements."

Goshawk sat in contemplation for a while after the girl with the black eyes, clean dress, and grubby accent had left his cairn.

"There seems little harm in letting her back within the walls," he said at last. "If she is successful, so much the better. And if not . . . there is a limit to how much damage she can cause."

A smaller Locksmith in a big coat shuffled out of the darkness at the back of the cairn, mopping meekly at his forehead. "Eponymous Clent seems to be playing a complicated game."

"Clent?" Goshawk narrowed his meltwater-colored eyes. "I wonder if he even knows she was here."

30

Goodlady Sparkentress,
bringer of the autumn flame

Can you hear that?" Laylow crouched in the darkness of the nonexistent sickroom, head cocked to listen. Her voice was hoarse with whispering, for she had received no response for some time. "The bells of Clamoring Hour, Brand!" Sure enough, one could hear the muffled cacophony of Toll's dayfolk ringing their bells in worship of the Beloved. "That means 'tis eleven o'clock. This day of the year is sacred to Sparkentress between eleven and one o'clock—that is right, is it not? Brand, can you hear me?" She reached out and prodded gently at the invalid's shoulder with her unclawed hand. "Happy name day, Brand," she muttered. "Eighteen years old, you are. I . . . I have no gift for you."

The mound of breathing darkness beside her shifted and spoke for the first time in an hour.

"I . . . would settle for some water."

Brand's fever had burned itself out for now, as had his temper. There had been a long sotto voce quarrel between Laylow and himself on the subject of Beamabeth Marlebourne, and now they sat exhausted amid the cinders of that argument in what was almost a truce.

"All gone. I will tout and fetch you some after change-over, when I can go out in the munge."

"I still have no idea what you are saying half the time." Brand's weary laugh was almost inaudible. "What are you going to do—run to and fro feeding and watering me like a mother bird with a nestling till you get caught? Why are you doing all this?"

"You simkin, Brand Appleton," spat Laylow. She aimed a kick at his unseen shin, but not hard enough to hurt. "You pea wit."

Silence.

"Did the teacher ever return? The foreign girl?" muttered Brand.

"No. Said she was running off to fetch you thistle wine, never came back."

"Perhaps she fell foul of some knife in the night," Brand whispered. "Or . . . or perhaps she went straight to the Locksmiths." A sigh. "Laylow, listen. The Locksmiths are bound to find this room sooner or later. I cannot run, or be of use to anyone anymore—you should hand me over to them. At least that way *you* could live to see another night, perhaps even persuade them to go and rescue Miss Marlebourne—"

"I will not bargain for the sake of that prissy vixen!" hissed Laylow with force. "If I make terms with the Jinglers, it will be to keep you alive, you noddy! I know what old Goshawk wants—he wants me to work for him. Join the Locksmiths. And I shall—I shall do even that."

"I always thought you *wanted* to become one of them." Brand sounded surprised. "Your chocolate smuggling—I thought it was meant to impress Goshawk, so that he would ask you to join."

"What? No! Brand, I was born under Wilyfell. So I am born to lure other folks into vice. It is my Beloved-given nature—I am doomed to it. So I sneak in chocolate because it is a vice that does a scratch less harm than gin or dice or poppies or—" Laylow halted as her companion succumbed to helpless snorting and snuffling. "What is so devil-speckled funny about that? And the money from chocolate was good too—I wanted to save enough that I could leave and never *need* to join the Locksmiths. When you take their mark, they have you. Life and soul. No going back."

"Then why in conflagration are you thinking of joining them?" whispered Brand. "Stupid girl. Promise me you will not. Whatever happens."

"But . . ."

"Please! Promise."

A few moments ticked away, followed by a slow release

of breath through teeth. "All right. You have my promise."

In the darkness, two temporarily nonexistent hands brushed fingertips, and neither flinched away.

"Laylow," Brand whispered after a while, "are you sure all that noise outside is Clamoring Hour?"

Mosca was not completely surprised to discover that the Locksmiths had a tunnel leading into Toll from outside. In fact, knowing what she did of the Locksmiths, she would have been rather more surprised if they had not. As far as they were concerned, being confined to one side of a wall or another was something that happened to other people.

It was narrow, musty, and supported by graying wooden struts that had clearly seen better days. As she followed the Locksmith in the blotchy gray coat, she could not help noticing that she was occasionally stepping on what looked like half-buried helmets or dank scraps of clothing. This tunnel, though she did not know it, had been dug as part of a failed siege during the Civil War.

The tunnel ended in a rough stone face and a ladder leading upward. Mosca's guide halted and held up his lantern, inviting her to climb by its light.

"Where does this go?" Mosca's lilac dress was thin cotton, and she was starting to shiver from the cold. She tugged her shawl around her, her hand brushing against the new pale day badge the Locksmiths had loaned her, its symbol a conveniently indecipherable muddle. "You coming with me?"

"No." It was almost the first word her guide had given her since they'd entered the tunnel. "Bring the Marlebourne girl as close to this entrance as you can. We will be waiting for her."

Feeling numb from head to foot, Mosca started to climb. There was nothing else she could do now. At the top she found a hatch and pushed it up, to find herself squinting at a crisscross wooden lattice and a glare of green. She had come up through the floor of the pavilion of the pleasure garden, just next to the broken chair.

It was only when she peered out through the door and saw the promenaders in the garden, with their parasols and lorgnettes, that it came home to her what she had done. Her die was cast, and suddenly she could not believe that she had run headlong back into Toll with only half a plan—and furthermore, half a plan that might get her killed even if it worked.

If there was one thing more dangerous than blackmailing Aramai Goshawk, it was lying to Aramai Goshawk. And the fact was, while Mosca had not said anything to him that was precisely and provably untrue, she had been guilty of misleading him. She had, in fact, no intention of luring Beamabeth Marlebourne to the tunnel, much as she hated the older girl. On the contrary, she had a rescue mission in mind.

She could think of only one way by which she could

both stop the Locksmiths from claiming Toll and prevent Sir Feldroll from marching on Mandelion. And for that she would need the help of the only person who might be able to sway the people of Toll more than the mayor's chain or Beamabeth's charm or Goshawk's menace or Sir Feldroll's guns. Paragon Collymoddle, the so-called Luck of Toll. She needed to find and rescue him.

She did not know where the Locksmiths had spirited Paragon away, but she had a shrewd idea *when* they had done it—during the hours of Saint Yacobray, when they could be sure that the streets were empty and that nobody would see where they took him. Only of course the streets had *not* been empty. There had been no less than three false Clatterhorses chasing one another around Toll. Mosca and the Leaps had seen nothing of the Luck's kidnapping, of course, and if Skellow had seen anything, he was no longer in a position to talk about it. But Brand and Laylow had also been running around in their sheep-skull horse, and Laylow had gone back after Brand's injury to look for the ransom. They might have seen something of the kidnapping without even understanding what it meant. On the downside, as nightlings Brand and Laylow were nonexistent right now, but on the upside, Mosca had a pretty good idea *where* they were nonexisting.

Mosca had one other reason for wanting to find Brand Appleton before he could be hanged by the authorities or quietly murdered by the Locksmiths. Beamabeth had gone to considerable effort to cover her tracks, and Brand was the only track that she had not yet eradicated, despite her best efforts. He might have letters, information, something that could be used against his treacherous ex-fiancée.

To have any chance of reaching Brand and Laylow, Mosca would need chaos. Fortunately, chaos was likely to be available very shortly. Mosca squinted up at the sun, noting that it was nearing the high point of its arc. She was just in time. Soon it would be noon, and Sir Feldroll's ultimatum would run out.

"So which way *was* the wind blowing before it died?" Sir Feldroll narrowed his eyes at the drifting clouds, trying to read meaning in their shapes. "Yes, of course it matters! We are not attempting to burn the town to the ground. These will be a warning, nothing more. From the north, you say? Good—then land it just inside the south wall, if you can. That way if the wind rises again, sparks will not be blown into the rest of the town."

He had hoped for a message before now, perhaps from the mayor or from Beamabeth Marlebourne. But the minutes had passed, and now he was steeling himself to give the order to fire.

There were still qualms in his mind about raining fire on the town, but he quashed them. Toll-by-Day needed to be shaken out of its complacency. It might shrug at a few cannonball holes in its perimeter wall, but there was nothing like a threat of conflagration to put a walled town into a state of terror. One cry of "Fire!" and a whiff of smoke would be enough. They might even lose a little faith in their precious Luck.

It did occur to him, as he gave the signal for two of the mortars to be made ready, that after this day the mayor might have a few choice things to say about the prospect of Sir Feldroll as a son-in-law. However, running through the core of Sir Feldroll was a steel wire of self-confidence that told him that he would yet manage to carry all before him. That the mayor, once cowed, could be brought around. That Beamabeth Marlebourne, given time, could be successfully besieged with gifts and the promise of estates in Waymakem.

He checked his watch, squinting at the glint of pale sunlight on its face. Twelve o'clock. He gave a nod and stared out at Toll as orders were shouted down the line.

Two mortars were traversed to point at the southern side of Toll. Two crude bombs, little more than metal cans full of oil and debris, were loaded into the barrels. Two lit fuses were pushed into touch holes to light the waiting powder. Then there was a duet of deafening explosions, and two mortars leaped back in their tracks like singed cats, filling the air around them with blue smoke.

Mosca heard the double detonation from her hiding place under the hatch and saw the promenaders react with shock and dismay, dropping reticules and lapdogs. The distraction was sufficient for her to pull herself up out of the hatch and pretend she had always been in the pavilion.

As she was staring about at the scattering dayfolk, she caught something out of the corner of her eye, something moving rapidly through the sky like a big black bird swooping. Even as she was turning toward the motion, there was a far louder and nearer explosion, perhaps a handful of streets away. Another, nearer to the center of town, followed so closely on its heels that for a moment her bewildered mind took it for an echo.

As the sound of the blasts faded, she could hear in all the surrounding streets frightened cries filling the air, like a cloud of birds startled from a field by a gunshot.

It was the easiest thing in the world to follow those running from the pleasure garden and join the confused muddle in the narrow streets. Staring up past the tall houses at the ragged band of sky, she could see two faint trails of smoke adrift, and a sooty cloud rising a little way to the east.

Toll-by-Day had limited experience of emergencies, and the double explosion had confused them. They could not tell which way they should be fleeing, if indeed they should be fleeing at all. Some had run out of their houses to gape and ask one another pointless questions.

But this was bewilderment, not panic; confusion, not chaos. Mosca's black eyes flicked around the street, taking in face after face, all doped with uncertainty. Then she took a very deep breath.

"FIRE!" she screamed, pointing a skinny finger toward the miasma of rising black smoke.

Half a second later, there were rather a lot of other people doing exactly the same thing.

It was clear from the roll of Saracen's strut that, for him, finding a military camp was like coming home. There were people bellowing, and buff coats that tasted of cowhide when you chewed them. Best of all, it turned out that hardened cavalry horses, inured to explosions, gunshots, screams, and the smell of blood, could be thrown into fits of hysterical rearing by small flapping things in their peripheral vision, such as wind-chased papers or an unexpected fluttering of white wings.

For now he was happy turning his beak to and fro to watch as two of the tall not-Moscas of his acquaintance took turns shouting loudly at each other over the wonderful clicks, rumbles, and yells of the camp.

"That was all she said!" explained Mistress Leap. "She handed me this letter to give to you, told me to look after the goose while she was gone, and said she would try to be back by dusk."

"Songs of the celestial!" Clent shook the paper in his hand, covered in Mosca's scrawl. "Do you know what the child has done? She has absconded to talk to *Aramai Goshawk* and ask him to let her back into the town!"

There were a lot of other words that Clent used after this, mostly to describe his opinion of Mosca's conduct. None of them were profane, but all of them were long and highly specific, and Mistress Leap might as well have been a goose for all the sense she could make of them.

Over Toll, the gunpowder-scented smoke that had been rising lazily was suddenly tugged and pulled apart like a dragged cobweb. Birds that had been beating their wings spread them and soared, wash lines came to life, and the town's few weather vanes started awake with a quiver and swung to point the opposite way.

Outside the town, Sir Feldroll twitched, stared about him, then wet his forefinger and lifted it into the rising wind.

"Hellfeathers! The wind has risen again, and now it is blowing from the south! Where did those mortars land?" From the trails of smoke it was clear that one had, in any case, landed closer to the center than intended. Mortars were hard to aim at the best of times, and on such uneven ground the times were anything but best. "Have our diplomats gone in yet to negotiate the mayor's surrender? No? Good. Hold them back until we can see whether the fires in the town get out of control."

Eponymous Clent puffed into earshot just in time to catch Sir Feldroll's words.

"Sir Feldroll—am I to understand that the town is

now in real danger of burning?"

"The wind changed direction," snapped Sir Feldroll. He had been shaken by this new lesson in the imprecision of war. He was many things, but an experienced soldier he was not. "But the townspeople must have arrangements for such . . ." He did not finish his sentence. Perhaps, like Clent, he was thinking of Toll's complacent reliance on their Luck to defend them against calamity.

"Sir Feldroll, I . . ." Clent closed his eyes as if in pain, made a few grimaced attempts to continue, then pressed his fingertips together and steeled himself. "I would like," he went on, with an expression that indicated the very opposite of liking, "to volunteer to take the place of your diplomats and approach the mayor for you. Fate— fate has clearly allotted me this role. After all, I belong to neither of your cities—what better intermediary could you choose?"

"Mr. Clent!" Sir Feldroll stared at him, his features managing a remarkable tug-of-war between gratitude and suspicion. "After all that has happened, you are happy to go as my ambassador into Toll?"

"Happy? No. Willing? Barely. Compelled by some pustule of honor I shall lance if I survive the day? So it would seem."

One of the canisters had rattled down to street level, where it had blown in shutters, shattered windows, and left its fragments smoking on the cobbles and a little stream of flaming liquid running down the drainage ditch at the center of the street. But the second had lodged in a cluster of chimneys, where its explosion had scattered burning oil over tile and thatch. Now the wind was stroking the young flames, and dozens of tiny red-gold sparks were taking wing like thistledown.

They blew out across a town full of timber and plaster, covered in facings of wood light enough be moved at dusk and dawn. A crowded town where flames might leap from house to house and never be made to halt. A town just waiting to be burned.

"Fire! Fire!" Mosca ran from street to street, screaming it at the top of her voice, and heard it echoed everywhere. "We got to stop it spreading! We got to tear houses down so it cannot spread along the rows!"

That was what had been done in the Ravens, the soot-blackened neighborhood where Clent had met with Skellow in Brotherslain Walk. There had been a fire, and in spite of all their rules about who should be locked indoors at which times of day, the people of Toll had all grabbed something heavy and torn down houses, locked doors and all, to stop the spread of the flames.

Mosca was counting on them doing the same now, if she could fill them with enough panic. Brand and Laylow were on the wrong side of a locked door, and so was the Luck. She could reach them only if the barriers started to fall. Everybody was terrified of the Locksmiths, but you could fight fear with fear. If there was anything that the townspeople would fear more than the Locksmiths, it would be fire. And it didn't matter whether it was a dangerous fire, providing everybody thought it was.

"Fire! F—"

Mosca smelled smoke, turned a corner into a wave of unexpected warmth, and gaped at a blazing street. Windowpanes were popping, plaster blackening, black smoke churning between timber joints. This was no smoke display. Sir Feldroll's "warning" had decided to carry itself out in good earnest.

"Oh, dung buckets!" she exclaimed breathlessly, then turned to yell at other fleeing figures. "Hey! HEY! Come back! We got to tear down these houses! There are people locked in there!"

"Lass! Come away!" A tall man in a smith's apron ran out and seized her by the arm, dragging her away from a large shower of sparks. "Lass, what—"

He stopped dead. Now that he had joined Mosca in the street, he could hear what she could hear, a chorus of thin, muffled cries from behind the plasterwork of the buildings.

"Goodlady Syropia's mercy! The nightlings!" His honest features contorted with indecision as his eyes flicked between the blazing timberwork and the gleaming Locksmith locks just visible at the edges of the facings. She could see the agony of fear and superstition, and she thought for a moment he would flee and pretend he had not heard the cries. Then he spun Mosca around and took her by the shoulders. "Run down to my forge— corner of Tattle Street—and find my brothers. Tell them to bring as many hammers as they can, and rally some strong arms willing to wield 'em."

Mosca was running even as he finished his sentence and was soon back with a gaggle of the smith's family and friends. The smith seized the largest hammer out of his brother's hand and ran forward to confront the locks that held the nearest facing in place.

"What are you doing?" Another man ran forward, catching at the smith's arm as he raised the hammer to strike at the locks. "What about the Locksmiths—have you gone mad? And the nightlings, you will release them upon us all!"

The two men struggled for the hammer, and Mosca felt the watchers stir, uncertain which side to help. Then the smith knocked his attacker down with a short, sharp punch to the jaw. He stared around belligerently, then stepped back toward the lock, raising his hammer once again.

"Beloved preserve me," he muttered tremulously, and brought the hammer down upon the locks with shattering force.

Everybody flinched with each blow of the hammer, and when the locks finally splintered and the facing was slid aside to reveal a door, most people there took a step back, as if they expected night to ooze out of it like star-infested gravy and drown them. But when the door opened, all that staggered out was a young woman with dull fair hair, wild, bitter eyes, and an implike boy of six clasped in her arms. She shivered in the daylight and flinched with fearful hostility from the dayfolk around her. The surrounding gaggle gawked aghast at the pair, who were clearly the worse for smoke, shuddering coughs shaking their pitiably thin frames.

"Break these doors down!" shouted the smith. "Smash those locks and take the sliding house fronts off! Do the same on that side! You, boy, run to the mayor and tell him what's happening!"

Nobody noticed a twelve-year-old girl stooping next to a charred timber, testing its warmth with a fingertip, then using the soot to smear her face, arms, and dress.

In shattering that first day-night door, the smith appeared to have broken a spell. Breaching the barrier between day and night was still dreadful to the dayfolk, something that could barely be managed without trembling, but at least now it was possible, thinkable. The nightfolk who scrambled coughing out of their cramped homes might be fear maddened, ragged, and earthworm pale, but none of them had slitted pupils or needles for teeth. They were people. And so more and more daylighters set about wrenching the false faces off the houses, kicking in doors, and battering their way past shutters. The impulse spread outward across the town from that first hammer blow, like a ripple from a dropped stone.

Mosca was not slow to help it spread. Satisfied that here at least people were starting to deal with the fire, she was soon running down another street.

"Fire!" she shouted as she went. "Fire in Myrtle Street!"

"Fire in the Winces!" she shouted a few streets later.

"Fire in Scupper's Way!" soon became her war cry. "We got to tear down the houses to break up the rows!"

As she suspected, people were a lot more ready to believe her declarations about the fire when she looked slightly singed. And naturally it was not enough to have people tearing houses down and breaking down doors near the fires. She needed it to be happening all over Toll, which is why she needed to spread the panic far and wide.

Of course there was one house in particular that she wanted to see torn open, and soon she was cursing Eponymous Clent for selling her map. She had been to Laylow and Brand's hideout only once, and then it had been dark and half the streets had been in different places.

At last she found what looked like the right street. Naturally there was no door there for her to recognize, only an expanse of innocent-looking plaster crisscrossed with timber, but she was fairly sure that behind it lay

Brand Appleton's sickroom.

"Please, sirs!" Her cry halted a set of tradesmen who were hurrying past with hammers, chisels, and a set of thatching tools. "Can you help me break into this house? There's a fire a few streets down, and . . ." *And I need you to help me break into this house in particular for reasons I can't tell you.* "And . . ." She inhaled and took it at a run. "And I had a little baby sister born a month ago and she was born to a night name and they took her away nightside and I think she's living in this house because I hear her crying through the wall some days and can you break in for me please before the fire gets here and roasts her like a piglet?"

Whether her story would have been believed if she had been wearing a dark Palpitattle badge will never be known. However, with her borrowed day badge and cast-off gown, she had magically become a respectable young lady in distress, albeit a slightly sooty one. She watched hungrily as the false front of the house was levered away with a crack to show the stained wall behind. The dingy door gave in to a few solid kicks.

"Go find your sister." One of the men chucked Mosca under the chin, and then the group of them hurried on. Gingerly Mosca pushed open the splintered door and jumped back just in time to avoid a claw in the face.

It was probably as well that Laylow had not been the first nightling to stagger into daylight. She was doing a very good impression of the dayfolk's worst nightmare, squinting ominously against the sun, her metal claws raised ready to strike, and various bruises and cuts livid on her face.

As she peered at Mosca, however, bemused recognition clouded her eyes.

"You . . ." She peered, and her face hardened. "Seisian, is it? Teacher, is it? You're no more a foreigner than I am! You're one of those visitors I helped get dayside some nights ago! What's your game?"

"I scarce know meself anymore. But we'll all lose if we don't play on the same side. Listen—the mayor's gone limp, Sir Feldroll's gone mad, the Locksmiths are taking over, and the town's on fire. Beamabeth Marlebourne is safe, and as long as she is, nobody else will be. And now we need to rescue the Luck. Can I come in?"

31

GOODLADY ZANACHE,
KNIGHT OF THE GLORIOUS BLUFF

GABBLING THROUGH THE truth behind Beamabeth's actions to Brand Appleton was a grisly and unnerving business, but Mosca could see no way to leave it out of her story. At first he simmered at the slightest insinuation against Beamabeth, but as she went on, she could see him taking her words on board, and a terrible lost expression crept over his face. Even Laylow looked away, her blunt features pained and embarrassed.

"So"—Laylow crushed the silence as she would have done a poisonous bug—"you say you have a plan? A way out of this?"

Mosca nodded. "We rescue the Luck."

Laylow rasped a laugh. "From the Jinglers? Are you mad? How would that help us anyway?"

"It *will* help—if we save him from *everybody*. From

the Locksmiths, from the mayor, everybody. Get him outside the town walls."

"Outside the walls?" Brand glanced at Laylow, who returned his look of shock, and Mosca remembered that they were born and bred Toll folk, brought up on stories of the Luck's protective power.

"Oh Prill's snout—don't tell me you believe the town will fall off the cliff if the Luck steps outside!" Their expressions suggested that they might. "Well, and what if it does? This town is *rotten*. All that matters is the people in it, and most of them want to get out of it. Any town that has to keep folk inside it using walls an' guns an' fear is wrong to its roots. And if a town needs to lock up some lad just to feel safe, then maybe it don't deserve to feel safe.

"Right now, dayfolk are pulling the Locksmiths' walls down. You know what that means? Just for once, nobody's surprised to see nightfolk running about the streets. You can slip out of this house, maybe head to the gate, and as long as nobody recognizes Mr. Appleton, people will jus' think you were let out because your street was burning.

"There's panic in Toll-by-Day now, but that's nothing compared to what there will be if we get the Luck out of the town. The men guarding the walls by day, they're not like the Locksmiths—they're just guards belonging to the mayor. Once they know the Luck has left, they'll be too busy running to stop people from leaving the town. Which means that you two can get out. And so can everybody else that wants to.

"And then . . . you can even run off to Mandelion if you still want to. Nobody will chase you, because with the Luck gone nobody will trust the bleedin' bridge." Including Sir Feldroll's troops, Mosca added in the privacy of her own head. A distrusted bridge meant a safe Mandelion.

"I say we take the risk," Brand said after a pause. "If we do nothing, it sounds like the Locksmiths take over the town and the sun goes down on Toll forever, trapping everyone in the dark. If Toll falls . . . it might as well do it with a splash."

Laylow looked more reluctant but eventually nodded. "So, where is the Luck being held, then?"

"I was hoping *you* might know," Mosca confessed. "You were runnin' around the streets the hours of Yacobray, looking for that radish after the rest of us were hidin' and prayin'. Laylow—do you remember seeing anybody else out on the streets after we all ran away? Anything that could have been the Luck being kidnapped? Any sign of the Locksmiths doing anything funny?"

Laylow crooked an eyebrow at her.

"You mean apart from jigging about in a ghostly great horse?"

Mosca blew out her cheeks and raised her eyes to heaven. "The *horse*," she muttered. "Oh, I might as well sell my brains to a surgeon for all the good they do me. A lamping great horse, big enough to hold a gang of men with swords—and a skinny Luck lad to boot, no doubt. Did you see where the horse went?"

Laylow nodded. "Headed northeast. After Brand hit the cobbles, I dragged him back up those steps." She shrugged. "'Twas all I could think of. The Jinglers' Clatterhorse was on wheels, so it could not follow, and the bravos inside could not get loose to give chase straightaway. Bought us just enough time to duck under a bush and lie there mum while they ran about looking for us. I dared a peek, though, when the Clatterhorse left at last, saw it heading toward Blithers Yard. Wondered why it wasn't snatching vegetables as it went."

"Probably went there to hide Paragon somewhere first, then came back for the tax turnips." Mosca bit her lip. "Well . . . that narrows it down to Blithers Yard, anyway. Not far from the fires. And if the Locksmiths get the fright like everyone else, they might run to pluck Paragon from his hide hole to take him somewhere safer."

"So. This was as far as your plan went." Laylow grimaced and rasped her callused palm back and forth over her cropped hair. There was no contempt in her tone, however; it was just a blunt statement of the case. "All right, we search Blithers Yard then, and look out for the Locksmiths trying to move this lad. I take the roofs, Mosca the streets, and Brand stays here. What does this Luck look like?" She listened intently as Mosca described Paragon.

"And if you see him before I do," Mosca finished, "then . . . tell him the soot girl sent you to set him free."

Laylow, who had put her head out through the door to peer at the roofs, ducked it back in again. "We need to shake our shambles and move—this hubbub will not last forever." She glanced back at Brand and looked irresolute.

"I will do very well here," Brand reassured her hastily. "Go!"

Eponymous Clent had not been quite sure what manner of disaster he would be facing when he approached the walls of Toll under his white flag. If, as her letter suggested, Mosca had approached Aramai Goshawk about returning to Toll in order to avenge herself upon Beamabeth Marlebourne, he did not give much for her chances. Even in the unlikely event that Goshawk had let her live and helped her inside the town, he thought it most probable that by now Beamabeth had used her silken influence to have Mosca thrown into prison, possibly for the theft of a lilac gown. For this reason he had asked to reenter the town as an ambassador who could not be so easily imprisoned, to see whether words would extricate his wayward secretary.

"She is an insufferable burden," he had muttered to himself, "but I suppose I cannot leave her trapped in a cell in a burning town."

However, the escort that met him at the gates made no mention of Mosca having been hauled off to the Grovels, and Clent started to wonder whether his uncharacteristic impulse of loyalty had been a blind and futile one. Unfortunately, his escort did not seem inclined to let him bob them a bow and duck out the town gates again, and instead insisted on taking him through the streets, which, Clent could not help noticing, were filled with a good deal of smoke and noise.

He reached the castle courtyard to find the mayor in the middle of a stand-up row with a number of subordinates, and in no temper to talk to ambassadors.

"Tearing the faces off the houses? Well, stop them! We cannot have nightlings running around the streets! There is no danger of anyone burning to death! The Luck will protect the town. Tell everybody to go back to their homes and behave in a civilized fashion!" Tiny furry fragments of ash chased through the grass at his feet.

Seated by the door with her sketchbook was Beamabeth, who flinched very slightly when she saw Clent and then gave him her usual sweet smile, but there was something flat about the expression in her eyes, something appraising. He made haste to her side.

"Miss Marlebourne, what luck!" He thought she winced almost perceptibly at the word "luck." "I was afraid I might miss you."

"Mr. Clent! I thought you had left town."

"Without bidding farewell to Toll's most precious jewel? Unthinkable. We owe you at *least* that much."

Clent had the satisfaction of seeing a glimmer of unease and uncertainty pass through Beamabeth Marlebourne's eyes.

She was confused by his return, he guessed. She was gauging him, trying to work out what cards he had up his sleeve. For now he might be able to keep her off-balance by smiling meaningfully and dropping hints, delaying the moment in which she realized that she held all the cards, and that his well-brushed sleeves held nothing but his arms.

"Wait—this door has been broken in already. Have the people left?"

Brand, who had lolled back onto his mattress in a state of helpless torpor, fought to open his eyes and look toward the voice. He could just make out two dark and fuzzy silhouettes against the door. Perhaps they would not see him.

"Look, over on the bed! An invalid! We cannot leave him here—the wind is so changeable. Let us take him to the doctor."

The one time Brand needed daylighters to be callous, here they were rescuing him from the dark safety of his stop hole and dragging him into the daylight where he could be recognized. He tried to protest when strong arms lifted him and his mattress, but his voice and limbs were too weak to prevent them from bearing him outside.

He flinched as a shaft of daylight fell across his face. There was a gasp from one of his mattress bearers.

"Wait—I have seen him before—this is Appleton! The radical! The man who kidnapped Miss Beamabeth!"

The mattress was set down roughly on the cobbles, and Brand opened his eyes to find himself confronted by the uncomfortable ends of a hook, a rake, a cleaver, and a chisel. The terror in his enemies' faces suddenly tickled him unbearably, and despite the pain in his side he started to laugh, so breathlessly and helplessly that the other four took a step back, evidently fearing madness.

"Yes," he choked. "The radical. The terrible radical." The absurdity was too much for him. "Bravo! You have captured the great Brand Appleton, the king of the radicals! The mayor will be very proud of you. *Ow.*" He clasped his hand to his side as his laughter threatened to reopen his wound. The very hopelessness of his position made him feel free and giddy all of a sudden. He was at death's door, but his captors were the ones who seemed terrified.

"We should take him to the mayor," whispered the hook wielder.

"Yes, to the mayor and his saintly daughter." Brand gave them a bruised and crazed grin. "What are you waiting for? Take me to them—do you think I will tell anyone but the mayor about my crimes? All these flames—that was me too, did you not know?"

"What? You . . . you cur!"

"Blame my birth." Brand winced as he was roughly dragged to his feet, his arms slung over two sets of shoulders so that he could be carried. "Blame Sparkentress, the wicked minx. Blame the mayor for sending me to Toll-by-Night, where I could mix freely with others of my seditious kind, plotting his overthrow and the destruction of Toll!"

Ah, so it ends, he thought as he was dragged along the streets by his captors. *And it seems I will be visiting the mayor and his daughter again, after all.*

He would see Beamabeth one last time. And yet, when he thought of her, he could only remember a set of golden ringlets and a warm glow, with no actual face. Instead he found himself thinking of a surly, crop-headed figure with a cut lip, and thanking the Beloved that Laylow had not been caught up in his arrest.

Let us hope Laylow and Mosca find the Luck. I am all out of luck, it seems. But perhaps I can help them . . . by forcing the Locksmiths' hand. If I can persuade everybody that the town catching fire is a sign that the Luck is dead—then the Locksmiths will probably have to bring him out of his hiding place to prove he is still alive. That might give Mosca and Laylow their chance. . . .

"You are all closer to death than I!" he declaimed, in a carrying and manic tone. "I have already doomed you all!

There is nothing to stop the flames now, nothing! Last night I slew the Luck myself!"

Let us see the Locksmiths ignore that.

The reaction to his pronouncement was all he could have hoped for, and more.

Toll-by-Day was blinding, and Laylow could barely keep her eyes open. As far as she was concerned, the whole world might just as well have been aflame. The colors burned, from the murky green of the yews to the red cloaks of respectable housewives. Even her good friends the roofs had developed leeringly bright patterns of moss and scratch tracery. The sky was an ache, and the sun a searing, shapeless hole, so different from the gleaming penny of the moon. The air smelled different as well, and not just because of the smoke.

Her own hands, as she found holds on ledges and chimneys, looked strange to her, the calluses yellow, the scars snail white. She felt exposed, as if everyone must be able to see her every instant. In actual fact, however, most people were too busy with thoughts of the fire to wonder whether a claw-gloved girl might be running along the rooftops.

There was a lot more noise in the streets than she was used to in the night town, but some fragments floated up to her.

". . . says the Luck is gone! Flames spreading because the Luck is gone!"

". . . captured Appleton and he says he cut the Luck into pieces and threw them over different walls . . ."

Laylow stiffened, and her claw tips made squeaky sounds as they etched tiny white marks into a roof tile. Brand had been captured. He was a prisoner and had come up with exactly the sort of mad defiant lie that would see him torn apart by a hysterical crowd. Did he *want* to die?

For a little while she could not breathe and thought about running to the jail to find him. But what good could she do against armed guards and a tower of stone? None.

What now? Would rescuing the Luck help her save Brand? It was so hard to think in this blazing, clattering daylight. If she was lucky, it would help somehow. She pushed on toward what she prayed was Blithers Yard.

Looking down, she saw two men stop dead and exchange glances as they overheard the report of the murder of the Luck. Both were wearing gloves. They conversed hurriedly, then broke into a run. Face puckering in concentration, Laylow set off along the rooftops, keeping pace with them.

She had to hope that these men were going to check on the Luck, make sure that he was still alive and well, and to report the rumors circulating. She almost knew where she was now. Laylow knew the Jinglers' favorite shortcuts to most places, having conned them by rote when planning her chocolate delivery routes.

In an alley, the two men met with two more, also in gloves, and Laylow craned to hear something of their furtive conversation.

". . . says we should move him . . . breaking into all the houses down there . . . move him farther from the fire . . ."

And on they went, now as a foursome. *Jingle-jing, jingle-jing,* the faintest silvery sound of hidden keys chiming as they ran.

No doors had been beaten in yet in Pritter's Lane, but the house tearers were only a street away. Casting quick glances up and down the lane, the gloved men fumbled quickly with the locks on a house facing and slid it aside to show a small red door. This was opened, and after more conference two figures came out, a large and burly man and a boy in his teens. Laylow could not tell how closely he matched Mosca's description of the Luck because there was a thick cloth draped over his head, as if to protect him from smoke.

If she did not act, they would lead him to another part of the town, pull him in through another door, fasten it, and vanish. But there were five of them and only one Laylow. What could she do?

Only one thing.

The five Locksmiths were on the alert. Two kept an eye up and down Pritter's Lane. One was casually keeping watch at the corner, another attending to locking the door behind them, the last making sure the hooded boy did not run or do anything sudden. None, however, were looking *up*, and so none were ready when a grim and wiry figure dropped down in their very midst, yanked the Luck backward by his collar, and placed the tips of three sharp iron claws to his throat.

"Get back!" hissed Laylow. "Or it's an unlucky day for all of us! Step away!"

During the following long pause, the Locksmiths glanced at one another and sent furious messages using eyebrow semaphore, but there was nothing that any of them could actually do without endangering the Luck. Carefully, but with an air of barely reined menace, they moved backward away from her.

The boy whose collar she was gripping was trembling. His feet were turned inward, and his hands were big and clumsy. He was taller than she, but he was making tiny, squeezed, sobbing noises under his face cloth, like a little child crying under its pillow.

"Soot girl sent me," Laylow whispered, and the crying noises stopped. "She says you want to be free. That true?" The clothy head shape nodded. "Me too. Stick with me and we will be." She reached up and tugged off the cloth, and the Luck blinked at the world around him, jaw hanging open. "I will not hurt you. But we must hoodwink these people so they think I will. Trust me."

Paragon nodded again.

"Hah," he gasped. Pale sunbeams sat on his lashes for the first time since he was three, and his world was full of floating angel halos.

32

GOODMAN HOOKWIDE,
CHAMPION OF THE TURNING WORM

BY THE TIME Brand Appleton reached the castle grounds, he had acquired a significant crowd. Never in the history of Toll had one man needed so many people to arrest him. The mayor looked up to find a quarter of the town surging out into the castle courtyard before his house, the grinning "radical" lolling in their midst.

There was a tumult of noise, declarations of Brand's crimes, and suggestions for immediate punishments, most of which seemed to involve a length of good stout rope and the nearest tree.

"No! NO!" The mayor stalked forward. "We are not animals! He shall be arrested, questioned, tried, and executed according to the law! There will be no lynching on my lawn!" He drew closer, and his features took on a granitelike angularity as he started to decipher some of the shouts from the crowd.

He rounded on Brand. "Is this true? Have you dared to harm the Luck of Toll?"

The crowd hushed, all eyes on Brand. His gaze flitted over the pale, downcast features of Beamabeth, the gray stone face of the mayor's house. *I was invited to supper here not so long ago,* he thought. *She played the spinet.*

"Yes," he said.

"This is a lie," declared one of the mayor's new Locksmith advisers, a graying, distinguished-looking gentleman who wore his chatelaine visibly. "The Luck is safe and well—"

"Prove it," demanded Brand. "You cannot. The Luck is dead."

"I do not believe you!" stormed the mayor.

"No? Perhaps I killed the wrong person then. About so tall, dark hair, fifteen years old, brows meeting in the middle? Green velvet frock coat too small for him? Gangly, clumsy ways of moving? Does that sound like your Luck?" Brand saw the mayor go waxen with horror. The Locksmith adviser looked somewhat uncertain as well. Neither could know that Brand was using Mosca's hasty description of Paragon.

"It is true. Beloved above—it is true!" The mayor turned on his Locksmith adviser. "You lied to me! You all lied to me!" He stared wildly about him, seeing his panic reflected in every face, and then turned his head slowly to regard his daughter. A strange mixture of emotions fought across his features—conflict, regret, pride, relief, anguish, and resolution.

"Silence!" The mayor's cry hushed the crowd, which had started to seethe with hysterical and panicky murmurings. "Listen, everybody! All is not lost. A cruel and terrible blasphemy has been committed, but there is still a Luck within Toll. This radical cur is just trying to stir us into unthinking panic, with his talk of flames unchecked. But you all know as well as I do that the Luck is the person with the best and most virtuous name in Toll—and when one Luck dies, the person with the next finest name succeeds them as Luck. Only taking the Luck outside the town bounds removes its protection. Behold! The new Luck! My own daughter . . . Beamabeth!"

Beamabeth's eyes were wide dinner plates of blue terror. All the color had blanched from her face, and the little freckles at the corners of her eyes started from her skin with unusual vividness. Like a trapped animal she gazed around her for rescue, and saw only rapt faces basking in her presence as if she was the newly risen sun. Usually she used the adoration of others to escape her problems, but here their adoration *was* the problem.

Clent, however, suppressed any sense of pity without the slightest difficulty. His brain was busy with the icy clockwork of calculation. If only this young woman's fears were justified! Beamabeth Marlebourne would be unlikely to threaten anybody, locked away inside the

Luck's cell for the rest of her life. Such a fate had a tempting poetry to it too, given that she really *was* the Luck of Toll, and had been all her life.

However, if Mosca was to be believed, Brand was lying. He had been prone in a fever since before the Luck was kidnapped, and would have had no chance to kill anyone. Clent was not certain why Brand had told an untruth that would set everybody against him. He could only assume that the young man had decided that, since a noose was awaiting his neck anyway, he might as well cause as much panic and chaos as he could in the meanwhile. In any case, Brand's claims would be shown as false as soon as the Locksmiths could haul forth Paragon Collymoddle, and Beamabeth would be safe again. But perhaps something could be achieved before this happened.

"Ah . . . actually, my lord mayor, I am rather afraid that you are mistaken about the identity of the Luck."

Everybody stared at Clent—Beamabeth with the stunned hope and terror of a drowning swimmer who finds herself being rescued by a shark.

"I fear I have a peculiar story to tell, but Miss Beamabeth . . . if I may still call her that . . . will be able to verify it. I have of late become acquainted with a certain midwife, who confessed to me that on one occasion she took pity on a small and sickly child, and pretended that it had been born at a slightly different time so as to give it a daylight name. . . ." And so he told the tale of

Paragon's birth, choosing his words very carefully so as not to mention the name or the sex of the baby.

"Miss Beamabeth," he said at the end, "you have known this story for a while. Why do you not tell everyone the identity of that little child?"

The mayor's daughter gaped at him, hardly believing that he was offering her an escape route, a lie that would save her from the cell of the Luck. But Clent had not actually crossed the line between truth and falsehood; he had simply opened the door for her to do so and made it plain that he would back her up.

"I . . . yes." A trapped animal will always scrabble for the chink of light. "Yes—it was myself. I . . . was not really born under the Goodman Boniface."

A murmur of surprise and consternation swept through the crowd.

"So you must have been born under . . . ?" Clent prompted helpfully.

Beamabeth's kitten face furrowed as she tried to remember which Beloved followed Boniface in the calendar, and she could not suppress a shudder of distaste as she remembered.

"Palpitattle," she whispered.

Perhaps she really believed that such news would not affect her standing among the people of Toll. Perhaps she thought her charm was such that nobody could think the less of her, nobody could imagine sending her away to the night town. If that was her belief, then a moment's glance around the listening crowd would have been enough to disabuse her of this delusion.

A slow ripple of recoil was passing through the crowd as the townspeople seemed to awaken from a dream and regarded Beamabeth with newly sharpened and hostile eyes. She was no longer sacred to them. She was a fly child, and so everything about her must smack of trickery and lies.

A shocked silence like this was far too good to waste.

"Well," Clent rubbed his hands, "since we are telling stories, I think I might tell another. It is a curious tale of a kidnapping—or should I say an elopement—or should I say a betrayal. . . . You shall make up your own minds, gentle friends. Really Mr. Brand Appleton should be telling it, since he has been the most cruelly abused in this affair, but I suspect that he is gagged by chivalry. I, however, appear to have woken in a lamentably unchivalrous mood this morning, so . . ."

By the time a messenger panted his way into the castle courtyard to inform the mayor that Paragon Collymoddle was alive, well, and being held at claw point on the Toll bridge, Clent had finished telling the story of Beamabeth's villainy, and several score of the Toll folk were staring at the mayor's adopted daughter as if they had seen her bite a kitten in two.

Laylow and Paragon had reached the bridge before they found themselves stalemated. At first the growing crowd around them was content to give them a wide berth, fearful eyes upon the metal claws so close to Paragon's throat. When they stepped out onto the bridge, however, their escort realized that this strange clawed girl really did intend to take their precious Luck out of the town.

Now the pair stood in the middle of the bridge. On the eastern side, the town end of the bridge, an ever-growing crowd of watchers gathered to gawk from the archway and the clock-tower windows. On the western side, the gate to freedom and the road to Mandelion were tantalizingly visible, but the way was blocked by a small crowd of waiting guards and a heavy portcullis. Even the life-size wooden Beloved statues that flanked the walkway along the length of the bridge seemed to regard the fugitive pair with relentless hostility.

Laylow herself could barely see them, blinded by daylight and the spray rising from the Langfeather. She had shouted herself hoarse over the roar of the river, and even when her words did carry across, it did not always help.

"I want everyone let out of the nask and brought here!" she was screaming. "Particularly a redheaded bird wit called Brand Appleton! And I want those drumbelos with the muskets out of our way and the gate open, or your precious Luck is gone to Peg trantums!"

"Did anyone understand a word of that?" asked the Raspberry, who had come out of his office in the clock tower to discover the cause of the rumpus. A dozen people shook their heads. "Oh, for pity's sake . . . run and find somebody who speaks cant!"

"Hah," said Paragon again. Laylow glanced at him, noticing the tiny jewels that the spray had left on his hair, cheeks, and grin. Then she looked down over the edge of the bridge to see what he was smiling at and nearly lost track of where she was. She had lived all her life hearing the breath of the Langfeather, so that was as much a part of her life as the taste of the air and the touch of her own skin. Now she saw it, a gleaming surge of ostrich-feather white more powerful than a hundred lions, blue shadows cast upon it by the jutting rocks above. Even the air was strung with the faint arcs of rainbows. It seemed alive, it seemed female. She had been living above a goddess her whole life and had never been allowed to see it.

Nobody was obeying her anymore, she realized. They knew she was trying to take the Luck out of Toll. Some of them were starting to edge toward her along the bridge. She bared her teeth by instinct, like a cornered dog.

"Get back!" she shouted, but her ferocity only slowed them. As she had feared, her threat was losing its power.

"Why do they not do as you say anymore?" Paragon whispered.

Because they would rather see you dead than free.

"They are afraid for your life, but they are more afraid for theirs," Laylow muttered unwillingly. "They think the whole town will perish if you leave Toll . . . but if you die instead, at least another Luck will take over."

The wind rose, and Paragon whooped aloud. Laylow felt sorry for him. Did he even understand what was happening, that their plan had run aground, that there would be no freedom for them after all? What was the point in further attempts to explain? Let him be happy for the moment.

"Can I shout orders now?" he asked.

"No," Laylow said through her teeth. "You are the hostage, remember? The hostage does not get to shout orders."

If it had been night and she had been a little less dazzled, she might have been ready for Paragon's next move. As it was, she was caught off guard as he slipped from her "restraining" arm and dodged to the edge of the bridge where the Beloved statues posed. He gripped the horns of Goodman Fullock and swung himself out so that his feet were resting on the very edge of the walkway, the rest of his body leaning out over the long plummet to the Langfeather's foamy embrace.

"What about now?" he said, grinning like a string of pearls.

There was an almost universal gasp of alarm, seasoned with a few shrieks, and followed by the sounds of muskets being readied and aimed at Laylow.

"No shooting!" shouted the Luck, loud enough to carry to both ends of the bridge. "No shooting at us, or . . . I fly away!" He bounced on the balls of his feet, to the consternation of the crowd, which clearly thought he was mad enough for anything.

Laylow ducked between two statues to make herself a small target, breathing heavily and waiting for the rain of musket balls. None came. After a while she peered out to dart a glance up and down the bridge. The guards had ceased their stealthy advance and stood frozen, staring at the capering Luck in shock, frustration, and terror.

"Listen!" Paragon's unguarded laughter bounced off the overhanging cliffs. "Everybody listen to me now!"

And they did. Even the Locksmiths, who pushed stone eyed through the crowds at the town end of the bridge to glower impotently at the delighted Luck. Even the mayor, who appeared at a second-floor window of the clock tower, looking down upon the scene. Most of the town-end crowd was watching Paragon's precarious slithering and capering with their faces set in a wince, both hands raised as if to placate or fend off a blow. The eyes of many watchers crept to the sheer fall below, the merciless bellowing engine of the water.

It took Laylow several stunned seconds to understand why his threats were working where hers had not. Her words had not been lost on him after all, she realized now, and in one swift, canny move he had turned the tables on everybody.

None of the spectators wished to see a careless boy fall off a cliff to his death, particularly one saintly enough to have such a good name. But nearly all of them were much more worried about the whole town following him. A dead Luck was a tragedy; a murdered Luck a shocking blasphemy. But a Luck who "left Toll" by jumping off a bridge *before* dying a watery death could be a catastrophe. In their minds, if Laylow cut Paragon's throat, then the next-best name would become the Luck and the town itself would be none the worse. However, if he jumped or fell, he would have left the town while still living, taking Toll's luck with him once and forever. Who could say what would happen then, or how quickly? Would people even have time to run for the gates before calamity struck?

"Now . . . everybody . . . make the gates be open!" Paragon's eyes were shining.

This was the great test. All eyes rose to the mayor, who was clutching the sill of his window with such force, it seemed he might tear it apart like pastry crust.

He bristled and gave a short, sharp nod. The small group of guards at the gate end of the bridge boggled, then set about cranking up the portcullis.

"All the gates!" crowed Paragon. "All the gates and doors open! All over the town!"

Even from below it was possible to tell from the mayor's strained body language that the prospect of obeying was tearing at his very soul. He gave another curt nod.

"You heard the Luck! Tear down the house facings! Open all the doors! Do everything he says!"

Nobody felt like telling the mayor that a lot of his citizens had been doing that for some time.

The townspeople busy battling the fire had need of every strategy they had to hand, for the fire was hungry and ingenious. It leaped from balcony to jutting jetty with the agility of a burglar, crossing streets in a single flurry of sparks. It found hidden stores of gunpowder, oil, and liquor in cellars.

However, the people of Toll were fighting back. Some grabbed small barrels, butter churns, and leather buckets and formed chains, passing water in a line from the wells to the blaze. Others ran for ladders and axes for making firebreaks, or even came up with proper long-handled fire hooks for tearing down roofs and masonry.

At first breaking through the Locksmith barriers had been an impossibility, then the recourse of a courageous few, then a terrible necessity. But the mood had changed. Now the self-appointed firefighters attacked the locks and barriers with a passion. Daylighter and nightling fought the flames side by side, without a glance at one another's badges. The only enemy was the fire.

The fire was not ready for this solidarity, and as the wind dropped, it grew dispirited. It let itself be cornered, drenched, covered in wet hides. It waited for another wild wind, a chance to show the town what it could do. But the wind did not come, and a lane at a time, the flames were beaten back.

It was then, while the front-line troops were gasping and soot stained, hammers and axes still in hand, that word came through. The mayor had ordered the destruction of every Locksmith barrier and lock in the town. Why? Nobody cared. With a new and wild intoxication, bolts were yanked from their frames, locks burst, walls cloven. No terrible Locksmith vengeance ensued. The townspeople plunged on with the glee a very young child feels the first time she realizes that her parents are not all-seeing and that plates break very easily.

Then another whisper rushed through the town, like a cold rain through a desert wasteland.

"The gates! The gates are open!"

Most of the newly released nightlings responded to this news with admirable promptness. The resourceful ran home, seized their belongings, and fled through the eastern gate, heading for the plumper, richer counties around Waymakem and Chanderind. The even more resourceful did the same, but with other people's belongings.

The shivering shantytown on the western bank of the Langfeather was only slightly slower. Abandoning their makeshift shacks, they hoisted their packs on their backs and were through the portcullis of the western gate, across the bridge, through Toll, and out through the eastern gate before you could say "starvation." On the Luck's insistence, the western gate guards followed them across the bridge, so that nobody now guarded the portcullis. Laylow was hunched next to Paragon, ready to slash out at anybody who made a lunge for her or for the Luck. Everybody gave them a wide berth.

On Paragon's orders, all prisoners were released, including the weary, lank-limbed members of the toil gangs and everyone in the clock-tower jail.

"And . . . Brand Appleton has to be brought here. To *this* gate," insisted Paragon, in response to Laylow's muttered prompting.

The hushed crowd had to wait for two solid minutes while the mayor emitted sounds like a man gargling with starlings. Then he made a choked *gah!* noise and gave a wave of his arm, which his guards correctly took as a sign of consent. Five minutes later a bruised, battered, red-haired man of eighteen years limped onto the bridge, one hand gripping his clumsily bandaged flank. When he drew level with the two fugitives, Laylow stepped out to join him and placed a supporting arm around him.

"Mandelion better be all you say," she muttered. She gave Paragon a glance of concern, but he cackled and capered, waving her away toward the unguarded gate.

The mayor could only glare helplessly as Brand limped across the bridge, supported by Laylow, and vanished through the gate to a world beyond his control.

At last there was only Paragon Collymoddle on the bridge. The sun had gone in, extinguishing the rainbows, and he was shivering with the chill of the wind and the drenching from the spray.

"Cold now," he said through chattering teeth.

The mayor came down to the bridge and ventured out onto it. His steps were slow, for he was acutely aware that nobody now stood between the Luck and the open portcullis.

"Come, boy," he said, not without kindness and some reverence, for was this not the Luck? "Enough is enough. You are not used to this light or this cold, are you?"

Paragon shook his head. He pulled himself up enough to hug the head of Goodman Fullock as if his arms had grown tired of the strain.

"It is all over. We will take you and make you warm and safe. No more troubles. No more dangers." The mayor cautiously took step after step. "Just . . . take my hand and come home. You are needed here. You have a job. You know that, do you not?"

The boy laid his cheek against the wooden head of the Beloved as if suddenly tired, and nodded. "Yes. Job. Save everyone," he murmured. Then he laughed, waved at somebody in the crowds behind the mayor, and with the same unexpected speed he had shown before, swung himself back onto the bridge and broke into a run.

"Quick!" spluttered the mayor. "Shoot . . . leg . . . something!"

Musket fire vented in a patter like applause, but Paragon's run was lolloping and unpracticed, and so lopsided that the bullets missed him. He leaped through the arch of the gateway and was gone.

"After him!" shouted Marlebourne.

Nobody moved but for one guard bolder than the rest. He darted forward onto the bridge and sprinted past the gesticulating mayor, who was already headed back to the safety of land himself. Two steps later, however, there was a splintering crack, and one of the planks of the famous unshakeable bridge of Toll gave under the guard's feet, so he dropped halfway through the hole. Desperately clutching at the boards, he was able to halt his fall and managed to haul himself back up and drag himself to safety.

There was a deathly hush, of just the sort that never lasts.

"Flee! The Luck has run out! The Luck has flown away! The bridge is falling down! Flee the town!"

With such cries all around, the mayor glanced behind him to see who the Luck had waved to before his flight. But there was only a heaving crowd full of faces made anonymous by fear. And in the corner of his eye, just a fleeting glimpse of a lilac-colored gown.

33

GOODMAN DOUBLETHREAD, KING OF CONSEQUENCES

Toll emptied with surprising speed. The inhabitants of Toll-by-Night had needed little prompting, and now that their Luck was gone, those of Toll-by-Day had lost their golden sense of self-assurance. People took what they could carry, push, or drag, and they left. By dawn the next day, the town was entirely empty.

Of all those who had been within its walls the preceding dawn, only three left from the western side, namely Brand Appleton, Laylow, and Paragon himself. It was widely supposed that Brand and Laylow had headed to Mandelion. As for Paragon, nobody had any idea where he had gone or even intended to go. He had plunged into uncertainty at a gallop, and the moors kept his secrets for him.

Everyone else had poured out of the east gate, to the

bemusement of Sir Feldroll, who saw more people pouring out of Toll than he had had reason to believe lived
there. Worse still, he found that his armies absolutely
refused to advance across what they all now firmly
believed to be a cursed bridge. They were not alone. As a
matter of fact, virtually nobody was willing to go near it.

There are, of course, exceptions to every rule.

In the gray of dawn, at what would once have been first
bugle time, a solitary figure could be seen stepping onto
the eastern end of the bridge of Toll. As a matter of fact,
it did not simply step, it stamped. Then it put its full
weight on the board, jumped up and down with all its
might, and moved onto the next.

Mosca had her shawl wrapped tightly around her
to shield her from the wind and her pipe clamped hard
between her teeth. She slammed her clogs into the
weather-beaten timbers as hard as she could.

When she had seen the guard put his foot through
the bridge, just for a moment Mosca's convictions had
been shaken into a jumble. Briefly she had believed that
Paragon must have been the real Luck of Toll after all, and
that his flight had left nothing holding up the bridge or
protecting the town. Even when she had gone to sleep that
night, on a blanket loaned by one of Sir Feldroll's soldiers,
she had still half believed it. And she knew that if she left
things at that, she would always partly believe it.

"All right," she said through the teeth clenched about

her pipe, "show me how cursed you are, then. Show me that it wasn't just a plank getting weak because hundreds of people came crowding across the bridge all at once. Go on, drop me then."

She was so caught up in her experiment that she did not notice another figure walking, a good deal more quietly, toward her from the other end of the bridge. Thus it was only when she caught sight of a pair of boots in the corner of her vision that she stopped midclump, slowly straightened, and looked Aramai Goshawk in the eye.

He was dressed in the same simple black she had seen him wear before, but with a traveling cloak over the top, and cream-colored kid gloves.

"I believe you owe me a town, Mye."

Mosca's heart lurched as she remembered her words to Goshawk the previous day. *You can have Toll.* Mosca pulled the pipe out of her mouth and gave a twitch of her arm toward the town behind her. Toll, with its dull windows, its doors creaking open, and ash flakes still chasing across its empty streets.

"Take it, Mr. Goshawk. Toll's yours. Nobody to quarrel over it with you. Not even a pigeon."

"A town is more than the sum of its bricks and the tons of its mortar. Toll numbered several hundred souls, now all flown."

"But you didn't care about the souls, did you, Mr. Goshawk? All you wanted was the bridge."

"A useless bridge."

576

"And you wanted it to be useless. You'd have pushed it into the Langfeather if you could."

"Indeed? Why would I do that?"

Mosca risked a glance at Goshawk from under her lashes. "Because you're in the fear business, Mr. Goshawk. Its frightened people come running to you, wanting you to deal with radicals, or criminals, or spiders under their bed. They're the ones that give their towns to you and let you tell them what to do.

"So you know what I think? I think maybe Mandelion turning radical was the best thing that happened to the Locksmiths for a long time. Because now everybody's seein' radicals in the closet, radicals in the fruit bowl, radicals hiding in every drawer. They're terrified. I bet there's dozens of governors all bobbing and doffing at you in their best wigs, beggin' you to stop the radicals jumping out of their suet pudding. But that all ends if somebody marches into Mandelion and puts some puffy-wigged noble back in charge.

"So it wasn't enough for you to hold Toll-by-Night. You had to hold Toll-by-Day as well, to make sure no armies marched through without your say-so."

The air was particularly cold, and the morning frost had left the Beloved statues with dandruff. Goshawk's face was impressively impassive as he gazed down at the Langfeather.

So far Mosca had been lucky. She had never quite crossed swords with Goshawk. Rather, their aims had chanced to slice in parallel, like a pair of scissors. Granted, a pair of scissors with one blade finger length and the other half a mile long, cutting out the sky and slashing buildings in two as it hissed through the air. However, this time she wondered if she had pushed things too far. Perhaps she should have pretended more stupidity, let him dismiss her as a foolish little girl caught up in things she did not understand.

"Mye, do you ever think of the future?"

"Do I get to have a future?"

Once again, her sidelong observation showed her a slight dimpling in his pocked cheeks, like fingerprints pushed into lumpy dough. It was that rare and unnerving phenomenon, the Goshawk smile.

"Are you still in fellowship with Eponymous Clent, the Stationer spy? I suppose he is a useful enough model for a starting apprenticeship . . . but sooner or later you will need to make some decisions. About your future. Your loyalties."

Mosca steadied herself against the wooden forehead of Goodlady Syropia and felt a prickle as ice crystals melted against the skin of her palms.

"I . . . I think Mr. Clent can still teach me a lot of things right now, Mr. Goshawk."

"Very well. Someone will come and speak to you on your next name day to see if you have had any more chance to consider. In the meantime, remember that I am still looking for that missing ransom jewel."

Sir Feldroll's encampment had become the hub for a sprawling temporary camp of the refugees from Toll. As Mosca returned to it, she found that many were already hoisting their goods onto their backs again and setting off for the cities to the east. In the distance Mosca could see the Raspberry, blinking bemused at the bookless wilderness. Farther down the road were the nightlings Blethemy and Blight, the former carrying a babe who looked a lot like the gobbet. Evidently there had been a family reunion.

Clent, with his usual shamelessness, had managed to find space for himself and his secretary in one of the campaign tents, as temporary diplomatic attachés to Sir Feldroll, and it was here that she found him quietly scrawling some notes in his black book under the heading ǀ ƒ ﬅ

Kidnappings, it read. *Bone horse—FIRE—no more town.*

"Ah, Mosca." Clent glanced up at her and passed her a letter that lay beside him. "Another consequence of your ingenious double-dealing, I believe."

Dear Mr. Scragface Pimplenose,

I am not overfond of jests, and I am even less fond of traps. My long wait at the time and place agreed for our meeting was wearisome and disappointing, but not nearly as wearisome and disappointing as the sight of a gaggle of ruffianly individuals staggering into the

*market square at an hour after the appointed time, and
then settling down to crouch behind the stocks under the
apparent impression that they were invisible.*

 *The Guild of Pawnbrokers informs me that your
breach of the terms of a contract it has brokered leaves
it likewise disappointed. Indeed I am to inform you that
unless substantial recompense is made to them and to me,
your rights will be revoked.*

Your obedient Servant,
The Romantic Facilitator

"That dozy footman Gravelip!" exclaimed Mosca. "I
was right! He and the rest of the mayor's men *did* let the
Romantic Facilitator slip out the net! Blunderin' in, all
red eyed and an hour late."

"Do you not curse them too wildly—I daresay their
young mistress probably gave them a tot or two of rum
to share the night before, enough to ensure their failure
to rise early." Clent sighed. "Ah well, it would seem that
we can now add the Guild of Pawnbrokers to the list of
people who would be lethally upset with us if they ever
found out precisely what we had done."

Mosca thought he was probably right. She had seen
the Pawnbrokers "revoking rights" during the auction,
and she still had a vivid memory of watching the revoked
individual plummeting down a mine shaft.

"Fortunately," continued Clent, "I believe if we vacate
the scene nimbly enough, most of the blame will land

580

upon the odious Skellow and the Marlebourne creature. I suppose you know that she and her adoptive father have vanished?"

Mosca nodded. The Marlebournes had emerged from the eastern gate with the general exodus, Beamabeth veiled in a vain attempt to avoid the new scorn with which she was widely regarded.

"I still feel . . ." Mosca narrowed her eyes. "I feel like she got away with it."

"Would you have her birched in the public square? Baited by dogs perhaps? Madam, we have destroyed her good name, and she will find the world a much colder and darker place as a result. Even now her father is probably changing her name to Buzzletrice.

"And you may comfort yourself with the thought that you have been the caltrop under her satin shoe every step of the way. You misdirected the Romantic Facilitator she had hired, you turned up in her own house and reported her plans to her father, and when she was on the brink of snatching the ransom, you careered in from stage left dressed as a pantomime horse and threw everything into disorder. And then, just when she was probably working her way toward claiming a second ransom, you *rescued* her."

This did indeed make Mosca feel a good deal better. *After all,* she reflected, *I got an idea what happened to that radish of hers.*

"I wonder what did happen to the first ransom,"

Clent reflected wistfully. Evidently his own thoughts had strayed in a similar direction.

"No idea, Mr. Clent," Mosca declared, her eyes two spoonfuls of black innocence.

"Alack. Well, child, at least I have good news. I chanced upon a member of the Company of Stationers, and after only a little scuffing of the truth made it plain to him that we had nobly and ingeniously prevented a town from falling into the hands of the Locksmiths, for the sake of the Stationers. Once again, madam, our star seems to be in the ascendant, our colors climbing the pole. In short, it appears I shall have buyers for my poems . . . and we might not need to live on rocks and grass this winter."

He glanced across at Saracen, who was happily tugging at the grass with his beak, his neck a muscular loop, the grass giving with a deep, meaty ripping sound.

"Though one of our number seems to favor that diet. I can understand the grass . . . but why *does* that perilous creature of yours eat pebbles?"

"'Cause he's only got teeth for biting, not chewing," answered Mosca, not quite meeting Clent's eye. "He swallows little rocks and they sit in his crop and roll around each other, grindin' his food up like little grindstones." She gave Clent a brief, needle-sharp glance, but his interest seemed to be idle. She decided to change the subject completely.

"Mr. Clent? I . . . I just had a word with Mr. Goshawk."

Clent looked up sharply. "Well, you appear to be still breathing, though your countenance is not reassuring. What did Mr. Goshawk have to say?"

"He . . . he didn't quite offer me a job, and I didn't quite say no."

"I see. Well, I suppose there is only so long one can make a hobby of deciding the fates of cities before it attracts attention. Did he quite manage to say whether the morn will find our battered bodies in the river's embrace?"

"I told him you still had a lot to teach me, an' he said he'd send somebody to ask me again on my next name day." Mosca gave a grimace. "Borrowed time, that's all."

"I generally find," Clent murmured after a pause, "that it is best to treat borrowed time the same way as borrowed money. Spend it with panache, and try to be somewhere else when it runs out."

"And when we get found, Mr. Clent, when the creditors and bailiffs come after us and it's payment time . . ."

". . . then we borrow more, madam, at higher interest. We embark on a wilder gamble, make a bigger promise, tell a braver story, devise a more intricate lie, sell the hides of imaginary dragons to desperate men, climb to ever higher and more precarious ground . . . and later, of course, our fall and catastrophe will be all the worse, but that *later* is our watchword, Mosca. We have nothing else—but we can at least make later later."

Saracen showed no distress at being scooped up with

every sign of haste. His world was one of disaster and near disaster, and he was used to sudden exits, often accompanied by screams, pursuit, and the smell of smoke. Another day, another exodus. He met the future with tiny, black, and fearless eyes, his bully brow full of goosely daring, and a crown jewel of the Realm in his crop.